The Confidence Game

A WHITE-COLLAR CRIMES ROMANCE
BOOK ONE

ALEX BERG

Prologue

THE MUSEUM LUDWIG IN COLOGNE, GERMANY WASN'T what most people would consider an architectural masterpiece. The building didn't have the undulating titanium walls of the Guggenheim in Bilbao or the inverted disco ball aesthetic of the Museo Soumaya in Mexico City, but it nonetheless had one architectural feature Natalia Levin adored: every gallery on the top floor featured a span of connected skylights that flooded the rooms below with natural light.

At least, they did during the day. It was 3 AM at the moment, but the natural light wasn't a selling point for Natalia. She simply appreciated having access to so much glass.

The skylight in front of her groaned and snapped as her glass cutter came full circle, but suction cups kept the freestanding piece from falling into the museum. Natalia moved it aside with the aid of a swing arm she'd mounted to the adjacent skylight. With a practiced ease, she slid the glass circle off the cups, set it aside, then disassembled the swing arm and the cutter and packed both at the bottom of her duffel bag. An experienced thief didn't leave evidence behind, and Natalia didn't like abandoning equipment either.

With her tools squared away, she tightened her rock climbing harness and went through her mental checklist. Her cell phone pressed against her thigh from the stash pocket on her black leggings, and a multitool weighed against her obliques from underneath her lightweight black jacket. Her running shoes were snugly tied, and her touchscreen gloves were pulled on tight. She tested the bun at the back of her head, and when she was convinced none of her long blonde locks had escaped, she pulled a thin black ski mask over her face. She clipped her harness to the belay rope and gave it a test tug, but it didn't give. She grabbed her empty black sling bag, threw it over her shoulder, then lifted her wrist and pulled back the sleeve to expose her watch. She opened the clock application, and with her finger hovering over the timer, she paused.

It was at this point in a heist that many thieves became overcome with fear, especially those Natalia dubbed Planners. They were the ones who were meticulous to a fault. The kind who never moved on a target until every security system was hacked, every camera feed spliced, every guard bribed or diverted, and every contingency planned for. They were intellectuals, people who'd become thieves for the payday and little else. Despite their slow and ponderous approach, they were still better than the second group of thieves, the Thugs. Those were the type to race into a museum waving a crowbar and a gun and hoping for the best, thieves who were high on brawn and bravado but short on brains. And then there was the last group. The Naturals. They didn't possess superior intellects or deft physical skills, though those certainly helped. They were Naturals because of their cool demeanors, because of their love of the game, and most importantly, because they absolutely *thrived* under pressure.

Natalia's fingertips tingled, and adrenaline flooded her system as she tapped her timer. The numbers had barely started moving before she jumped through the open hole in the skylight. Her rope hissed as it slithered across her figure eight descender, and Natalia's lithe, lean form landed light as a feather at the bottom of the twenty foot drop. She gave the darkened room a quick scan as she unclipped her harness, then darted toward the far wall.

On it hung *Lady in Green Jacket*, an expressionist piece by August Macke from the early nineteen hundreds, about a foot and a half square including the frame. Under different circumstances, Natalia might've taken a moment to appreciate the simplified forms, the warm autumn colors, and the isolation of the titular woman in the green jacket, but here every second counted.

Natalia pulled her sling bag off her shoulder and tossed it to the floor as she simultaneously withdrew the multitool from her pocket. She pried the painting off the wall, snipping at the fasteners behind it that kept it in place. As soon as she sliced through the wires, a silent alarm would've sounded. If the museum security hadn't already noticed her black-clad blur in the cameras, they'd definitely know about her now, but she didn't let fear overtake her. She pocketed the multitool and tucked the painting, frame and all, into her bag before zipping the whole thing shut and throwing it over her shoulder. She darted back to the rope, her timer ticking past thirty-five seconds as she took the rope in both hands and climbed. If the distance were any more than twenty feet, she would've needed to clip into the harness for safety. She probably would've used handheld ascenders or even a mechanical winch to make a faster exit, but she was fit and experienced enough that it was faster to climb the twenty feet by hand. With a few wraps of her feet around the rope and a few tugs of her arms, she reached the lip of the cut glass and pulled herself to the roof.

Her timer ticked past a minute as she tucked the sling bag into her duffel, grabbed the latter, and raced to the end of her belay rope. She unclipped it from the emergency ladder she'd used as a support, quickly looped it and stuffed it in the duffel, and set off across the rooftop at a run.

By this point the police would be on their way, and the guard who normally sat in the first floor security booth would probably be approaching the gallery. If he was smart (which he wasn't) and he'd noticed Natalia enter through the skylights (which was unlikely given the darkness), he'd have headed straight for the central stairwell rather than the gallery, but even if he made all the right choices and took the most direct route, he wouldn't burst out of the rooftop access door until Natalia's timer hit a minute and fifty seconds (she'd timed the route herself).

All of which meant he was already too late to catch her.

Natalia slowed as she approached the zip line she'd set up a couple hours ago. Placing it between the Ludwig and the hotel across the street hadn't been trivial, but by stringing a guide wire between the two buildings via drone, she'd then been able to ratchet a sturdier cable across without alerting anyone at street level. She gave the line a quick tug to test the tension, then clipped her harness into the line and dove off the edge. Her heart fluttered in that fleeting moment when she hung weightlessly in midair, but then the harness caught and she went skittering across the *Bischofsgartenstraße*, five stories off the ground.

Natalia could hear the faint wail of approaching sirens as she landed in a run upon the roof of the hotel. Without wasting time, she unclipped herself from the harness and pulled her phone from her pocket. After a few quick taps, she heard a faint pop as the electronic quick-release atop the Ludwig unlatched, and then the electric winch atop the hotel whirred into action. Natalia stepped out of the way as the cable retracted lightning-quick across the gap, wishing the process wasn't so noisy, but there wasn't anything she could do about it. Hopefully anyone who was up would be more intrigued by the sound of the sirens than the skittering slither of the cable being sucked up by her winch.

The whole process only took a few seconds. With the cable spooled, Natalia lifted the winch off its attachment. The thing was too heavy to take with her, so she lugged it behind a rooftop air conditioner where no one would notice it until she could come back for it later. Once done, she hefted her duffel, set foot to the fire escape at the back of the hotel, and with the melody of the police sirens serenading her, she disappeared into the night.

Natalia's duffel hit the floor with a thud as she stepped inside the entryway of her apartment following her long trek home from Germany. She closed the door behind her and latched it, then slid her sneakers off and tucked them in the shoe cupboard by the coat closet. She rubbed the sore spot at the base of her neck where the duffel strap had dug into her as she padded her way into the kitchen.

The refrigerator puffed as she opened the door, and the bottle of Perrier she pulled from it sparkled and fizzed as she cracked it open and took a sip. Otherwise, the apartment was silent. No dog barked and ran up to her, wagging its tail. No cat mewled from her bedroom, too lazy to make the trek out, and no boyfriend wandered out with a smile on his face, ready to pull her into a hug. The apartment was quiet, private, and empty.

Much like her.

Natalia sighed, set the bottle of sparkling water on the counter, and headed back to her duffel bag. She unzipped it and pulled out the cardboard parcel box in which she'd packed her stolen painting. She brought it with her to the kitchen, using a box cutter to slice through the packing tape holding it closed. After pulling *Lady* free, she brought it with her to the living room and hung it upon the south-facing wall, right in the spot she'd picked out for it before departing for Cologne. Then she stepped back, crossed her arms, and examined it.

In the bright light of mid-afternoon, the painting looked exactly as it had during Natalia's scouting trips in the Ludwig. The vibrant greens of the trees, the bright blue of the sky, and the warm browns of the forest floor all contrasted against one another beautifully, and while the focal point of the painting stood front and center in her green jacket, she somehow felt miles away from the other two couples depicted in the piece. It was a wonderful example of early nineteenth century expressionism, perhaps her favorite piece of Macke's, but as she stood there absorbing it, Natalia felt... nothing.

Well, almost nothing. She felt a sense of pride at how smoothly she'd stolen the piece, same as she always did, but the euphoria that accompanied the theft had been more fleeting than usual. It used to be whenever she stole a famous piece, she'd feel as if she was on top of the world for weeks at a time, months even, but this time the feeling hadn't even lasted through the journey home. The buzz of adrenaline she'd felt while breaking into the museum had almost been longer lasting. But why? Did it have something to do with the painting itself? *Lady* was nice, but it wasn't exactly a piece she'd lusted after. Could it be that she wasn't pushing herself, testing her limits, and learning new tricks of the trade anymore? Was she simply getting *bored?* Or was it something else entirely? Was there some void inside of her that she was trying and failing to fill?

Natalia waited, hoping the answers would come to her if she was patient, but none did. After a couple minutes, she shook her head and turned away. Her plan had been to enjoy *Lady* for a while before selling it, but even though the spot on the wall was perfect for it, she didn't think she'd be getting much enjoyment out of the piece after all.

She was still wondering which fence she should move it through when her phone buzzed. She pulled the device from her pocket, noting the unknown number. The text read:

Grow your business fast with this one weird trick. Text 44375 for more information.

Natalia's brow creased. To the untrained eye, the text looked like spam, but to her, it was the exact phrase potential customers contacted her with. Even the five digit passkey was correct.

She texted back.

Who is this?

My name is Diego. I have a business proposition I was hoping to discuss.

Business propositions were better than the other kind, which Natalia had also received her fair share of.

Who gave you this number?

A mutual acquaintance. Someone well known in our arena.

It was a good thing he hadn't said mutual friend, otherwise Natalia would've known he was lying. But acquaintances? She had a few of those. Probably one of her fences.

You're looking to hire, I assume?

Not exactly. What I wanted to discuss is more of a partnership.

I'm not interested in stock options. I expect my services to be paid for in cash.

You misunderstand me. I'm putting a team together. I'd like for you to be on it.

Natalia scoffed, and a bit of her inner Aussie sneaked out.

Sorry, mate. I work alone. If you'd done your research, you would've known that.

Natalia thought that might be the end of it, but apparently Diego wasn't the type to take no for an answer. After a long pause, her phone dinged again, and a lengthy message appeared.

I've done enough research to know you're the best, which is why I reached out, and for what I have planned, only the best will do. Trust me, the job I have in mind will have the art world talking for decades. Even someone as talented as you would want it on her resume.

Natalia paused, staring at the phone. She could've put it to sleep and stuffed it back in her pocket, but something kept her from ending the conversation. Maybe it was the fact that she loved a challenge, or maybe it was the persistent voice in the back of her head telling her that getting out of her comfort zone might reinvigorate her and help her rediscover the passion that had been missing from her latest heist.

Or maybe it was simpler that that. Sometimes a little flattery can go a long way.

I'm listening.

Apparently that was all the urging Diego needed, because he sent her another text, then another. And another. He sent twelve in total, and with each one, Natalia's eyes grew a little wider, not only because he'd been telling the truth. The job he described was big, bigger than any Natalia had pulled off, but more important than the job itself was the target: a piece known across the globe, one Natalia herself had, oddly enough, long coveted.

A piece Natalia wasn't sure she'd be able to steal on her own.

And even though the thought of working alongside a number of people who she didn't know, let alone trust, almost had her breaking out in hives, the bubbling excitement in her belly was too strong to ignore. But Natalia was smart enough not to sound too eager, lest that set off warning bells for Diego, nor was she impulsive enough to agree to anything without doing a little research first, so in reply she simply typed:

Let me think about it.

Chapter One

Natalia landed at Oslo Gardermoen Airport at a little after noon, local time. With her sling bag over her shoulder, she grabbed a quick sushi lunch before eschewing the baggage claim and taking the escalators to the railway station under the main terminal. There she boarded a train headed to Oslo proper. Given the state of subways and bus systems across the globe, voluntarily stepping foot onto public transportation might be considered grounds to be declared legally insane, but the train from the airport was modern and clean. Not only that, but the map app on her phone assured her it was faster than taking a cab. The first half of the ride was scenic with rolling fields and stretches of thick forest visible from the windows, but as the train approached the city, it dipped underground into a featureless tunnel. After a number of stops, it reached the *Nasjon-altheatret* station in the city center, where Natalia exited and climbed to street level.

Natalia zipped her lightweight jacket to the base of her neck as she stepped onto the sidewalk outside the station. The mid-September sun shone bright in the sky, but a breeze heavy with North Sea salt whipped through the air, sending an involuntary chill through her. It almost made her wish she'd packed something heavier, a nice down coat, perhaps, but Natalia chose her attire for function, not form. It was rare for her to wear anything other than leggings, running shoes, and a form-fitting top, because in her line of work, you never knew when you'd be pressed into action. Tight-fitting clothing didn't snag as often, making it easier for her to fit in narrow spaces. If someone tried to grab her, snug clothing gave them less to hold onto, and in the event she had to take off running, it was useful to blend in with other joggers trying to keep their fitness in check.

But that meant you sometimes suffered the odd wintery nip.

Natalia got moving, figuring the activity would help her warm up. According to her phone, her hotel was a mere ten minute walk away, but instead of heading straight there, she took a quick detour. She ventured south until she reached the waters of the Oslofjord, headed across a wide plaza known as the *Rådhusplassen*, and stopped at the foot of the newly constructed *Nasjonalmuseet,* or National Museum.

The architecture wasn't particularly spectacular as far as museums went, just a sprawling building meant to fit the block it had been placed on, though Natalia imagined the twenty-four hundred square meter light hall that stretched across the top floor would be more impressive at night. Natalia had half a mind to head inside and indulge herself a little, but between perusing the artwork and casing the security, she'd almost certainly lose track of time and miss her meeting. Instead, she reluctantly tore her eyes from the building and continued down the waterfront, past a number of restaurants until she arrived at her destination: a hotel known as The Scoundrel.

With a name like that, Natalia would've booked a room even if the place was a rat-infested flophouse. Luckily for her, it was anything but. Between the *Nasjonalmuseet*, several nearby contemporary art museums, and a selection of upscale galleries, downtown Oslo was a bit of an art mecca, and several of the local hotels had cashed in on the craze. The Scoundrel was one of the most unique. As she pushed her way through the tinted glass revolving door, black, pink, and rose gold enveloped her. A lobby sparsely furnished with black leather chairs and tables the color of champagne stretched to her left. A curved wall covered with graffiti art served as a backdrop, but it wasn't crude gang signs sprayed onto the polished concrete. Rather, the scene depicted a warrior prince and an armored bear fighting off an army of ice giants. Natalia supposed the scene might've been based on Norwegian mythology, but if so, there was surely some poetic license involved. Above her, a chandelier consisting of a hundred free-hanging Edison bulbs bathed the lobby in a warm glow. The bulbs swayed as Natalia stepped further into the hotel, her brow furrowing as she tried to make sense of it.

"Try standing directly underneath it," said a feminine voice with a lilting, musical quality to it.

Natalia cast a glance at the clerk who stood at the front desk before stepping to the center of a rose gold circle inlaid into the black tile. Sure enough, when she looked at the chandelier from that vantage the scene transformed from a jumble of lights into a cohesive image, that of a small bird with spindly legs.

"It's a white-throated dipper," said the receptionist. "The national bird of Norway."

Natalia approached the desk, still absorbing the unique art pieces around her. Everything was a different style, but somehow it all worked together. "You have quite a foyer."

The woman behind the desk smiled. "Thank you. Welcome to The Scoundrel. You are staying with us?"

"I am. Natalia Levin."

The receptionist's fingers tapped at a keyboard. "Welcome, Ms. Levin. I have you checking out in two weeks?"

Natalia didn't actually know how long she'd be in town, but she suspected the job would only take a week to ten days. She could always cancel the rest of her reservation if she didn't need it. "Correct."

"Excellent," said the receptionist. "If I could have a credit card for incidental charges?"

Natalia pulled one from her bag and slid it across the polished marble. "My luggage should've been delivered yesterday." Airport CT scanners didn't exactly pair well with the sorts of items she traveled with, so she used bonded carriers instead.

The woman nodded as she typed. "I see a note that we have two items waiting for you. I'll have them sent up. You'll be in room five-oh-five. Elevators are to your right." The receptionist handed Natalia back her card, along with a magnetized key card. "If you have any needs, do not hesitate to ask. Enjoy your stay."

Natalia thanked the woman and headed to the aforementioned elevators, passing a minimalist bar by the name of Snøhytta en route. Sleek, laser-engraved signs pointed to a spa and pool further in back. Natalia hadn't included any bathers in her bags, but she made a mental note to check out the spa services if she had some downtime.

The elevator dinged and spit Natalia onto the fifth floor. The lock on her room whirred and clicked as she inserted her key, and she pushed her way in. While her room didn't feature any experimental art, it was nicely furnished. A king size canopy bed with a matte black frame took up the majority of the space, though there was a reading nook with a suede chaise and a narrow desk underneath the wall-mounted television. A subtle floral scent drifted across her nose—lavender, maybe?—and when she peeked into the loo, she found a pair of candles had been left burning on a shelf above the sink. Everything was sleek and modern, but it was the shower that caught her eye, with a mosaic tile design that transitioned from sky blue to navy to a metallic black at the top.

Natalia had just slipped off her shoes when she heard a knock. She opened the door to find a bellhop with her luggage on a cart: one standard suitcase upholstered in black ballistic nylon, and a worn steel trunk with black leather sheathing and reinforced corners. The bellhop gave Natalia a small bow. As he brought the suitcase inside, he asked where she'd like the trunk. She told him to put it in the corner by the bed. The man grunted as he picked it up and maneuvered it inside, but he didn't ask her what was in it. In Natalia's experience, most people assumed it was a musical instrument.

Natalia dug a fifty krone bill out of her bag and handed it to him as he finished. The bellhop tipped his head, wished her a good day, and Natalia closed the door behind him. She picked up her suitcase, set it on the bed, and opened it. On first glance, it looked like any other travel case, because for the most part it was. Natalia had need of underwear and socks and toothpaste, same as anyone else, but once she'd stored her clothing in the room's dresser, she reached the secure compartment at the bottom of the case. Though the trunk looked more imposing, it was actually her nylon bag that held the most expensive pieces of equipment: the electronics. Natalia opened the compartment and checked to make sure everything was undamaged. There was a tablet computer as well as two additional smartphones, an electronic card reader, several dongles for connecting to different security systems, a wireless signal jammer, and a featureless black box that was often referred to as a code grabber, not to mention several spare passports, driver's licenses, and cash.

Natalia slipped one of the spare phones into her backpack before moving to her trunk. The items within it were more robust—coring drills, an angle grinder, a reciprocating saw—but there was one item she wanted to have on her person, so she popped open the lid, retrieved her favorite set of lock picks, and tucked those into her backpack, too.

Natalia checked the time on her phone. She still had an hour to spare, but she was too amped up to lie in bed and watch TV, so she slung her pack over her shoulder and headed out. She checked the spa and pool on the first floor—the latter of which was lit by magenta lights, making it seem like a better spot for late night pashing than swimming—before heading to the bar. There, she ordered a Moscow mule, extra lime, and nursed it for a half hour before eventually running out of patience and hailing an Uber on her phone.

There was a bus stop not far from her hotel that provided a perfect place to wait for her ride. Once the car arrived, Natalia gave the driver the address and off they went. Instead of weaving his way through the tight downtown Oslo streets, the driver hooked a left at a roundabout, performed a U-turn, and headed into a subterranean tunnel, one that curved and weaved for at least a kilometer before popping aboveground. There was another short section of tunnel after that, followed by a stretch of freeway, but they hadn't gone far before the driver exited and headed into a more commercial portion of town. Natalia didn't spot any factories or tall chimneys spewing smoke, but she noticed all the trappings of an industrial park: a hardware store, a commercial glass place, and an appliance repair shop, all with the same bland off-white siding. The driver pulled into a mostly empty lot and parked in a spot beside the appliance repair.

"Here we are," he said in his accented voice.

Natalia thanked him and stepped out. The instructions she'd received told her to look for a second floor industrial loft with access from the outside. Sure enough, as she rounded the corner of an empty store with what she assumed were Norwegian "For Lease" signs hanging in the windows, she found a metal staircase leading to a second story door. She didn't head right up, though. Natalia took her time making a full circuit of the building, looking for secondary exits, fire escapes, security cameras, and anything else that might seem out of place. Only when she was convinced she wasn't walking into a trap did she head up the staircase to the door above. There was a spot next to it where a placard with business information could be hung, but it was empty.

Natalia knocked on the door and waited.

After about twenty seconds, she heard the clack of a latch, and the door pulled open. In the open frame stood a man who just about filled it. He was tall, maybe four inches over six feet, with broad shoulders, a broad chest, hell, *broad everything*. He had the build of a former rugby player, except even a prop or a hooker wouldn't have as many scars as the man in front of her did, nor his hands. The man rested one of his thick mitts on the frame of the door, a heavily muscled hand that suggested he was either a semi-professional arm wrestler or a blacksmith.

The big man was mostly bald, and the rest of his hair was shaved super short, about the same length as his five o'clock shadow. He stood there in a loose-fitting T-shirt and jeans, staring at Natalia with hazel eyes that were surprisingly bright for how weathered he looked. "Oy."

"Oy yourself," said Natalia.

The big man frowned. "Y'alright?"

The man's tone was gruff, his accent thick as molasses. Natalia couldn't place it, but he was definitely working-class British. A Londoner, maybe?

"I'm quite well," Natalia replied. "How are you?"

The big man rolled his eyes as if Natalia had committed some faux pas. "What can I do for ya, muva o' pearl?"

Now it was Natalia's turn to frown. *Mother of pearl?* "I'm Natalia. I'm here for the job."

The big man's face brightened and he stepped to the side. "Well, why didn't you say 'smuch? Come on in."

Chapter Two

Natalia knew that following heavily-muscled, rough-around-the-edges types into enclosed spaces wasn't a bright idea, but the way the big man reacted when she told him who she was suggested his job was to keep undesirables out, not her in, so she nodded and stepped into the loft.

The door clattered shut as she took in her surroundings. Other than a partitioned section at the far side that might've been a toilet, the loft was wide open. Sunlight streamed through a half-dozen south-facing windows, illuminating trapezoidal patches across the aged wooden floors. A quintet of columns held up a vaulted ceiling, but there was precious little filling the space. A few desks had been set up outside the direct light, on which were a number of computer monitors and custom built rigs, all connected by a jumble of cables. There was also a hangout corner: a trio of couches arranged in a C shape that faced a bare wall. There was no television, but a projector on a coffee table pointed at the bare spot.

The big man stomped up next to her, about as subtle as an elephant wearing tap shoes. "So... you're the fief."

"That's me, a parcel of land, held on condition of feudal service."

The bruiser's brow furrowed, and he looked at Natalia sideways. "You 'ard of 'earing or somefin', or are you off yer trolley?"

Natalia took a breath to steady herself. She shouldn't bully this poor man over his accent. It wasn't as if he was *trying* to obfuscate her. "No, I'm not hard of hearing. My apologies. I am the thief. Natalia Levin. You are?"

The big man blinked, looking taken aback. "Goodness, where are me manners? Name's Eddie Wheeler, but me china call me Wheels. Pleased to make yer acquain'ance."

Natalia frowned. "I'm sorry. *China?*"

"Yea. Me china. China plates. Me mates."

Natalia's brow creased in confusion, then went slack as she had a revelation. "You're cockney."

Eddie snorted. "Come off it, ya muppet. Ya can't *be* cockney, ya *speak* cockney. I'm from Wappin', born and bred."

Natalia had no idea where that was, but since Eddie hadn't denied the cockney bit, she assumed it was somewhere in east London. "I take it you're the muscle."

Eddie shook his head. "Nah, I'm the driver. Why do ya fink me mates call me Wheels?"

Natalia blinked. "Your last name is literally Wheeler."

"And?"

Eddie stared at her for a good five seconds before busting out in an earth-shaking laugh. "Oh, I'm just takin' the piss. Don't get cheesed. 'Course I'm the muscle. But drivin's me specialty. Drove an 'Ackney in London fer a long lemon."

"A long lemon?"

Eddie sighed. "Lemon and lime. Time. A long time."

Natalia nodded. "Got it. Sorry. You'll have to cut me some slack. I'm not up to snuff on my rhyming slang."

Eddie shrugged. "S'alright. Yer pickin' it up faster 'an Midge did when we first met."

Natalia was glad to know she wasn't the only one who had a hard time parsing Eddie's dialect, but his assurance nonetheless left her with more questions. "Who's Midge?"

A deadpan voice cut through the air. "It's Miriam. Not Midge."

Natalia might've jumped if she didn't have so much practice keeping cool under pressure. Nonetheless, her eyes widened at the outburst. She took a few steps toward the couches. From her new vantage, she was able to see there was someone lying on one of them: a woman with warm, terra cotta skin, her black hair held in tight braids. It was always hard to judge a person's age based on appearance, but Natalia guessed she was younger than her, maybe early twenties. She wore loose-fitting athletic pants and a pink cotton hoodie, and she seemed fully absorbed in the game she was playing on her mobile phone.

Eddie clomped up beside her. "'At's Midge, but if anyone calls 'er 'at, she frows a wobbly. Best you use 'er proper name 'less you want a taste of 'er Oliver Twists." Eddie put up his fists for emphasis.

"You get a pass for some reason?" Natalia asked.

"Per'aps if you spend a few donkey's ears building up a proper relationship, you too can earn a li'le lee along the way."

Natalia glanced at Miriam's phone. The game she was focused on was rendered in an anime style and featured a youthful protagonist beating up monsters with a flurry of attacks. Based on the frequency with which numbers flashed across the screen, Natalia guessed it was fairly complicated, but Miriam didn't appear to be putting in much effort. "Does she talk other than when she's correcting your mistakes?"

"When I need to," said Miriam without looking up from her phone.

"She's not much of a people person," said Eddie. "Prefers to spend 'er lemon with 'er pistol and shoo'ers."

Natalia's first instinct was that Eddie was talking about her fighting game, but she had to remind herself his slang was all about rhyming. Lemon meant time because the pair of lemon was lime, so pistol and shooters would be...?

"Ah." Natalia smiled as she turned her gaze back to Miriam. "Computers. You're the hacker."

Miriam, again without looking up, replied: "I'm the hacker."

Eddie crossed his arms across his broad chest as he stared at Miriam's phone. "God's 'onest truf, I can't understan' what she gets out 'o fose games. Maybe it's a generational fing."

"Really?" said Natalia. "You don't seem that old."

Eddie arched a thick eyebrow at her. "Not sure if 'at was a complimen' or not, but I work had to keep meself fit as a fiddle, Tom 'anks."

"Tom Hanks?"

Eddie snorted. *"Fanks."*

"Right. Thanks." Natalia shook her head. Even Eddie's explanations could be hard to understand.

Eddie turned his attention away from Miriam's phone. "So... how long ya been tea leavin'?"

Rather than continuing to ask what the heck he was talking about, Natalia took her time. He was technically speaking English. If she put her mind to it, she could figure out his meaning. "I've been *thieving* since I was a child, but I didn't become a professional until I was an adult."

"Pulled any jobs I might've 'eard of?"

"That depends on how attuned to the art world you are," said Natalia. "Are you familiar with *The Cardsharps*?"

Eddie's brow furrowed. "What's 'at? You mean a card *shark?*"

"It's a painting," explained Natalia. "By Caravaggio. I stole it from the Kimbell Art Museum three years ago."

Eddie looked at her blankly. "Never 'eard of it."

Natalia got the impression Eddie couldn't tell a Picasso from a Pissarro. "There are others, but I won't bore you with the details. How about you? Been in the business long?"

Eddie smiled. "Been knockin' 'eads since I 'ad two teef to me name, but I never pinched anyfin' 'till a few donkey's ears back. 'en 'at blighter Diego crashed into me life, and fings ain't been the same since."

Right. Diego. Despite the texts they'd shared, Natalia's research hadn't unearthed much information on the man, which she assumed was by design. In this business, the fewer personal details you shared with your business partners and prospective buyers the better. The less everyone involved knew, the less likely they were to incriminate everyone else if things went sideways. It was one of the reasons Natalia preferred to work alone, if not necessarily *the* most important reason, that being that she just didn't trust anyone.

"You've worked with Diego before, I take it?" asked Natalia. "He recruited you for a previous job?"

Eddie chuckled. *"Recrui'ed.* 'at's a crackin' way to put it. I was workin' in me off hours bouncin' blokes for a bettin' parlor in the East End when me pitch n' toss told me to collect a few fousand quid from some pain in the arse wanker. Turned out to be Diego, o' course, and by the end o' meetin' 'im, not only was 'is face not flat as a Scotch pancake, but I found meself with a new Uncle Bob."

Natalia blinked a couple times. "He *adopted you?*"

Miriam snorted loudly and started laughing. The laugh turned into a cough, and she had to sit up and clear her throat to make it stop. Even then she kept laughing.

Eddie slapped the top of the couch—not in anger, more the way you'd pop a friend who was annoying you on the arm. "You done 'aving yer giraffe, Midge?" He looked back at Natalia. "Don't be daft. Diego offered me a *job.* Could'a called it a dog's knob, instead, but I was tryin' to watch me language 'round the two of you."

Natalia couldn't help but grin at the exchange, but it wasn't due to her gross misunderstanding of Eddie's speech. It was the way Eddie and Miriam reacted to each other. Admittedly, Natalia didn't have much experience working on a team, but Miriam seemed at ease around Eddie despite his gruff manner. In turn, Eddie appeared to have a soft spot for Miriam despite her total lack of social skills. Clearly, Eddie hadn't been lying about the two of them having a history, and from the way he told it, he and Diego had been working together even longer.

That made Natalia the odd woman out—which, to be fair, was the position Natalia was accustomed to working from, but she'd nonetheless have to be careful not to let her guard down around any of them, no matter how nonthreatening Eddie and Miriam might seem.

As Natalia contemplated the pair's relationship, she heard the clack of a latch and the groan of a set of hinges. She turned to see a man entering the loft, pocketing his keys as he let the door swing shut behind him. Unlike Eddie or Miriam, he was dressed to the nines. He wore a tailored charcoal suit over a crisp white shirt, his jacket reaching to his wrists and a perfect three-quarter inch of cuff peeking past that. His shoes were a glossy midnight black and his tie a deep navy with white polka dots, both of which paired nicely with his dark hair and tan skin. His attire wasn't the only part of him that was put together, though. The man was broad in the shoulders but narrow-waisted, not big and bulky like Eddie, and his form-fitting trousers hinted at lean, muscular legs underneath.

As he turned from the door, he stopped and fixed his eyes on Natalia. His mouth opened, perhaps in surprise, and his eyes widened a little, too. He stood there staring at her, and Natalia stared back for what seemed like the longest three seconds of her life. Eventually, he gave his head a shake, blinked a couple times, and came over.

"Hello," he said in a pleasing baritone with the barest hint of a Spanish accent. "You must be Natalia."

The words he spoke were easy to parse, not at all like Eddie's cockney word salad, yet she still had a hard time processing them. She was too distracted by his dark eyes, which smoldered like coals. She didn't think they radiated *actual* heat, but the room nonetheless felt warmer than it had a moment ago.

A voice in the back of Natalia's mind reminded her she'd been asked a question, so she forced out a response. "Uh, yes... that's right. Natalia Levin."

Eddie leaned in between them. "She's the fief."

As the man ripped his eyes from her to face Eddie, Natalia felt a tangible snap, as if the force of his gaze had kept her under a spell.

"Thank you, Eddie, I'd already figured that out." He turned back to Natalia. "I'm Diego Cabrera. It's a pleasure to finally meet you."

He hesitated, as if he wasn't sure whether to greet her with a European kiss on the cheek or a more informal handshake, but after a moment's indecision he extended a hand. A tingle shot up Natalia's arm as she took it. His hand was firm and strong yet soft, and he didn't squeeze her excessively, as if trying to prove a point.

As quickly as the sensation accosted her, so it fled when Diego let go. He clasped his hands before him and gave Natalia a bright smile. "Well. Let's get started, shall we?"

Chapter Three

Diego waved toward the sofas as he headed toward the computers. "Please. Make yourselves comfortable. I need to grab something before I start the presentation."

Miriam snapped her fingers and shot a set of fingers guns toward the sky. "Way ahead of you, boss."

Natalia watched Diego's back as he sifted through the jumbled computer equipment. While Diego had locked eyes with her, her breath had caught in her throat and she'd felt as if someone had turned the IQ dial on her brain down by a couple notches, but now that he'd left her personal space, she'd started to feel normal again. What. *The hell.* Was going on?

The man was undeniably handsome, but he wasn't exactly Natalia's type, at least in features if not body shape. If Natalia could be accused of having a wandering eye, it was toward men with fair hair, blue eyes, and a smooth jaw, not men with Diego's scruff that was several days past designer stubble but still a week or two shy of becoming a true beard. And while Natalia could be wooed by a sexy Latin accent, Diego's was barely there, as if he'd been born abroad but had the spice beaten from his tongue through years of international school. He was impeccably-dressed—with true high end attire, not cheap knockoffs—and he wore the clothes well, but a tailored suit alone had never made Natalia weak in the knees.

Regardless of what made her suffer a momentary lapse in reason, Natalia knew she couldn't let it happen again. While Diego, Eddie, and Miriam seemed to have a level of familiarly and trust with one another, Natalia wasn't here to make friends. She'd come to complete a job—and not precisely the one Diego had invited her to do.

As Diego came around the edge of the sofas with a tablet in hand, Natalia picked a spot by herself on the edge of the couch nearest the door, giving herself a wide berth from Eddie and Miriam. Diego pressed a button on the projector with his free hand and plucked a remote from its side. The device whirred to life, splashing a loading screen on the bare wall across from them.

"Here we go." Diego tapped his tablet a few times before putting the thing down. "Before we start, let me offer my apologies for being late. I'd intended to greet you myself when you arrived, Natalia, but an unavoidable engagement drew me away. Nonetheless, I see you've made introductions with Eddie, and I assume with Miriam."

Natalia glanced at Miriam, who was still on her phone. "Perfunctory introductions, yes."

Eddie snorted. *"Perfunt'ry?* I thought I put me best foot forward, if I say so meself."

"I'm sure we'll all acclimate to one another as we go, but for the time being, perhaps the best way to come together is to discuss why we're all here." The projection behind Diego switched to that of his presentation software, which was dominated by a single, striking piece of artwork. "Ah. Perfect timing. Ladies and gentleman, if you don't mind me calling you that, Eddie... Let me present to you our reason for being here. Edvard Munch's *The Scream.*"

The image projected on the wall was bumpy, not so much from the quality of the projector but due to the texture of the wall. As a result, it gave *The Scream* a rugged graininess lacking in the original, yet nonetheless, Natalia felt a pang inside her at the mere sight of the reproduction.

This was why she was here.

Natalia couldn't remember when she'd first realized she loved art —the simple fact that she *couldn't* indicated it was at a young age— but she could recall the first piece of art she committed to memory: *Water-Lilies* by Claude Monet. More specifically, it was the *Water-Lilies* painted by Monet between 1916 and 1919 and currently held in the Musée Marmottan Monet in Paris, because as Natalia would later learn, Monet had painted about two hundred and fifty water lily pieces. As an adult, Natalia had seen *Water-Lilies* in person at the Musée Marmottan, but that's not how she remembered it in her mind. The version she remembered had been reproduced on a tattered poster and hung on the water-damaged wall of her temporary foster home, not the first she'd lived in and not the last. The poster was yellowed around the edges, with a thick crease down the middle and numerous holes in the corners where tacks had been placed and pulled and placed again, but it was the most beautiful thing in the entire house all the same. Those simple lilies with their bright pink flowers, shaded by hanging vines and floating in an endless pool of pastel purple and pale blue, spoke of tranquility and peace, of a simplicity and beauty intrinsic to even the simplest things in life.

And it was all a lie.

Perhaps it hadn't been to Monet. Natalia doubted he'd have painted so many water lilies if the act had been some sort of convoluted charade, but to Natalia the peace and natural beauty depicted in the scene was nothing but a sham. A wish. A fantasy. Natalia's world had been one of revolving doors, of terse words and sharp rebukes, of adults who claimed they had her best interests at heart but who jumped to get rid of her when the first, easiest opportunity presented itself. For Natalia, the idea of a state of languid calm had never existed. She'd never known tranquility. For her, there were no water lilies.

The Scream, on the other hand—now that was a painting that had captivated her from the moment she laid eyes on it. Every aspect of the piece spoke of the inherent loneliness of existence. The ghostly central character, hands pressed against their cheeks, face distended in some combination of terror and horror. The fierce orange red sky, boiling with anger even as the cool ocean underneath swirled with mystery. And perhaps Natalia's favorite part, the faceless couple in the background walking along the docks, either oblivious to or uncaring about the plight of the screaming stranger before them. So many times in her life she'd felt the way the stranger in the painting did, wanting to scream but knowing there was no one there to hear her. No one who really cared.

As Natalia stared at the projected image of the painting, at the raw emotion on the stranger's face, their pain, their need to be heard, Natalia thought to herself, *I hear you.* And also, with a bit of a grin, she thought how much better the painting would look on her living room wall than *Lady in Green Jacket* had.

Miriam snorted, bringing Natalia out of her thoughts. "Really, Diego? Powerpoint? What is this, a community college course?"

"I figured you of all people would be in favor of me using the projector," said Diego. "Would you rather I'd purchased a chalk board?"

Eddie grunted. "Don't be daft, D. 'At's not what Midge is sayin' a' all. It's 'at 'is format is so formal. We're all china 'ere. Can't we just talk about the old Uncle Bob?"

Diego turned to Natalia. "Where do you stand on visual aids?"

Natalia snuck a glance at Eddie as she tried to figure out the team dynamics. "We can always pull up references if we need them."

"Very well. To be honest, I prefer a dialogue myself." Diego returned the remote to the table and turned off the projector, but he remained standing facing the couches. "So let's discuss why we're here. *The Scream.* Edvard Munch's magnum opus. Painted in eighteen ninety-three—"

"The *original* was painted in eighteen ninety-three," interrupted Natalia. "One of the pastels also hails from the same year. The others came later."

Eddie frowned. "Overs? 'ers more 'an one?"

Diego gave Natalia a piqued glance, his eyebrow rising slightly. "Indeed, there are. As Natalia has pointed out, Munch created four versions of the same piece, two pastels and two paintings. One of each was crafted in eighteen ninety-three, the pastel perhaps as a preliminary study for the painting. He then drew another pastel in eighteen ninety-five, and he revisited the work in paint form many years later in nineteen ten."

"And there are black and white lithographs as well," said Natalia. "Also from eighteen ninety-five. It's unclear how many survive, but only about four dozen were pressed."

Diego's second eyebrow joined the first. "Someone has done her homework."

Eddie crossed his arms across his chest. "'An all 'ese versions are 'ere in Oslo?"

"Most of them," said Natalia. "The second pastel was sold at Sotheby's to an American investor, but the other three are all here. The original painting is at the National Gallery, and the other two are at the Munch Museum."

Miriam had put her phone to the side. Amazingly, she looked somewhat interested in the conversation. "So which one are we going to steal?"

"The original painting, of course, as it's the most valuable," said Diego with a smile. "And amusingly enough, we will not be the first ones to do so."

"Technically, both versions of the painting have been stolen over the years," said Natalia.

Diego snorted. He waved his hand toward the couches. "Perhaps you'd prefer to give the presentation instead."

Natalia didn't stand, but she turned toward Eddie and Miriam. "The original was stolen in nineteen ninety-four, the day of the Olympic opening ceremonies in Lillehammer. The painting had been moved to a more prominent location as part of the Olympic festivities, and two men broke in and took it, even leaving a note thanking the National Gallery for its poor security. The painting was recovered undamaged later that year following a sting operation.

"The nineteen ten version of *The Scream* was stolen in two thousand four, and that was even more of a smash and grab job. Masked gunmen swarmed into the museum and stole it, as well as Munch's *Madonna*—or rather, one version of it. Like *The Scream*, Munch painted several. For a while, it was feared the thieves had burned the paintings to remove the evidence of their crime, but that rumor proved unfounded. Police recovered the paintings in two thousand six. Both had sustained damage, but neither was beyond repair."

"Good to know," said Miriam. "So I'm going to hazard a guess that the security has been beefed up at both museums to prevent this type of thing from happening again."

Diego had crossed his arms. He gave Natalia a sideways look before addressing Miriam. "That would be why I've recruited all of you rather than hired an assortment of thugs with firearms."

Eddie nodded in agreement. "Truf be told, I'm a bit of a bully meself, but I'm with D on this one. Best not to pull out the old lady from Bristol if'n ain't needed."

"So what's the plan to steal the painting, then?" asked Natalia.

Diego cast an annoyed look toward Miriam. "Well, I had the details in the presentation, but to boil it down: we wait until after hours, subvert the museum's security, and walk out with the piece, all without anyone being alerted to our presence until the painting is found missing the following morning. Miriam will be tasked with dealing with technology and computerized security, Eddie will handle the driving—and combat, if necessary—and Natalia is our expert on museum-specific security protocols and theft logistics."

Natalia frowned. "And what do *you* bring to the table?"

Diego smiled. "I am what you would call a conman, my dear. Unlike the rest of you, I've been in Oslo for several weeks, establishing my identity as a wealthy donor and known aesthete."

"A what now?" asked Eddie.

"A lover of art and all things beautiful," said Diego. "Specifically,

I've been running a confidence game with the curator of the National Gallery, learning about possible road bumps along our path to steal the painting and facilitating access to certain security systems that might otherwise be too difficult to gain entry to. And, perhaps most importantly, I'm the one who's secured a buyer for *The Scream.*"

"Big deal," said Natalia. "I know plenty of people who buy stolen art."

"Yes, and I'm fairly sure I know all the same people you know," said Diego. "But I'm not talking about a fence. I have a *buyer*. Someone with deep pockets."

Miriam leaned forward in her seat. "Speaking of... what *is* the take?"

"Twenty million apiece," said Diego. "Plus a little extra for myself since I was the one to negotiate the deal with the buyer."

"How much extra?" asked Miriam.

"Ten million."

Natalia snorted. "Ninety million in total? That seems a little low given the pastel from eighteen ninety-five sold for almost a hundred and twenty million dollars a decade ago."

Diego smiled at Natalia. "If the original we plan to steal were to sell at auction, I have no doubt it would fetch at least two hundred million, maybe two and a half times that, but that's the difference between a painting legally traded at auction and one sold on the black market. Buyers, even those with a hundred million dollars to spare, aren't keen on the idea of their wares being repossessed by angry government agents should the wrong person let their tongue wag."

"Seems plenty 'igh to me," said Eddie. "Would'n' catch me spendin' ninety million quid on a paintin', 'ats for sure."

Natalia would. She'd spend whatever it took to get this particular painting—or *do* whatever it took.

Diego spread his hands. "So. Any questions?"

"Plenty," said Natalia. "But none that are going to make me walk away from *this* job. Not with everything that's on the line."

Eddie sucked on his teeth. "Could'na said it better meself. What about you, Midge?"

Miriam nodded slowly. "For twenty million? You'd better believe I'm in."

Diego clapped his hands together. "Excellent. Now the real work begins."

Chapter Four

DIEGO TOOK A SIP OF ICE WATER FROM HIS VANTAGE beside the couches, letting it sit on his tongue for a moment before swallowing. After his pitch, he'd spent over an hour going through his slides with Eddie, Miriam, and Natalia, discussing and hashing out the finer points of his plan with the trio. To be honest, he hadn't anticipated the scope of questions Natalia would have at this early stage. When they finally executed their theft, every movement of theirs would have to be planned down to the second. To pull off the heist without leaving any trace of their presence, they'd have to become a well-oiled machine, with pristine communication and rock solid teamwork. Diego didn't harbor any doubts they could get there, but he hadn't been ready to answer mission specifics today, not before he'd had a chance to get a sense of Natalia's skills.

Diego peered across the room to where Natalia stood, focused on one of the computers while Miriam showed her a set of museum schematics. He'd known almost nothing about Natalia when he reached out to her, only the stories he'd heard through the grapevine about the jobs she'd pulled off. Because of those stories, he knew she'd be a capable thief, but he hadn't anticipated how clever and knowledgeable she would be. She knew more about Edvard Munch than perhaps even the curator of the National Gallery did, and he got the sense that the breadth of her art knowledge didn't stop at Norwegian borders. Sure, her manner left a bit to be desired. She came across as a know-it-all—which, to be fair, she seemed to be. She was also on the brash side, though he didn't expect any less from a thief of her caliber. Still, her confidence and intelligence had caught him off guard— among other things.

When he first entered the loft and laid eyes on her, he'd felt himself rooted to the floor in shock, his mouth hanging open for so long that a migrating bird might've thought it a convenient place to nest for the summer. Even now as he watched her from across the room, he couldn't believe how gorgeous she was. She was tall, with the lean, toned legs of a professional dancer and a shock of golden blonde hair that contained the perfect amount of body to contrast against her long, supple frame. Her face was almost perfectly symmet- rical, her lashes long, her eyes a piercing pale blue, like an arctic glacier that had started to melt in a bright patch of sun. She had the look every Hollywood director knew would turn their cheesy melodrama into a box office smash, except she pulled it off without a single scrap of makeup or, as far as Diego could tell, effort of any kind.

Diego couldn't remember the last time he'd been caught so off guard by a woman, and the strangest part was that she wasn't even his type. While Diego had found himself attracted to women of just about every body shape—tall, short, thin, fit, voluptuous—he none- theless preferred women with Latin features. In his opinion, women with dark hair, dark eyes, and tan skin were simply sexier than their counterparts, and they needed to have either an impressive display of cleavage or an equally impressive derriere to catch his attention. Preferably both. Yet here was Miss Levin, checking none of his boxes and looking like a Norse goddess all the same. It made him feel as if he was back in school, casting furtive glances at the pretty girl in class.

It was *not* a feeling he enjoyed.

Diego had worked hard to get where he was. It wasn't necessarily the financial or career success he was most proud of, although he'd worked hard to achieve those as well. It was the fact that he'd built himself into the kind of man he'd always wanted to be, brick by painstaking brick. He hadn't always been suave, confident, and stylish. Much the opposite. He'd taught himself to gather and command attention. He'd trained himself to act in a way that would intrigue and enamor women. He especially had to work at his ability to lie naturally and effortlessly. He wasn't born a conman. He'd grown into one.

Perhaps the most important facet of his success was in learning to control his emotions, both how he displayed them and how they affected him on the inside. And he hadn't done a particularly good job of either since locking eyes with Natalia.

Still, he'd always believed every challenge that presented itself was an opportunity, and Natalia presented plenty. There was the professional one, of course, in that she needed to be integrated seamlessly into his team if they were to succeed in their theft of Munch's *Scream*, as well as the personal challenge she presented, forcing him to shore up his emotional facade in the face of her beauty and wit. And perhaps there might be the challenge of persuading her to crawl into bed with him—although that was a dreadful idea given the nature of the job ahead of him. But he couldn't keep the thought from crossing his mind.

Diego set down his water, took a breath to compose himself, and headed for the far side of the room, where Natalia continued to peruse Miriam's architectural model of the museum while Miriam looked on, arms crossed and a look of ennui plastered across her face.

"Excuse me, Miriam," said Diego as he approached the pair. "I was hoping to get a moment of Miss Levin's time."

Natalia looked up from the schematics, though she didn't straighten or release the mouse. "I prefer Natalia. I'm not a big fan of my last name."

"Really?" Diego cocked his head. "I find that surprising. It's a powerful surname."

At that Natalia stood tall, giving Diego a sideways look. "What do you mean by that?"

"Well, Levin comes from the Russian *lev* for lion. The king of the jungle, so to speak. Because of your first name, I assumed you were of Russian heritage, although given your Australian accent, it's possible Levin is a Jewish surname instead. If so, still a good name."

Natalia's brow furrowed. "You speak Russian?"

Diego thought Natalia's puckered lips gave her a cute, piqued sort of look. "Not fluently, but I've picked some up over the years. I sell goods to a wide clientele."

Natalia cocked an eyebrow, as if not totally satisfied by his answer. "I see. Well, Levin *is* Russian, but I have no ties to the name or the country. I emigrated when I was very young."

Diego got the impression there was more to the story, but Natalia's tone made it clear she had no intention of telling him about it. Not that Diego could blame her for not wanting to come clean. Who among them didn't have skeletons in their closet, or at least a few bones?

Diego decided to tack into a new direction. "I understand you're responsible for the theft of two different Degas from the Hermitage Museum in St. Petersburg, not to mention a Caravaggio from Fort Worth, Texas."

Natalia snorted. "You're familiar with Caravaggio, are you?"

Diego responded with his own cocked eyebrow. "Born Michelangelo de Caravaggio, he spent most of his career in either Milan or Rome. He was a violent man, and was convicted of murder following a brawl, for which he was forced to go into exile. However, he's probably best remembered for his strong use of *chiaroscuro*, extreme contrast between light and dark, and for his influence on Baroque painting. Is there a reason I shouldn't be familiar with him?"

Natalia's expression softened. "Sorry. When I mentioned I'd stolen Caravaggio's *Cardsharps* to Eddie, he looked as if spoken to him in Mandarin. I assumed you were cut from the same cloth."

Diego glanced at the restroom, into which Eddie had disappeared. Miriam, meanwhile, had retreated to her smartphone as soon as he and

Natalia began speaking. "Eddie is more cultured than you might imagine, but he's not particularly interested in fine art. The same is true of Miriam. To her, a *Matrix*-inspired desktop wallpaper is as impactful as a Renoir."

Miriam responded without looking up from her phone. "Right here, you know."

Diego continued, undeterred. "I'm think I'm the only one with a real interest in the medium—or I was until you joined our team."

Natalia shrugged as she glanced back at the schematics. "I like to be prepared for the jobs I take, that's all."

Diego frowned. "I think it's more than that. I've met meticulous thieves before. People who plan every one of their steps before they move a muscle—"

"Planners," said Natalia.

Diego lifted an eyebrow. "Pardon?"

"Sorry," said Natalia. "That's the name I use for that type of thief. Planners."

"Right," said Diego. "Well, I try to be similarly meticulous when the consequences of failure are twenty-five years to life, but the way you spoke about Munch's *Scream* showed this is more than an intellectual exercise to you."

Natalia turned her attention away from the computer and regarded Diego carefully. She took her time answering. "If art doesn't invoke emotion, then it has no purpose. *The Scream* is pure emotion in physical form. That's why I'm here."

Diego thought about that for a moment. "You choose your jobs based upon the piece. Art theft is more than a way to keep the lights on. This is about passion."

Natalia gave Diego a sly smile, with her lips pressed together and one corner curling up, creating a dimple in her right cheek. Natalia had smiled a few times throughout his presentation, but they'd all been cursory sorts of things. This one was the genuine article, and it lit Natalia up like a bonfire.

"I have bills to pay, same as anyone," said Natalia, "but generally speaking, I enjoy what I do. I didn't get into antique art theft for the money alone."

"I did," said Miriam.

Diego glanced at her, as did Natalia. Noticing the silence, Miriam looked up, if only briefly. "Well, I did. Just saying."

"My point is," said Natalia, "there are easier ways to steal fortunes than trying to pluck them from armored fortresses plastered with security cameras. Many of them legal, depending on where you live and how clever your lawyers are."

"You're referring to hedge fund managers?" asked Diego.

Natalia flashed that devilish smile again. "I was thinking politicians, myself."

Diego caught himself as a chuckle escaped his lips. He hadn't intended to laugh. Laughing shifted the power dynamic in a conversation toward the person who had elicited the response, in this case Natalia, which was the opposite of what he'd intended to do when he first walked over, but Natalia had caught him off guard—again.

He hesitated, rubbing thumb against forefinger as he tried to make sense of the woman in front of him. Here was a stunningly beautiful woman, a woman who was confident and intelligent and well-traveled, a woman with a mysterious past she wasn't proud of but who could sneak humor past his guard without even trying. Perhaps most confusingly, she was an accomplished art thief who seemed to pursue her profession not for the money but for the love of the game.

The fact that Diego couldn't immediately understand what made her tick maddened him—and strengthened his resolve.

"You know," said Diego, "given the amount of work we have ahead of us, it would behoove us to get to know each other better. It's nearly six. Why don't we continue this conversation over dinner?"

Almost as soon as the offer left his lips, Natalia's smile vanished, replaced with the same icy look of suspicion she'd borne as he first approached. "Yeah... That's a hard no."

Chapter Five

Diego blinked at Natalia's response, looking befuddled. "What do you mean, no?"

Natalia sighed, her estimation of Diego crashing from what had started to look like a promising peak. Regardless of how clever or cultured a man might be, all of them seemed to have a hard time understanding such a simple word. "No. The opposite of yes. It means I'm going to pass on dinner."

Diego pursed his lips. "To be honest, it wasn't really a request, even if I did phrase it that way. I don't know how many of your thefts have been solo jobs as opposed to group endeavors, but the most important key to our success going forward isn't our individual skills. It's our ability to work together as a team. To do that well, we have to establish a level of familiarity with one another."

"That's a very reasonable response, Diego," said Natalia, "but I'm afraid the answer is still no. I'm not interested in going on a date with you."

Diego frowned. *"A date?* Who said anything about a date?"

Natalia lifted an eyebrow. While the man's acting was commendable, did he really think he was going to fool her? "So I suppose Miriam will be joining us? And Eddie, too?"

"Well, they could if—"

Natalia turned to the seated Miriam. "Dinner then, Miriam? Diego's treat."

Miriam glanced up from her phone, looking uncomfortable. "Honestly, I want no part of whatever's going on here."

"As I was saying," continued Diego, "Miriam and Eddie are welcome to join us, but I'm already familiar with their personalities. Their styles. I know the way they operate. You're the unknown quantity. That's why it's imperative I get to know you better. But the road goes both ways. Surely you'd be more comfortable working with me once you learn my background and understand my tendencies?"

Natalia smirked. She had to give Diego a point there. He knew she was just as invested in feeling out his edges as he was in hers— metaphorically speaking, of course. "Point taken, but I'm still not going on a date with you. I came here to do a job. No more, no less."

Diego sighed and threw his hands into the air. *"Caramba.* I'm not trying to dupe you. I don't know how else to say it, unless you'd prefer I use another language. *No es una cita.* Or maybe you'd prefer Russian. *Eto ne svidaniye.* It's not a date."

"So what would you call a meeting, over dinner, between two individuals who just met with the implicit purpose of *getting to know each other better?"* Natalia added air quotes for emphasis.

"How about a meeting?" said Diego. "Or a rendezvous. Or simply dinner would suffice. Regardless of what you call it, the reason I suggested it remains valid. And quite frankly, this whole exchange makes it all the more obvious you need to join me. If we're to become a well-oiled machine by the time we pilfer *The Scream,* we'll have to work together as a team. You're going to have to learn to trust me."

And there is was. *The T word.* Natalia assumed Diego would utter it sooner or later, but she'd hoped it wouldn't come for another day or two. The fact of the matter was that as good as Natalia was at deceiving people, it wasn't something she particularly enjoyed, and yet already she was being forced into a position where she was going to *have* to lie to Diego, if only to convince him that she did, in fact, trust him.

Even though there was no way in hell she ever would.

It wasn't that she didn't trust Diego in particular—although, to be fair, she'd be a fool to trust him. He was a conman dressed in an impeccable suit and armed with a smile that could inspire women to disrobe. It was that Natalia didn't trust *anyone.*

And why should she? People, as a general rule, sucked. People leveled rain forests to make way for strip malls. People drove gas-guzzling trucks and SUVs while the world burned around them. People didn't slow for animals and didn't tip enough and threw trash at their feet as they walked. People were *awful.*

But individuals weren't much better. Miss Gramercy at her first foster hadn't been. She'd preferred to get munted on cheap whiskey and malt liquor rather than buy groceries for the fridge. Mr. Penbrook hadn't been any better. He made Natalia taste the back of his hand if she showed even the slightest bit of spine. Then there was Jeremy, her boyfriend in secondary school. He'd seemed decent enough, until he ratted her out to the cops following a bungled burglary of a sneaker shop, claiming he'd been nothing more than an accessory as opposed to the architect of the hare-brained plan. Not that the cops believed a dim-witted Shiela like Natalia could've been anything more than a pawn, otherwise she would've spent the next three year in juvenile detention, but Jeremy had sold her upriver nonetheless.

And then there were her parents, wherever and whoever they might be. In her more charitable moments, Natalia liked to think there'd been a pressing reason why they'd given her up. Not her father, who undoubtedly had been some drunken lout, but perhaps her mother had been forced into making the gut-wrenching decision to leave her. Perhaps she'd had no more than two rubles to her name and lived in a bombed out wreck in the most remote corner of the former Soviet Union. Maybe she'd worked the streets and refused to expose Natalia to the same life. But most likely she just hadn't cared enough to be there. Hadn't wanted to put in the effort to nurture a nascent soul into a fully-formed person.

Nobody had ever cared. Not really. It was a lesson Natalia had learned early, one she'd had reinforced over and over and over again. There was no one she could rely upon to help her. No one she could trust but herself. And Diego's flashy smile, no matter how pretty a face it belonged to, wouldn't get her to think otherwise.

That said, Natalia *did* need Diego to trust *her*, and perpetually coming across as standoffish, rude, and as inflexible as a brick wall wasn't a good way to win over the hearts and minds of her new team. Some pushback would be expected—she was the rookie member of the crew, after all, and a thief to boot—but at some point it would be expected of her to relent.

And really, what was the harm in dinner? It *had* been a long day, and the sushi she'd grabbed at the airport hadn't exhibited much staying power. She also needed to win Diego over so he'd stop prying into her past, lest he find any red flags that might make him doubt her ability, or worse, her sincerity. Plus, Diego seemed to be cultured and charming, with a rather impressive knowledge of art history, among other things. He'd be far from the worst dinner companion.

Not to mention, he was cute as hell.

Natalia chewed on her lip, making a protracted display of mulling Diego's offer over. She lifted an eyebrow as sharply as she could. "Where are you proposing we eat?"

Diego tried to keep his expression even, but Natalia noticed a relaxation in his shoulders. "That depends upon your tastes. We could grab a quick meal at a cafe, or if you're looking for something more decadent, Oslo is home to any number of wonderful restaurants. Might I recommend *Hyse Fisk?* The name translates to Haddock Fish."

"A seafood restaurant, I hope?" said Natalia.

Diego flashed his smile. "With a name like that, I wouldn't trust it if it weren't."

Natalia checked her watch. "Very well. I'll meet you there at seven. Hopefully we won't need a reservation."

"I can handle it if we do," said Diego. "But it's not far from seven now. My car is here. I could drive you if you prefer."

"I do not prefer," said Natalia with a tight-lipped smile. "I have things to attend to first. But I appreciate the offer. Miriam." She gave the young hacker a nod, and then, as she spotted Eddie emerging from the restroom, gave him a polite wave. "Eddie. Good to meet you. And I'll see *you* at the top of the hour."

Without hesitation, she gave Diego a polite nod and headed for the door.

Chapter Six

Diego watched Natalia as she pulled open the loft door and slipped outside. He watched as the door clattered shut behind her, then kept watching after she'd gone, all while pondering a simple question: Why was he so attracted to such an infuriating woman?

It wasn't as if Diego had ever lacked for female companionship, or at least he hadn't once he'd figured out the way he carried himself and the way he directed a conversation had as much impact on his charm as the way he looked. Young adulthood had been a challenge for him, as it was for most adolescents, but once he developed his interpersonal skills to the point where he could swindle people out of their antiquities, getting women to fall for him proved not much of a challenge. He'd had countless trysts over the years. He'd dated a model or two, a powerful, jet-setting CEO, an aspiring pop star, even the wife of a wealthy oligarch, which could've resulted in him being thrown into a river while shackled to a half-dozen cinderblocks if the oligarch ever found out about it. With the exception of that last one, Diego didn't regret any of the relationships. He'd gained something from each, from prestige to knowledge to the thrill of conquest, not to mention a few thoroughly fulfilling sexual encounters. None of the flings had been particularly deep or lasting, but that was to be expected. His profession didn't allow him to build meaningful relationships. Those required a little something called honesty, as well as the ability to live in one spot for more than a few weeks at a time. But all the relationships he'd been a part of *did* have something in common: he'd been the one in control.

Which wasn't the same thing as being *controlling*, mind you. Diego wasn't one of those alpha creeps who kept women as little more than pets, dictating what they should wear and what they could eat. It was simply that in every relationship he'd ever been in he felt as if he was the one driving the car. He was the one who set the final destination, decided where and when to turn, and if he determined it was time to take an exit ramp off the relationship freeway, he'd make that choice, too.

With Natalia, he constantly felt as if she were reaching across his seat to take control of the wheel. Admittedly, all they'd shared were a few short conversations, but conversation was what Diego prided himself on. His entire job revolved around making people believe what he told them, but Natalia resisted. Not just his obvious exaggerations, either. She was a thief, after all. She knew to be wary around him, but she didn't defer to him on the slightest thing. She fought him for control of every exchange, as tenacious as an Olympic wrestler, and even when he thought he'd pinned her, there she was again, reversing his hold and climbing back atop him.

Perhaps that was what intrigued him about her. Diego had always appreciated feisty women, but there was something else that drew him to Natalia like a moth to a flame. There was an element of mystery about her that transcended her problematic past. She was hiding something, whether it was her personality, her true feelings, or something more tangible. Natalia presented a puzzle, and Diego wanted to solve it. If he did that, perhaps he'd be satisfied.

Though he wouldn't mind seeing her naked, either.

"Oy, D. Ya got a crick in yer ol' Gregory Peck, or did the door start a fight with yer mum?"

Diego blinked to find Eddie standing next to him. "What?"

Eddie nodded toward the exit. "Ya been starin' at the wall so long I'ma 'ave to dust ya off. Y'alright?"

"I'm fine, Eddie," said Diego. "I got lost in my thoughts."

A wide grin spread across Eddie's face. "Sure ya did, mate. And I suppose 'at fief ain't got nofing to do wit why you've lost yer marbles all o' sudden."

Diego glanced toward the door again. "Natalia is intriguing, I'll give you that."

Diego didn't think it was possible, but Eddie's smile grew wider. He elbowed Miriam, forcing her to look up from her phone. "'ear 'at? Diego fancies 'imself the ol' tea leaf."

"I wouldn't say I fancy her," Diego lied. "But she's undeniably interesting. She knows enough about *The Scream* to qualify as an amateur Munch biographer, and she's the most accomplished art thief I've ever met, myself excluded, of course."

Miriam rolled her eyes. "And it doesn't hurt that she's easy on the eyes, I'm sure."

Eddie frowned as he shook his head. "Eh. She's bog-standard, mate."

Diego blinked. *"Bog-standard?* I don't even know what that means, but I can assure you she's anything but."

Miriam looked at Eddie as if he'd lost his mind. "Are you blind? I don't swing that way, and even I can tell you she's freaking hot. She should've been the one to pursue a career as a grifter, not Diego."

Diego peered at Miriam, his brow creasing. "What's that supposed to mean?"

Eddie ignored him. "I calls it like I sees it. I prefer me twist and twirls wif a li'l more meat on 'em. And she's too posh. Be'er to get wif a bird 'at's not as 'igh maintenance. Like Midge, 'ere."

Miriam's cheeks darkened. She shrugged deeper into her hoodie as she turned her attention to her phone. "Um... thanks, I guess."

"Look, Natalia's appearance is irrelevant," said Diego. "What matters is that we integrate her seamlessly into this operation so we all walk away with twenty million dollars in our pockets rather than ending up in jail."

"Firty million quid fer you, mate," said Eddie.

"If *you'd* rather befriend the powerful mobsters and CEOs who have a hundred million dollars to burn on a stolen painting, be my guest."

Eddie held up his enormous, calloused hands. "Ain't got no problem wif the deal, mate. Twenty mil is more 'an enough fer me. Ain't got no problem if you fancy Natalia, nei'ver. Just wanted to make sure we was on the same page. 'At you was focused on makin' sure she was legit and all, and comi'ed to gettin' 'at paintin'. 'At's all."

Miriam looked up from her game, the color gone from her cheeks. "For real, Diego. We need to make sure we can trust her."

Diego crossed his arms, tapping his fingers against the side of his rib cage. "That's why I invited her to dinner, obviously. I have to get a sense of who she really is. If I get the feeling she's not the right fit or that we can't rely on her, I'll be the first to admit it and call the whole operation off, at least until we can find a replacement. Fair?"

Eddie nodded.

"As long as you have the right focus," said Miriam.

Diego glanced at the door once more. "Trust me, I am laser-focused on getting our hands on *The Scream.*"

And he was. Mostly.

Chapter Seven

Hyse Fisk WAS LOCATED ON A WHARF THAT PROJECTED A hundred meters into the deep blue waters of the Oslofjord. The interior of the restaurant was sleek and modern, with black glass tables and polished concrete floors, but Diego preferred the view from the patio. Out on the wharf, with the cool breeze whipping off the water to rustle his hair, the creak of joists and riggings from nearby sailboats in his ears, and the rough feel of the weatherbeaten wooden tabletop under his fingertips, he almost felt as if he were at sea himself, albeit without the queasiness that a real ride upon the North Atlantic's choppy waters would bring.

Diego closed his eyes and took a deep breath. Though the predominant scent of the sea was a salty one, it was far from one-note. Some people claimed it smelled fishy. If you had the misfortune of walking along a shore during an algal bloom then that description was both accurate and overwhelming, but most of the time the fishiness was a part of a larger whole. A smell of freshness, of clear sun and cool rain brought ashore on sea-swept breezes. There was a smell of openness, a smell of the wild unknown, and of... *lavender?*

Diego opened his eyes to find Natalia standing over his table. She looked the same as when she'd left the loft an hour ago, still wearing her black leggings and lightweight running jacket and with her hair pulled back in a ponytail. The vain part of him thought she might've hurried to her hotel and slipped into something more revealing as a way to catch his eye, but clearly whatever business Natalia had attended to wasn't of the personal grooming variety.

Natalia met his gaze evenly, but she wasn't motionless, frozen by his eyes like a deer caught by headlights. Rather, her look was more calculating. While it stopped short of being malicious, Diego nonetheless had a sense of what it might feel like for a rabbit to come face to face with a lynx, one who'd yet to decide whether it was hungry enough to bother chasing down its lunch.

Natalia arched an eyebrow, and she *almost* smiled. "You know in our profession, it's best to have a sense of awareness of your surroundings at all times. Otherwise you might be caught unawares."

Diego pictured the lynx in his mind before he smiled in return. "You didn't catch me unawares. I smelled you approaching."

Natalia frowned, her mirth vanishing as if whisked away on a stiff sea breeze. *"Excuse me?"*

Diego sat up straighter. "Sorry. That came out the wrong way. I simply meant I noted your perfume. Lavender, correct?"

Natalia rolled her eyes and sighed. *"Ugh...* It's those damn candles. Now I'm going to have to wash my clothes."

Diego lifted an eyebrow. "Candles?"

Natalia pulled out the chair opposite Diego and had a seat. "At my hotel. In the toilet. The staff had them lit when I arrived, and I never blew them out. Now they've infused their stink into my jacket."

"I wouldn't call it a stink. Lavender is a pleasant smell."

"But it's a *recognizable* smell, nonetheless," said Natalia. "While not being caught off guard is an important part of our profession, not being caught at all is more important. A smell of any kind—lavender, citrus, sage, whatever—can be tracked. If someone who was looking for me knew nothing else about me other than I smelled like lavender, they'd have a hard time tracking me down, but give them one or two other clues, my shoe size for example, maybe the lunch I ate one day, that might be enough for them to decipher my identity. Once they know that, it's game over."

Natalia flicked her fingers across her throat for emphasis. It might've come across as a more vicious gesture if her neck wasn't so lovely.

Diego grasped the Gimlet he'd ordered, the glass still cool to the touch. He took a sip and held the liquor in his mouth to savor the flavor. "You realize we're here for dinner, not a job, right?"

Natalia's annoyance wicked away, disappearing behind a devilish smile. *"Really?* I was under the impression this event was work related, so I figured we should abide by the same standards we normally would. Or is this dinner *not* the team building exercise I was led to believe it was?"

Diego snorted as he rested his glass on the table. "Your lunge strikes true. Point to the lady. Care for a drink?" He held up a hand, signaling to the nearest waitress before awaiting her response.

"I had a cocktail at my hotel when I arrived this afternoon," said Natalia. "I'm fine."

"Well, one more couldn't hurt. My treat." Diego turned to the arriving waitress. "Hello. My guest would like order a drink."

"Water, please," said Natalia before the waitress could respond. "With *extra* ice." She glared at Diego as she said that last part.

The waitress smiled and nodded. "Certainly. I will—"

Diego stuck a finger in the air again, feeling a little miffed. "I'm sorry, but the lady hasn't had a chance to see the drink menu. Perhaps if you have one."

The waitress nodded again. "Of course. I—"

Natalia gave her head a taut shake. "No, thank you. Water will be fine."

Diego frowned. "You can leave the menu. In the meantime, why don't you bring her a Caipirinha, assuming you have any cachaça. If not you can use mild white rum."

Natalia's brow furrowed. She kept her eyes on Diego as she spoke. "The drink is for him, to be clear. Just the water for me."

The waitress glanced between the two of them as she set a menu down, clearly unsure of herself. "I'll see what the bartender has in stock."

Natalia kept staring at Diego as the waitress scuttled off. "*A Caipirinha?* That's an interesting choice of cocktail to force on me. I would've expected you to order something bland like a Cosmopolitan."

Diego ran his finger along the rim of his glass. "You're clearly not a bland sort of woman. On the contrary, you seem quite spicy this evening, so I ordered you something that might help cool you down."

Natalia's eyes drifted to Diego's Gimlet. "And I don't suppose a Caipirinha would be a drink *you* would enjoy in the event I stick to my guns and don't drink it."

Diego shrugged, but he couldn't help but flash a sly smile. "That might've been a secondary consideration."

Natalia met Diego's gaze once again. She considered him carefully, and for a moment Diego thought she might get up and leave, but whatever she had on her mind she eventually dismissed. She sighed, sagging into her chair. "I'm sorry. I came here more guarded than I needed to be. How about I make you an offer? I'll try to be more open and less *spicy* if you meet me halfway."

"Halfway where?"

Natalia cocked her head at him, as if she thought he might be dense. "To opening up. To putting this facade aside and being more genuine."

Diego hesitated. A small voice in his head whispered to him, *she knows,* but outwardly, he smiled. "But of course. I'm as open as a book."

Natalia scoffed. "Right. My mistake. Enjoy the Caipirinha." Natalia's chair squealed as she pushed back from the table and stood.

Diego hadn't intended to shoot out of his own chair, but reactions moved faster than conscious thought. "Wait."

Natalia eyed him expectantly, teetering on the edge of leaving.

Thoughts swirled in Diego's mind. On the one hand, he didn't know why he'd become so invested in this woman he'd just met. She was beautiful, yes, but also difficult and quarrelsome and too smart for her own good. But for the sake of the heist, he couldn't let her leave. Her departure would make things significantly more complicated and delay theft of *The Scream*. Perhaps more importantly, however, he didn't *want* her to leave. Something told him there was more to this woman than met the eye, something far more complex than anything a model or a pop star could offer, and despite all warnings of curiosity leaving a trail of dead cats in its wake, he wanted to know what it was. He wanted to unearth the hidden core inside her, to see what Natalia was hiding that she was so protective of, but what she was asking for, for him to be *genuine*, was simply out of the question.

Other than perhaps the odd moment with Eddie, Diego hadn't been genuine with *anyone* in at least a decade. It wasn't who he was. Not anymore. Besides, the personas he'd worked hard to develop were far more interesting, mysterious, and alluring than anything the original Diego had to offer. That old personality, the one he'd grown up with, was dull, bland, and boring. It wasn't deserving of even a passing interest, much less affection. For that reason, Diego had buried and forgotten it, focusing instead on building new and interesting personalities.

Natalia had already seen through his first one, his prominent, suave personality that he shared with most marks, but this wasn't Diego first rodeo. What sort of conman would he be without a backup plan? So, rather than digging inside himself and shining a light into the deep recesses of his soul in search of what he'd once hidden away, he simply donned a new suit and did what he did best.

He kept lying.

"I'm not used to this, you know," Diego said with a sigh. "I've partnered with Eddie and Miriam before, but most of the time when I run a con, I do it alone. I'm used to plying my trade on a mark, not an equal, and I suppose I'm finding it difficult to shift my train of thought accordingly. So I apologize. Though I cannot guarantee perfection, I will do my best to be more open and forthright, and I promise I won't force any more drinks on you. Deal?"

Natalia thought it over for a moment. "For now."

Natalia returned to her seat, but she didn't settle into it. She perched on the edge, like a bird ready to take flight should a predator threaten her. Clearly, Natalia didn't fully believe him, as she shouldn't. Diego would have to be careful to come across as credible and genuine, even if he wasn't. One slip up and Natalia might take flight again. He needed to be charming but relatable. Come across as honest without being overly revealing. Most importantly, he needed to figure out some way to keep Natalia on the hook so he could learn what made her tick. Diego had no doubt he could win Natalia over eventually, but he needed time to do it.

Diego settled into his own chair. "You're a hard nut to crack, you know that?"

"I don't crack," said Natalia. "So. In the interest of coming clean, why don't you tell me the real reason you asked me to dinner tonight?"

"I actually told the truth in that regard," said Diego. "You intrigue me. You're an art thief who's passionate about art, Munch in particular unless I'm mistaken. As someone who appreciates art, that's an immediate draw. I also wanted to get to know you more, but not just on a personal level. It's important that I make sure you're going to be able to work well with me, Eddie, and Miriam. The stakes are high, and I don't intend to rush into our job until I'm confident in your abilities."

Natalia sniffed as she scooched further into her seat. "You don't need to worry about my abilities. Frankly, I don't think the security at the National Museum is that impressive. I could probably pull the job on my own if I wanted."

Diego took note of Natalia's response. So she was cocky. Good. He could use that to help reel her in, but he needed more. "I like a woman with confidence, but justified confidence is even better."

Natalia arched an eyebrow at him. "You're the one who came to *me*. Are you saying you don't believe the stories about the jobs I pulled off?"

"I do my research," said Diego, "so I know the stories are true. Whether you were the protagonist of the stories is to be determined, but I have no reason to believe you're not who you say you are. One thief taking credit for another's work would cause quite a stir in the circles I hang out in, and I haven't heard of any such thing. So yes, I believe the tales. That doesn't mean I wouldn't want to hear them again from a first person perspective."

Diego dropped his voice as the waitress returned.

"One water, and one Caipirinha." She set the later down in front of Diego. "Can I get either of you anything to eat?"

Natalia made eye contact with the waitress this time. "I'm not picky. I'll take whatever your chef thinks is their best dish."

"Certainly." The waitress looked at Diego expectantly. "And you, sir?"

Diego shrugged. "Why not? Make it two."

The waitress bobbed her head and left. As she headed inside, Natalia leaned across the table and snagged the Caipirinha. She took a sip, her expression brightening as she did so. "Not bad. Sweet but not cloying. I like it."

"See? I wasn't trying to poison you." Diego waved his hand. "So. I believe you were going to tell me about your successes. Maybe the St. Petersburg job? Rumor has it you pulled an Irwin Allen to clear the museum floor."

Natalia took another slow sip. *"An Irwin Allen?* You might be the first person I've ever met who knows what that is."

Diego snorted. "Please. I'm a professional. Of course I know what it is. So is the rumor true? I mean, it makes sense given the museum suffered broken windows to the third floor, but I can't figure how you pulled it off. Maybe a depth charge on one of the foundation pylons?"

Natalia chewed her lip in a seductive way, but she shook her head. "No, I don't think so. That's too good of a story. You haven't earned it."

Diego blinked. "Pardon?"

Natalia flashed that devilish smile again. "Do you think I'm going to give that story away for free? Come on. Stories are currency, and the best ones are worth a pretty penny. Besides, it seems entirely unfair that you seem to know so much about me when I know absolutely nothing about you. Why should I be the one to bare myself when you haven't even given me a glimpse?"

Diego sat there for a moment, probably looking rather foolish, but an ingenious thought had just come to him, a way to keep Natalia leashed so she couldn't run away—or rather, so she wouldn't want to. And it didn't involve any coercion or blackmail or anything smarmy at all. Rather, it took advantage of one of Diego's best skills, one he'd been honing for half his life: his ability to tell a darn good yarn.

"So, what you're saying is, before you tell me about your history in the business, you want to know how *I* got started?"

Natalia took another sip of the drink she'd commandeered. "It seems only fair."

A smile spread across Diego's face. "Well. Funny you should ask, because that *is* an interesting story..."

Interlude 1

The first thing you have to understand is everything I'm about to tell you is one hundred percent true. Some of it might sound outlandish, but that's simply a testament to the sort of life I've led.

The second thing you have to understand is that I have an impeccable memory. Not a single event I've ever experienced firsthand has been lost to the sands of time. All of them are locked tight in my mind, each of them in their own cage, perfectly sized to the memory in question. I like to think of myself as having a keyring at my side. When I need to access a particular memory, I pluck at that ring and pull the appropriate key from my side (it always seems to be the first one I pick). Then when I unlock that cage, *presto*. The memory pops into my mind as pristine as if I were experiencing it for the first time, the colors bright, the smells vibrant, the sounds clear as crystal.

Now you might be excused for thinking a perfect memory is my talent, the unique gift that has been passed down through my bloodline for generations, but that's only half of it. This story is about the other half.

But I'm getting ahead of myself. You see, everyone in my family has a gift, some minor, some impressive. It's not something any of us have had to work at, either. The gift comes naturally to us, either at birth or shortly thereafter. My older brother Rodrigo, for example, has the gift of language. He was able to speak fluently—Spanish, of course, as we grew up in Andalusia—by the time he was nine. Not years, mind you. *Months.* By three years of age, he was fluent in English, French, German, Portuguese, and Italian, all from watching cartoons on television. He met a Kenyan at the age of seven and was able to pick up a rudimentary understanding of Swahili within an hour, simply from context!

But his gift is nothing compared to my sister's, who happens to be three years older than me to the day. In some ways, Antonia's gift is also one of speech, but not like Rodrigo's. Her talent is something even members of my own family, who are used to this sort of thing, consider *unnatural,* because her gift is the ability to speak... *to the dead.* In fact—"

Chapter Eight

"WHOA, HOLD ON." NATALIA HELD UP A HAND. "ARE YOU seriously trying to convince me your sister could talk to *ghosts?*"

"Still can," said Diego. "She's alive and well. And while *I* would say they're ghosts, Antonia has always described them more as lost souls. She's more religious than I am—perhaps because her gift has convinced her there is an afterlife—but she claims these are the spirits of folks who haven't yet passed to their final destination. Which if you ask me sounds a lot like what a ghost is, but she's adamant there's a difference."

Natalia stared at Diego, dumbfounded. Before she could stop it, a laugh escaped her, echoing across the patio.

Diego lifted an eyebrow. "You find ghosts funny?" He stared at her intently. *Seriously.*

"What I find funny is you're sitting here with a straight face while you spin this ridiculous web of lies."

Diego exaggerated a look of shock, even going so far as to press a hand against his chest. *"Lies?"*

Natalia snorted. "Sorry. That was too kind. I meant to say bullshit."

Diego gave her a sly smile, his white teeth flashing. Natalia knew it was an insincere gesture, but gosh darn if it didn't make him look incredibly appealing. He'd probably practiced it a million times. "Perhaps you weren't paying attention. You see, when I started my story I made it clear everything I was going to tell you was one hundred percent factual. I even cautioned you to withhold your sense of disbelief because I knew you'd react this way."

Natalia rolled her eyes. "My mistake. How could I possibly think anything else of this completely believable tale you've embarked upon."

Diego shrugged, this time feigning ignorance. "I don't know. Perhaps you're so used to most people's boring, mundane lives that when you come across someone who's led an existence worth chronicling, you're too overwhelmed to process it."

Natalia might've rolled her eyes again, but she feared she might strain something. "Of course. But putting aside for a moment your *completely factual, incredibly honest* anecdotes about your family, do you mind telling me what any of this has to do with my original question?"

Diego clasped his hands before him. "Well, you asked how I got started in this business."

Natalia would've felt exasperated if it wasn't so obvious Diego was playing her. "Exactly. I didn't ask about your family or whatever weird personality quirks you claim to have. I just wanted to know your background."

"Which is what I'm giving you," said Diego.

"Your background *in the business.*"

"Ah." Diego shrugged again. "Well, that's the thing. Every action we take in life shapes us. Every experience is formative, some more than others. Often it's the strangest situations that have the biggest impact on who we become. So if all you care about is *how* I got into the confidence game business, that's a short, dry account. But if what you care about is *why*, then you have to understand a few keys events that transpired first."

"And this business with your siblings will explain the why?"

Diego waved his hand. "My siblings are irrelevant to this particular story. I was simply using them to explain how strange gifts run in my family. But I assure you, understanding this particular story is key to seeing how I got here. As a great poet once said, if you want to know where I'm going, all you need to know is where I've been."

Natalia frowned. She'd heard that line before, or some formulation thereof, and it didn't come from any great poet. Far from it. "Is that... a quote from the movie *Cars?*"

Diego cocked his head and pursed his lips. "No. I don't think so."

Natalia felt a smile creep onto her face. "It is. *It absolutely is.* You just quoted a hillbilly tow truck from an animated children's movie."

"Pretty sure it was Maya Angelou, actually," said Diego. "And I'm the one with the impeccable memory, so I would know."

Natalia dipped her head, wiping a couple fingers across her brow as she tried to hide her mirth. When she'd asked Diego to be more genuine, she certainly hadn't expected *this,* though the exchange had nonetheless been a welcome change from the self-assure rake she'd had to deal with previously.

"To be honest, I'm not an expert on quotes from children's movies," said Natalia, even though she was *certain* she was right. "So I'll let you have this one if you'll just get on with it."

Diego leaned forward. "Are you sure? Because I could give you the dry version if that's what you'd prefer. Drop a few names. The man who introduced me to the seedy underbelly of society. Maybe make a bulleted list of the jobs I've taken part in."

Natalia smirked. She knew what he was doing, but her dinner had yet to arrive, so what was the harm in letting him work his mouth a little? Besides, he was finally starting to amuse her. "No. Tell it your way. I'll try not to interrupt this time."

Diego's smile widened. "Very well. Now, let's see. Where was I..."

Interlude 2

To recap: My brother's gift is of speech, my sister's of touching the afterlife, and mine, at least in part, is of memory, which is how I'm able to relate this story. You see, the tale takes place when I was just eleven months old. Most individuals would have to rely on other people's recollection of events at such a young age, as most people don't form lasting, permanent memories until at least three or four years of age, but I recall it all clearly.

Let me tell you, it's an odd experience to be able to perfectly picture the world as an infant. Everything is so big. Rooms the size of amphitheaters. Chair cushions that reach to your nose. And the people! I can still picture my father, who was roughly the size of a giraffe, though much better looking. I'd reach up as far as I could to grasp his hand and he'd stretch just as far down to grab mine, his eyes wide as saucers but full of a kindness I've never seen elsewhere.

But I digress. This story begins with my parents leaving home for an evening out. They went to the movies to watch *Ferris Bueller's Day Off*, though in Spain the movie was titled *Todo En Un Dia*, which translates to Everything in a Day. Regardless, my parents ate an early dinner with me and my two siblings, and after my mother gave firm instructions to my brother Rodrigo about proper bedtimes, she and my father headed out at seven o'clock sharp.

Now keep in mind that Rodrigo, whom my mother left in charge, was just seven years old at the time, and Antonia was not even four, but my mother was nonetheless confident in Rodrigo's ability as the oldest sibling to take care of the rest of us. Don't judge her too harshly. The prevalence of gifts in our family makes everyone more confident then they should be, something of which I'm occasionally guilty of myself, but my mother was more susceptible to that because of her own particular gift. More on that later.

In any case, after my parents left, my brother carried me upstairs to the play room and Antonia followed us. Now if you think I should've been in bed at the time, you're probably right, but Antonia wanted to play a game and Rodrigo figured I'd be entertained enough watching. So while the two of them set up and began to play a board game, I watched while drooling on myself and playing with a rattle.

What board game?

Natalia, please, this is my story. It's quite rude of you to interrupt.

My mistake. I figured someone with an impeccable memory would remember the game and include that detail in the story.

If you must know, it was a dreadfully boring Pac-Man game, in English, that my brother translated into Spanish for my sister. All went well for the first half-hour or so, until the phone rang. Rodrigo got up to answer it, and while he was busy, Antonia rearranged the board in her favor, because as anyone with an older sibling can attest to, being constantly beaten at board games by your brother gets irritating fast. When Rodrigo returned, however, he was perfectly aware that Antonia had cheated, which Antonia vehemently denied, and this set off a heated argument between the two that may have involved some kicking and biting.

I wasn't impressed, and I took it upon myself to explore the world while the two of them were distracted. I was just learning to walk at the time, so I crawled to the nearest door, used the frame to pull myself up, and stumbled into the hall. My bedroom was down the hallway, as were Rodrigo and Antonia's, but I knew what was there. Nothing interesting, that was for sure. So I wobbled my way to the banister at the top of the stairwell, grabbed it for support as I eyed the front door, and took my first step toward all the freedoms that door promised.

Needless to say, it was a bad idea. The floor fell out from under me, I tipped forward, and the next thing I knew I was flying. Well, falling, and without much style, I'm afraid.

Is that another children's movie reference?

Hush. The point is I pitched forward, crashing painfully into one step, then another, as I tumbled down the entire length of the stairs, whacking my shoulder, my thigh, my ribs, and most notably my forehead, before eventually rolling to a stop at the base of the steps, not five feet from the front door.

I lay there for a moment in a daze. I might've been mildly concussed due to the sharp crack I took on my head, but as the world started came back into focus around me, one critical sensation coalesced before all others.

I hurt. *A lot.*

And when you're not even a year old, there's only one response to a sudden flood of pain: to scream. So I did. I yelled at the top of my lungs, filling the house with my panicked, pained cry. Upon hearing me, Rodrigo and Antonia broke off their bickering and came running, both of them moving so fast they almost tripped and flew down the stairs themselves. Upon seeing the condition I was in, Rodrigo immediately blamed my sister for distracting him, to which Antonia retorted that he was the one who'd started the fight upon seeing the revisions she'd made to the board, but both of their arguments dissipated quickly in the face of my relentless screaming.

Rodrigo picked me up, poking me in the arm, the leg, the chest, all through which I continued to scream and Rodrigo's features became increasingly more worried. He paled as he took a look at my face and told my sister to examine the large lump, or *chichon* as we say in Spanish, that had already formed on the side of my forehead.

With a trembling hand, he reached out and touched the lump in question.

The feel of his fingertips on my head felt foreign, as if he were touching some part of me that wasn't really there, but even more strangely, as soon as my brother pressed his fingers against the still growing lump, I *knew*. I knew that my screaming wasn't helping anything, and that my brother and sister would be better able to help me if I stopped. So I did.

You see, while I might've already had a perfect memory, I was still an infant at the time. I couldn't count. Couldn't speak. Couldn't understand speech. It's only now as I recall what happened that the words Rodrigo and Antonio spoke make sense. At the time, they didn't. Until that touch, at least. At the time, with my limited understanding of the world, I thought it was my brother's touch that had changed me, releasing perhaps some hidden gift that none of us knew about, but over time it would become obvious it was the lump itself that was responsible for the shift.

Rodrigo startled as I calmed, but he didn't ignore my condition. In fact, he thought quite the opposite, that perhaps me going quiet was a sign I'd taken a turn for the worse. My sister assured him I was fine, that the spirits around her didn't see me passing over at that moment, but Rodrigo wasn't pacified by her belief that I wasn't immediately dying. He knew I needed to see a doctor right away, but how to get me to one?

In those days, cellular phones were something only the rich and famous had access to. Certainly, my parents didn't have one, so Rodrigo had no way of letting them know the situation. My brother could call the theater where my parents were watching their movie, try and have someone locate them, tell them what happened, and have them rush back, but in doing so, he'd have to admit he let me fall down the stairs while he and Antonia bickered over a game.

"We need to take him to Dr. Alvarez," said Rodrigo. "He'll know what to do."

Antonia was too frightened to argue, so she nodded and followed Rodrigo to the garage.

Luckily, our pediatrician, Dr. Alvarez, lived only a few blocks away, even if his practice was downtown, but Rodrigo had skinned his knee badly on a Sunday once and the doctor had my parents bring him over to his home instead, which was how Rodrigo knew where to go. Rodrigo didn't know how to drive and my parents had the car, besides, so he attached a wagon to his bike, placed me inside it, and headed out, with Antonia following on her tricycle.

Now given everything else that had been transpiring, my siblings could be forgiven for not noticing that a large storm was moving in. As Rodrigo set out with me trailing him, the wind was picking up, sending leaves skittering across the sidewalk into the road. Thick clouds rolled in overhead, shrouding the fading light of dusk with a foreboding darkness. There was a crackle in the air, as well as the smell of oncoming rain.

Now as it turns out, there happened to be a graveyard on the path from our house to Dr. Alvarez's, and the quickest route between the two happened to be across it. We made our way through the entrance gates as the first droplets of water started to fall. Throughout this, Antonia had followed diligently on her tricycle, complaining about the pace Rodrigo had set, but as we wound along the cobblestone path, Antonia suddenly burst out in that little voice of hers: "Wait! Stop!"

Rodrigo did, asking what was wrong, to which Antonia replied that the spirits were swirling, telling her something bad was about to happen. Rodrigo always thought her gift was more theater than anything else, but he knew better than to publicly doubt her, especially with me battered and bruised in the back of the wagon, so he told her the spirits were right. If we didn't hurry, not only would we get soaked, but we might blow away in the coming storm. Antonia fought him, telling him he was wrong, that the spirits said we needed to turn back, but Rodrigo told her to swallow her cries and hurry up.

At that moment, as Rodrigo put his feet to his pedals, the sky turned white and a blast like none I'd ever heard rent the sky. A lightning bolt crashed down from the heavens, splitting the old cork oak that had loomed over the cemetery for generations, sending shrapnel flying in all directions. A large chunk knocked Antonia off her tricycle with a thwack, and wouldn't you know it, but another chunk hit me right on the *chichon*, same place where I'd cracked my skull on the stairs.

This blow hurt even worse than the first, but along with the rolling waves of nausea and pain that sent me reeling onto my back in the cold metal wagon came a new sensation. An increased sense of self, of my place in the world, of Antonia and Rodrigo's conversations, and about the weather events unfurling around me. Everything was starting to make *sense*.

I lay there, stunned as much by the blow as by my newfound understanding of the world, when I finally heard Antonia's cries. I dragged myself to the side of the wagon, and when I did, I found her on the ground, her arm hanging limp at her side and Rodrigo looked even more pale and concerned than when I first fell down the stairs. Perhaps more importantly than Antonia, though, was that I could now see out of the corner of my eyes my own rapidly growing forehead bump, which at this point projected from my skull like a rhinoceros's horn.

But the bump was not the only of our worries. The storm had arrived in force, with the wind howling, rain beating on our heads, and lightning crackling across the sky every few seconds. Rodrigo knew we needed to find shelter, especially since the only tall tree in the graveyard was now little more than splinters, but with Antonia's arm broken (which we'd find out later), we couldn't move quickly.

To make a long story short, we walked the rest of the way to Dr. Alvarez's home, with Rodrigo pulling the wagon by hand and the three of us taking shelter under trees when possible. We didn't get struck by lightning, but in the twenty minutes it took us to march to his house, the rain soaked us to the bone and chilled us to the point that everyone's teeth were chattering—well, except mine. I only had a few of them at the time. Most importantly, the *chichon* on my head continued to grow, like Pinocchio's nose. It was almost at the point that it might snag on passing branches.

It was a good thing Dr. Alvarez was an accomplished pediatrician. He would've had no problem getting us warm and getting the bump under control if he'd been available, but unfortunately, he was not. As we arrived at Alvarez's home, we found a quartet of police vehicles parked out front, and Dr. Alvarez was in the process of being escorted into the closest one. Apparently, for as good of a doctor as the man was, he was equally as poor of a criminal, which the police had recently discovered during a sting of the Ponzi scheme he was running alongside his practice.

I clearly recall Rodrigo's look as he gazed upon the police cars, his face as pale from shock as from the cold. I also remember the look on the officer's face who first approached us, his brow furrowed as tightly as a caterpillar as he asked what in the world we were doing there.

Once the officer got over the shock of having three young children approach him, wet, bedraggled, and in the middle of a summer squall, his eyes quickly moved to the zeppelin-like projection coming out of my skull. That's when his training kicked in. He shouted for help, and other officers came running. I lost track of what was going on, because from my point of view, every inch of real estate had become filled with enormous servants of the law, but in no time at all, I'd been pulled into the arms of an officer. He held onto me tightly as his partner backed their cruiser out of Alvarez's driveway and shot down the street like a rocket.

Doctors and nurses were ready and waiting for us when we arrived at the hospital. Antonia accompanied us as well, as had Rodrigo, but it wasn't Antonia's arm the doctors had amassed for. It was the giant *chichon* that caused an outpouring of concern. I remember being rushed to an exam room as doctors poked and prodded me, more thoroughly than Rodrigo had by a factor of ten. The oddest part was that I understood every one of their conversations. Me, an infant of eleven months, knew all about subcutaneous hemorrhages and the blood brain barrier and intracranial pressure, just as much as the doctors did. And I wasn't particularly worried about my injury, because I knew what was causing it. I knew the blow I'd sustained had generated a lump that was applying pressure on the right half of my frontal lobe, which was in turn putting strain on the cerebellar-parietal component and causing new neural pathways to form with the cerebellum and temporal lobes of my brain. Don't ask me how I knew.

I just *knew*.

But as they continued to poke and prod and as someone called the theater where my parents were getting out of their showing of *Ferris Bueller's Day Off*, the *chichon* suddenly began to shrink. I was perhaps the first to notice, as I could still see it from the corner of my eyes, but soon everyone in the room noticed. The lump shrunk from the size of a horn to that of an overly large nose to eventually that of a grape, and as the lump dissipated, so too did the effects it had on my intellect.

By the time my mother arrived, sobbing and worried out of her mind, the lump had all but disappeared, as had the effects it brought with it. Or so I thought. Because as it turns out, a blow upon the same spot on my head would reactivate those neural pathways years later, and good thing, too. Because without them, I never would've survived my very first con...

Chapter Nine

DIEGO TRAILED OFF. NATALIA EYED HIM EXPECTANTLY, BUT
he didn't continue.

"Well?"

"Well, what?" said Diego.

Natalia could tell Diego wasn't that dense, but he seemed intent
on playing a role. "So what's this first con that you wouldn't have
survived if not for your concussion-induced intellect?"

"It wasn't induced by the concussion," said Diego. "The concussion was a side effect of the blow. My brain power was enhanced by
the bump itself and the neural pathways it established. Weren't you
paying attention?"

Natalia wished she could say she hadn't, that the story had bored
her to tears and put her to sleep several times, but sadly, that wasn't
the truth. As ridiculous and contrived as the whole thing had been,
Diego clearly had a knack for storytelling. There was an easy rhythm
to the yarn he spun. He never tripped and stumbled on his own lies,
never contradicted his own story. Even when Natalia interrupted he
kept going, coming up with the perfect detail to flesh out his tale.
Although the story was a hundred percent false and he was *not* being
genuine with her as she'd asked, in a sense there *was* something

genuine about the act he'd put on for her. He'd shared a talent with her, put it on display knowing she'd be the harshest of critics.

And frankly, she'd enjoyed it. But she couldn't let Diego know.

"If I'm being honest, I faded in and out a few times," said Natalia. "For a story that was so obviously contrived, you could've made it more exciting. Added an earthquake or a runaway train. That moment with the lightning brightening the sky? It could've been aliens coming to abduct you. It was a missed opportunity. And if you're going to insist on stealing ideas from film, you should move outside animated movies. The thing about your family's gifts? Pretty obvious."

Diego smiled, causing dimples to become visible through his cheek scruff. "Once again, you besmirch my good name. I promised you everything in the tale was true, and here you go again."

"Don't try to make this about me," said Natalia. "You're deflecting, and you need to get on with the story. About how this all ties into your first con? Or did you forget this whole exercise started because I asked you about your origins as a grifter?"

Diego's smile turned into a smirk. "So you *do* want to hear more. I can't imagine why. According to you, everything that's come out of my mouth this evening is lies. Bunkum. Hogwash."

Natalia rolled her eyes, but she couldn't stop a bit of a smile from creeping onto her lips. "It is, but that doesn't mean you can stop halfway. If I were to watch a movie about time-traveling star-crossed lovers and the credits rolled mid-feature, you can be sure I'd be upset."

Diego tipped his head toward Natalia. "Fair enough. But unfortunately, the rest of the story is going to have to wait. The evening grows late, and I fear this restaurant might close around us."

Diego might've been exaggerating, but he wasn't far off the truth. The spots on the table before them were clear, but not because the food had yet to arrive. Much the opposite. Throughout the course of Diego's tale, their entrees had arrived—a delectable soy-marinated arctic char served with risotto and a microgreen salad—then been consumed. Natalia had finished her Caipirinha and the second one she'd ordered when the waitress arrived to clear their plates. The sun had set over the hills west of the fjord, leaving little more than wisps of purple and navy in the sky, and a chill had seeped into the air despite the presence of a few commercial patio heaters spread around the deck.

Natalia checked her watch even though she knew more or less what time it was. "It's not *that* late. If you're getting cold, we could move inside and you can tell me the second half of your story there."

Diego snorted, but it wasn't a harsh sort of snort. "If *I'm* getting cold. How thoughtful of you. But no. If you want the rest of the story, you'll have to show up on time tomorrow."

"Show up on time to *where* tomorrow?"

"The National Gallery." Diego checked to make sure he'd returned his credit card to his pocket before standing. "You have a lot to learn, and as nice as Oslo is, I don't plan on being here for the next month."

Natalia blinked. "Excuse me. *I* have a lot to learn? The art thief who you specifically reached out to for expertise?"

Diego paused in front of his chair, adjusting his jacket as he did so. "Well, let's say we have a lot to learn about each other. As I've tried to make clear, teamwork is what will determine the success of this endeavor. Besides, we need to perform reconnaissance at the Gallery, and as talented as Eddie and Miriam are, I doubt they'll notice the same details you will. I'll meet you in the lobby. Ten o'clock sharp."

Natalia ran her tongue across her teeth. Him complimenting her on her ability to pick out museum security at a glance wouldn't make up for his gaffe. "AM or PM?"

"AM of course. The Gallery isn't open that late."

Natalia gave him her best withering glance. "Details matter, and we're not the sort to be dissuaded by locked doors. I figured I should clarify."

Diego dipped his head, responding with a slight chuckle. "Very true. Ten AM tomorrow morning. I'll see you then, Natalia."

Natalia pondered if she should wish him goodnight, but instead she just acknowledged him with a nod. He nodded back, headed onto the wharf, and disappeared into the night.

Natalia picked up her Caipirinha and drained the last of the slightly sweet ice melt from the bottom of the glass, glancing up the wharf after Diego and wondering what exactly she'd gotten herself into.

Diego was a liar. A darned good one, that much was clear, but she'd expected nothing less from a professional conman. Like any grifter, he was disingenuous and occasionally smarmy, and he seemed to have an overly high opinion of himself, something Natalia detested in anyone much less some man trying to ingratiate himself to her. But there were parts of him Natalia didn't detest. He could hold a conversation well, he was quite the talented storyteller, and despite the overblown assertions about his magical intellect, he was clearly quick on his mental toes. Those, too, were qualities she'd expected to see based on her few interactions with him via text (and frankly, if he wasn't a smart, silver-tongued liar, she'd be having serious reservations about the heist right about now), but she hadn't expected him to be passionate about art, too. The way he spoke about Caravaggio and Munch made it seem as if he actually cared about the craft. It was hard to know for sure given the front he insisted on showing her, but why would he make up such a thing? He might grin and wink and whisper sweet nothings to gain her trust or in hopes of luring her to his bed, but why lie about his passion for art? Natalia didn't know what to make of it.

She also didn't know what to make of the stubborn yearning desire she felt when she gazed at him. It didn't help that the man looked like a fashion magazine cover model, what with his perfectly combed dark hair, his thick eyebrows, and that short beard of his that he must meticulously trim every morning to achieve the perfect slovenly but hot look.

Natalia told herself that despite his broad shoulders he was probably a little pudgy under his jacket (which she didn't quite believe) and that because of his meticulous grooming habits he was probably insufferable to share a bathroom with (which she did believe). Regardless of how he might or might not look, Natalia acknowledged that she needed to be careful around him. As she reminded herself for probably the fifth time today, she'd come to Oslo for one reason and one reason only: to get *The Scream*. Not to work with Diego or Eddie or Miriam. Not for the money, but for the painting itself.

And Diego stood in her way.

So what if he was pretty? So what if his stories kept her on the edge of her seat and if his smile made her smile in return? It was immaterial. She needed to get close to him, to make sure she could pull off the job she'd come here to to do, and if Diego wanted to let her get close, all the better.

Natalia took a deep breath of the salty sea air. Yes, working with him wouldn't be as bad as it could be. She'd get as close as she'd need to—for work—and not one step closer.

Chapter Ten

DIEGO STOOD IN THE LOBBY OF OSLO'S *NASJONALMUSEET,* watching tourists enter through the tall, clear glass doors. It was his fourth visit to the museum since arriving in the city, and while he wasn't the biggest fan of modern design, he'd come to develop a certain begrudging respect for the building, which had opened a few months prior. The galleries were spacious and open. Those situated on the edge of the building were flush with natural light, and those that weren't featured diffused panel lights that made the rooms as bright and welcoming as the others. The floors were laid with a light colored wood that featured a distressed patina, and while the walls in some parts of the museum had been painted with gaudy murals, the ones in the galleries were muted solid colors, allowing the pieces on display to attract the attention. Diego had been in some museums where it seemed as if the designer's intent was to force the visitor's gaze onto some gaudy architectural monstrosity, with the centuries old paintings surrounding it relegated to the role of also ran. That rubbed him the wrong way. Not that architecture couldn't be art in its own right, but in a museum of fine art, the latter should be the focus.

Although, even as the thought crossed his mind, his own focus drifted from the exhibits in the lobby to the woman entering it. Natalia strode toward him, sporting similar clothing to what she'd worn the day before: a lightweight mauve jacket, wine-colored tights that accentuated the muscles in her long, lean legs, and a pair of bright white running shoes. Her golden hair hung in a tight braid rather than being relegated to a ponytail, and even though she refused to wear makeup, she did sport a pair of small gemstone studs in her ears, maybe apatite or citrine based on their color. Diego was surprised he noticed them at all, not because of their size but because he was too engrossed in the way Natalia moved across the wide open floor. She didn't strut like a model but had an effortless, graceful gait, like that of a ballet dancer.

It was intoxicating, and Diego's heart beat harder just watching her.

She came to a stop a few feet in front of him, her shoes making not so much as a whisper on the polished floor. To make processed rubber as quiet as moccasins was a talent in and of itself.

Natalia cocked her head at him. "You grabbed a map?"

Diego blinked. He couldn't let himself get caught off guard by this woman, not when he'd left last night's dinner in a position of control. Good thing he was so adept at keeping his composure.

Diego gestured with the brochure he'd picked up at the front desk. "In case we get lost. Also, holding this makes me look more like a tourist. I see you dressed for the occasion, by the way."

Natalia lifted an eyebrow.

Diego tapped his earlobe. "It's a joke, given you accessorized so heavily."

Natalia frowned. "Do you have a problem with the way I dress? Because what I'm wearing is far more functional than what you have on."

Like Natalia, Diego hadn't deviated in his dress from the night before. He wore a crisp suit, this time a deep navy in color, which he'd paired with a brilliant white shirt and burnt umber Italian loafers. "Perhaps it would be more accurate to say your outfit is suited to what you do, whereas mine serves the purpose I intend of it."

Natalia's brow relaxed, and her tongue flicked out to wet the edge of her lips. "I guess that's a fair point."

Diego suppressed a smile. *So you don't mind my dress after all, do you Natalia?* He glanced at his watch. "You're punctual, I'll give you that."

"As we established last night, details matter," said Natalia. "If you wanted me here at nine fifty-five or five after, I assume you would've said as much, but you said ten AM, and here I am. So what are we here to do?"

"To scope the place out, so to speak," said Diego. "I already purchased a couple tickets on my phone, so we're free to explore. The ground floor mostly contains artifacts: tapestries, glass, historical attire, that sort of thing. The fine art is upstairs. I thought we might start there, although if you'd prefer to sweep the ground floor first I'll understand, given how meticulous you seem to be."

Natalia's eyebrow crept up again. "Do you have a problem with my meticulousness?"

"I'd be questioning the validity of the stories I'd heard about you if you weren't." Diego held out his hand. "After you."

Natalia gave a slight nod and headed toward the stairs. Diego followed her closely, his eyes once again drawn to the gentle sway of her body. She held herself with such poise, such natural balance. Diego supposed it was a good quality for a thief to have, though he wondered where she'd perfected it. Natalia reached the steps a few paces in front of him, bringing the small of her back to eye level as Diego put foot to the stairs, giving him an excellent view of her legs and the roughly two-thirds of her butt that her jacket didn't cover. It may not have been as large as he liked, but the shape was damned near perfect.

Diego chuckled silently to himself. He always acted the perfect gentleman, but there were benefits to having ladies go first beyond simple altruism.

As they reached the top of the stairs, Diego pulled even with Natalia. He was content to let her take the lead, so he walked a couple paces at her side, following her through one gallery and then another. Diego had initially thought to broach a new topic of conversation, but as soon as he'd joined her, he'd noticed a shift in her demeanor. Her shoulders had tightened, and her brow had tensed. Her eyes were sharper, darting toward the corners of the rooms, at the security cameras above, at the emergency exits, at the occasional passing guard. Her eyes took note of everything, from the orientation of the rooms to the position of benches to the placement of the air vents on the walls.

Everything except the art itself, it seemed. *Strange.*

"You missed a vending machine," said Diego. "On the right, near the elevators."

Natalia blinked and turned toward him, as if noticing him for the first time. "Pardon?"

"It's a joke. You seem very focused."

"Whereas you seem not nearly focused enough."

Diego shrugged. "It's my fourth time here, and I've studied Miriam's plans countless times. The building is starting to feel like an old friend."

"An old friend that will get you arrested if you aren't careful?"

"I mean, sure. Who among us hasn't had a mentor who's tried to betray us, am I right?" Diego pointed into the gallery outside which they'd stopped. "Would you care to look at the Dahls while we're here?"

Natalia looked at him blankly. *"Dahls?"*

"Yes. Johan Christian Dahl?"

Natalia followed his finger. "He was a landscape artist?"

Diego shook his head. Given Natalia's seemingly encyclopedic knowledge of Edvard Munch, he couldn't quite believe what he was hearing. *"Some sort of landscape artist?* JC Dahl is the father of Norwegian landscape painting. The founder of the golden age of

Norwegian fine art. Maybe the first romantic painter in all of Norway."

"Ah. *Romanticism.*" Natalia nodded. "That would be why I haven't heard of him."

"You don't care for the movement?"

Natalia shrugged. "It's fine, I guess."

Diego scoffed. *"Fine?* No, no, no. Come here. Look at this."

Diego tucked his map into his pocket before taking Natalia's hand, which was warm and soft but with a roughness at the tips that made it clear she worked her fingers when needed. There was an instantaneous moment of hesitation as Diego took it, but it was instinctual, not planned. She didn't pull away as Diego led her into the gallery, stopping before Dahl's *Winter at the Sognefjord.*

Diego reluctantly let go of Natalia's hand as he gestured at the painting. "Look at this. The jutting mountains. The snow-swept vistas. The glassy reflection off the water. I can almost feel the bitter chill of the fjord just looking at it. This doesn't speak to you?"

To her credit, Natalia didn't immediately dismiss the artwork. She gave it a careful examination with the same focused eyes she'd previously committed to dissecting the museum's security. "Sorry, but no. It doesn't. I like art that invokes emotion."

Diego blinked. "This doesn't invoke emotion for you? Romanticism was all *about* emotion. Well, and individualism. And idealization of nature, and glorification of the past. But mostly emotion."

Natalia laughed, her sudden outburst carrying across the gallery. A few people looked their way. Natalia composed herself and lowered her voice. "Sorry. You sound like a textbook on art history. And very defensive, I might add. Did I just insult your favorite artist?"

"Dahl?" Diego shook his head. "He's a good example of the genre, but not a favorite of mine. I'm just surprised. You were so passionate about Munch. I thought..."

Natalia smiled. "That I knew everything about every artist who's ever spread paint across a canvas and was as passionate about every single one?"

Diego scowled. "Now you're poking fun."

"As a general rule, I like expressionism and impressionism," said Natalia. "For me, those movements captured the emotion of the human experience, but I don't limit myself to certain movements or periods. Art just has to... make me feel something." Natalia's eyes crinkled as she said that last part, and a wistful look crept into her eyes.

Diego studied her. "And what emotion do you prefer that art invoke?"

Natalia took a slow breath. She looked up, locking eyes with Diego. Her irises were so blue, so piercing, and so... eager? Wistful? Conflicted? Diego couldn't tell.

Natalia looked away. "Ah... I don't know. Depends on the piece, I suppose. We should keep moving."

Natalia headed into the adjoining walkway, but her focus seemed to have been lost. She no longer glanced at the security cameras and emergency exits with the same ferocity as before. If anything, she looked pensive, but she remained as quiet as she had while first scanning the property.

As they passed a gallery containing works by the Dutch painters Ferdinand Bol and Daniel De Blieck, Natalia spoke. "It's strange. I think you might be the first person I've met in this business who cares about the art. You asked if this job was about more than the money for me, but it's the same for you, isn't it?"

Diego didn't want to play too much of his hand. "Don't get me wrong. The money is nice. Necessary, even. But yes. Why pick a career you hate?"

Natalia was quiet again as they passed Jacob van der Ulft's *Seaport*. "Can I ask you something? Why do you do what you do?"

Diego snickered, feeling a tug on the line he'd cast the night before. "I'm not sure this is the right time to continue my story. I wouldn't want to distract you from your sweep of the museum."

"No," said Natalia. "I'm not asking *how* you came to be a conman. I'm asking *why*. Why this? Why not something else?"

Diego stopped in mid-stride, causing Natalia to pause and wait for him. It wasn't often that Diego was caught off guard, but Natalia had managed it. Again.

Why *did* Diego con people for a living? The money was a draw, of course, and it was more important now than it ever had been for reasons he didn't like to think about, but the money hadn't been there when he'd been getting started, when he'd worked at his craft. He'd gravitated toward art cons over time because he enjoyed the visual arts, but he hadn't gone into art himself. He'd always been terrible at it. His paintings looked as if they'd been drawn by a child, and when he'd tried his hand at sculpture, the resulting atrocities had been more reminiscent of abstract horror than the realist pieces he'd intended them to be.

Diego wasn't used to telling the truth, so he surprised himself with his response. "I guess... I became a conman because I'm good at it, and because it makes me feel good to excel at something."

Natalia pursed her lips. "Even if that something is being a spectacular liar?"

"Aren't you proud of being a good thief?"

Natalia cocked her head as she thought it over. "I suppose I am."

There was a voice inside Diego, one that normally told him dispiriting things he tried not to listen to: that he wasn't as good of a charmer as he thought, that the facade he showed the world had cracks, that he'd get caught sooner or later because of mistakes that were entirely his fault. The voice spoke to Diego again, but it didn't whisper to him the usual fallacies. This time, it whispered that maybe, *just maybe,* the woman in front of him might understand what he'd been through. That maybe she of all people *wouldn't* judge him for his choices, and that telling her the truth, at least some of the time, might not be the worst idea ever.

But Diego ignored the voice, slapping it into obscurity, and not a moment too soon. Though Natalia hadn't moved from the spot in front of him, she'd adopted that same focused look as before as she glanced at the security cameras and the people around them.

Well, maybe not the *exact* same look as before. She wore a malicious grin that Diego remembered from last night's dinner.

"You're up to something," said Diego. "Why are you up to something?"

Natalia smiled. "You're not the only one who studied Miriam's blueprints. Follow me. We might as well do something useful while we're here."

Chapter Eleven

NATALIA CROSSED THE GALLERY TO THE FAR SIDE OF THE room, to a service door installed flush with the wall. Natalia took a quick glance at the cameras above and at the folks in the gallery: a couple examining another series of landscape paintings and an old man sitting on a bench, peering near-sightedly at his phone.

Natalia tested the handle to the door, which was locked. She nodded to Diego. "Keep an eye out."

"Keep an eye out?" Diego eyed the door uncertainly. "What are you doing?"

"Performing a stress test." Natalia reached into her jacket and produced a soft leather case, from which she produced two tools: a torsion wrench and a rake pick.

Diego's eyes widened. *"No.* Are you insane? Miriam isn't in control of the security yet. Why in the world do you even have those with you?"

"A thief never leaves home without them," said Natalia. "And we're not going to be doing anything illegal, so you can quit your worrying."

"Nothing illegal? Last I checked, breaking and entering was against the law in Norway, same as it is everywhere else in the world."

"Breaking and entering is the act of entering a building without permission with the intent of committing a crime, which we are not doing." Natalia returned the case to her pocket. "For one thing, this building is a public space which we entered legally, assuming you weren't lying about buying the tickets online. Second, we're not going to steal anything today."

Diego glanced at the security cameras. "Yes, I'm sure the security guards who apprehend us will be swayed by your generous interpretation of the law."

Natalia stuck the wrench and the rake into the keyhole. "Those cameras point toward the paintings, not this service entrance. We're out of their field of view, so the only reason a guard might approach us is because you failed to keep an eye out." The lock clicked reassuringly as Natalia twisted on the wrench. "Which you didn't do, did you?"

Diego's eyebrows rose as Natalia cranked on the handle and cracked the door. "That was fast."

"Of course it was," said Natalia. "I'm not an amateur."

She glanced behind her one more time to make sure no one was paying them any attention, then pushed through the open door.

Diego followed her closely into the plain hallway beyond, closing the door quickly behind them. "Well, mission accomplished. No alarms went off. Are you satisfied?"

Natalia snickered. Could it be that Diego was nervous? It was the first time she'd seen him the slightest bit flustered, perhaps with the exception of the instant at dinner when she'd threatened to leave. "My picking the lock wasn't the stress test. I need to know what security is like in the parts of the building that are off the beaten path. That's why we're here." And because Natalia hoped to find some of the art nobody else was getting a chance to see, but she didn't want to let Diego know that yet.

"So your plan is to bumble around until we run into a guard? Wonderful idea."

"Relax," said Natalia. "We're not going to get into trouble. After all, we're just a clueless tourist couple who got lost. A guard is going to help us get back to the museum proper. I assumed a criminal mastermind like you would've figured that out by now."

Diego looked almost offended. "Don't patronize me. You won't find anyone better at ad-libbing than me, assuming of course I've been made aware that I'm taking part in a production."

"Well, consider yourself informed. Now stop being a baby and come on."

Natalia gave him a nod and headed down the hall. While the architecture of the *Nasjonalmuseet* in many ways felt uninspired, at least the rooms were spacious and flowed into one another with sense of direction. The back area into which they'd stepped reminded Natalia more of a commercial office space than anything. As she walked, she passed a couple rooms with signs on the doors, but the signs were in Norwegian, so she wasn't sure what the rooms contained. A broom closet? A conference room? Probably not the latter, as there weren't any windows adjacent the hall.

There were, however, windows across the front of the room which faced them as they reached the end of the corridor. Inside this room were a number of items Natalia recognized: easels, tables on casters draped with moving blankets, and in the corner, tables laden with microscopes, swing arm lamps, and photography equipment.

"Let's check out the restoration room," said Natalia. "There's sure to be something good in there."

Diego responded with something that was halfway between a sigh and a grumble, but he didn't argue. He followed her inside the room, the door to which was unlocked.

As soon as Natalia stepped inside, she felt a rush of excitement. It wasn't so much that she wasn't supposed to be there. Over the years, she'd pulled enough jobs that she'd grown used to the flood of adrenaline that washed over her when she lifted a priceless piece of art off a wall. As she'd told Diego, she wasn't worried about getting caught, but there was nonetheless a thrill associated with being in close proximity to famous works of art. To Natalia, it seemed like stepping into a time machine. She might never travel to Norway of the late eighteen hundreds, or Italy during the Renaissance, or Egypt during the reign of the pharaohs, but she could get up close to a piece of artwork created during that period, see what the creators saw, even reach out and touch the same artifact as those peoples of yore. If she hadn't become an art thief, going into art restoration might not have been a bad career choice, though it probably required more schooling than she had the patience for.

The thrill inside her intensified when she saw which painting was propped on the easel in front of her. "Diego, we hit the jackpot. Look. It's Munch's *Death in the Sickroom*. Well, one of them anyway. He—"

"Painted more than one, yes," said Diego. "I've caught onto the theme with Munch."

Natalia was tempted to stick her tongue out at him, but she settled for a scowl. "You can't blame the man for needing to earn a living. It's easier to paint multiple versions of the same painting than paint new pieces all the time. But look at it. The strokes are so simple. Almost amateurish, and yet consider the emotion evoked by it. God, I can feel the sorrow of every one of those individuals. And look, there! That's *Love and Pain*. I thought it was at the Munch Museum. Maybe they brought it over for restoration."

"Could be a different version." Diego gave her a smug grin.

"I know you're poking fun, but he actually painted... I want to say six of them?" Natalia approached the painting in question. "Now that you mention it, it could be. I think the original was more blue rather than dark grey?"

Diego feigned shock. "You mean there's something about Munch you don't know? I'm disappointed."

The desire to stick her tongue out grew. "I don't have an encyclopedic knowledge of him. I just admire the man's work. He had a way of capturing the heartache of existence that few others have ever replicated."

"I can agree with that," said Diego. "But he was also rather morbid, don't you think? *The Scream? Death in the Sickroom? Love and Pain?* They're all so... sad."

"Well, Munch did have a nihilist as a mentor. He was also an alcoholic, and he suffered a nervous breakdown later in life."

Diego lifted an eyebrow. "You're undercutting your own argument about lacking an encyclopedic memory."

"Come on," said Natalia, gesturing at the painting. "You can't tell me this doesn't move you more than that dopey Dahl did."

"As I tried to make clear, I'm not especially into landscapes."

"Just look at the painting. Don't you feel something?"

Diego opened his mouth as if he wanted to say something, but then he thought better of it. He turned toward *Love and Pain* and studied it. He stood there for a good minute and a half, gazing upon the two individuals depicted, the man with his head bent low, the woman hugging him, her fiery red hair cascading over his head and her arms alike.

As he looked at the painting, Natalia looked at him. At his eyes, deep and dark and thoughtful. At the smooth slope of his nose, and the plump projection of his lower lip, just the perfect shade of pink. As he studied the work of art, he brought one corner of said lip into his mouth, ran his teeth across it, and let it back out, now gleaming with a thin, wet sheen. As Natalia watched him, she found herself doing the same thing—and wondering what it might feel like to have those lips pressed against hers. She envisioned the scrape of his rough stubble against her skin, the warmth of his breath, the press of his body against hers.

Diego turned his eyes from the painting to her, and Natalia's breath caught in her throat. He didn't say a thing, simply regarded her with the same intensity he'd brought to the painting. His lips parted, as if once again he wanted to share something, but nothing came out.

For an instant, Natalia thought she should lean in and find out for herself if the kiss she'd imagined resembled the real thing, but she didn't. She hadn't come to Oslo to be hoodwinked into falling for some smooth-talking grifter, no matter how captivating his eyes might be.

She cleared her throat and glanced at the painting to break the line of sight. "Well?"

Diego nodded, almost imperceptibly. "I feel something, all right."

The way he said it made Natalia think he wasn't talking about the painting, but before she could reply she heard the clack of a latch and the squeal of hinges. A suspicious voice followed. "Excuse me. What are you doing here?"

The man who'd poked his head into the restoration room wasn't a guard, rather some sort of administrative staff based on his attire, but his forehead was nonetheless creased with concern.

Natalia had a plan for how to deal with him, but Diego beat her to the punch. He pulled the map from his pocket and held it toward the man, and in a perfect Russian accent said: "Yes, help please. We try to find *Madonna,* but is nowhere. Map shows us here, no?"

The man in the doorway didn't relax. "Sir, you're not in the galleries. This area is off limits."

Diego looked around himself, blinking rapidly. "Is not gallery? Painting here. But no *Madonna.* Where is exhibit, please?"

Natalia stepped forward, ready to impersonate his own accent. "Um—"

Diego held up a hand, his voice harsh as he spoke. *"Tikho, zhenshchina. Pozvol'te mne govorit'. Dostatochno."* Then to the gentleman: "Apologies. She is very mouthy. I tell her, here, no *Madonna.* But always, she is talking. Talking, talking."

Natalia didn't have to feign annoyance, but she played it up for the sake of appearances. She even added an annoyed sniff, and muttered the one Russian curse word she knew for good measure. *"Mudak..."*

The man in the doorway glanced from Diego to Natalia and back, his expression shifting from one of concern to one of mere annoyance. "If you two could follow me, I can show you how to get to the *Madonna* exhibit."

Diego gave Natalia a sharp look, and he extended a firm hand in the direction of the door. Natalia responded with a piqued glance, but inside she couldn't help but be impressed. Despite the nerves he'd shown upon breaking into the back half of the museum, Diego had instantly transformed the moment a threat appeared. No hesitation. No delay. He'd just reacted.

As a fellow professional, Natalia had to appreciate the man's skill, but on a more personal level, she had to admit it was kind of hot, too.

Chapter Twelve

NATALIA WALKED AT DIEGO'S SIDE AS THEY EXITED THE museum and headed across the street toward the open *Rådhusplassen* she'd walked through upon first arriving in the city. The sun shone bright overhead, and a cool breeze whistled through the piers before diving into the downtown streets.

Diego gave Natalia a reproachful glance. "Just so we're clear, what you did in there was reckless."

"Oh, come off it," said Natalia. "Everything went exactly as I expected. We played the role of a lost couple, and the museum staff bought it. And for our efforts, we managed to get up close and personal with two different pieces that no one else in that museum will get to experience today."

Even after the attendant left them at the *Madonna* exhibit, the anger Diego had adopted as part of his Russian tourist shtick hadn't totally faded. "Look, I understand you're used to working alone, but when you're part of a team, you can't rush off and implement whatever plan pops into your head without discussing it with everyone else first. That's how accidents happen, and accidents can lead to arrests. Or worse."

"*Or worse?* What exactly did you think was going to happen in that restoration room?"

Diego gave Natalia another sharp look. "Did you forget that I've been running a confidence game with the curator of the museum? What if she'd been the one who'd run into us? Or it was someone else I've met over the past month? We're lucky it was some random administrator who could be so easily fooled."

"True, but if it *had* been the curator or someone else you know, I'm sure you would've modified your strategy to get us out. If you'd pretended to be an irate Russian after having established yourself as a wealthy philanthropist, I'd be seriously doubting your abilities as a conman."

"My point is your expedition to find more Munchs was completely unnecessary," said Diego. "That's not why we visited the museum."

"Maybe it's not why *you* visited the museum," said Natalia. "But I fully intended to partake in those. Besides, it was an integral part of the stress test, which you passed with flying colors."

Diego paused as they approached the statue at the center of the plaza, his face contorting into new and interesting positions. "Are you suggesting your stress test was about testing *me?* You're incorrigible!"

"Try to look at it from my perspective," said Natalia. "You contacted *me.* You've read my resume, so to speak, but I've had to take your word about the jobs you've taken part in. I haven't avoided the law as long as I have by taking people at their word, especially the word of such an accomplished liar as yourself. So, yes, I did make you follow me into the bowels of the *Nasjonalmuseet* under false pretenses, but I had to see how you'd react to an adverse situation. To see if you're actually a good conman or if you're just pretending to be one. And simply put, if I'd given you warning of my intentions, your reaction wouldn't have been genuine."

Diego scowled at her. At least *that* reaction seemed genuine.

Natalia sighed. "Look. For what it's worth, I'm sorry. Unlike you, I don't take pleasure in deceiving people. It's just a part of the job.

The good news is, I was impressed with your ability to think and react under pressure. You were quicker on the draw than I was, and that's saying something. Not to mention your Russian sounded very believable. That wasn't total gibberish, was it?"

Diego rolled his eyes, but his posture relaxed as some of the anger bled out of him. "I told you, I picked some up over the years. My grammar is far from perfect, but I doubt our Norwegian friend noticed."

"So... truce?" Natalia extended a hand.

Diego eyed her peace offering as if it might be hiding a joy buzzer, but eventually he took her hand and gave it a shake. As when he'd drawn her by the hand to view the Dahl, his hand felt firm and strong without being rough.

"I'm not one to bear a grudge, so yes, of course. But if anything, this exercise has proven that we have much more work to do than I thought. I knew you needed to work on your teamwork skills, but I assumed you were somewhere around here—" Diego held a hand to his ribs. "—when in fact your ability level is down here." He waggled a hand toward his feet.

"I can be a team player when I want to be," said Natalia. "Like I said, I had to get a sense of who I was working with."

"So is it enough for me to vouch for Eddie and Miriam, or are you going to ask Eddie to knock someone out and Miriam to brick your phone for you to trust them as well?"

"I'm willing to give them the benefit of the doubt," said Natalia.

"Well, that's something at least," said Diego.

The wind picked up, flicking Natalia's braid across her shoulder. "So. I held up my end of the bargain. Now it's time for you to hold up yours."

Diego peered at her through narrowed eyelids. "Excuse me?"

"I performed the reconnaissance you wanted of me, or at least, most of it. Now it's time for you to do what you promised."

Diego squinted harder. "Before I point out that we didn't even make it through half of the second floor, what is it I supposedly promised you?"

Natalia sighed. For as smart as the man was, he could act like quite the idiot at times. "The story. You were going to finish telling me how you got into the grifting business."

Diego pulled back. "Oh, no. *No, no, no.* That's not how this works. For one thing, I never promised I'd be finishing the story today, and for another, we didn't finish canvassing the museum, which was the whole point of today's exercise."

Natalia frowned. She may not have been the one with the supposedly impeccable memory, but she was pretty sure he'd used the story as a lure to get her to show up. "If you didn't promise to tell me the rest of the story, you strongly implied it."

"I believe I said that if you wanted to hear the rest of my tale, you'd have to show up," said Diego, "but I didn't say I would be telling it straight away. That's the difference between a necessary and a sufficient condition. Details matter. Someone told me that once."

Natalia pursed her lips. Frustration grew within her, but at the same time, what had she expected? Not only was she dealing with a lying conman, but she was dealing with one whose chain she'd yanked around for the past hour. "You're a duplicitous man, and you should know I don't like having my words used against me."

Diego brightened. *"Duplicitous?* Why, that's a wonderful word. I'll have to add that to my repertoire. And if you don't like having your words used against you, then hold on, because I was also recently told that stories are currency, and the best ones are worth a pretty penny. So I don't know why I should continue to share the enticing story of my life when all you've done so far is be deceitful and difficult. Need I remind you that the point of us visiting the museum was to evaluate security, not to mention begin developing a rapport which will help us function as a seamless team the night of the heist, though that's *clearly* going to take some effort."

At first, Natalia thought Diego was feigning his annoyance, but between the hard glint of his eyes and the way the muscles at the sides of his jaw bulged occasionally, she realized he was actually a little steamed. That was the problem with dealing with professional liars. You never really knew when they were telling the truth. She could've tried to appease him by letting him know she'd made a quick tour of the museum the night prior before joining him for dinner, or that she'd researched the building extensively before flying to Oslo, but she suspected that wouldn't make him feel better about the ordeal.

"I said I was sorry," said Natalia. "Is the problem that I doubted your abilities, or that I didn't let you know what I was planning? Because if you'd like to even the score, I'm fine with you asking me to perform a petty theft ahead of the heist to prove I can handle myself under pressure."

"Unlike you, I actually believe you know what you're doing," said Diego. "The problem is one of trust. That's what we need to work on."

There is was again. That T word. Natalia didn't like it at all. "What are you proposing?"

A sly smile returned to Diego's lips. "I think we need to take part in a trust building exercise. All of us. You, me, Miriam, and Eddie. I'll set something up for tomorrow morning, and participation will be mandatory."

"A trust building exercise?" Natalia spat the words. "Oh, God. You want me to go on some ropes course with you and do trust falls and other asinine garbage?"

"As entertaining as that might be, no," said Diego. "I have something else in mind. Frankly, it'll be a good exercise for Eddie and Miriam as well. But that's a required activity. If you want to hear more of my story, you'll have to do something extra."

Natalia cocked her head, wondering what that smile he'd adopted meant. "It's not something creepy, is it?"

Diego blinked. "What? No. I just need a date. Not even a real date. A fake date. For tomorrow night's gala."

Natalia couldn't have been more surprised if he'd asked her to go jet-skiing. *"Gala?* What gala?"

"You'll recall I've been working a confidence game with the *Nasjonalmuseet's* curator? I actually need to meet her for lunch soon." Diego checked his watch. "Anyway, there's a charity gala in support of the museum tomorrow night at the Hotel Maximillian, which you'll be unsurprised to learn is where I've been staying. Not only will the curator be there, but so will many of the museum's management staff, including the head of security. It's the perfect opportunity for us to gain access to security systems that we'll need on the night of the heist. While I could probably do it myself, you just offered to prove your mettle under pressure. And, if I'm being honest, you'd fit in much better than Eddie or Miriam would."

Natalia's brain seemed to be running slower than it should've been. She was stuck one speech behind schedule. "You want me to go to a *gala?*"

"Yes." Diego held up his hands. "Is that a problem?"

Of course it's a problem, thought Natalia. *It's a problem because I'm not good in social situations. I'm a thief who prefers to work alone, and I'm already having a hard enough time trying to pretend I can work well on a team without you asking me to rub noses with the upper crust at a charity ball. It's also a problem because I'll be there with you of all people, with your dark eyes and that smirk of yours and those lips that seem quite perfect for kissing.*

But Natalia *did* have to get close to Diego. For her plan to work the way she wanted it to, she did, *damn it all.* She absolutely did.

"No," said Natalia. "It's no problem at all. Except that no one told me I'd be attending a gala, so I don't have a dress, or shoes, or proper jewelry, or an appointment with a hairdresser, or anything that I would need to be able to attend such an event without looking completely out of place."

Diego's face lost its hard edge. "I doubt you could look out of place there if you tried, but you do have a point about the dress and the shoes. We'll have to do something about that." He glanced at his watch again. "I really should be going, but what do you say I pick you up outside your hotel at... four? PM. Details matter. Unless you'd rather take a ride share again."

"Pick me up to go where?" said Natalia.

"Dress shopping, of course," said Diego. "Don't worry. I'll pay. So, four?"

Once again Natalia reminded herself that she needed to do this, even if she didn't want to. Except that she sort of did want to, and that was the problem.

She forced out a smile. "Four it is. See you then."

Chapter Thirteen

NATALIA DIDN'T ACTUALLY SEE DIEGO PULL UP, BUT SHE did hear him.

As she stood at the bus stop near her hotel, watching people stroll along the nearby wharf and wander into the galleries that resided there, she heard a deep, throaty rumble, almost reminiscent of a proud jungle cat roaring his virility for all the tigresses of the savanna to hear. When she turned, she found a sleek metallic green Aston Martin gliding to a stop in front of her. It was a two-door coupe with a long hood and a mesh grill at the front. The body was smooth and elegant, the panels molded seamlessly to minimize drag. The wheels were a matte black aluminum, and the windows were tinted a similar shade.

The beast rumbled again, more of a mechanical chuckle than a sound an engine should've made. The window nearest Natalia rolled down. She bent down to find Diego sitting behind the wheel.

"Subtle," she said.

"Don't get too attached to it," said Diego. "It's a rental."

"They didn't have it in red?" asked Natalia. "Because honestly, how am I supposed to know your penis is *enormous* if the car isn't red?"

Diego cut loose with a hearty laugh, which, if Natalia was being honest with herself, was a much more pleasing sound than the car's imitation of the same. Diego shook his head. "Sadly, there was no red."

"Well, that *is* disappointing." Natalia glanced into the back of the car. "Not a lot of storage. You realize we're going shopping, don't you?"

"I guess you'll have to buy a small dress." Diego pushed a button on the dash, and the door nearest Natalia swung open automatically. "Well? Are you going to get in? I'd rather not anger any bus drivers if I can avoid it."

Natalia hesitated, but she'd already committed to this charade, so she couldn't pull out now. With a slow breath to steady her nerves, she got in the car and closed the door behind her. The Aston Martin's bucket seat enveloped her, soft as down but supportive in the places it needed to be.

Diego eyed her expectantly. "Are there any particular brands of dresses you prefer over others?"

"Um... not really." Natalia's seat belt clicked as she latched it into place.

"What about stores? Any favorites?"

Natalia didn't see any reason to lie. "I don't do a lot of dress shopping. They're not terribly functional for running or climbing through access hatches, and they're not very subtle either."

"Fair enough," said Diego. "I know a place not far from here that should have a good selection."

Diego put the car into drive, the engine rumbled as he pressed his foot against the accelerator, and they pulled onto the main thoroughfare.

Natalia trailed her hand across the soft leather of her seat—lambskin, maybe?—then did the same to the leather on the dash. It was lush and smooth to the touch. "I have to admit, I didn't picture you as much of a car guy."

Diego shrugged as he drove, his shoulders stretching the fabric of his blazer. *Damnit. He really wasn't pudgy under the suit, was he?*

"I'm actually not," said Diego. "I don't even own a car. Eddie, on the other hand, *loves* cars. I guess it shouldn't come as a surprise given he's a professional driver, but the man could go on about British automobiles for days. And he has. When he found out I'd rented an Aston Martin Vantage, he proceeded to give me the entire history of the model going back as far as nineteen seventy-seven. He even knew how many foot pounds of torque the original version had. Who knows that?"

"Alright, honest question," said Natalia. "Do you understand what he's saying most of the time?"

Diego shot her a quick smile before turning his attention to the road. "You have to think of his dialect as a foreign language. You pick up bits and pieces along the way. Eventually you get to a point where you start to think of his rhymes as true synonyms. The other day while walking into a building he asked me if I wanted to take the lift or the apples and pairs, and I didn't even blink twice."

Natalia had to think about that one before she got it. "So you don't own a car?"

"I'm always traveling," said Diego. "It's the life of a conman. Two months here, three there. I have a condo in Majorca, but I haven't spent more than a handful of weeks there in the past year. I wonder if I should sell it."

Natalia nodded, feeling the gentle vibration of the car underneath her. "I understand. Sometimes it feels as if all I have is a home base rather than a true home."

"And where is home base for you?"

Natalia eyed Diego suspiciously. It took him a moment to catch the look.

"Right. I suppose I haven't earned that yet. My mistake." Diego turned off the main roadway onto a side street, one lined with expensive-looking businesses.

Natalia ran her hand across her leather armrest once more. "So if you're not a car guy, why bother with the Aston Martin?"

"I have appearances to maintain," said Diego. "What sort of

wealthy philanthropist would I be if I drove a thirty-year old broken down jalopy?"

Natalia smiled a devious smile. "And the choice of vehicle wouldn't have *anything to do* with overcompensating for failures in other areas, I imagine."

Diego laughed as the car slowed. "I could assure you that's not the case, but I'm a professional liar, so why would you believe me?" He veered into an open spot at the side of the road and killed the engine. "Here we are."

Natalia followed Diego's finger to a store about thirty feet away by the name of Werner Johansen. The front of the store was all glass, and from what Natalia could see of the interior, there was a lot of empty space and not a lot of goods on display. That probably meant it was exorbitantly expensive. Good thing Diego was paying.

Natalia exited the car and followed Diego to the store. Upon entering, Natalia was greeted with a minimalist experience. A number of mannequins wearing carefully crafted outfits dotted the floor, but there were vanishingly few displays. Those were confined to cubbies along the walls, each of which held ten or twelve items apiece: a mixture of jackets, slacks, jeans, dresses, and skirts, with shoes and accessories relegated to shelves below the main displays. Despite the store's low density, it was *large*, with a second story accessible via marble staircase.

A young woman wearing a pert blouse and skirt and with a silk airline scarf around her neck approached them. "Hello," she said in the lilting Norwegian accent Natalia had become used to. "Can I help you find something?"

Given the sort of place it was, Natalia was surprised she hadn't first offered them sparking water and canapés.

Diego nodded. "Yes, thank you. My friend is in need of an evening gown. Something formal but which won't require tailoring, as the event we're attending is tomorrow night. I'm thinking of something with a bias cut, but we can be flexible. Definitely no trains or overly large skirts, though."

Natalia looked at Diego askance. It was one thing for him to order her a drink at dinner, but it was quite another for him to dictate how she should dress. "Excuse me? I'm capable of deciding what to wear on my own, thank you."

"Are you, though?" said Diego. "Because in the car you admitted you don't wear dresses because of how impractical they are. If we were going shopping for a track suit or rock climbing gear, I'd have no qualms about letting you dictate the conversation, but it seems to me that here I might be better suited to the task at hand."

Natalia felt annoyance bubbling up inside her. As correct as Diego might've been, that didn't give him the right to start mansplaining dresses to her inside of a women's boutique. "I can pick for myself."

Diego took a half step back. "My apologies. By all means."

The poor saleswoman looked at the two of them uncertainly, giving Natalia a nervous smile. "So... what can I help you find?"

What, indeed? Natalia had an idea in her mind of what she looked good in. More form-fitting dresses tended to fit her better than those enormous puffy things wannabe princesses wore, but she wouldn't want something too plain either. Those sheer dresses that clung to women like lingerie were incredibly trashy, and given what Diego had said about their plans at the gala, she didn't want to attract *too* much attention. So what then? Something strapless or over the shoulder? Maybe with a bunch of folds. Those always looked elegant. What were they called again? Rushes? Ruches? *Oh, damn it all.* She didn't know.

"Um... Well... Let's try something with a bias cut. And no trains or overly large skirts, either, though a medium-sized skirt would be fine."

Natalia snuck a glance at Diego, daring him to say something, but not only did he remain silent, he had the gall not to look smug. What a jerk.

"Of course," said the saleswoman. "I have some ideas I think could work. Please, follow me."

She led Natalia up the stairs to the second floor, which contained more elegant clothing than the main floor. Here, the mannequins stood on pedestals, each of them wearing dresses of rich silk or layered lace and toile and with their arms held out in an imitation of motion, as if they were being twirled during a dance.

The saleswoman crossed to the side of the store and began plucking dresses from the cubbies. "Do you have a preference on sleeves? Short, long? None? And color?"

"Ah... sleeveless, most likely. And as far as color..." Natalia glanced at Diego with a little less sharpened steel in her eyes than the last time.

To his credit, he perfectly understood her intent. "Well, black is always in fashion. I think that royal blue one looks phenomenal, and there's another one over there that's sort of an eggplant color that could be quite nice. I'd avoid red, though. It's too flashy, and you wouldn't want anyone to think you're overcompensating for anything."

Natalia snorted, but she tried to hide it by clearing her throat. "I don't think women have anything they need to overcompensate for."

Diego smiled. "Only some of them."

Natalia eyed the man as the saleswoman left in search of the purple dress. She eyed the curve of his lips, the dimples in his cheeks, the twinkle in his eyes. If Natalia didn't know any better, she'd think he was taking her for a ride, but she'd met conmen before. More importantly, she'd met *men*. She could spot their sycophantic smiles from miles away. Pick out the ingratiating tones in their voices when they urged her to move a little closer and press her lips against their own. She could feel their unctuous fake confidence as it oozed through the air toward her.

Diego carried a bit of the latter, it was true, but it wasn't entirely contrived. There was a playfulness to his demeanor. A quiet knowledge he didn't flaunt. Natalia didn't for a moment think he was being truly genuine, no matter what he might've claimed at dinner, but there was something he was sharing that felt true to her.

He also, apparently, had quite the eye for fashion. The saleswoman came back with an armful of dresses, including the purple one

Diego had spotted from afar. Even hanging lifelessly from the sales-woman's arms, it looked like something a starlet might wear to the Oscars.

"I think this is a good start," said the saleswoman as she led Natalia toward the changing rooms. "If you find the styles are not to your liking, I will find others. Would you like my assistance with the gowns?"

Natalia didn't relish the thought of having a strange woman help her try on clothing. "No, thank you. I'll manage."

"Of course. Let me know if I can be of help." The woman finished hanging the gowns inside the changing room and stepped aside.

Diego settled into one of the plush chairs outside the dressing rooms. "Likewise, although I probably shouldn't help with the changing part. But I'd be happy to give you my opinion on the dresses. I have a discerning eye if I say so myself."

Natalia smirked at him. "How kind of you. I'll let you know if I need anything."

Natalia stepped inside the changing room and closed the door. It was one of those silly three-quarter length things that left about eight inches of open space at the floor and an equal amount open above her head, perfect for peeping toms who had foot fetishes or things for professional basketball players. Natalia slipped her shoes off as she gazed at the wall of dresses in front of her. The saleswoman had only picked six gowns, but it was an intimidating wall nonetheless, full of straps and clasps and copious amounts of fabric.

Natalia heard the saleswoman's voice, speaking to Diego. "I will be downstairs. If you need me, just call." She heard footsteps recede and fade, followed by Diego clearing his throat and a rustle as he rearranged himself on the loveseat.

Natalia frowned as she stared at the dresses, unsure of where to start. "Um... just so you know, this could take a while."

"It's all right." Diego's voice drifted into the room through the finely stacked door slats. "I've taken part in numerous long cons. Patience is my middle name."

"Sharing secrets about yourself already? I thought I hadn't earned those, yet."

Diego chuckled. "You haven't, but you're getting closer."

Natalia unzipped her jacket and lay it on the bench next to her. "How close, exactly? Because a story might help pass the time."

"Are you using this situation to extort more of my story out of me? For all I know, you're a world-renowned quick change artist and this is an elaborate ploy."

Natalia's voice was thick with sarcasm. *"Right.* This is all part of my devious plan to have you invite me to a gala I have no interest in attending and have you buy me a dress I have no interest in wearing. Very underhanded of me. But have it your way. Sit in silence. I *love* silence."

Diego lasted about fifteen seconds. *"Fine.* You win. Now where was I? I was eleven months old?"

Natalia pulled her shirt over her head and tossed it atop her jacket. "Absolutely not. Do not continue this story from when you were a toddler. Get to the good stuff."

"My life story is nothing *but* good stuff," complained Diego. "But I understand what you're getting at. You still want to know how I got started in the business, so to speak. So let's fast forward to when I performed my first big job..."

Interlude 3

OR THE STORY OF HOW I PUT TOGETHER MY VERY FIRST CREW

You'll of course remember that everything I'm about to tell you is true, no matter how ludicrous it might sound, and I'd appreciate it if you don't interrupt with any protests or complaints, as it interrupts my flow. The other thing I want you to keep in mind is that everyone involved in this story ends up better off as a result of the events that transpire, with the possible exception of Principal Rosales, but I wouldn't worry too much about him. He always was a bit of a jerk.

This story begins with me during my final year of secondary school, and if you think that's a little early for someone to be planning their first big heist, you wouldn't be wrong. Especially because—and I hate to admit this—I was what you might call a screwup. Not like my brother Rodrigo, who by this point had established himself as the premier international real estate agent in all of Andalusia, or my sister who had recently traveled to the jungles of Columbia to continue her training with the *brujas*, or witches, who lived in the foothills of the Andes. I wasn't doing anything of the sort. I was just getting into trouble with the wrong sorts of people.

You see, by this point in my life I'd already come to the realization that some of the activities I was best at were the ones frowned upon by the police. Lying, stealing, tricking people into handing over their money or valuable information. I was pretty good at keeping my activities hidden from my mother, who would've killed me if she'd known what I was up to, but unfortunately, that same knack for keeping my talents out of the public eye was also keeping me from being noticed by the right people.

Speaking of, you never did mention what your mother's gift was. You said it was important during the last story, but you glossed over it.

What did I say about interrupting? You have a hard time following directions. Anyway, my mother's gift isn't important to this story. What is is that going into my final year in secondary school I was determined to make a name for myself, and in the town I lived in, that meant being noticed by Santiago de la Paz. Señor de la Paz had his finger in every pie of questionably legality that you could think of, from protection rackets to smuggling to investment scams. Remember Dr. Alvarez from my last story? Señor de la Paz had been implicated in that Ponzi scheme as well, but he was never charged with a crime, probably because he made sure to share his profits with the officers of the law, something Dr. Alvarez never learned. So I knew that if I wanted to get into the game, so to speak, my foot needed to be planted squarely in Señor de la Paz's door.

The opportunity to do so came early in that final year of secondary school. Santiago's son, Hernando, attended the same school I did. He was much more popular than I was, and he was constantly surrounded by his dimwitted cronies, not to mention the girls who wanted to date him. But luckily for me, Hernando wasn't much smarter than his hangers-on. One day at lunch, I noticed a crowd around him, and when I joined them, I saw what he was showing off: his father's famed signet ring that had run in the de la Paz family for generations. As the girls fawned over Hernando, I asked one of his cronies if Señor de la Paz had forged a new one for him, but the thick-headed lunk told me it was the original. As I wondered how Hernando had gotten hold of it, his moronic friend confided in me, in hushed tones, that Hernando had *stolen* the ring from his own father, as if that was a feat to be proud of rather than a stunning act of stupidity. But it gave me an idea. If I could return the stolen ring to Señor de la Paz, that might ingratiate me enough to the man for him to consider taking me under his wing, even if it might simultaneously anger Hernando.

So, during the period between the final two classes of the day, I swung by Hernando's locker. I don't think Hernando bothered carrying any books with him, but his locker was nonetheless the prime spot for him to hang out. Sure enough, there he was, getting one of the girls to swoon over his stolen signet ring. As I wondered how I might steal it from him, he slid the ring back into his pocket, instead pulling out his cell phone. As the girl giggled and gave him her number, I knew I wouldn't get a better opportunity. I walked in their direction, and as I passed them, I stumbled, falling into Hernando before ricocheting off him and sprawling across the floor alongside the contents of my backpack.

I was all too aware how everyone would react, and my fellow teenagers didn't disappoint. They all pointed and laughed at my misfortune, calling me names, but because of the mean-spirited taunting, none of them noticed I'd snatched Hernando's ring from his pocket. I mumbled my apologies as I scooped my books into my bag, trying to get away from the taunting as soon as I could, and I would've gotten away scot-free if not for the hole that had torn in my bag while I'd fallen. For you see, as I slipped the ring from my hand into the side pocket of my bag, the ring fell right through the hole and bounced off the floor with a ringing, metallic peal.

Because of my incredible memory, I can remember perfectly the look of raw hatred Hernando gave me as he realized what had happened. He screamed at me, "Thief!," before charging and tackling me to the ground. It was a good thing Hernando's muscle-bound cronies weren't with him, because I had a hard enough time shielding myself from Hernando's blows alone, but I was able to survive long enough to have Hernando pulled off me and be dragged to my feet myself.

By none other than Principal Rosales.

The principal was a large man, large enough that I sometimes wondered if he moonlighted as a bouncer or a longshoreman. He also had a scowl that could cut through glass. He shot that scowl at me and Hernando alike as he gathered the ring, grabbed each of us by the arm, and marched us to his office. There, he demanded we explain what was going on. Hernando of course told him I'd stolen his family signet ring, and I pled my innocence, saying I'd merely fallen and the ring must've been knocked from his pocket by accident. I don't think Principal Rosales believed either of us completely, but he was smart enough to know the ring in his possession belonged to Señor de la Paz, not Hernando. Being a rough-around-the-edges type, he was also smart enough to know Señor de la Paz was not to be trifled with, so he told us he'd personally return the ring to Santiago after the parent-teacher assembly that Friday evening. Then, the man expelled us from his office and told us that if he ever caught us fighting again, we'd face expulsion or worse.

I didn't know what *worse* was, but Hernando had a suggestion: my complete and total demise. As soon as we were out of eyesight of the school's offices, he grabbed me by the scruff of my neck and told me that his father didn't know the ring was gone, and if he found out, he'd disown him. More importantly, Hernando informed me that if I didn't get the ring back for him before the assembly, he would personally turn me into a stain on the school floor. Given Hernando's family ties, I had reason to believe him.

Now before I go on, there's something I have to point out. While I may have been a fledgling conman who dabbled in petty theft, I wasn't anything approaching the man I am today. I didn't have the skills I needed to break into the principal's office to steal the signet ring, in part because that office was *an impenetrable fortress*. Harder to access than the Louvre, better guarded than Fort Knox, harder to escape than Alcatraz. Getting in there was simply impossible.

Oh, come on. It was a principal's office.

Well, I might be exaggerating a little, but for someone of my abilities, it felt that way. There were multiple doors between myself and the ring, a cabinet that would be locked at all times, and several secretaries who always seemed to be around, watching the lobby like hawks for any sign of trouble. For Hernando to tell me I needed to get the ring back for him within five days, he might as well have told me to steal the *Mona Lisa*.

So you can imagine how despondent I was as the day's final bell rang. Instead of heading home, I sat on one of the benches outside the school and pondered my fate. Perhaps being reduced to a gelatinous goo wouldn't be so bad, I told myself. Puddles of goo didn't have nerve endings, after all, so after my initial pounding I might not feel anything at all. It would be an existence of sorts.

But even at that moment, with my life seemingly over, the fates had one more cruel joke in store for me, because as I sat there with my focus firmly on my future, a football, or soccer ball as the Americans would say, flew through the air and struck me square in the forehead.

I won't lie. The blow was potent enough to daze me, and I tipped off the bench. As I blinked away the birds that swirled around my head, chirping gleefully, I found a young man hunched over me, stammering his apologies. I didn't know him well, but I recognized him. He was one of the special needs children. Rojo, we called him, because he refused to wear anything but red, *ever*. He was very apologetic as he helped me to my feet. Even though I was still confused from the blow, there was also a tingle at the front of my head, for the soccer ball had struck me in the same spot where the *chichon* had grown on me as an infant. Whatever the reason, that blow reactivated senses that had lain dormant for over a decade. Neurons started to fire, and an inkling of a plan started to take shape.

For you see, as an apology, Rojo had drawn me toward his friends, two other special needs children who were playing a game of soccer on the pitch behind the school. There was Chiquitín, who despite his nickname was not tiny at all but rather massive in every way: tall, broad, heavy-set. I'd never seen him wearing anything but sweats because any other kind of clothing wouldn't have fit him. And there was Maria, who didn't have a nickname because she referred to herself in the third person and so everyone knew her real name. So as I stood there, with Rojo inviting me to join them in their game and my brain crackling with fresh creativity, I knew how I was going to steal back Señor de la Paz's ring.

Chapter Fourteen

N<small>ATALIA WAS ONLY HALF-DRESSED, SO SHE COULDN'T</small> leave the changing room, but she nonetheless cracked the door and stuck her head out. "Oh, no. *No, no, no.*"

Diego looked up in surprise. "Oh, no, what?"

"You're a monster!"

Diego blinked. "What do you mean? What did I do?"

"What did you do? You decided to impersonate a special needs child so you could steal a stupid ring, that's what. So you could waltz into the office without anyone paying you the attention you deserved."

Diego frowned. "No, I didn't. How would that even work? Everyone at the school knew I didn't have a mental disability."

"Are you sure about that? Because it seems as if the only time your brain is actually working is when you've been struck in the head. You should probably get that checked out."

Diego sniffed. "I didn't impersonate any of the special needs children, and I'm not a monster."

Natalia was glad there was no one else in the store, because even though Diego couldn't get a glimpse of her naked shoulders from his seat, someone else at a different angle surely might've. "Well, that doesn't excuse what you're about to do. You're going to use those poor special needs children in some way. Abuse their trust to your own sick ends. It's abhorrent."

Diego smirked at her. "You really do have a hard time listening, don't you? I told you at the beginning of this tale that everyone involved with the exception of Principal Rosales came out better as a result of the events that transpired. That includes Rojo, Chiquitín, and Maria."

"Do you even know their real names?"

"Of course I do," said Diego. "Though at the time, those were the names I knew them by, so I figured it made sense to call them that in the story. For the record, Chiquitín loved his nickname. Still does."

Natalia frowned at Diego. On the one hand, she couldn't believe the turn Diego's story had taken, but on the other, it was just a story. Some ridiculous tale he'd made up. A tale that was a little too similar to another one she'd heard... "You know, there *is* another option. One that doesn't paint you in a horrible, conniving light."

"Which is?" asked Diego.

"That you admit you've made this all up," said Natalia. "That you based it all off the plot of *The Score.*"

"The Score?" said Diego.

"The movie?" said Natalia. "With Robert De Niro and Edward Norton? Where one of the main characters pretends to be a mentally-handicapped janitor so he can gain access to a museum?"

Diego waved a hand. "First of all, I'm familiar with the movie. And it's a customs house, not a museum. More importantly, my story is nothing like the plot of *The Score.* It doesn't involve any bejeweled scepters or depth charges, and it certainly doesn't involve any back-stabbing. It's an uplifting story."

A smile grew across Natalia's face. "So you *are* a movie buff. I knew it. I have to admit, it's nice to know you watch movies besides those intended for children."

Diego gave her a long look. "Are you done?"

Natalia shrugged, though the door hid her shoulders from view. "I guess."

"No, really, are you done? You've been in there forever and I've yet to see you in a single dress. I thought you were going to show me them as you went along."

Natalia smiled again. "These dresses take time to shrug into. And I never said I was going to display them for you."

Diego kept that flat stare on her, his eyes narrowing slightly. "You know, given I offered to pay for this outfit, you could try to be more accommodating."

"I'll show you once I've picked the right one," said Natalia. "In the meantime, you can sit there and wait, Mr. Diego Patience Cabrera."

Diego clasped his hands. "Fine. I can sit."

Diego turned his attention to the mannequins. To his credit, he abstained from twiddling his thumbs and whistling.

"You still have to finish your story, though," said Natalia.

"What?" Diego blinked. "No. You don't want to hear it. I'm a monster, after all. It's a repugnant tale."

Natalia scowled. "You really are infuriating, you know that?"

Diego pursed his lips, saying nothing.

Natalia sighed. "Fine. I'll withhold judgement on whether or not you're a monster until the end of your story. Fair enough?"

Diego thought about it. "I'm also going to need some assurances that you're not going to mock me for my choice in movies."

"Oh, get over yourself." Natalia closed the door and returned her attention to trying to figure out how to wiggle into the purple dress.

Diego's voice once again drifted through the slats in the door. "I'll take that as a guarantee. Now, where was I…"

Interlude 4

OR THE STORY OF HOW I PUT TOGETHER MY VERY
FIRST CREW (PART 2)

As I stood there with Rojo, Chiquitín, and Maria, my plan began to take shape, but first, there was the immediate concern of the soccer game, so I joined the three for a light-hearted scrimmage. Really, it was little more than kicking the ball between the four of us, but that was fine by me. If you're thinking I might've been mortified to play with the special needs children, you'd be wrong. Fact of the matter was, I wasn't a particularly popular child at school. I didn't have many friends, which I know is shocking for someone of my intellect and charm, but it's true. So I didn't mind a little company, especially given how poorly my day had gone.

Soon enough, the parents of Rojo, Chiquitín, and Maria arrived to take them home, at which point I had to convince them to let me invite their children to my home for an after school get-together. The parents were suspicious, of course, having become protective of their children due to their unique circumstances, but after Rojo explained the soccer ball incident and given that it was just me and not some disingenuous group of bullies, they eventually relented and drove us all to my place.

At this point, I should probably explain my plan for obtaining the ring. It was all dependent upon the fact that prior to the parent-teacher assembly on Friday evening, there would be a school wide assembly for the students during the day on Friday to share information relevant to the parent meetings. Mainly, it was an exercise in making sure everyone would be on their best behavior and to ensure the school would come across in the best possible light. The important point is that attendance was compulsory for *everyone* in the school: students, teachers, even most of the support staff, with one notable exception.

The special needs students.

Oh, brother, here we go.

You said you wouldn't judge me until the end, and I'm going to hold you to that. Now the plan I came up with was two-pronged. The first part would involve Rojo, Chiquitín, and Maria enacting a series of distractions to get the few remaining eyes in the school's front office off of Principal Rosales' room, and the second part would involve me breaking in and stealing the ring. Despite what you might think, I was not going to implicate any of them in my theft, only use them in the way that best suited their talents.

You may be wondering, though, how I could steal the ring while confined to the assembly in the gymnasium. As it turns out, there were a series of tunnels underneath the school which I'd stumbled across two years earlier while pulling off a prank during one of the school's musicals. You see, it was an old school that used hot water to heat the various rooms through radiators. The tunnels contained pipes that carried the hot water from the central boiler to the edges of the school, but the tunnels were big enough for a skinny teenager to sneak through them without much difficulty. There was no access hatch to the tunnels in Principal Rosales' office, but there was one not far outside in the hallway, not to mention one in the gymnasium and another in the main janitor's closet, where a skeleton key that could open any door in the school resided. So my plan was to sneak into the service tunnels during the assembly, steal the skeleton key from the closet, head to the front offices, wait for my new friends to distract the remaining secretary who would've stayed behind in case of emergency, and then break into Rosales' office while no one was the wiser.

And all I had to do to make it happen was gain Rojo, Chiquitín, and Maria's trust over the next three and a half days.

Now this is the part of the story where surely you think I took advantage of them, and I'll admit I started out with that intention. But as I spent that first evening with the three of them, and then the next one and the one after that, I came to get to know these three individuals who'd I'd largely ignored for the last decade of my life. And you know what? Their mental impairments didn't make them any less charming or engaging or worthy of friendship. Rojo, despite his serious quirk about the color red, was incredibly generous and caring. The incident with the soccer ball was no fluke. Any time he thought his actions had caused anyone harm, he would apologize profusely, no matter how much you assured him he'd done nothing wrong. Chiquitín loved to laugh. He had a laugh that was even bigger than his prodigious size, and he laughed at just about anything. But more than that, he was funny, too. His laugh was so infectious that when he inevitably laughed at his own jokes, you'd find yourself carried along for the ride. And Maria? Well, they say she had a mental disability, but I wasn't so sure. For her, it was simply a difficulty in translating her thoughts into speech, and in that respect I'll admit she had a hard time. But you could tell from looking in her eyes that she understood everything perfectly. To this day I'll argue she might've been one of the most clever people I've ever met.

Anyway, I won't bore you with the details, but I grew close to those three that week. While I initially thought to lie to them about why I needed them to practice their elaborate distractions, in the end I told them the truth: that Hernando had picked on me, and that if I didn't get his ring back from Principal Rosales' office, my life would become a living hell. And you know what? They understood quite well what that was like. All of them had been picked on, ridiculed, and embarrassed over the years, and if they could help stop that from happening to someone else, they were only too eager to help. Moreover, no one, not even their teachers or parents, had ever entrusted then with the sort of job I had. Everyone coddled them, held their hands, whereas here I came, asking them to perform a critical role in a daring plan to break into the principal's own office. If they failed, I would fail. I needed them to perform flawlessly. That wasn't lost on them. In fact, it meant the world to them that I'd put that much faith in them. Even though we didn't have much time to practice, by Friday not only was I confident in their abilities, but they were confident in themselves.

Come Friday, I was nonetheless a mess of nerves, but nothing that happened that morning was of any importance, so I'll fast forward to the assembly. The entire student body gathered in the gymnasium, packing onto the bleacher seats while Principal Rosales looked on with that dour frown of his. While everyone was being seated, I slipped underneath the bleachers, opened the access hatch to the tunnels, and dropped inside.

That's when I encountered my first problem. You see, I'd pulled my prank during the musical at the end of the school year, when heat was the concern rather than cold. Then, the boiler had been shut off, which wasn't the case at the moment in late October, with a cold front that had blown in two days prior. As I dropped into the tunnels, a blast of blistering, Saharan air knocked me to my knees. I nearly burned myself through my shirt as I brushed against the boiler pipes. For a moment I reconsidered my entire plan, but the prospect of becoming a human punching bag for Hernando still sounded worse than roasting to death, so I turned on the flashlight I'd brought with me and set off in search of the janitor's closet.

Now I'll admit, I should've scouted the tunnels before heading down, but I knew the school like the back of my hand. I figured that knowledge would translate underground.

It didn't.

Even though the janitor's closet was situated close to the gymnasium, within two minutes I was hopelessly lost. I took a left when I should've taken a right. I doubled back when I should've kept going. I second-guessed every decision, all while my cheeks became flushed and sweat poured down my face. My breathing became ragged, as much from the panic that was setting in as from the intense heat. I seriously considered going back to the gymnasium and accepting whatever fate befell me at Hernando's hands, but I'd become so lost I didn't know how. So I switched plans and began looking not for the janitor's closet but for *any* way to escape my underground hell. I stumbled and staggered, occasionally burning myself on the blistering steel of the boiler pipes while the sweat on my skin turned to steam before my eyes. My shirt provided little protection against the heat of the boiler and had soaked through completely, so I stripped it off and kept going. Dust caked my fingers, decades old cobwebs attacked my face, and my hair stuck to my head like glue. Just when I thought the tunnels might become my grave, I suffered a sense of déjà vu, and with a cry of sudden glee I knew where I was. Within a few seconds I'd located an exit, popped open the hatch above, and crawled out to the sweet, sweet freedom of the theater, where I'd pulled my prank two years prior.

I'll admit I took a moment to catch my breath and thank *Dios* for delivering me to safety, but as I checked my watch, I realized my plan had crumbled around me. Not only had I failed to secure the skeleton key from the janitor's closet, but Chiquitín and Maria should've been pulling off their distraction at that very moment (Rojo, of course, having already thrown a tantrum in their class as a means of allowing Chiquitín and Maria to slip out undetected).

But even with my plan in shambles, I didn't give up. I burst out of the theater into the chilly October afternoon, racing across the grounds, dirty, shirtless, slicked with sweat, and no doubt looking like a madman, all while my mind raced to come up with an alternate plan to retrieve Señor de la Paz's ring. I burst through the front doors to the school, still not having been seen by anyone thanks to the assembly. As I approached the lobby, I caught the tail end of Chiquitín's performance. You see, he'd lurched into the offices, moaning and groaning about his belly, all while Maria mumbled over and over that he needed help. I arrived as Chiquitín stumbled into the arms of the secretary, who was roughly a third his size. Somehow, she and Maria managed to drag Chiquitín in the direction of the nurse's office, probably because Chiquitín helped just enough so they didn't have to support his full weight. And wouldn't you know it, that big fellow caught me out of the corner of his eyes as he stumbled away from the scene of the crime. Rather than gape at my disheveled state, he just gave me a wink and a smile.

And so there I stood, staring through the windows into the front offices of the school with no one to stop me and yet with no way to get through the final barriers that stood between me and the ring.

Chapter Fifteen

THE DOOR CREAKED AS NATALIA STEPPED FROM THE changing room. She took a step toward Diego and held out her hands. "Well. What do you think?"

Natalia had eventually decided upon the purple satin dress, though after consideration she'd determined it was more violet than eggplant. It was a cowl neck backless dress, with slender rolled straps that crisscrossed between her shoulder blades. The dress lay smooth against her right hip, but the fabric had been intentionally bunched over her left, leading into a slit that exposed almost the full length of her left thigh and calf. Currently, the dress dragged along the ground, but once paired with a set of four inch heels, it should clear the floor by a finger's breadth.

Natalia would've preferred to choose one of the dresses the saleswoman picked instead of one of the two Diego pointed out, but the truth was it fit her best. It was revealing while still elegant. The satin felt smooth and lush against her skin, and the lack of arms meant her movement wouldn't be restricted in the event that she needed to lift keys or a wallet off one of Diego's marks. Most importantly, it fit her body shape without adding tons of superfluous ruffles or lengthy trailing sections she might trip over.

Judging from the look Diego gave her, he thought it fit well, too. He stood, his face slack. He blinked a couple times, and though his lips moved, all he managed to force out was a breathy, "Um..."

Natalia smiled. She'd seem him flustered at the National Gallery when she'd forced his hand and broken into the back before he was ready, but this was a different beast. This was the first time Natalia had broken his shield of confident charm, and all it took was a little dress.

Natalia took another couple steps toward Diego, enjoying herself. "Hello? Diego? Did you hear me? What do you think of the gown?"

"I... I think..." Diego closed his eyes. He gave his head a shake, and when his eyes reopened he regained most of the composure he'd lost. "I think everyone at the gala will be sufficiently distracted by it."

"Sufficiently distracted? Is that all that matters? If that were the case, why didn't you buy me a neon poncho or a chicken suit?"

For a moment, the mask of composure Diego armed himself with again slid off. His dark eyes were soft as he gazed at Natalia. His long lashes fluttered as he blinked. His lips parted, and a soft breath escaped his chest. He reached out and touched Natalia gently above her elbow, his fingers strong and gentle and slightly rough. A tingle ran up her arm in response to his touch, one that shot to her spine and made her shiver. The breath Diego exhaled seemed to flow into her, catching in her throat, and her heart, normally so steady, might've missed a beat.

Diego spoke in a low voice, breathy and measured. "You look breathtaking, Natalia. Any man would be lucky to have you as his date."

As his fingers lingered on her arm, a pressure built inside Natalia's chest. It pushed on her ribs, constricting her lungs and making it hard to breath. At the same time, the nervous tingle that had started in her arm and made it to her spine travelled to her legs, and she had to focus to keep them from wobbling. *What is this?* she asked herself. It wasn't as if she'd never experienced attraction before. She'd dated many men, handsome men, and when she desired, she let the relationships become sexual for a time, but she'd never felt this uncomfortable sensation in her chest. Why this, why now, and why with Diego of all people? Because this thing she was feeling would not, *could not*, work.

Natalia forced herself to focus. "Fake date, you mean."

Diego drew his hand away. He chuckled, and the tension between them broke like a pane of glass. "Yes. Fake date."

Natalia swallowed, trying to force some saliva into her suddenly dry mouth. "So, what happened?"

Diego squinted. "What do you mean?"

"In your story," said Natalia. "You left yourself standing there, shirtless and sweaty outside the principal's office. How did you get the ring?"

"Oh." Diego shrugged. "It isn't that exciting. I can finish the story another time."

"Like hell you will," said Natalia. "You made a promise to tell me the whole story."

Diego smirked, and he cocked his head. "Did I though?"

Natalia sighed, wondering how this infuriating man had made her feel weak-kneed a moment ago. "It was an implicit promise. When someone tells a story, they don't leave the listener hanging mere moments from the conclusion. They see it through to the end *unless* they're some sort of monster, which by the way is a judgement I've yet to pass on you."

"Fair enough," said Diego. "But the ending to the story isn't that exciting, because believe it or not, Principal Rosales' door wasn't locked. I didn't even need the skeleton key to get in."

Natalia felt as if a balloon had deflated in front of her. "Are you serious?"

"I'm serious."

"So you just walked in and grabbed the ring?"

"No," said Diego, "because even though the office door was open, the cabinet drawer in which the ring was stored was locked. And in retrospect, the skeleton key wouldn't have helped me open that anyway."

"You know, for someone with a supernatural intellect, you really failed to think a lot of things through."

"I blame the soccer ball," said Diego. "Though the blow spurred me to creativity, the bruise it left had long since faded before I descended into those hellish underground tunnels."

"So how did you get the ring?" asked Natalia.

"A letter opener," said Diego. "I took it from Rosales' desk, jabbed it in the cabinet's lock, and twisted."

Natalia frowned. "That's not how you pick a lock."

"I know," said Diego. "The opener snapped in half, and it messed the lock up something fierce as well. Then I took a bronze statue from Rosales' desk, smashed it into the lock a few times, and whole thing splintered and fell apart. From there it was a simple matter of pulling open the drawer and running off with the ring."

"So in the end, the best you could come up with was a smash and grab?"

"It wasn't pretty, but it was effective," said Diego. "And I did warn you that things worked out well for everyone *except* Principal Rosales."

"And Rojo? And Maria and Chiquitín? What happened to them?"

"Nothing bad," said Diego. "Their confidence grew as a result of the heist, and though the adults never suspected them of having anything to do with the theft, a pervasive rumor spread through the school that they'd engineered the whole thing."

Natalia eyed him sideways. "And did you stay friends with them afterwards?"

Natalia expected Diego to smile and beam at her and make some outlandish claim about them moving onto the Museu Picasso in Barcelona next, but instead he looked wistfully off into the distance and gave a slow nod. "I did."

Despite Diego being the smoothest liar she'd ever met, something about the way he said it made Natalia half-tempted to believe him. "Alright. I've made my decision."

Diego lingered in thought for a moment before bringing his attention back to Natalia. "About whether I'm a monster?"

Natalia smiled again. "I'm upgrading you from monster to fiend. Depending on where the story goes next, you might rise all the way to rascal status."

"Unfortunately, that's the end of the story," said Diego. "It doesn't go anywhere else."

"That's not possible," said Natalia, "because you *still* haven't shed any light on how you actually got into the business."

"Oh, that," said Diego. "That's a different story altogether, one that involves the ring and Señor de la Paz and some very angry Portuguese mobsters, but seeing as you've finally picked your dress, that story will have to wait until another day."

Natalia snorted. "Of course it will. What a surprise."

Diego nodded toward the dressing rooms. "You should probably change into your own attire. In the meantime, I'll see if I can find some shoes and jewelry to match that dress—assuming you trust me to pick something that works, of course."

Natalia didn't trust anyone to do anything, but she could admit Diego had an eye for fashion. Probably a better eye than she did. "I suppose I could entrust you with that."

Diego glanced at her feet. "Size seven and a half?"

"Eight, actually."

Diego nodded. "Perfect. Meet me at the register."

Natalia figured it would take him longer to pick out a pair of shoes than it would for her to wiggle out of the dress—it was easier to get out of it than in, after all—but knowing Diego, he'd probably assumed she'd pick one of the dresses he told her to try on and had already spotted shoes that worked. Natalia might've changed a little more quickly than she otherwise would've to test her hypothesis, gathering the purple dress and leaving the rest behind, but despite her speed, she nonetheless found Diego waiting for her at the bottom of the marble stairs. Behind him on the checkout counter was a shoe box, on top of which sat a pair of golden ankle strap stilettos, as well as a couple of smaller boxes that probably contained a necklace and earrings.

Diego noticed her gaze. "Care to try them on?"

Natalia didn't need to. She knew they'd be uncomfortable and difficult to move in, but they'd make her legs look fantastic and as long as they were size eights, they should fit her as best as could be hoped. "They'll do."

Diego took the dress from her arms and added it to the pile. "That'll be it, I think."

As the woman rang up the items, Diego turned to Natalia. "I have to admit that took longer than I was expecting. Care to join me for dinner after this?"

Natalia eyed the display as the woman scanned the tags. She'd expected the dress to cost an arm and a leg, but *seven hundred dollars for the shoes?* She almost felt as if she owed Diego a dinner after this. "I assume this would be another necessary evil for building team unity?"

"Not really," said Diego. "I'm simply getting hungry, and I enjoy your company."

There it was again. That pressure building inside Natalia's chest. The strange flutter of her heart that shouldn't have been there. The tingle in her extremities. The subtle sensation of longing that was going to *doom her,* damn it all.

Diego noticed her hesitation. "It doesn't have to be anything fancy. We could pick a casual restaurant. Alternatively, I could buy you another dress to wear while we sample Oslo's finest, assuming you don't extort another long story out of me while you try it on."

Diego looked at her hopefully. She averted her gaze to avoid having to stare into the deep wells of his eyes. "Ah... I'm flattered, but I'm going to have to decline. It's best we stick to the business in front of us."

Out of the corner of her eyes, she noted his nod. When he spoke, there was a hint of disappointment in his voice. "Of course. I'll give you a ride back to your hotel as soon as I'm done paying."

Chapter Sixteen

THE SUN HUNG LOW IN THE SKY, CAUSING SHADOWS TO stretch between the buildings of downtown Oslo as Diego drove toward Natalia's hotel. He'd tried to broach a few topics of conversation since pulling away from Werner Johansen, but while Natalia had answered his questions, she hadn't offered more than necessary, responding with simple yeses or nos. She hadn't taunted him or ribbed him. She hadn't stuck her tongue out, nor squinted at him with that twinkle in her eye that suggested she was loving giving him a hard time. Ever since he'd asked if she wanted to join him for dinner, it was as if a wall had been airlifted and dropped into place between them. There was no doubt that question had resulted in the change in her behavior, but for the life of him Diego couldn't figure out why it had done so.

After all, he'd asked her to dinner the night before, and though she'd resisted—strongly—eventually she'd relented. And the oddest part was at that time, she clearly hadn't wanted to spend any time in his presence at all, whereas now he could've sworn she did. Was she playing hard to get, or did she not actually like him? His ability to read women wasn't that poorly honed, was it?

Perhaps he was simply rushing things. After all, they'd only met in person a little over a day ago. Even as Diego considered that fact, it seemed ludicrous, because it felt as if he'd known Natalia for weeks, although to be fair, they had been texting that long. Still, something had already blossomed between them that he hadn't felt in any of his other relationships, even the ones that lasted close to a year. There was an easy rapport between them, a fluidness of banter and an understanding that things they told each other would be exaggerated and embellished. Maybe it was because they were both in the business. They were used to dealing with people who kept secrets and who only let others to within arm's length.

The strangest part was that even as Diego continued to lie to Natalia and as she hid aspects of herself from him in turn, he felt himself wanting to be more *genuine,* much as he knew he couldn't. Even as he'd told her the story about his youth, he found himself adding details that, while overstated, actually contained an element of truth to them, some of which were quite personal. He hadn't done the same thing with his first story, which had been completely fabricated except for the fact that he *had* fallen down the stairs as a small child. Why was he sharing these details with her? Natalia wouldn't know the difference between truth and fiction so long as he sold it properly, and sharing anything about his true life was sloppy. It put him at risk should their heist backfire.

And yet... there was a part of him that had enjoyed telling her those details. A weight that had lifted when Natalia hadn't recoiled in horror following his sharing of them. Sure, she'd joked about him being a monster, but in the end she'd deemed him no worse than a knave, and her eyes suggested she thought he was anything but. She'd enjoyed hearing about his youth—but only through the sensationalized, fictional version he provided. Diego's true story wasn't thrilling. It wasn't inspirational. If anything, it was pitiable and sad, and he couldn't risk telling Natalia *that* story. After all, the story was the only thing keeping Natalia at his side. The previous night proved it. Natalia had been ready to leave and let him eat his arctic char in silence before he started to spin his yarn. Like Scheherazade in *One Thousand and One Nights,* Diego's story was the only thing keeping Natalia on his hook. If anything, he'd need to make his narratives *more* enticing if this wall Natalia erected remained in place.

Diego slowed as he pulled into the bus stop near Natalia's hotel, the Aston Martin purring beneath him. He put the Vantage into park and turned toward Natalia, adopting his most charming persona. "You're sure I couldn't convince you to join me for dinner? I've heard interesting things about a molecular gastronomy restaurant not far from here, assuming you're into foams and sauces that have been suspended in solids."

Natalia gave him a brief glance before turning away. "Ah... no. Thank you. Could you pop the trunk?"

To say the car had a trunk was an overstatement. Diego would've been hard pressed to fit two carry-on suitcases behind the bucket seats, but the spot was large enough to pack Natalia's dress and shoes. Diego briefly considered cajoling her into staying, but experience told him that too much coaxing would push Natalia away as forcefully as a hard shove.

He pushed a button and the trunk unlatched. "Enjoy the rest of your evening. And don't forget about our exercise tomorrow morning."

Natalia paused with her hand on the door handle. "Ugh. Right. Your ropes course."

"You'll find it a little more engaging than that," said Diego. "I was thinking we should get started about nine o'clock. I can give you a ride, or I'll text you the address if you'd prefer to get your own transportation."

Natalia popped the door and hopped onto the sidewalk. "I appreciate the offer, but I'll arrange my own ride."

Somehow, Diego wasn't surprised by her response. He leaned across her seat, bending low so he could see her fully through the open door. "The offer stands if you change your mind. Good night, Natalia."

She nodded back, her face a mask devoid of emotion. "Good night, Diego."

There was a thump as the trunk closed after Natalia collected her things. Diego didn't immediately pull onto the thoroughfare, busses be damned. He watched Natalia walk away, enjoying the gentle sway of her hips. She kept her focus in front of her, but as she reached the tip of the wharf on which her hotel was situated, she turned and looked back. Diego couldn't make out her eyes from that distance, but he was sure she was looking in his direction.

So. There is *a crack in the wall.*

A call rang on the Aston Martin's speakers, rerouted through his phone's bluetooth. Diego accepted it as he put the vehicle into drive and pulled onto the street. "Diego speaking."

The voice that responded was meaty and gruff, with a thick Russian accent. "Diego. Is long time since we talked."

Diego felt a nervous tingle in his spine, but he was experienced enough not to let it enter his voice. "Mr. Kovalyov. My apologies about that. I've been very busy lately, and I haven't had time to reach out."

"Tell me about progress."

Kovalyov wasn't one to beat around the bush. He got to the point, *quickly*. In anyone else, Diego could've appreciated the quality, but with Kovalyov it gave him the impression that if you didn't provide the man with exactly what he wanted when he wanted it, there would be serious repercussions. In fact, Diego had seen some of the repercussions firsthand.

"The plan is coming along nicely. We're still working out a few kinks, but we should have full access to museum security by tomorrow night. Once we have that, we'll have to carefully parse the museum's safety protocols, but I have no doubt we'll be able to make our move shortly thereafter."

"How long?"

"Five days, maybe," said Diego. "A week at most."

"Is longer than you said would take. I am not pleased, Diego."

Diego swallowed. "Mr. Kovalyov, this isn't the sort of thing where you can rush in waving a gun. People have tried that before, multiple times. Every time the painting was recovered and the people involved caught. This is a delicate operation. If we want to get out alive with the painting in hand and not have an international task force take it back by force in six months to a year, we have to plan carefully. We have to do it my way, with my team, on my schedule."

"Is team capable? Is team ready?"

Eddie was. Miriam was. But Natalia? The truth was Diego didn't know. He didn't doubt her abilities, but there was something she wasn't telling him, and that was a separate issue from the strange relationship brewing between them. Diego had known it was a bad idea to mix work and pleasure, yet he'd let his interest in her smolder anyway.

But he didn't tell Kovalyov that. That would've been the definition of a bad idea. "Very capable, Mr. Kovalyov. We *will* be ready. I guarantee it."

Silence lingered long enough for Diego to wonder if Kovalyov had hung up, but he hadn't heard any click. After a lengthy pause, the Russian spoke. "You have five days. Do not test patience, Diego."

Now the line went dead, the dial tone merging with the steady hum of the road. Diego unclenched his fingers, which he only now realized had been gripping his steering wheel with unnatural force. Five days wasn't a lot of time, but he could make it work.

He'd have to.

Chapter Seventeen

THE UBER DRIVER LOOKED SUSPICIOUSLY OUT THE passenger's side window as he parked the car. "Are you sure this is where you are going, Miss?"

They'd returned to what Natalia considered the more industrial part of Oslo, not far from the loft, but at least there were businesses in the vicinity of that structure. The address Diego had given her this time led to an empty lot surrounded by chain link fencing and with numerous weeds sprouting through the concrete. In the distance, she could see an enormous rail yard packed with hundreds of shipping containers and beyond that some sort of trucking and distribution hub.

The expansive lot was empty except for three cars: a white delivery van, a black sedan, and a metallic green Aston Martin.

"This appears to be the right spot." Natalia exited the car and strode through the open gate into the lot itself. A cool breeze whistled through the air, but the sun shone brightly in the clear sky overhead. Chances were it would warm up sooner or later.

As Natalia approached the trio of vehicles, the door to the Aston Martin opened and Diego climbed out. He wore a third different suit in as many days, but like the others this one was cut from rich cloth and impeccably tailored. If anything, it fit him even better than the previous two. His broad shoulders stretched the blazer across his back, and his slacks fit snugly against his muscular thighs. *Nope,* thought Natalia. *Definitely wrong about him being pudgy under the jacket.* As he came to rest in front of Natalia, he placed his hands in his pants pockets, further stretching the fabric over his legs as well as what lay between them. His jacket fluttered open, revealing a cream-colored shirt, the top two buttons of which had been tantalizingly left unbuttoned.

Diego smirked at her. "I take back everything I said about your punctuality. You're five minutes late. This is unacceptable."

Natalia snorted, willing herself not to get absorbed into Diego's mind games, or his unnecessarily tight pants. "Blame my driver. He's not used to dropping tourists off at abandoned lots."

"You should give him one star in the app," said Diego. "Teach him a lesson."

"Oy. Don't do 'at."

Natalia turned to see Eddie extracting himself from the front seat of the sedan. The car lurched as he pulled his weight off it, and Natalia had to wonder how he'd folded himself inside it in the first place.

"You can't give the man one star," said Eddie, his T-shirt flapping in the breeze. "A driver's ratin' is 'is liveli'ood. You do 'at and ya might as well be snatchin' quid from 'is rockets."

"It was a joke, Eddie," said Diego. "I didn't mean it."

"It weren't an egg. Yoke's is supposed to be runny." Eddie nodded to Natalia. "Mornin', Natalia."

"Good morning, Eddie." Natalia spread her hands wide. "So, I'm here for the team-building exercise. What's the plan? Did you bring a Frisbee?"

Diego smiled. "It's too windy for that, and I neglected to bring a cooler full of cold beers, much to Eddie's dismay. I have something else in mind. Have you ever seen *Scent of a Woman?*"

Natalia blinked. "What?"

"The movie. *Scent of a Woman.* With Al Pacino and Chris O'Donnell?"

Natalia stood there staring at Diego. "You know, I was kidding earlier when I teased you about being a movie buff, but you are one, aren't you?"

"I'm surprised you're not given how much you seem to like stories," said Diego. "But I take it you haven't seen the film. It's about a student, played by O'Donnell, who accepts a job to take care of a blind man, played by Pacino. Pacino is suicidal and an alcoholic, and there's a plot point about the school O'Donnell attends, but ultimately it's about the bond that forms between the two characters. It's a good movie. Pacino won the Academy Award for best actor."

"So that's what this is?" asked Natalia. "Movie night? Or morning? Is there a projector in the van?"

"Not exactly," said Diego. "You see, in the movie there's a scene where O'Donnell's character tries to cheer Pacino's character up by taking him on a joyride in a Ferrari. Pacino doesn't care for it until O'Donnell allows him to drive. Remember, Pacino is blind. But O'Donnell talks him through the activity, and Pacino trusts him enough that they manage to get through the experience unscathed, even if they do get pulled over by a police officer at the end."

Diego pulled his hands from his pockets and reached inside his suit. From the interior pocket he pulled a black sleep mask, which he held toward Natalia.

Natalia looked at the blindfold. Her eyes stretched wide. "Are you *insane?* I'm not driving blindfolded anywhere, no matter who's coaching me."

"Of course you're not," said Diego. "Eddie will."

Natalia and Eddie both reacted at the same time. *"What?"* Then Natalia, to Eddie: "Wait, you didn't know he was planning this?"

Eddie cast her a glance that clearly revealed he did *not* know. "Diego, drivin' blind spells Barney Rubble. Them folds is for bedrooms and firin' squads."

"It'll be all right, Eddie," said Diego. "I'll be with you every step of the way. Besides, we're in a wide open parking lot."

Eddie nodded, as if that made sense. "'At's true, but it's stiw a bit bonkers, mate. You might as well be askin' me to drive without using me German bands."

Diego took a step toward Eddie. "Do you trust me?"

"Well, sure, mate, but—"

Diego held the big man's gaze. *"Do you trust me, Eddie?"*

Eddie thought about it for a second. "Yeah, Diego. I trust ya."

Diego gestured toward Natalia with the sleeping mask again. "Could you inspect it please?"

Diego might as well have thrust an enormous furry spider at her. "I think that blow you took as a child did more harm than good. *I'm not driving anywhere blind.* Eddie might trust you that much, but I sure as hell don't."

Diego snorted. "That's precisely the point I'm trying to make, but again, I don't want you to put it on. I just need you to check the blindfold to make sure it's not see-through."

"Oh." Natalia accepted the mask. She held it to her eyes without pulling the strap over her head. A diffuse glow made it through the fabric, but that was all. "I can't see a thing."

"Great," said Diego. "Eddie?"

Eddie accepted the mask from Natalia and started to draw it over his big egg of a head.

"Not yet, Eddie," said Diego. "Wait until you're in the car. Natalia?" Diego nodded toward the black sedan.

Natalia shook her head. "Oh, no. I'm not getting in that thing. If you want to put your life in Eddie's hands, that's on you, but I'm rather fond of my internal organs. I'd like to keep them where they are."

Diego took a couple steps toward Natalia and placed his hands on her upper arms. His grip was firm and strong, and at the feel of his touch, a warm sensation spread through her chest, same as it had when he'd touched her at the boutique. Normally, Natalia hated unnecessary physical contact, but rather than making Natalia feel trapped, she felt protected by Diego's grasp.

Diego smiled at her, not one of those fake grins he'd initially plied her with. This smile was small and thoughtful. "Look, Natalia. I know you don't trust me. Maybe you don't trust anyone, but the whole point of this exercise is for you to trust, just a little bit. I'm not asking you to jump off a cliff or dive into a pool of starved piranhas. I'm asking you to give an inch, maybe two. Can you at least believe I won't let any harm come to you?"

Natalia eyed the man carefully. Diego was right. She didn't trust him. She didn't trust anyone but herself. How could she after the way the world had treated her? After all the people who'd lied to her and ignored her and left her to fend for herself in foster home after foster home? Everyone lied to her. Everyone told her what they thought she wanted to hear, and Diego, a professional conman, lied more frequently and thoroughly than anyone else. Yet for some incomprehensible reason as she stood there in his arms, held gently but with a hidden strength coursing through the man in front of her, she did feel safe. Protected. At ease. She couldn't remember the last time she'd felt that way, especially in the presence of someone else.

But she couldn't let Diego know that.

Natalia glanced toward the sedan. "You'll be in the car?"

"Of course. I'll be talking Eddie through it every step of the way."

Natalia allowed herself a smirk. "Well, I suppose I can believe you won't let any harm come to *yourself.*"

"That's the spirit." Diego let go of her arms, and Natalia sighed instinctively. "Come on. Let's get buckled in."

As soon as Diego no longer held her, she once again questioned the sanity of what she was about to do, but her entire plan revolved around getting Diego and the rest of the crew to trust her. If she didn't play along, they surely wouldn't afford her the same courtesy. Besides, what was the worst that could happen? As long as they didn't crash into the Aston Martin or the van, they'd be fine, right?

Natalia swallowed her hesitation and got in the back of the sedan. She fastened her seatbelt as Diego settled into the front passenger seat.

Eddie was in the process of checking his rearview and side mirrors. Diego gave him a long look. "Ah... Eddie? You remember you'll be driving blind, right?"

Eddie blinked. "Oh. Right. 'abit."

"You can go ahead and put the blindfold on," said Diego. "Here's how it'll work. At any point during the exercise, if I fail to say anything, that means to keep doing exactly what you're doing. Generally, that'll be on the straightaways. If I want you to go faster, I'll say faster. Slower, I'll say slower. Acceleration or deceleration should be gentle unless otherwise specified. Stop means a rapid stop. We're all wearing our seatbelts, right? For turns, right or left means a ninety degree turn. Shallow left or right is forty-five degrees. Sharp will be more than ninety, about a hundred and thirty-five. Otherwise, I'll be your eyes and ears. Any questions?"

"What about puttin' 'er in reverse?" asked Eddie.

Diego clapped Eddie on the shoulder. "I think we'll avoid that this time around, even though you are—"

"Oh, God," said Natalia. "Don't say it."

Diego turned to look at her. "Say what?"

Natalia blurted it out. "That he's the world's best backwards driver. We're already enacting a scene out of a movie for adults, why not pick a memorable quote from one of those rather than one for children?"

Diego looked at her as if she'd lost her marbles. "I was going to say that he's more than capable, but whatever. You ready, Eddie?"

Eddie slipped the blindfold over his head and settled it over his eyes. "Ready as I'll ever be, mate."

"Alright," said Diego. "Let's pull her out, nice and steady."

Eddie gave the car some gas, and the vehicle pulled forward smoothly, much more so than if it were Natalia blindfolded behind the wheel. Despite the fluidity of the motion, Natalia nonetheless felt her heart skip a beat. *Good Lord,* she thought to herself. *We're really doing this aren't we?*

"Very nice," said Diego. "A touch to the right. Now we're straight. A little more speed would be fine."

The car accelerated. The car went *thump-thump* as it rolled over stretches of cracked pavement. Natalia glanced at the dashboard where the speedometer informed her they'd already reached forty-five kilometers an hour. The chain link fence at the end of the lot, though still a ways away, was approaching too rapidly for her comfort.

"Perfect, Eddie," said Diego. "We're at about fifty-five right now. Let's slow and take a right."

The car decelerated smoothly and Eddie pulled the sedan into a turn. The car practically glided across the pavement as the acceleration pushed Natalia sideways in her seat. Eddie evened the car out, and suddenly they were traveling parallel to the fence they'd been barreling toward a moment ago.

"'Ow's 'at?" asked Eddie.

"Excellent," said Diego. "A touch to the right. Now we're spot on."

In what seemed like no time at all, they were approaching the next piece of chainlink fence at the back of the lot, but Diego gave Eddie more instructions. After another smooth right that put them heading back the direction they'd come, Natalia felt her nerves start to ease. Even blindfolded, it was clear Eddie was a very experienced driver.

"How are you feeling, Eddie?" asked Diego.

"Fi' as a fid'le," he said. "So far, it's brilliant, mate."

"Great," said Diego. "Should we push the envelope a little?"

Natalia straightened in her seat, the tingle in her extremities returning in force. "Wait, what? *No.* The envelope stays where it is."

"I'm feelin' confident if you are," said Eddie.

"That's what I like to hear," said Diego. "Take a right."

Eddie pulled the car through another smooth turn. Diego had him adjust a smidge to the left, and suddenly Natalia could see exactly where they were headed. "No. *No, no, no.* We're heading for the exit. Eddie! Do something!"

Eddie cocked his head slightly as they rushed past the parked van and the Aston Martin. "Diego?"

"Don't worry," he said. "There's no traffic. Slow a little. Okay. Now right."

The sedan shuddered as they drove down the parking lot entrance onto the adjoining street, but once again Eddie performed a perfect ninety-degree turn before straightening the car.

"Very good, Eddie," said Diego. "The street curves to the right. More. More. Excellent."

Natalia stared out her window at the trees that flicked by one after another, her heart thumping hard in her chest. There wasn't any oncoming traffic on the other side of the street, but some could appear at any moment. "This is insane. We're on a public road."

"And Eddie is doing a phenomenal job navigating it," said Diego. "A little to the left. Accelerate a smidge. That's it."

"Accelerate?" said Natalia. *"Are you nuts?* We need to pull over. Eddie, pull over."

"Don't listen to her, Eddie. You're doing great, though we are approaching another right. Slow. And... shallow turn."

Eddie followed Diego's instructions to a T as they merged onto a busier thoroughfare. This one did have moving vehicles in the lane opposite theirs, vehicles with actual human drivers who could undoubtedly see that Eddie was blindfolded if they only bothered to pay attention. Not only that but there were cars parked on the side of the street and even a pedestrian or two on the sidewalks.

Natalia's heart hammered against her ribs. How had she ever convinced herself Diego had her best interests at heart? She'd believed him, him and that stupid lying face of his. She'd swallowed every last falsehood, hook, line, and sinker. What an idiot she was. What a rube. "Oh, God. We're going to die. We're going to crash and we're going to die and we're going to ruin someone else's car."

"Nonsense," said Diego. "Eddie, you're doing wonderful. A smidge to the left."

"He is *not* doing wonderful," snarled Natalia. "He's trash, and this is reckless and insane. He's not Al Pacino and you are not Chris O'Donnell and *this is not a god-damned, mother-fucking movie!*"

"Relax, Natalia," said Diego. "I guarantee you I'm in complete control of the situation. Now will you please—"

A car parked not fifty meters down the road started to pull onto the street. Natalia screamed and braced herself, planting a foot in the back of Eddie's seat while she simultaneously jammed a hand against his headrest and another against her door. Before Diego could warn Eddie, the car screeched to a halt. Natalia slammed forward in her seat, as did everyone else, but their seatbelts kept them from losing more than their breath.

Eddie ripped the blindfold from his face. "What the..."

Diego grunted as he pulled the seatbelt from his chest, trying to get it to unlock. "I told you I was in control. Or rather, Miriam is. We outfitted the sedan with a bunch of exterior cameras and a wireless override. I've even got an interior camera so she could follow along." Diego pointed to the dash on the right side of the car, where a tiny microcam stared at them from the base of the windshield.

A grin spread across Eddie's face. "You *wanker.*" He leaned toward the camera. "Mornin', Midge."

Natalia heard their conversation as if through ten feet of water. Her breath froze in her lungs, and her seatbelt pressed across her chest, crushing her, immobilizing her. *Trapping her.* She clawed at the release, then at the door handle, her heart pounding like a drum inside her chest.

She gasped for air as she escaped the vehicle, stumbling onto the sidewalk. She grasped a parking sign to help give her balance while a random passerby looked at her with concern. Even now as she stood in the clear Oslo morning, she couldn't catch her breath. Her chest heaved as she tried to fill her lungs with air, but they stubbornly refused to cooperate.

Somewhere behind her, she heard the thump of a car door. Then Diego's voice. "Natalia. Are you all right?"

She glanced back to find Eddie had parked in the spot vacated by the car that pulled out in front of them. Natalia's chest still ached, but she was able to get enough breath to speak. "Stay away from me. *Stay away.*"

Diego must've noticed something in her eyes, because he did just that. He leaned down and spoke into the open car window. "Maybe you should talk to her."

Natalia focused her attention on the street behind her, so she didn't see Eddie approach. Eventually she felt his presence, though it might've been his shadow that fell across her. "Y'alright, Natalia?"

The boa constrictor crushing her lungs had traded places with a smaller, weaker cousin. She finally felt as if she wasn't starved for breath. "No, I'm not all right. Diego just tried to kill me. All of us."

Eddie clicked his tongue. "'Sa bit o' a stretch, don't you fink? Like 'e said, Midge was watchin' us the 'ole lemon."

Natalia turned to face the enormous man, who stood there cool as a cucumber, his thin T-shirt hanging across his muscular frame. "Did you really not know?"

"'At Midge was watchin'?" He shook his head. "Don't get me wrong, I knew she was in the van, but I fought she was just playin' one o' fose games o' 'ers on the dog and bone."

"So you had no idea? And you're not angry?"

"Cheesed? Nah. I'm proper chuffed, I am. First time drivin' blind and I made it 'is far wifout Midge havin' to step in."

Natalia felt as if her brain wasn't working properly. "Clearly I'm missing something. Diego put your life in his hands and you're not upset with him."

"Me life was in me own 'ands seein' as I was doin' the drivin', but I understand what ya mean. But no. Diego asked me to trust 'im, and I did. Simple as 'at."

Natalia blinked. "Really? Someone asked you to trust them *with your life,* and you did? Simple as that?"

"Not some bloke. *Diego.*" Eddie put a hand on Natalia's shoulder. It felt as if someone had left a seventy-two ounce steak there. "Y'see, I didn't know what 'e 'ad up 'is sleeve, but I knew 'e wouldn't put us in danger if 'e 'adn't fought it frough first. And I wouldn't 'ave let 'im drag you innit if I did."

Natalia glanced toward Diego who leaned against the side of the sedan, his focus on the storefront before him. "So... you actually trust him? Like, *for real?* Even though he's a smooth-talking grifter?"

Eddie shrugged, his shoulders moving like mountains during an earthquake. "Ever 'eard 'at sayin' 'at 'ere's no 'onor among fieves? Well, not wif us. We's is all criers and cheats, Natalia, but we trust each ofer. You should give it a try."

No, I shouldn't, Eddie, she thought, *because there is no honor among thieves. You should stop acting as if I have any, and you and Diego alike really need to stop believing in me, because I'm going to let you down. I promise.*

Natalia swallowed hard as she glanced at Diego. "I don't think I can trust the way you do, Eddie. I'm not built the same as you."

Eddie laughed. "Ain't 'at the truf. You need to eat a pork pie or two. Come on. Maybe I can convince Diego to let me swing by a pub afore we 'ead back to the lot. And don't worry. I won't wear the blindfold 'is lemon."

Now that she knew Miriam was watching, the blindfold was the least of Natalia's worries. The bigger one was how she'd look herself in the mirror after screwing over someone as good-natured as Eddie.

Chapter Eighteen

DIEGO STOOD IN THE LOBBY OF THE SCOUNDREL, admiring the graffiti art on the far wall and the chandelier full of Edison bulbs above. The receptionist at the front desk, a young blonde woman in a dark blazer, had asked him if he was staying with them, to which Diego replied he was waiting on a friend. To that the receptionist had stared at Diego's outfit: at the glossy shine of his black jacket and pants, at the silk satin trim on his lapels, pockets, and the outseam of his trousers, at the crispness of his collar and the rumpled flair of the pocket square above his left breast. The receptionist had lifted an eyebrow as if to question why a man would go to such lengths over a mere *friend,* but she hadn't commented other than to point out the bar should he find himself waiting longer than expected.

And in fact, Diego *had* found himself waiting. He checked his watch, which confirmed it was five past seven. He'd chided Natalia on being a few minutes late to their morning meeting, but he'd believed it was the fault of her driver, not her own. This was a different story. Diego stood in the lobby of her own hotel. Unless the elevator had gotten stuck, she'd have to take full responsibility for the tardiness, and Diego would enjoy giving her a hard time about it. Not that tonight's timing was critical, but it would be for their heist. Natalia already knew that of course, which was why chiding her over it would serve to frustrate her that much more effectively.

Diego wandered into the bar, declining the bartender's offer of a drink as he thought about why he liked to tease Natalia so. Some of it was the faces she made when he prodded her. The cute way she pursed her lips. The narrowing of her eyelids that was far sexier than it was intimidating. The tensing of her jaw, and the glimmer in her pale blue eyes. Every time she reacted that way it made Diego want to laugh. Sometimes he couldn't help himself, though he tried to keep his mirth under control. But he did love those honest moments of reaction, those jibes that were a hundred percent real even if they didn't mean a thing.

Diego shook his head. Why was he suddenly so concerned with authenticity? He'd always prided himself on his ability to lie fluidly, and he never expected total honesty from the people he worked with, nor with the women he involved himself with romantically. He didn't expect any more or less from Natalia so long as she performed her role in the heist, and yet... he craved that devious smile of hers. The one that was mischievous and maybe a little malicious but nonetheless a hundred percent *genuine*.

Diego shuddered at the thought of the word. As he did so, he heard the *click clack* of high heels behind him, followed by Natalia's irritated tone. "Sorry I'm late. It took me longer to prepare than I thought it would. One more reason I avoid getting glammed up whenever possible."

Diego turned, and as he caught sight of Natalia, a fuse inside him fizzled and blew. His eyes widened. Though he'd seen her in the dress she'd picked out, he hadn't seen her *like this*. Not with her long blonde hair lightly curled and cascading over her bare shoulders like a golden waterfall. Not with her piercing blue eyes accentuated by a smoky eyeshadow, and her lips glossed with a nude lipstick that, while subtle, gave them an added plumpness and shimmer that made him want to kiss her right then and there. Not with a thin golden necklace dangling from the perfect creamy skin of her neck, drawing his attention into the folds of the cowl that covered her breasts, and not with her left leg, made even longer and leaner by her sparkling heels, completely bared by the split at the dress's side.

Diego tried not to stare, but he failed. He failed *spectacularly.* He stood there, drinking Natalia in as if she were a firehose and he a man who'd spent the last two decades roaming the Sahara. He couldn't tear his eyes off her, no matter how hard he tried. His only saving grace was that Natalia seemed to be having a similarly hard time focusing on anything but him. With her small clutch gripped firmly before her, her gaze drifted up and down the full length of his tuxedo. She bit her lip, and Diego thought he heard a faint moan escape her lips, though it was possible he imagined it.

Diego tried to focus. *Come on,* he told himself. *You're a grifter. An internationally renowned conman. You've bedded models and online influencers. Act like you've been there!*

But he hadn't. Not with a woman like this.

"Uh... You... You're..."

Natalia averted her gaze, gave her head a shake, and when she looked up, she was back in control of herself. "Late. I know. I accounted for the dress and even the makeup, but the hair got the best of me."

I wasn't going to say that, Diego wanted to say. *I was going to tell you you're the most beautiful woman I've ever met, and that it's not even close. That compared to you, every other woman is the light of a candle, and you shine bright as the sun. That they're a drop of water and you the ocean. That until I'd met you, the desire I'd felt for other women was a pinprick, but now my entire body aches with it.*

But he couldn't tell her that, for many reasons. For the sake of the job they needed to complete. Because he was certain she didn't feel the same way about him. But most importantly, because he couldn't bare himself that way to anyone, especially not a woman he'd just met.

Diego cleared his throat, any thoughts of teasing Natalia vaporizing under the heat of her brilliance. "Your tardiness isn't an issue.

The gala will be going all night. I doubt anyone will notice if we're ten minutes or even an hour late. Besides, I'd say your efforts were well worth the time. You're breathtaking."

Natalia looked away again, and for the first time Diego noticed a hint of red on her cheeks. Was that rouge or an actual blush? "Ah... thank you."

Diego forced himself to continue, because if he stopped talking he feared he might start staring again. "Look, Natalia. I wanted to apologize for this morning. I won't say what I did was reckless or dangerous, because Miriam was in control of the sedan at all times. She knew that sooner or later she was going to have to jump in to save us from crashing, because I made it clear to her that I would push Eddie until it was necessary. That said, I do regret putting you in that situation in the first place. I wish I could've told you I had safeguards in place, but that would've defeated the purpose of the exercise which was to show you that Eddie, and Miriam by extension, trust me completely. To show you that I won't put them in harm's way unless I've done everything I can to keep them safe. I hope that message came across through the general panic I put you through."

Natalia looked at Diego carefully, in a way he couldn't quite decipher. "You don't need to apologize. I understand what you were trying to do, and I can't blame you since I already did the same."

Diego lifted an eyebrow. "Am I suffering from early onset dementia? Because I don't recall you stuffing me in a car and driving me around at high speed."

"Not that," said Natalia. "When I forced you to follow me into the back of the National Gallery, I was putting you in a position you weren't comfortable in and doing so without warning. I was asking you to trust me, and you did. Frankly, I performed much worse than you did."

"Well, your stunt didn't involve the risk of sudden, painful death."

Natalia smiled, that mischievous grin he'd fantasized about. "Fair. I take it back then. You're a jerk, and you remain in my debt."

Diego smiled in return, and the warmth from a genuine interaction, no matter how irrelevant, once again filled him. "We should probably get going. Eddie's waiting for us, and eventually he'll get ticketed, his charming personality be damned."

Diego extended his arm, and after a brief hesitation on her part, Natalia slid her arm inside his own. Together, they headed into the cool Oslo evening. Natalia didn't say anything as they walked along the wharf toward the bus station. Diego didn't know what to say, either, so he simply enjoyed the sensation of Natalia's arm upon his and tried to keep his gaze from drifting toward her bare back and the subtle curve of her derriere below. Diego thought Natalia might struggle in heels given her penchant for athletic shoes, but she walked with the same ballerina's grace she always did.

The black stretch limousine remained where Diego had left it, and if any police officers or angry bus drivers had come by in his absence, they hadn't left any evidence of their presence. Diego opened the back door for Natalia, his heart suffering a sharp pang as her arm left his, before following her inside the vehicle.

As he ducked inside the cabin, he heard Natalia's voice, chillier than it had been. "Oh. Miriam's here."

Diego settled onto the back seat as he closed the door behind him. Natalia had slid onto the bench on the right side of the vehicle, while Miriam sat behind the driver's cabin. She wore sweatpants and a hooded sweatshirt, a laptop resting in her lap.

"Took you guys long enough," said Miriam. "Eddie, we can go now."

Eddie's voice drifted through the partition at the front. "Ontoppit, Midge."

Diego heard the grumble of the engine, and the limousine pulled smoothly onto the adjoining street. Natalia sat upright in her seat, her face more composed than it had been inside The Scoundrel.

"I didn't realize you'd be joining us, Miriam," she said.

Miriam snorted. "Are you kidding? I'd rather have my toenails removed with hot pokers than join you and Diego at a gala. I'm just along for the ride to get you two properly outfitted."

"Outfitted?" Natalia gave Diego a questioning glance. Diego was sure it was supposed to be a stern look, but he could've melted into it regardless.

"You won't need to change, if that's your concern," said Diego. "Miriam is referring to our electronic accessories."

Natalia turned her glare toward Miriam, causing Miriam to sigh. "Have you not explained how this is going to work to her yet?"

"I went over the general plan," said Diego. "I figured we could go over the specifics now. Natalia, as I believe I've mentioned, the primary focus of tonight's gala is to gain access to the *Nasjonal-museet's* security. The head of security, a man by the name of Nils Olsen, will be there. Miriam has been performing surveillance on him while I've been working on gaining the curator's confidence. While we don't believe he can remotely access the museum's security system through his phone, we have reason to believe the secure login information on his phone will allow us to hack our way in."

"Us?" said Miriam. "Diego, you don't even know the difference between keystroke logging and clickjacking. Don't act like you're going to be involved in any hacking." Miriam pulled a slim black phone from the console beside her. "Here's what you need to know. Olsen uses an iPhone. You need to steal his and pair it with this one, like this." Miriam unlocked the phone and went into the settings, tapping through menus as she went. "We'll need his passwords. Just use the Airdrop feature and transfer everything. Easy, right? Except to do this you'll need to unlock his phone, and for that you'll need his thumbprint."

Natalia glared at Diego. "So I'm not just lifting his phone? I have to get him to unlock it first?"

"If you want," said Miriam. "But there's an easier way." She pulled something else from the console, a packet of translucent strips that looked like adhesive tape. "If you can snag a glass he held, press one of these against his thumbprint. Peel the print off and press it against the phone's home button. Should unlock right away."

"Wonderful," said Natalia as she accepted the phone and the strips. "I'll slip these into the tactical pockets that have been sewn into this dress. *Oh, wait...*"

Diego leaned over, gesturing for her to hand the items over. "I'll keep hold of anything you need me to, including your purse, if you'd like."

Natalia gave him the phone and the strips. "You know, it seems to me this is a job you could pull off yourself."

"Could?" Diego smiled. "Probably. I mean, I'll have the attention of the curator on me, and I imagine my fingers aren't as sticky as yours, seeing as you have a hundred times the experience I do, but I could probably manage. The issue, really, is that one doesn't attend an event such as this without a date, real or fake."

Natalia's voice adopted an icy chill. "And you didn't think to invite the curator as your plus one?"

"That's not the sort of relationship we have," said Diego. "It's more of a donor grifter mark sort of thing. Like anyone running a charity, she's after my money, nothing else. So... do you have any questions?"

Natalia eyed the phone in Diego's hand. "I'm assuming you'll need me to return the phone to Olsen's pocket, otherwise we wouldn't bother pairing it in the first place."

"He's not an idiot," said Miriam, "so if he notices his phone is missing, he's going to change all his passwords. You'll have to work quickly and not tip him off. I've also got earpieces, if anyone wants them. Any takers?"

Natalia shook her head, a look of quiet determination overtaking her. "I don't think that'll be necessary. This should be a walk in the park."

Chapter Nineteen

EDDIE PULLED THE LIMOUSINE UNDER A BROAD PORTICO supported by marble-lined Corinthian columns. Whereas The Scoundrel was an amalgamation of contemporary and new age, the Hotel Maximillian was the definition of old world swank. The building was constructed of thick granite blocks, worn smooth from age, and the roof of the hotel was shingled with tarnished bronze that shone a deep sea green in the fading light of the setting sun. The front double doors of the hotel were flanked by a pair of gentlemen dressed in red and black frock coats, looking as if they'd been transported through time from the middle of the nineteenth century, and an honest-to-goodness red carpet descended the stairs before stopping at the base of the road.

Natalia gave Diego a questioning look. *"This* is where you've been staying?"

"It was a strategic decision due to the gala," said Diego, "though I'll admit the hotel has a nice gymnasium in the basement. And the breakfast spread is top notch, but I'm getting sidetracked." He tucked Natalia's clutch into one of his interior jacket pockets. "One thing I forgot to mention is the curator of the museum, Malin Hanssen, knows me as Jorge Muñoz. I was thinking I could introduce you as Aurora Bello."

Natalia wasn't the most adept at deciphering the meanings of names, but this one was straightforward. *"Beautiful dawn?"*

"Why not?" Diego smiled a shy smile. "You have a certain... glow that reminds me of sunlight cresting over a horizon."

Natalia felt her cheeks flush, and she hoped Miriam hadn't noticed. "That's... kind of you. But it's a ridiculous pseudonym. It sounds like something a professional wrestler would use."

Diego balked. "What? No, it doesn't. Miriam, it's a lovely name, isn't it?"

Miriam cleared her throat. "Sorry to break it to you, boss, but Natalia's right. It's half Disney princess, half exotic dancer. She can't use that."

Diego leaned back in his seat, blinking in confusion. "Well, I liked it."

"I'll go by Charlotte King," said Natalia. "It's a very Australian name to match my accent, and I've used it before so it'll be easier to remember. Assuming you haven't already mentioned me by name to the curator?"

"No. She only knows me." Diego tucked the phone Miriam had given them into his left pants pocket along with the fingerprint strips, forcing the fabric tighter against his muscular legs. Natalia forced herself not to stare. "Are you ready?"

She nodded. Diego popped open the door and stepped out, pausing as he reached back for Natalia's hand. She gave it to him, letting him pull her to her feet. Once again Diego offered his arm, and Natalia snaked hers inside his. She shivered in the rapidly cooling evening air, but within a few strides they'd made it to the hotel, with the doormen in their antique attire smiling as they held the doors open.

Once inside, the lobby delivered everything the hotel exterior promised. There was white marble everywhere, excessive amounts of crystal, and everything that might normally be polished steel had instead been gilded. Diego led her down a broad hallway with high ceilings before taking a right at the first opportunity. From there, another short hallway funneled them into an expansive ballroom. People in tuxedos and evening gowns mingled in small groups while waiters carrying trays of hors d'oeuvres and champagne made their rounds. At the far side of the room, a ten piece band complete with trumpeter, trombonist, and saxophonist played a lively tune while at least a half-dozen couples danced on the glossy floor before them.

Natalia scanned the room, taking note of the displays set up in each of the room's four corners. There were two sculptures, one traditional and one modern, as well as a piece of framed art and an ornate dress that probably hailed from the 1700s. Now Natalia understood why the museum's head of security would be at the gala. "Thank goodness there's no table with name tags. Having mine be handwritten would make it clear I was some floozy you brought along for the ride."

Diego chuckled. "I think the people organizing this are more concerned with the aesthetics. Name tags aren't posh enough for an event like this." He shot a thumb toward a bartender's stand. "Care for a drink?"

Natalia suppressed a smile. "I don't suppose they'd be able to make me a Caipirinha?"

Diego flashed his white teeth. "I doubt it, but I'll ask. Should I get you a daiquiri if they have the gall not to carry cachaça?"

"That'll have to do."

Diego left to go stand in line, leaving Natalia on her own. She scanned the various groups who stood around the ballroom, trying to decipher which one contained the curator. Probably the one whose group was biggest, though she'd probably never stick in one group for more than five to ten minutes. A waiter came by with a tray of smoked-salmon canapés and pieces of bruschetta topped with a red pepper, pine nut, and Parmesan mousse. Natalia's grumbling stomach reminded her that she'd only had a snack several hours ago to tide her over, so she helped herself to three of each as she eyed another waiter who carried a tray of Chinese soup spoons full of ceviche.

Natalia had just popped the last of the bruschetta into her mouth when Diego returned. He extended a martini glass toward her while reserving a lowball glass of what appeared to be gin and tonic for himself. "Can you believe the bartender didn't even know what a Caipirinha was? And when I asked for a daiquiri, he thought I wanted one with frozen strawberries. Honestly, the staff at some of these events leaves something to be desired."

Natalia continued to munch, holding up a finger as she accepted her drink.

Diego's brow creased. "And... I'm only now realizing I didn't mention a full dinner wouldn't be served. My mistake."

Natalia swallowed. "That would've been good to know. Unless your plan was to keep my stomach empty so you could get me munted on a single glass of grog."

"My experience with women has taught me that keeping them starved is antithetical to my social agenda." Diego pointed at one of the nearby waiters. "He looks to have fritters of some sort. Do you want me to grab you—?"

"Yes," said Natalia before he could finish. "And some of the ceviche spoons. I saw a tall woman carrying them."

Diego nodded, perhaps realizing by the speed of her reply how serious the food situation had become. Natalia sipped her drink, which despite the bartender's confusion was delicious, and within a minute Diego had returned. He held a small plate stacked with two of the spoons and a trio of fritters.

Natalia reached for the plate, but Diego kept it. "I'll hold it. You'll need a free hand to eat, after all."

"Oh. Right. Thanks." Natalia popped one of the fritters into her mouth, then another. There was a creamy filling inside them that Natalia wasn't in love with, but she was still at the point where her stomach would prefer something over nothing. Still, manners were a thing that existed that she should probably remember.

She held the last fritter toward Diego. "Want one?"

"You take it. You still have a shark-like gleam in your eye."

Natalia polished off the last fritter, then moved to the ceviche. There was enough on the spoon that she had to take it in two bites, but both were delectable. The red onion was crisp, the fish properly acidic, and a spicy pepper had been finely chopped and mixed throughout.

Natalia washed the mouthful down with a healthy gulp of her daiquiri. "These spoonfuls are delectable. You should try one."

Diego shrugged. "It's fine. Go ahead."

Natalia's hunger was finally abating, otherwise she would've pounced on it. "Come on. You're a Spaniard. If you eat anything, this should be it."

Diego smiled. "I enjoy ceviche, but my hands are full. You eat it."

There were any number of solutions to the problem. Natalia, who'd now set her empty spoon on the plate, could've taken the dish and held it while Diego fed himself, but that's not what Natalia did. For some incomprehensible reason, she picked up the spoon and held it toward him.

"I'll help," she said. "Open up."

Diego's brow furrowed. His lips parted a little, as if he wanted to say something rather than eat, but after that moment of hesitation, they parted wider. Natalia slid the spoon inside his mouth and tipped it up. She drew it out slowly, allowing Diego's plump lips to slide along the surface of the spoon as he licked it clean.

The entire process played out slower than Natalia thought it should've, and it felt far more sensual than she'd intended. Diego watched her with those dark, gentle eyes of his as his lips pulled off the tip of the spoon. He kept them on her as he chewed, and Natalia couldn't force herself to look away. She couldn't look away from his perfectly straight nose. From his high cheeks and strong jaw, with the scruff recently trimmed to an even length. From his gaze, which seemed to notice nothing but her. He'd never seemed more kissable to

Natalia than at that very moment, despite the fact that his mouth was full of raw fish.

After what seemed like an eternity, Diego swallowed. He gave Natalia a shallow nod. "You're right. That was delicious."

Natalia suddenly felt quite warm, and not just in her cheeks. She placed the spoon on the plate and forced her gaze into the sea of party-goers. "So, ah... where's Nils Olsen?"

Diego took a sip of his drink as he placed the empty plate on a passing waiter's tray. "Far side of the room, to the left. Near the sculpture of... what would you call that? A Möbius strip? He's the barrel-chested one with the salt-and-pepper hair."

Natalia spotted him right away. He didn't look as intimidating as she'd pictured him in her head. He looked more like a portly grandfather than a hired gun. "Great. I'll—"

"Hold that thought," said Diego. "Malin is waving to me. Come. I'll introduce you."

Diego held out his arm again, and Natalia once again took it. The feel of his upper arm felt nice under her fingertips, the muscle of his biceps hard even under the satin fabric of his jacket. Natalia forced herself to take a steadying breath as she walked with him toward a group of six people, at the edge of which a middle-aged brunette in an elegant black dress was smiling at them—or at Diego, at least.

The woman spoke in a more polished accent than most, though there was still a hint of a musical quality to it. "So good of you to come, Jorge. I do hope you are enjoying yourself. Please, let me introduce you to a few people. This is Per Kristiansen and his wife Astrid, two patrons of the arts like yourself. Then we have Malik Ohakwu, one of the members of the Nigerian consulate, and Ingrid Bjørnstad, who works at the museum in the restoration department."

Everyone bobbed their heads or gave greetings.

"Good evening," said Diego. "I'm Jorge Muñoz. This is my good friend Charlotte King."

That drew more waves and greetings. Natalia nodded and smiled politely. "Good evening."

Malin smiled a wide smile, her eyes glimmering as she rested a hand against Diego's upper arm. "Now be honest, Jorge. What do you think of the pieces we brought? You were right to suggest we not bring the bust of Ole Jacob Broch, by the way. It would've been a bureaucratic nightmare, not to mention a logistical challenge."

Natalia felt her arm tighten upon Diego's at the sight of Malin pawing Diego's other side. It wasn't a conscious thought, simply a reaction. As soon as Natalia realized she'd done it, she relaxed her grip, but the reaction had been there all the same. Why? She couldn't possibly be jealous of Malin's touch, could she? Diego hadn't reacted to the curator the way he did to her. His eyes hadn't widened, he hadn't frozen in shock at her touch, and the smile he'd given her was perfectly professional, not the smirking grins he'd given Natalia when he teased or tested her. Diego clearly had no interest in the woman, just as he'd claimed, but even if he had, why should Natalia feel any jealousy? With the exception of this one-time gala, they weren't dating, not for real. Really, Natalia had only just met the man, and she had no interest in him besides. She was here for *The Scream*, not him. But even as she told herself that, she knew it wasn't true. That may have been her intention when she'd landed in Oslo two days ago, but it wasn't now.

She *was* interested. *Damn it, all!*

Diego and Malin had begun discussing the pieces on display, which Diego must've known about because he hadn't had a chance to investigate them upon arrival. Natalia glanced across the room toward Nils. Seeing that he was roughly three-quarters of the way through his drink, she forced herself to release Diego's arm. She had a job to do after all.

As Malin spoke, Natalia leaned close to his ear. Diego smelled incredible, with a faint hint of cologne barely masking his own clean, woodsy musk. Natalia tried not to let it distract her while she slid her hand into his left pocket, her fingers brushing against his thigh as she grabbed the fingerprint strips. "Be right back."

Diego gave her a shy smile and nodded as Natalia left the safety of the group. She drifted to the nearest corner, pretending to take notice of the painting there—a picture of a man at a window, painted by Lars Jorde—while watching Nils out of the corner of her eye. As a waiter passed by, Natalia snagged another spoonful of ceviche before continuing her trek. She would've stopped at the vintage dress if she hadn't noticed Nils finishing the last of his drink, so she picked up her pace. She'd crossed halfway across the dance floor when she saw Nils place his empty lowball glass on a waiter's tray. Natalia tipped the last of her cocktail into her mouth as she moved toward the same waiter, grabbing his attention with a flick of her index finger. He lowered the tray toward her, and with the practiced ease of a stage magician, Natalia set her cocktail glass down and swept Olsen's off as she pulled back her hand. The waiter never noticed a thing, distracted as he was by the smile Natalia froze him with.

Natalia turned away as she snuck a glance at the glass she'd stolen. She turned it toward the light, catching a hint of the smudges along the edge. One of them stood alone, near the base where a thumb would've rested. She pressed one of the fingerprint strips against it as she walked, palming the newly printed strip before depositing the glass upon another waiter's tray mid-stride.

With every motion, Natalia's confidence grew, and she found herself drifting back to the days in her youth when she'd lifted people's wallets in crowded outdoor markets. Her movements became more fluid, her gait as smooth and elegant as a dancer's. She smiled and nodded, captivating people with her eyes while keeping their attention off her hands. As she approached Nils from behind, she noticed a slim bulge from the man's front right pocket, as well as the watch upon his left wrist.

As he spoke to a colleague, she wrapped an arm around his back while resting another upon his left arm. "Beg your pardon, but do you have the time?"

Nils suffered a moment of surprise at the closeness of Natalia's body before he realized what he'd been asked. "Ah... yes, of course. It's —" He glanced at his watch. "Eight thirty-five."

Natalia had palmed his phone by the time he thought to respond. "Thank you so much."

Natalia turned away, making sure to hide his phone with her body should the man be watching her walk away, which in this dress with her back bared almost to her ass was a sure thing. She waltzed across the ballroom, a lightness in her step that almost made her want to step onto the dance floor. She moved around other groups of minglers like a fish gliding through water before once again sidling up to Diego. Maybe it was the warmth of the rum working its way through her, or perhaps it was the high of the effortless ease with which she'd lifted Nils's phone, but she pressed herself close against him from behind, letting herself enjoy his scent as she once again drew close to his ear.

Natalia's stomach brushed against Diego's backside, and she pressed her fingers against his hips, where they met a solid core lacking even an ounce of flab. "Care for another drink?"

Diego straightened at the sensation of Natalia's touch. He turned his head to meet her gaze. "That would be wonderful. Thank you."

"Gin and tonic?"

"Gin fizz, actually, though you might have to coach the bartender if he's forgotten how to make it."

"I'll do my best." Natalia slipped her hand back into Diego's pocket. This time she didn't use a light touch. She let her hand slide along his thigh before palming Miriam's phone.

Diego turned, watching her as she stepped away. Natalia shot him a jaunty smile before turning her back to him and heading toward the bartender's stand. She pressed the fingerprint strip against Olsen's phone, activating it without any issue. With a few quick presses on his phone as well as an equal number on Miriam's, she initiated the transfer. She held the phones together, face to face, as she approached the bartender. "One gin fizz and one daiquiri, please."

The bartender seemed to know what he was doing. The phones in Natalia's hand pinged as the man finished shaking the beverages. She clasped the two phones between fingertips and palm while pinching the stem of her cocktail glass between thumb and forefinger, leaving her free hand to grab Diego's lowball glass.

Natalia returned with the two beverages. Diego had his back to her, once again chatting with Malin, but perhaps he felt her presence, like a magnetic attraction. He turned as she arrived.

Natalia held out his gin fizz. "Your cocktail."

Diego accepted it and took a sip. "Delicious. Did you bribe the bartender?"

Natalia slipped the phones into her free hand. "Turns out when you're beautiful, men make an effort to do things the right way."

Diego kept his eyes firmly on her. "I believe that."

Natalia leaned in for the third time, finding she was growing to like being so close to him. She slipped Miriam's phone into his pocket, again trailing her hand across his firm thigh as she whispered to him. "Once more unto the breach. Wish me luck."

Diego blinked slowly, his mouth hanging open. "Good luck."

Natalia smiled and swept across the open floor, her feet feeling light and airy, as if she were walking on clouds rather than polished wood. She took a few sips of her daiquiri and eyed the centuries old dress again before setting off across the dance floor in the direction of Nils. The older gentleman still stood in front of the Möbius-like sculpture, talking to another gentleman with short brown hair. Neither of them noticed Natalia as she passed behind them and slipped Nils's phone into his pocket, light as a feather.

Natalia could've wandered off, but something made her stay. She settled herself in front of the sculpture, taking sips of her drink as she tried to find meaning in the smooth lines and gentle curves.

After a minute or two, she noticed the conversation beside her had ceased. She looked up to find Olsen's eyes had drifted her way. He wasn't staring at her in a lecherous fashion, simply eyeing her with curiosity.

"It's a Rygh," he said. "One of her Möbius series, which were her most famous works. Do you like it?"

Natalia answered honestly. "There's a certain simplicity and fluidity I enjoy, but I don't really appreciate modern sculpture. I would take a good Hellenistic depiction of the human form over this any day."

Nils chuckled. "Whether or not I agree with you, Hellenistic statues are hard to come by, especially in Norway. They also happen to weigh a ton. Not the sort of thing you want to lug to a hotel for a party."

"I suppose not."

Nils blinked. "I probably should've introduced myself when you asked for the time. I'm Nils Olsen. I work with the museum."

"I think *I* should've been the one to introduce myself seeing as I bumped into you." Natalia extended her hand. "Charlotte King. It's a pleasure."

Olsen shook her hand. "You're here alone?"

The way he said it didn't make it seem as if the man was hitting on her. He seemed quite cordial, actually. More like a grandfather than a security mastermind. "No. I'm Jorge Muñoz's plus one." She pointed toward Diego's group.

Nils followed her finger. "Ah, yes. I've seen him before with Mrs. Hanssen. He's making a sizable donation to the museum, isn't he? Very generous of him."

If he actually makes it, thought Natalia, but she nodded in response.

Olsen looked at Diego before turning his attention to Natalia. "If you don't mind my asking, Miss King, if you're not a particular fan of modernist sculpture, then what are you doing over here?"

Natalia suffered a sudden fear that Nils suspected her true motives, but she was disciplined enough not to show anything. "Pardon me?"

"Well, if I had someone as handsome as Mr. Muñoz looking at me the way he's looking at you, I surely wouldn't be over here talking to an old man like myself."

"What? No. I don't think he's looking at me. He's busy having a conversation with Mrs. Hanssen."

"Are you sure of that?" said Nils. "Because it seems to me as if he's not entirely aware that Malin exists at the moment."

Natalia looked toward him, and sure enough, though Malin continued to chat Diego's ear off, he stood there, looking across the ballroom straight at her, as if she was the only woman in the entire room, maybe the only person in the whole world.

And Natalia didn't mind his attention one bit.

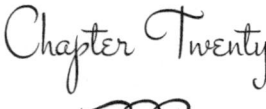

Chapter Twenty

NATALIA FINISHED HER SECOND DAIQUIRI AND PLACED THE empty glass upon a waiter's tray as she approached Diego's group. Diego watched her, excusing himself to Malin out of the corner of his mouth as he moved to intercept her. He deposited his own glass upon an empty tray before meeting her a few feet from the edge of the dance floor.

"You were finally able to get away," said Natalia. "I feared we might have to set up your gravestone right here in the middle of the ballroom."

Diego smiled. "Malin is loquacious, that's for sure. I'm assuming everything went to plan? Miriam already texted to say she's received the data."

"Nils didn't even know I was there," said Natalia. "Well, at least not while I lifted and returned his phone. He noticed me eventually."

"Yes. I saw you two speaking. What about?"

"Sculpture," said Natalia. "And you."

Diego lifted an eyebrow. "Me? I didn't think he knew me."

"He doesn't," said Natalia. "He just noticed that... well, never mind."

Diego stepped closer, his broad shoulders blocking her view of anything but him. He wore a gentle expression of concern. "Is everything okay?"

"Fine." But even as she said it, she wasn't sure Diego would believe her. Her breath caught in her throat, and she wanted nothing more than to lean into him, to breathe that subtle, woodsy oder that clung to him. To cling to his arm and feel his muscles through his jacket. To drown in his dark eyes and ignore everything else she'd come here to do. "Do you, ah... I mean... would you like to dance? Assuming you know how, of course."

This time, both of Diego's eyebrows rose. "I... I'd love to. I didn't know if you'd be able to in those heels."

"It's been a while since I've worn any," said Natalia. "But the balance of wearing them returned to me quickly. I've always been agile, after all."

"You've certainly shown it." Diego extended a hand.

Natalia took it, and together they stepped onto the dance floor. Natalia didn't know what song the band was playing, something with a slow to medium beat, but she didn't really care. All that mattered was that Diego was the one dancing with her.

Diego took her hand in his, wrapping his right arm around the small of her back. His fingers pressed against her bare skin, his pinky trailing against the edge of her dress. He pulled her close, placing his right leg between hers as she draped her arm over his broad shoulders. She felt the strength in them immediately, not bulging muscle like one might find in a bodybuilder but a lean strength that spoke as much to his exercise routine as to his confident dancer's stance. Diego's grasp kept her close, her breasts pressing against his jacket, her thighs straddling his, his hip on her midsection. Natalia's heart fluttered, and she hoped Diego couldn't feel that, too.

"Can you follow a simple triple step?" asked Diego.

Natalia swallowed to get a little saliva in her mouth. "If you can lead it, I can follow."

Diego smiled, a small, demure sort of thing. "Confidence. I like it. I didn't expect anything less from you."

Diego stepped out, drawing Natalia along with him. His lead arm was solid as a rock, the one at her back firm and decisive without gripping too hard. He didn't push her where she needed to go, nor drag her, but rather gave her clues with his body as to where to go. Within a half-dozen steps she found herself gliding across the polished wood alongside him as smoothly as if they were connected. They rotated counterclockwise slowly, backward and to the side and then forward before repeating the pattern. Natalia felt herself falling into him, sinking into his embrace. She wanted nothing more than to nuzzle into Diego's neck and breath deep as he hugged her, but before she knew what was happening, Diego's arm rose and the hand at her back propelled her forward.

Without thinking, she spun perfectly only for Diego to catch her as she completed the rotation, sliding right into the pocket at his hip where she'd been. Diego smiled, and so did Natalia, but now Diego's arm was gliding across her body, his hand pushing her in the opposite direction. Natalia spun the other way, and though she felt mildly disoriented, once again Diego was there to catch her, pulling her against him with a firm, gentle arm.

"You weren't lying," said Diego. "You're an excellent follower."

A warmth spread through Natalia. Some of it might've been from the activity, but they'd only been dancing for a couple minutes. No, this was a different sort of warmth. A warmth of desire that spread from her chest into her cheeks and between her legs. "And you're quite the lead."

"Well, I'm used to a leadership role," said Diego. "Your skill is more surprising."

"Why's that?"

"Because being able to dance is more or less required of a high-end grifter. The same isn't true of a thief."

Diego twirled Natalia again. The room spun around her but she floated right back into Diego's waiting arms. He caught her at just the right moment in just the right spot. "Where did you learn?"

A twinkle shone in Diego's eyes. "Funny you should ask. It was my final year of secondary school, a few months after the signet ring heist I told you about, and my school's end of year formal was approaching. It was normally a big deal, but this year was shaping up to be bigger than most because—"

"No," said Natalia.

Diego blinked at her. *"No?"*

Natalia pulled herself closer, though there wasn't much room to spare between them. "Not this time. Tell me the truth. Just this once."

Diego's brow furrowed. His lips parted, then closed, all as he kept Natalia pressed against him, the two of them rotating around the dance floor. He licked his lips, and he turned his gaze downward. "The problem is the truth isn't very exciting. It doesn't make for a good story."

Natalia pulled her arm from Diego's shoulder, trailing her fingers underneath his bristly chin. She tipped his head up, forcing his eyes back upon her. "I don't care. I want you to be honest with me for once, even if it is to tell me something meaningless."

Diego's brow creased. His grip upon her low back tensed, and his eyes grew soulful. He took a deep, shuddering breath, letting it out in a heavy sigh. In that moment, Natalia knew there was something he wanted to tell her, something that was the exact opposite of meaningless, something his heart ached to tell but his mind and body refused to allow. The very thought of speaking from the heart put his body into a panicked state and made his face go through contortions.

At the moment of greatest stress, Natalia thought he might let her go, that he might turn and leave the floor entirely, but Diego surprised her by doing the opposite. He pulled her deeper into his body, resting his head against the side of her own. She could feel his warm breath on the side of her neck, and his comforting musk filled her nostrils.

Diego spoke softly, as if from a place far away. "Her name was Ximena Márquez, but I called her Doña Márquez out of respect. I took lessons from her. She was about fifty-five and I just twenty-one, which made the lessons awkward at first, but she was a consummate professional. By the end of the first lesson, she'd fully established the relationship between teacher and pupil, and she was demanding and stern, which made it easier for me to focus on my footwork. She taught me the waltz, both conventional and Viennese. She also taught me the tango and tried to teach me the foxtrot, which I was so atrocious at that she gave up after three short lessons. An attempt was also made at teaching me the rumba, though practicing such an intimate dance with Doña Márquez was too much for me, even accounting for her professionalism."

Something about the way Diego told the story, without any embellishment, without any elements of the strange or unbelievable, and with no immediate threat to his body or reputation, made Natalia certain he'd told her the truth. The absolute truth, and it hadn't been easy for him.

"Thank you," she whispered into his ear.

Those two words, simple as they were, seemed to give Diego strength. His body, which had sagged into her as he'd told the truth, now regained its upright posture. His arm grew firm against her back, his lead arm becoming as solid as an oaken branch. He looked at her, not with the glimmer she'd seen so many times, the glimmer that signaled he was crafting some clever tale, but with an honesty and hopefulness and desire she'd never before seen.

"What about you?" he asked softly. "Where did you learn?"

Natalia surprised herself. She didn't deflect. She didn't bargain. She didn't lie. She just told him. "When I was seventeen, I was staying at a foster home a couple blocks away from a dance studio. There was a cute boy who worked there. He was a little older than me, maybe twenty or twenty-one. To me he seemed very suave and sophisticated, so I'd hang around outside the studio hoping he'd notice me, which wasn't very hard because most of the clients were middle-aged women."

The corner of Diego's lips rose in a smile. "This dance studio. It wasn't located on some sort of mountain resort, was it?"

"*Resort?*"

"You know. Like in *Dirty Dancing.*"

Natalia batted Diego playfully across the shoulders as she held onto him. "You and your movies. No. It was in suburban Melbourne. Anyway, it didn't take long for the young man to ask me if I was looking to dance, at which point I had to inform him I didn't know how. And of course, he couldn't let an injustice like that stand, so he taught me. Mostly latin dance. Samba and what he called salsa. A little bit of swing, too."

"Did he teach you any lifts?"

Natalia felt her cheeks dimple with an oncoming smile. "Like in *Dirty Dancing?* No. My feet stayed on the ground."

"What about dips?" asked Diego.

"Yes, he taught me how to—"

Without warning, Diego lifted his arm and gave Natalia a push from behind, spinning her. As she completed the turn, Diego's steady hand stopped her and gave her a sharp tug. She spun again in the opposite direction, gliding back into Diego's waiting arms, but unlike her previous spins, his arms didn't stop her. They merely slowed her, cradling her as the ceiling tilted into view and she fell toward the floor. But it wasn't really a fall. It was a controlled descent, and Diego's arms were iron pillows, simultaneously strong and soft.

Diego hovered over her, his face close, a shy smile on his lips. "Something like that?"

Natalia's heart beat hard in her chest, but not from adrenaline. Her arms lay across Diego's shoulders, the limbs firm but not locked into place by fear, her fingers relaxed rather than digging into the muscle of his back. They didn't have to. Diego was supporting her completely, but that didn't explain her reaction. She hadn't clung to him because she'd known deep down inside that Diego would never let anything happen to her. He'd never drop her. He'd never fail her.

So she'd trusted him. Implicitly, without thinking, without making any effort to protect herself. And he hadn't disappointed her.

Diego's face was still close to hers, his eyes kind, his smile gentle. "Well?"

Natalia took a breath to try and steady her beating heart, but it did little to slow it, nor did it slow the warmth that continued to spread throughout her body. "Something like that, but at the same time, nothing like that at all."

Diego drew her back upright. In the background, Natalia vaguely noticed the song the band was playing was ending.

Despite having stopped dancing, Diego hadn't taken his hands off the small of her back, nor had his eyes wavered. "I understand what you mean. I don't think I've ever had a dance quite like that."

Somehow, Natalia knew he was telling the truth again. "Um... we've done what we needed to do here, correct?"

Diego's shoulder's sagged. "Oh. Yes. Miriam has the data. Eddie left, but if you'd like to return to your hotel I can either call him back or I can drive you myself."

Natalia hadn't taken her arms off Diego, either. "That's not what I had in mind. You have a room here, right?"

Diego blinked. *Slowly.* "I... I do. Come on. Let's get out of here."

Chapter Twenty-One

THE HOTEL ROOM DOOR HADN'T EVEN FINISHED CLOSING behind them before she pounced on him. Natalia charged into Diego with the force of a bull, pushing his jacket over his shoulders as she pressed him into the nearest wall. Her mouth found his. His lips pressed against hers, soft and plump while the bristles on his upper lip and chin tickled her lips and cheeks. Normally, she didn't care for the sensation of a beard against her skin, but Diego's scruff against her only made her more ravenous. Her mouth opened, her tongue flicking against the inside of his lips, probing, tasting, relishing in the heat of his breath and the flavor of his mouth, all while his own tongue pushed against hers, but kisses weren't enough. She drew her teeth along his bottom lip, nibbling and pulling at him as her moans of pleasure mixed with his. Diego's hands pressed tight against her lower back and moved lower still, pushing her into him so that not a single gap remained between them. She felt a growing pressure push against her from between his legs as her hands roamed over his body, caressing his muscular chest and the hard abdominals underneath it. Her fingers raked across the short hair at the nape of his neck before entwining with the longer hair at the crown of his head, all while she took futile swipes at his jacket, which stubbornly refused to come off.

Diego tried to speak as she drank deep from his lips. "If I can... If I just... Spin, maybe..."

Natalia was too far gone in her desire to understand his intent, but she was aware of the movement of his body, sensing the useless shrugs of his shoulders. Realizing she still pinned him to the wall, she relented, letting him free himself. As soon as her pressure abated, he pushed himself off the wall, keeping her pressed against him with his right arm as he spun. He shook his arm once, twice, three times as the sleeve finally flapped free of him. Diego switched the arm that held her as he shook his other arm, flinging his jacket to the ground as he now pushed her into the wall, attacking her lips and mouth with the same ferocity she had his. His strong hands roamed across her back, along her sides, her hips, then gripping her waist. The pressure between his legs strengthened as his slipped his right hand along the bare skin of her thigh into the slit of her dress, then back, his fingers slipping underneath her underwear as he cupped her ass and squeezed. Natalia moaned in pleasure as she continued to devour his kisses. Diego's other hand moved over her stomach, up her ribs, then over the folds of her cowl neck dress to the swell of her breast. His fingers squeezed gently, probing for Natalia's peak. Another moan of pleasure escaped her lips as he found it, his fingertips squeezing and caressing Natalia's now fully erect nipple.

Diego tried to speak between their kisses. "Are you sure... I mean, do you want—"

A voice in the back of Natalia's mind reminded her why she was here, why she'd taken the job, why she'd agreed to go to dinner with Diego in the first place, why she'd played along on this fake date, but she swatted the voice away as easily as she might a gnat. "Yes. Yes, I'm sure."

Diego's right hand moved forward, over her hip while remaining underneath her underwear. He played with the thin strap that kept the undergarment in place, pulling it away from her before letting it snap into place. Then his fingers slid back underneath it, along the front this time, pulling the fabric away from her body and tucking it to the side, leaving her exposed to his touch. His fingertips found her slit. Diego's eyes widened as his fingers slid across the intense wetness he encountered and the sheer heat radiating from between her thighs.

"Whoa."

"Yeah," said Natalia, although *Whoa* was probably a more apt response. She was no stranger to men's bodies or their touch, nor did she have any issues becoming aroused when the time was right, but what was occurring between her legs was borderline ridiculous. She couldn't remember becoming so turned on so fast, and now that her underwear was tucked tightly against her thigh she could tell just how soaked the fabric had become.

Diego continued to kiss her as the tip of his middle finger dipped inside her. Natalia shuddered and moaned at his touch, then again as the finger slid further inside her to the knuckle. He drew it out slowly, stroking it between her legs and then back inside, using it to spread the natural lubrication that was pouring out of her over every centimeter of her folds. His fingertip slid north, into her uppermost tip, sliding across her swollen clitoris.

Natalia's legs wobbled as a ripple of desire washed through her. Her grip tightened upon Diego's shoulder and his biceps, and she felt herself slide an inch down the wall. Diego noticed, removing his hand from her breast and sliding it under the small of her back, giving her support while his middle finger delved back inside her. Natalia's pulse raced, her breath coming in ragged gasps as Diego increased his cadence. He thrust his finger inside her several times only to draw it back out and work more moisture into her lips, then he'd dip it back inside and work it in and out, sometimes three strokes, sometimes four or five. Natalia's fingers turned into claws, digging into the folds of his shirt. Again her legs wobbled underneath her. Natalia pulled her mouth away from Diego's simply to get a breath of air, and Diego took the opportunity to move his mouth lower, planting kisses down the length of her neck before licking at the soft flesh above her clavicle. Diego's finger moved faster and faster, and then suddenly there was his thumb, rubbing and stroking at her clitoris while his finger drove deep inside her. In what seemed like only a second, Natalia's body exploded in a wave of pure ecstasy. Her muscles shuddered as sheer bliss spread through her at the speed of sound. Her fingertips tingled, the hairs on her arms stood on end, and her legs stopped functioning. She would've crumpled and fallen to the floor if Diego's strong grip hadn't been there behind her back, holding her up, keeping her safe, just as he had on the dance floor.

Somewhere from deep inside her the voice spoke to Natalia again, telling her to stop, to be wary, but she barely heard it anymore. The voice spoke to her as if from across an ocean. It didn't matter now. All that mattered was the joyous ripple echoing through her. A euphoric cloud settled over her, making her brain feel as if it were vibrating inside her skull and causing it to work a little slower than it should've.

Natalia took another gasping breath as Diego drew his finger out of her and pulled his hand to her waist. He stood there, staring deep into her eyes as she caught her breath, his tongue raking his lips. Though her brain was still foggy and her legs still trembled, Natalia knew what she wanted, and she refused to wait. She pushed off the wall, forcing Diego into the middle of the room. As he stumbled backward, she tugged at his shirt, pulling it free from his trousers as she started to undo the buttons from the bottom up, quick as she could. Diego helped her, undoing them from the top until their hands met in the middle. Diego threw the shirt open, his arms whipping as he cast it aside into a corner.

As Natalia caught sight of his bare chest, she wondered how she'd ever entertained the thought that Diego might be pudgy. His broad shoulders, thick with muscle, made him seem twice as broad as her. She ran her hands across his chest, through the short black hairs that curled upon his pectorals before letting them drift onto his abdominals, which, while covered with a thin layer of fat, were developed nonetheless. Natalia leaned forward, kissing Diego's neck, breathing deep of his scent and nibbling none too lightly at his shoulder while her hands dropped to his belt. She tugged at it, trying to loosen it, but with her brain still clouded and the thing backwards (at least from her point of view) she only proceeded to make it tighter.

Diego, noticing her lack of progress, helped. Within a moment, the belt whipped free of its loops and sailed across the room, smacking into the far wall with a thud. Diego unbuttoned and unzipped his pants, pushing them down along with his underwear, causing his manhood to spring free, slapping Natalia in her midsection as it came to attention.

Natalia moaned again as she felt it pressing against her, throbbing and warm. Goodness, Diego was *big*. Bigger than he had any right to be. Natalia reached down and took him in her hand, stroking his shaft while she tried to push his trousers the rest of the way down his well-muscled thighs with her free hand. A deep, guttural sound rose from Diego's chest, and he helped her push, but with both of them standing and Diego gripped firmly in Natalia's hand, he couldn't quite reach. With a grunt of pent up desire, he pulled himself out of her grasp. For a fraction of a second, Natalia thought she'd done something wrong, but from the speed at which he moved it was clear he'd only freed himself so he could shed the rest of his clothing. His shoes went flying, as did his socks, and a quick shake of his leg left his pants and underwear on the floor. It was only when he'd finished that Natalia realized she should've spent the time undoing her dress instead of staring at Diego's lean, well-muscled body, but Diego didn't seem to mind her inaction. As soon as he finished he closed on her, his thick erection pressing against her as he tugged her dress down over her breasts to her waist.

It was at that point that he hit a snag. Diego tugged harder, but the dress wouldn't budge, refusing to slide over her hips. Natalia thought she heard a stitch rip, and the noise helped a thought worm through her fogged brain. "Wait. There's a zipper."

Natalia reached down, trying to find it as Diego's hands caressed her midsection. He leaned down, pulling her breast into his mouth and sucking lightly at the nipple. Natalia shuddered again, the space between her legs feeling unbelievably slippery as she tried to find the damned zipper. Natalia fumbled behind her, her eyes rolling back in her head as Diego's teeth raked against her nipple and his whiskers tickled the soft flesh of her breast. Only by luck did her hand come across the end of the fastener. With a desperate tug, she yanked on it, hoping it wouldn't snag, but it didn't. The dress came free and fell, bunching around her ankles along with her panties.

As soon as the dress fell, Diego wrapped his arms around her, one under her bum and the other around her back, and lifted. She popped into the air light as a feather, and with no other choice available to her, she wrapped her legs around Diego. It was only then that she realized she was still wearing her damned heels, but it was hard to give that more than a passing thought as her bare skin pressed against Diego's body, his firm erection pressing against her butt as he spun her through the air. Diego took two steps toward his bed and dropped her. For once he didn't catch her, but the bed did. Natalia bounced as she hit the mattress. She pushed herself up on her elbows and started to crawl backward, but Diego didn't let her. He wrapped his arms around her thighs, picking her up and pulling her toward him, positioning her bottom at the corner of the mattress. He ripped her heels off and tossed them aside, and then, just as Natalia thought he might plunge inside her, he hesitated, his sex pointing toward the ceiling, stiff as a rod.

"Wait," he said. "Should I get a condom?"

Natalia's heart raced, and there seemed to be precious little breath in her lungs, but Diego had asked her a question that demanded a response. She shook her head, forcing the right words out in the correct order. "No. It's fine."

That was all the encouragement Diego needed. He took one hand off her legs and used his fingers to spread her open. Then he leaned forward, easing himself inside her. Natalia gasped as she felt herself stretch around him, as she felt him slide into her and felt the strong, regular thrum of his heartbeat coursing into her legs. A sound that she wasn't aware she could make escaped her lips, and she melted into the mattress.

Diego paused. "Is everything okay?"

Natalia licked her lips. "Better than okay. *Phenomenal.*"

Perhaps Natalia shouldn't have said anything, because as he leaned forward, she realized he'd only entered her halfway. She felt herself stretch even further, sensing an incredible sensation of fullness and pressure radiating from between her legs and infusing every last scrap of her body from her head to her toes. Despite Diego's size, his presence inside her wasn't uncomfortable. Just the opposite. He seemed to fit perfectly, filling her completely. As he pulled out and drove back in, her intense wetness coated the full length of his shaft, letting him glide effortlessly in and out.

Diego started slow, running his hands across Natalia's thighs, her stomach, cupping her breasts and squeezing them, a little harder than he had before. With each of his thrusts, he pushed Natalia deeper into the mattress, and seemingly, he pushed deeper into her. Ecstasy and desire built inside her, like a clock being wound tighter and tighter with each push of Diego's hips. Along with the desire grew an intense heat. It was in her cheeks, in the breath in her lungs, not to mention between her legs. Sounds escaped her, sounds she had no control over, and her fingers dug into the sheets at her sides, grasping for any sort of purchase, any way to keep her grounded.

As Diego saw the pleasure on Natalia's face, he increased his tempo. His thrusts became stronger. Harder. Deeper, even though Natalia didn't think it possible. He drove his pelvis into her, his pubic bone striking her already stimulated clitoris, his short, groomed hairs stimulating her even further.

"Yes," Natalia cried. The sensation was so powerful. All-consuming. She couldn't remember the last time she'd wanted anything this much. "Yes. *Harder.*"

She didn't really think Diego could oblige her. She didn't think any cohesive thoughts at all except that she wanted *more*, but in response Diego moved his hands to her hips. He grabbed her around the waist and drove her into him with the full strength of his upper body.

With the sound of his pelvis slapping against her filling her ears, Natalia cried out. Her body stiffened, then shattered. There was no other way to put it. Every ounce of euphoria and desire that had built inside her from Diego's thrusts exploded outward, wracking her with as much power as an earthquake. Her body convulsed. Every muscle inside her clenched tight, especially those between her legs. Pure bliss washed through her, over and back, then over and back again, like tides breaking across a shore. Though some part of her suspected the moment must've only lasted a few seconds, other parts of her weren't so sure. Every nerve ending between her legs tingled, her stomach felt as if she'd done a hundred crunches, and her arms weren't moving, even though she was sure they should be able to.

The mattress moved underneath her. She felt Diego crawl beside her. Felt him helping her further onto the bed, though she wasn't sure how much she helped. Her arms and legs still weren't working, after all. A pillow appeared beneath her head, and she saw the headboard not far behind it. She blinked, and Diego's face was there, close to hers, a concerned look in his deep, dark eyes. "Are you alright?"

Natalia took a deep, shuddering breath. "I think you broke me."

Diego smiled. "I guess I'll have to put you back together, then."

Diego crawled on top of her, and for a moment, Natalia wasn't sure what was going on. She swiped at the euphoria-induced fog that cradled her, forcing herself to retrieve the memories of what had just happened. As difficult as it was, she *could* remember. While she'd screamed and convulsed and shattered into a million pieces, she hadn't felt that familiar throbbing pulse between her legs. Diego hadn't grunted and slumped into her, and when she looked down, her suspicions were confirmed. He hadn't climaxed. His erection stood as firm and proud as ever, glistening from her own wetness.

Natalia told her arms to move, and this time they obeyed her. She wove a hand into the hair at the back of Diego's head, playing with the short follicles. "Be gentle this time, please."

Diego nodded. "Anything for you."

Diego pushed her legs apart, and again he entered her. This time,

Natalia's body was prepared, though he still filled her just as fully. Whereas the first time Diego had stood at the edge of the bed, his body out of reach, now he was completely against her. His stomach pressed against hers, his powerful chest brushing her nipples. His mouth was once again within reach, and he leaned in and kissed her. Where once his mouth had been hungry (and Natalia's own, as well), now it was gentle. Patient. He kissed and pulled back, then kissed again, sucking lightly at her lips. As he kissed her, he moved in and out of her slowly. Rhythmically. The overloaded nerve endings between Natalia's legs settled down, reverting from a state of explosive shock to a blissful, even euphoria. Diego's abdominals contracted and relaxed with each of his motions, and Natalia ran her hand along them, relishing in the strength of his core. Her arm she wrapped around his back, feeling the muscles along his spine and across his broad shoulders.

As Diego's kisses moved to her neck, again Natalia's breath ran short, but it wasn't like before. It wasn't ragged or desperate but a sustainable, steady sort of thing, as if she were in the seventh kilometer of a 10K that she was confident she could finish. Diego's mouth moved lower, back to her breasts, but there too he was gentle. He sucked and licked, making Natalia's nipples grow even harder, but he never bit, at most raking his teeth gently against her.

Little by little, Natalia's body and mind came together, the pieces that had been shattered and thrown around the room coalescing. Desire and joy built within her, but rather than a spring being wound too tight, it was like a fire that continued to grow as more and more fuel was added. Diego caressed her breasts, caressed her thighs, caressed her bottom and squeezed it, causing Natalia to gasp a little each time.

As all traces of tension left her body, she could sense Diego growing more confident. He kissed her, not just on the lips but over every portion of her body he could reach. Natalia found herself moaning more frequently, whispering words of encouragement into his ear even though he had no need of them. He seemed to enjoy them, however, as he grew even firmer and stronger inside of her. As the flame Diego built turned into a bonfire, Natalia felt her breast start to rise and fall. She'd reached the ninth kilometer of the race, and the end was in sight, but just as she felt herself peaking, Diego pushed himself up on his arms and pulled out of her.

Natalia looked at him with confusion in her eyes, but all that was in Diego's was a twinkle. With his erection still ramrod straight, he probed her sheath, pushing in an inch before pulling back out. He did it again, and again, before plunging inside her and pulling back out again. Though Natalia couldn't see him well from her vantage, she could feel the tip of his erection hovering, feel the gravity and mass of it. The desire inside Natalia grew to white hot levels.

She grasped at his hips, trying to pull him inside her. Diego smiled, teasing her again and again with only a quarter of his length. Natalia's legs started to tremble, and still Diego refused to enter her fully.

Natalia locked eyes with Diego, her breath coming hot and heavy. She pleaded with him, her voice husky from unmet desire. "Please. Give it to me. *Now.*"

In response, Diego pressed his chest onto hers and drove deep inside her, pushing every last inch of himself into her. Natalia gasped, clutching at his back. Her legs wrapped around him, squeezing with every ounce of strength she had. Natalia didn't think the two of them could get any closer, but Diego wrapped his arm around the small of her back and *pulled*. Somehow he pushed himself even deeper inside of her, and the fire that had been building consumed her. She rocked against him, crying out in ecstasy, rubbing her pelvis against him. Diego's muscles tightened, holding Natalia tight against him as he too cried out. This time he did climax. Natalia felt his powerful rhythmic pulses inside her, pushing against her inner walls, driving her to new heights of pleasure. She screamed again, and though her muscles were failing, she tried to hold Diego in place.

She needn't have tried so hard. Diego lay atop her, his face in the crook of her neck, his bristles tickling her and his breath hot on her shoulder. He kept his weight on his forearms, but his body nonetheless pressed heavily upon her.

Natalia closed her eyes and focused on her breathing. Her entire body was numb and yet not at the same time. She felt tingly and breathless and bone tired. She felt as if her body had been drained of every ounce of energy, but her heart had simultaneously been filled with something far more worthwhile.

Diego groaned and pushed himself off her. Natalia gasped as he pulled out, her nerve endings so thoroughly frazzled that even the slightest touch between her legs made her shiver.

Diego lay on his side next to her, his arm tucked underneath his head. "That was amazing, Natalia. I don't think I've ever felt—"

It was a monumental effort even for Natalia to open her eyes. It was more of one for her to lift a finger to Diego's lips, and even more for her to speak. "Shh... Let's just enjoy this."

Diego's brow furrowed as Natalia turned on her side, tucking her naked body into his crook. His hand moved over her hips. With the last of her strength, Natalia took his arm and lay it across her stomach, relishing in the feeling of his body cradling hers. She nestled further into him, enjoying his strength and the comfort he provided. Her eyes fluttered, she took a deep breath, and she thought about just how well she fit against him as she drifted into sleep.

Chapter Twenty-Two

NATALIA DREAMT SHE LAY IN A LUSH MEADOW. HER BODY was bare, but her nudity didn't bother her. The grass was soft and spongy beneath her, the sun warmed her skin, and though there was a faint buzzing in the air, there didn't seem to be any insects nearby. A breeze whistled past, causing the bright white daisies and yellow ragworts to sway in the grass around her and shaking the trees at the edge of the meadow, their boughs thick with dark green leaves. Though Natalia knew the breeze should cool her, it couldn't. The sun above was too bright, its rays too strong. They beamed down on her, infusing her with a warmth that soaked through her skin and muscle into her bones. It filled her heart, suffusing her with a luscious heat that lingered in every part of her, but the sunlight provided more than warmth. It shielded her. Protected her, keeping the bugs away, keeping predators away, and keeping anyone from wandering through the meadow and laying eyes on her nude form. Natalia didn't know *how* she knew, but she was utterly certain of that fact. The sun shone for *her*, and if anyone else took pleasure or derived value from it, that was a mere stroke of serendipity. The sun was hers. It would never stop shining, and it would never leave her.

Natalia closed her eyes, relishing in the sunlight, at the heat and comfort it provided. She could've lounged there for a day. A month. A year. The sun provided everything she needed, and it always...

A chill swept over Natalia. Her eyes snapped open, and in the sky above her was a cloud. Just one, but it was thick and grey and malicious, and it hovered between her and her precious sun. But it was alone, and as soon as the breeze picked up, it would sweep the thing away and bring her sun back to her. In fact, the breeze was strengthening at that moment, causing the leaves on the trees to rustle violently. Natalia lifted her head, checking in its direction.

That's when she saw the storm. It choked the sky, covering the horizon with boiling, black clouds. It rushed toward her like an oncoming train, distant thunder pealing and the scent of rain thick in her nostrils.

And suddenly Natalia was aware of how utterly, completely vulnerable she was.

Natalia gasped and her eyes fluttered open. Gone was the meadow, and in its place, Diego's room had returned. A light somewhere still shone, casting a mellow glow across the room. A few distant lights glimmered through the room's partially-draped window, and the clock on the nightstand read 12:30.

Though the sunlight from Natalia's dream had vanished, the warmth hadn't. Diego still pressed against her from behind, keeping her backside toasty. His arm lay over her hip and across her stomach, and she could feel every inch of his body from his pectorals to his thighs pressed against her. His chest rose and fell, pushing into her with each of his slow, steady breaths that tickled her neck as he exhaled. His body cradled hers, keeping her close. Like in her dream, Natalia felt safe. Protected. But also like in her dream, there was a storm on the horizon, chilling her exposed thighs and breasts and promising wind and rain.

Carefully, Natalia lifted Diego's arm from her side. She inched away from him, trying not to wake him. They'd been pressed against each other for so long that her back and butt stuck to him. Diego stirred as she peeled herself off him, mumbling something and smacking his lips, but he didn't wake as Natalia put a good six inches between them. From there it was a simple endeavor to lay his arm back on the mattress and ease herself off the edge of the bed.

The room was in a state of disarray, their clothes littering the floor. Natalia padded across to Diego's pants. Her clutch with her phone was tucked in Diego's jacket, but his pants held Miriam's phone, and more importantly, his own. Natalia checked the bed to make sure he wasn't stirring, then slid Diego's phone into her hand. She crossed to the single lit lamp, turned it off, and slipped into the bathroom, turning the light on as she closed the door.

Natalia sat upon the toilet and began to pee as she unlocked Diego's phone. She'd watched him as he unlocked it before, memorizing the numerical code he used to back up his fingerprint. With four quick presses, Natalia was in. She swiped through his apps, looking for PDF readers and cloud services. She discovered a few, and with a few extra taps, she found what she was looking for: his plans for breaking into the National Gallery. It didn't take long for Natalia to see the plans were the same as the ones Miriam had shown her, but Natalia had to make sure he didn't have any unexpected surprises in store for her. Natalia then switched to Diego's emails, scanning the most recent messages before doing the same to his texts. The emails were mostly benign, and none of the texts between Diego and Eddie and Miriam gave her much pause either. A few mysterious texts between Diego and a number that didn't have a contact listed did, but there still wasn't anything in the exchanges that made Natalia second-guess her overall plans.

When Natalia finished perusing the texts, she stayed upon the toilet, even though she'd long since emptied her bladder. There was one thing she still needed to do, but she didn't want to do it. She'd already betrayed Diego's trust, but this next step was a bridge too far.

As if on cue, the voice that had failed to reach her as she'd torn Diego's clothes off spoke. *Told you so.*

Natalia sighed. It wasn't as if she hadn't known sleeping with Diego was a terrible idea. She just hadn't cared. It had been so long since she'd felt anything even remotely real. So long since she'd found herself drowning in desire. So long since she'd wanted to share a piece of herself that was honest and true. And she had. There on the dance floor, when Diego had asked her about her past, she'd shared it with him, without hesitation or regrets, and when they'd reached his room, everything she'd shared with him had been gloriously honest as well. She'd shared more than her body. She'd shared her wants and desires and a tender intimacy she hadn't shared with any of her short flings throughout the past decade.

Was it really so bad? She'd always known she'd betray Diego, and their intimacy hadn't changed that. If anything, when she finally left his side, they'd have this night to remember each other by. The bliss they'd felt, the sensation of each other's bodies, the heat of each other's breath and the taste of their skin. Natalia wouldn't forget any of that, and she doubted Diego would either. Knowing Diego's betrayal had always been in the cards, wasn't it better for them to have the memories of their night of passion than not?

Logically, it seemed to Natalia it was better to take life's simple pleasures when available and not worry about the rest, yet if this were the better choice, why did the thought of finishing the job she'd come to Oslo to do make her heart ache? Why were her lungs unable to fill themselves with air, and why did her stomach feel as if it had been replaced with a black hole?

Because it's easier to betray someone you don't care about, dummy.

Natalia bent over, holding Diego's phone against her cheek as she put her face in her hands. Her stomach roiled, her chest hurt, and a single strangled sob escaped her lungs, but even through it, Natalia forced herself to focus. This wasn't who she was, some flighty bird who made decisions based upon emotions and feelings. A lifetime of experience had taught her to trust only herself and value only herself, and as soon as she'd started practicing what she preached, she'd elevated herself from a scrawny pickpocket to an international jet setting thief.

This was who she was, and she just had to accept it.

Natalia swallowed back the lump in her throat and forced her head up. The phone had gone to sleep in her hands, so she punched the passkey back in and opened the app store. She didn't know Diego's password, just the four digit numerical code to unlock his phone, but she didn't need his password to download a free app. She found the software she was looking for, a tracking app that would store Diego's location data as well as a few other key metrics, and installed it on his phone. Once it finished downloading, Natalia signed in under her own account, ensuring the data would go straight to her. When she was done, she cleared the app from the main screen while making sure it remained active.

As she finished, she hesitated. A part of her was still trying to figure out if there was a way she could get out of this without hurting Diego, but there wasn't. Their goals were diametrically opposed, and no amount of thinking would change that. With one last sigh, Natalia flushed the toilet, gave her hands a wash, and slipped out of the bathroom.

Natalia had to give herself a moment to let her eyes adjust to the darkness, but as they did, she was able to see Diego hadn't stirred. Quietly, she put the phone back in his pocket and padded her way to bed. The sheets were trapped underneath Diego, but she managed to free the duvet from the base of the bed. She pulled it over herself and Diego alike as she slipped back into the nook created by his body.

This time, Diego did stir. His eyes fluttered, and his speech was mostly intelligible. "Natalia?"

Natalia hushed him. "Shh. It's okay. Go back to sleep."

Diego hummed, putting his arm back around her naked body as he pressed himself against her. Perhaps Natalia should've pushed him away, but that would've alerted him that something was amiss as surely as if she'd slapped him. Besides, she enjoyed his touch and his warmth, and if she was going to lose all of it, she might as well allow herself to relish in his presence one last time, no matter the consequences.

Chapter Twenty-Three

As Diego blinked and his brain coalesced into consciousness, he noticed a few things. First, the light in the room had been turned off, but a pale pre-dawn glow was brightening the windows. Second, a soft duvet covered him, keeping him warm. Most distressing, however, was that he had a powerful erection and Natalia no longer lay beside him.

Diego heard a rustle. He turned onto his back to find Natalia dressing herself in the middle of the room. She'd already pulled her dress on, the purple looking darker than he remembered in the low light, and now she was struggling with the zipper.

"Natalia?"

She looked up, her pale eyes hidden in shadow. "Hey. I was trying not to wake you."

Diego sat up, pulling the duvet along with him to hide his erection. It didn't seem like the right moment to let that spring free. "You don't have to leave, you know. It's not even dawn."

Diego heard the *brrrrrrr* of Natalia's zipper as she engaged it. She leaned over, searching for her shoes. "I wasn't planning on staying all night. I have things to take care of."

"Can't they wait? I'd love to have you back in bed." *And make love to you again and again,* Diego thought.

Natalia hopped, steadying herself against the wall as she pulled on one of her heels. "It's better that I go. Really."

Diego's erection started to fade as he realized Natalia wasn't coming back to bed. "Well... can I call you a cab, or order you a rideshare?"

Natalia slipped her second shoe on. "Already took care of it, but thanks."

Natalia started to head toward the door. Diego felt a moment of panic as he watched her go. He lifted a hand and called out. "Natalia! Wait!"

She hesitated at the edge of the hallway that led to the front door. Her hand trailed along the wall, the dress looking as marvelous on her as it had the night before. "Yes?"

Diego opened his mouth to speak, but nothing came out. It wasn't for lack of ideas. A million thoughts raced through his head, a million things he wanted to tell her, but which was the right one? Should he tell her he'd felt a bond form between them the night before, one that was genuine and honest and true? Should he tell her that as they'd danced, the bond had become a physical connection, and that in his hands she'd danced as beautifully as a professional salsa champion? Should he tell her that as they'd kissed and pressed their bodies against each other and Diego had teased his fingers between her legs that he'd grown so hard he feared he might rip his pants from the sheer intensity of his desire? Or should he just be forward, tell her he'd never felt the way he had around anyone the way he'd felt around her and ask her to please stay?

"I, ah..." The thoughts swirled, overwhelming him. "We'll need to get together later. There are a lot of issues to iron out with regards to the heist."

"Sure," said Natalia. "Give me a call."

She gave him a tiny wave, and then she was gone. Diego heard the clack of the door, a whine of air, and a soft click as it closed again.

Diego leaned back in his bed and sighed. Even though he'd clearly fumbled his final opportunity to keep her around, he didn't understand what had happened. The night before Natalia had laughed at his jokes, smiled at him, let her arm linger on his for far too long. She'd glided across the dance floor, held him close, and once in his room, she'd responded with ecstasy to his every touch. Why had she run off so suddenly? Had he done something wrong?

It wasn't the sex, of that he was sure. Like anyone else, he'd had a few unsatisfying sexual encounters in his life, ones where either he or his partner left feeling unfulfilled, but last night was *not* one of those. Everything had been magical. His and Natalia's bodies felt as if they'd been designed for each other. Every movement between them had brought intense pleasure and built additional desire. There wasn't an actress in the world talented enough to put on the performance Natalia had without truly feeling the passion and desire she'd displayed. So what then? What had he done to drive her away?

It must've been something he'd done earlier in the night, something Natalia realized she disliked once the passions of the night had cooled. But what? Something to do with Malin Hanssen? The woman had been overly handsy and had flirted with Diego to an excessive degree, but what fault of his was that? One of the most effective tools in the arsenal of a grifter was to get the mark to fall for you, and while he hadn't tried to seduce Malin, he hadn't downplayed his charm either. Still, that shouldn't have affected Natalia's choice to leave. If Natalia were jealous of another woman, she'd be more likely to stick by his side, wouldn't she?

Diego shook his head as he tossed the duvet aside. He dug some fresh underwear, a pair of sweatpants, and a T-shirt out of a dresser drawer and dressed himself as he continued to think. He'd watched Natalia carefully throughout the course of the prior evening, perhaps a little too close. He was honestly surprised Malin hadn't commented on how distracted he was, or that Natalia hadn't noticed him staring at her throughout the gala, but how could he not have stared? Dressed as she was in that clinging gown that exposed the length of her leg,

Diego had thought her the most beautiful woman he'd ever laid eyes on, and that was before he'd seen her *out* of the dress. Could that be it? Had she noticed his attention and deemed it too much? Maybe he was being too clingy. Then again, Natalia had tried to leave before Diego could attempt to pursue more amorous intentions, before he'd awoken in fact. It had to be something else.

Diego crossed the room to his crumped pants, pulling his underwear from inside them and removing Miriam's phone from one pocket and his from the other. As he pocketed both, he remembered Natalia's purse. He pulled his jacket off the floor, checking the interior pockets, but thoughts of a gallant return of her possessions fled as he realized the clutch was gone. Natalia must've grabbed it while he was still asleep.

Diego hung up his trousers and jacket, both of which would need to be cleaned and pressed. He plugged in his phone and set Miriam's beside it, then worked on collecting the rest of his clothing: his shirt, socks, shoes, and his belt, the buckle of which seemed to have dented the wall as it went flying during last night's lovemaking. Thinking back to the passionate session made him start to become aroused again, and that led to a fresh round of thinking about what had driven Natalia off.

The strangest part of Natalia's sudden departure was how content she'd seemed the night before. As she'd stolen Olsen's phone and returned it to his pocket undetected, she'd grown more fluid, more confident, more at ease. Even before they'd stepped onto the dance floor, her movements across the ballroom had started to resemble a dance, her arms swaying as she executed Miriam's instructions. She'd seemed entirely in her element, as free as a bird. Was that it? That her passionate lovemaking was a byproduct of her euphoria at a job well done? No, that seemed ridiculous. Natalia didn't come across as the sort of woman who would pounce the nearest man just because she was high on adrenaline. It must've been something Diego did. Something he'd shared with her that she found repulsive on further reflection...

And then he remembered. He remembered standing on the dance floor, Natalia held in his arms as he came clean. As he told her about Doña Marquez. As he told her *the truth*.

It was a terrible story. Bland and insipid and one that painted him as insecure and buffoonish. It was a shameful thing to have shared. It had physically hurt to pull that story out and shine the light of day upon it, but Natalia had given him no choice. She'd pleaded with him to share a glimpse of his real self, and in a moment of weakness he'd obliged. In a sense, it worked. By giving her what she'd wanted, it awakened her desires, causing her to pounce on him the instant they walked through his door, but in the cold light of dawn, she'd realized the true self Diego had shared wasn't one she wanted to associate with. And who could blame her? The only women who'd ever fallen for Diego had been those who'd fallen in love with his persona, the confident playboy grifter he shared with the world.

At least the solution to Diego's problem was straightforward. If he was to get Natalia back, he'd have to lean into his established persona, *hard*. He'd have to push his true self back into the dark recess of his soul where it belonged and trust in the charm that had gotten him this far.

Diego took a deep breath as he sorted his discarded clothing, grateful he'd figured out an approach to get himself back into Natalia's good graces, but at the same time, there was a pit in his stomach. An aching emptiness that shouldn't have been there. Why? Because some part of him had been happy to share his true self with Natalia? Well, he'd have to deal with it. Better to hold Natalia close and keep himself hidden than the alternative.

Diego went to the bathroom and relieved himself. As he came out, the sun was strengthening outside his window. Still feeling a little down, he decided to indulge himself in the one thing that always gave him pleasure. He sat at the desk near the windows and opened his laptop, clicking on the web browser before punching in the name of one of his favorite online poker sites. As he logged in, an alert popped up in the middle of his screen informing him that his account had been locked and he'd be unable to participate in any games until his outstanding balance was paid. Diego looked at the amount that he owed and blinked. It was more of a debt than he recalled having racked up, but then again, he had a habit of letting the sums get away from him. He punched another website into the browser and tried to get a game going there instead, but that one too had locked him out due to unpaid debts. Diego cursed. There were another three or four sites he'd used, but the two he'd already tried were the ones he was most confident were functional.

Diego sighed. On any other day, he would've taken the notices as a sign that he should stop playing, at least until he'd completed the *Nasjonalmuseet* heist and sold *The Scream,* but with everything that had happened, his itch demanded to be scratched. So he went to the only site he knew he could count on. He punched in the .ru address for Yevgeniy Kovalyov's betting site and navigated to the poker rooms.

As he was waiting to find a lobby, his phone rang. He crossed to his nightstand, and recognizing the name that appeared on the touch-screen, he answered.

"Hey, Miriam. What's up?"

Miriam's voice was strained. "Diego. We have a problem."

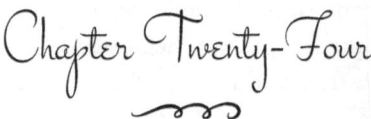

Chapter Twenty-Four

WHEN DIEGO PUSHED INSIDE THE INDUSTRIAL LOFT, HE found Miriam and Eddie seated in front of the bank of computers. At least a dozen windows were open on the monitors, some of them half hidden by others, showing everything from websites to schematics to terminals full of computer code.

Eddie bobbed his head as Diego joined them. "Mornin', D."

"Morning, guys." Diego pulled up a chair and pointed to the nearest monitor. "Is this the museum's security interface?"

Miriam nodded. "Yeah. I was able to log in remotely using the data I scraped off Olsen's phone. Once in, I created a secret account with the same permissions as Olsen, so there shouldn't be any issues with him being logged in at the same time as us, and no one knows we're in."

"Great," said Diego. "So what's the problem?"

Eddie snorted. "The problem, mate, isn't what we 'as, it's what we 'asn't. When the pistol and shoo'er fails, we's got to get the ol' German bands dirty, and 'is 'as frown a 'uge Judy Dench in the works."

Diego blinked. "I have to admit, a lot of that went over my head. Miriam, what exactly is going on?"

Miriam cast him a sideways glance. "What's going on is that security won't be as easy to control as we thought. Based on the schematics I had available going into this, I was under the impression that as long as we got into the system, we should be able take control of the specific cameras and sensors watching over *The Scream* and over our path in and out of the building. Turns out we *can* do that, but what I didn't prepare for was the existence of hardwired failsafes that are inaccessible from within the online system."

"What sort of hardwired failsafes are we talking about?" asked Diego.

"The kind where if you pulls a paintin' off the wall, all the Auntie Nells starts ringin' and the Bobbies come a'runnin'."

"So there's a hardwired connection between *The Scream* and its mount?" asked Diego. "If we remove the painting, that sends a signal straight to the alarms and they go off? And this connection isn't controlled via the security software?"

"Essentially, yes," said Miriam. "There are several other security measures that *are* controlled by the software, but this one isn't, and there's no way to disable it externally."

"Well, can't we intercept the signal somehow?" said Diego. "Keep the case from communicating to the alarm that it's been breached?"

Miriam's face scrunched up. *"What?* No. That's not how this works."

"Why not?"

She sighed. "I forget this isn't your area of expertise. The hardwired sensor completes a loop with the alarm so there's always feedback. If anything interrupts that loop for any reason, the alarm goes off. You can't, like, *punk* the signal into thinking something else is happening."

"Well, what if we cut the power?" suggested Diego.

"Won't work," said Miriam. "There's a battery backup. Not sure how long it would last, but I'm confident in saying it would be long enough for the police and museum security to investigate what caused the power to go out in the first place."

Eddie leaned back in his chair. "I still fink my idea's the best."

"And what's that?" asked Diego.

Miriam rolled her eyes. "Don't get him started..."

Eddie ignored her. "Smash and grab's what I say. 'S worked before, it'll work again."

"Two key points about that strategy," said Diego. "First of all, those attempts succeeded at the old national museum. This one is bigger, and it'll take us longer to get to safety with the painting. Second point, both of those attempts resulted in arrests. We're trying *not* to get caught."

Eddie shrugged. "Fose arrests came after the fact, mate. Seems fose tea leaves didn' 'ide their tracks well 'nough after fey ran off, y'ask me."

"Well, it's a lot easier to hide your tracks if you don't leave a trail of destruction in your wake," said Diego. "Besides, that's not how we operate. We stick to the shadows. None of us has ever been arrested—"

Eddie cocked his head.

"—*for stealing art,*" added Diego. "And I intend to keep it that way."

There was a click and a creak of hinges. When Diego turned, he saw Natalia entering the loft. Diego had texted her after his phone call with Miriam, but he'd harbored a fear that she might bail on them entirely after everything that had transpired the night before. That fear appeared to have been unfounded. Not only had she arrived almost as quickly as he had, but she looked as if nothing had occurred between them at all. Gone was the dress that clung to her body like a second skin, replaced instead with her usual leggings, long-sleeved running jacket, and tennis shoes. Her hair had been pulled into a tight ponytail, the traces of makeup she'd worn the night before had been scrubbed clean, and she wore a look of quiet determination.

The door closed with a thump as Natalia approached them. "So. What's going on?"

Diego's heart beat faster at the sight of her, but he knew had to keep himself composed. It was the only way he'd win back her affections. "Miriam gained access to the museum security using the data you scraped for her, but it's not enough. There's a hardwired sensor we can't access remotely."

"Pressure or contact?" asked Natalia.

"Contact, I think," said Miriam. "Closed loop. Battery backup."

Natalia nodded, as if she knew exactly what was going on from those few words. "That does make things tricky. Any delay?"

"Nope," said Miriam.

"Okay..." Natalia's eyes flicked to Diego. She held his gaze for a fraction of a second before shifting her attention to the monitors. She gestured at his chair. "Do you, ah... mind if I have a seat?"

Diego felt like an idiot for not having already offered. Here he was, supposed to be the suave, confident grifter of old, and he'd been too captivated by the sight of Natalia wearing basic running attire to make the simplest of gestures. "By all means."

Diego stood and Natalia took his chair, rolling herself closer to the monitors. She held up a finger. "Is this the schematic of the system?"

"Not the one specifically in the National Museum," said Miriam. "This is the generic schematic provided by the manufacturer, but it should be set up similarly to this."

Natalia rubbed her chin. "Do you have a paper and pencil?"

"Paper and pencil?" said Miriam. "What is this, the nineteenth century?"

"Hold on," said Diego. He patted his jacket pockets. Sure enough, there was a pen in one of them. He also carried a lighter, even though he didn't smoke. You never knew when a woman might need something to write with or someone to light her cigarette. Paper, on the other hand, was a trickier ask. He crossed to the edge of the furthest desk, digging through the built-in drawer. There wasn't any printer-sized paper, but there was a notepad in it about the size of an open palm.

"Will this do?" He held out the pad and the pen from his pocket.

"Good enough." Natalia took the pair, making sure not to make contact with his hand in the process. She leaned over and started drawing, talking to Miriam as she did so. "All we really need is to find the loop and make a device we can open and close remotely, allowing us to switch from their closed loop to a new one we're setting up. You think you can build this?"

"Sure, but that'll set off the alarm," said Miriam.

"That's the point. We'll set it off intermittently as we install it."

"Wait... You want to make it look like a loose connection?"

"Right. But they'll want to make sure it *isn't* a loose connection. They'll call someone in to look at it."

Miriam smiled. "So we'll need to tap the phone lines. Get a spare uniform or two."

Natalia nodded. "Exactly. You've got it."

Diego couldn't see over them. "Excuse me? What are you two talking about?"

Natalia turned toward him, showing him the sketch she'd drawn. "With a closed-loop, battery-operated system like the *Nasjonalmuseet* has, there's literally no way not to trip the alarm when tampering with the system, assuming the batteries are functional but that's a different story. So if we tamper with the system, we *are* going to set off the alarm. I'm saying fine. Let's embrace that. We go in early and place a simple device like this—" She waggled the piece of paper. "—which routes the signal into a new closed loop. That'll set off the alarm. If that happens a single time, it'll raise eyebrows. If, however, the alarm activates for a fraction of a second and turns off again, then does it again and again and again over a period of ten or twenty minutes, all while *The Scream* remains firmly in place with no one touching it, the security team will assume a connection got loose somewhere along the line. That's what this device does. It allows us to falsify the loose connection signal before eventually establishing a new closed loop that isn't connected to *The Scream's* contact sensor. But the *Nasjonalmuseet's* security won't trust themselves to solve the issue. They'll call the installer to come and validate the system, which means we need to intercept that call and send our own technician to tighten the connections and confirm everything is working as intended. I'm thinking Miriam, since she has the most technical know-how."

Miriam sighed. "Ugh. I hate having to go places and interact with people."

"So 'at's why you need the unis?" said Eddie. "For Midge when she sneaks inna the museum?"

"Probably for you, too," said Natalia. "I'm guessing the museum's security office has a land line, which means we'll need to isolate the pole that carries the call and install a tap. If people see you shimmying up a telephone pole without the proper gear and phone company attire, that might raise some eyebrows."

"Me?" said Eddie. "You want me t'a install 'at?"

"Well, it's either you or Diego," said Natalia. "And someone will need to take the call when the security office phones the alarm system installer. No offense, Eddie, but your accent doesn't make you sound like someone a professional security company would hire to a call center."

"And where does that put you during all of this?" asked Diego.

Natalia glanced at Diego, but again, she didn't hold his gaze for more than a second. "I'll be installing the device that establishes the new loop. Obviously, we can't install it near the contact sensor. If anyone is near *The Scream* when the alarm goes on the fritz, they'll be considered a person of interest. Luckily, I can install the device anywhere along the loop. I'm guessing there's a maintenance hatch somewhere that allows me into the crawl space between floors. If we can figure out where the wire is, we're golden."

"And 'ow do we figger 'at?" said Eddie.

"Well, assuming Miriam doesn't already have those blueprints..."

Miriam shook her head.

"Then we'll have a little work to do," said Natalia. "There should be an office of urban design that has them, but the builder is probably the safer bet. Maybe Miriam can hack into their system, maybe not. Honestly, if I were them, I wouldn't have this stuff on an internet-connected computer, which means we might have to go old school to get what we need."

"You mean a B and E?" said Eddie.

"Yes," said Natalia.

Eddie rubbed his hands together. "'At's what I'm talkin' about. Breakin' and enterin' is me speciality."

"Cool your jets," said Natalia. "There's no glass in need of smashing yet. This is going to require a lot of prep to get it right, and we want it to go perfectly. Besides, there's no rush."

Diego cleared his throat. "Actually, that's not entirely accurate."

Natalia turned to him, her brow furrowed. "What do you mean it's not accurate? Are we on the clock?"

"The buyer would prefer to take ownership of the painting sooner rather than later."

"How soon is sooner?" asked Miriam.

Diego took a deep breath and let it out. "Three and a half days."

"*What?*" said Natalia.

"Three and a half *days?*" said Miriam. "Well, at least we're not measuring things in hours yet. Jesus, Diego. What the hell?"

"I wasn't aware of the timeline until recently," he said. "Trust me, it's not my preference, either."

"Can't you tell the bloke to cool 'is 'eels?" asked Eddie.

"My buyer is not the sort of man whom you tell to wait," said Diego. "He's more the type who tells you to jump and you ask how high."

Natalia rubbed a hand across her forehead. "Christ. Are you telling us you've gotten in bed with a mobster?"

It was a funny turn of phrase given who she'd actually gotten in bed with. "People who are willing to drop a hundred million dollars on an illicit painting usually aren't on the up and up. But the deal is legit. If we deliver, we get our money, end of story."

Miriam groaned as she leaned into her chair. "Ugh. So that gives us a day to manufacture the loop splicing device, source uniforms and gear, and obtain the building schematics, another day to pull the job with the tap and the alarm, then we can hopefully have all our ducks in a row to pull the *Scream* heist the night after that. It's plausible, but it doesn't give us a lot of wiggle room."

Natalia exhaled forcefully. "It'll be fine. Maybe it's better this way. It gives us a deadline we have to meet. Three days of focused work and then we all go home with money in our pockets. We can do this."

Natalia started giving everybody instructions as far as the items and gear they'd need to procure, but Diego found himself suddenly adrift. He'd always held Kovalyov's deadline in the back of his mind, but it wasn't until now that he fully connected the dots. Three days to obtain the painting meant he had just three days to win back Natalia's affection. Perhaps he hadn't given it much thought because until this morning their relationship had been on an upward trajectory, but now that she'd pulled back, three days didn't seem like much time. He had just seventy-two short hours to win back Natalia's heart and convince her not to board a plane and fly out of his life. *Forever.*

Diego shook his head, trying to focus on the present. And what better time was there to make amends than now?

He touched Natalia lightly upon the shoulder, causing her to startle. She looked up at him, her eyes finally meeting his for more than a fleeting instant.

"Natalia, before we get too deep in the weeds, do you mind if we have a word? In private."

"Um..." Natalia paused, and it was a *long* pause. Enough for several blinks. "Sure."

Diego could've led Natalia to the couches, but the loft was wide open and sound carried. Instead, he led her out the front door onto the small landing at the top of the stairs. Fluffy clouds shrouded the sun and a cool wind blew. Natalia joined him on the landing, forcing them into close proximity as the door clicked shut.

Diego put on his best smile. "Hey."

Natalia seemed intent upon not meeting his gaze. She crossed her arms in front of her. "Um... hey."

Diego wanted to reach out. To touch her, to hold her in his arms, to kiss her, but her body language made it clear she wanted no such thing. "Can we talk? About last night."

Natalia shrugged, a dainty, slight motion. "What's there to talk about?"

What was there to talk about? How about everything! How about the way they'd glided across the dance floor, arm in arm and connected at the hip, as if there hadn't been another soul in the world except the two of them? Or the fireworks that had gone off in his hotel room, filling each of them with unspeakable pleasure? They could talk about how she made him feel like a teenage boy who'd never experienced love or attraction of any kind and had no idea how to deal with it, or how his heart fluttered and his pulse grew quick in response to her presence.

Diego had always prided himself on his vocabulary, but as the thoughts mobbed him, he felt as if his grasp of the English language had become tenuous. "Well, last night was... *amazing.* Wasn't it?"

Natalia sighed, her chest heaving with the effort, and finally she brought her eyes to his. "Yes. It was. It was... everything I wanted it to be."

Diego leaned closer, the urge to touch her growing stronger. "Then why did you leave so suddenly this morning?"

Natalia's eyes were so large, so blue, but there was a hint of sadness in them. "Diego... This isn't the right time. We have so much to do and there are only so many hours in the day. We need to focus on the job. Once we've gotten *The Scream,* maybe we can let ourselves consider what's going on."

Diego could've reached out. He could've pulled her into his arms and kissed her passionately, but he didn't. "I know, but I don't want to ignore what's between us. This isn't something we can brush aside."

Natalia blinked a few times, and Diego could've sworn her lashes batted away nascent tears. "Don't worry. We'll have time. It's just three days, right?"

Diego felt himself deflate, even though he tried not to. "The blink of an eye, really."

Natalia reached out, trailing her fingers along the edge of his jaw. In that moment, a shy smile spread across her lips, but then she pulled her hand back, as if what she'd done hadn't been a conscious choice. "I, ah... should get back to work. I have a lot of stuff to hash out with Miriam."

"Of course," said Diego. "Me, too. I'll be right behind you."

Natalia nodded and slipped into the loft, leaving Diego alone on the landing. He took a deep breath and blew it out forcefully. Three days. Three days to win Natalia back, all while she didn't want to be won.

By comparison, stealing *The Scream* would be easy.

Chapter Twenty-Five

NATALIA SAT IN THE PASSENGER SEAT OF THE BLACK SEDAN in which Diego and Eddie had psychologically tortured her, but this time, Miriam sat behind the wheel. The car wasn't moving. It was parked on a street corner, pointed toward the six-story offices of The Matthiessen Group, which was the architectural firm that had designed the National Museum, among many other museums and public buildings in Oslo. The sky behind the building was dark, the last vestiges of dusk having fled within the past twenty minutes, but a few lights were still on in the upper floors of the building. Natalia hadn't seen any movement in the windows while staring through her binoculars, but that didn't mean someone wasn't still there, working late. That meant all she could do was wait.

Natalia leaned back in her seat and sighed. Miriam cast her a sideways glance before returning her attention to the phone in her hands. Her thumbs tapped at the screen as faint sounds of gameplay drifted into the air: the clink of armor, the grunts of enemies, the metallic tinkle of gold being collected, all set over a melodic score. Natalia had never been a gamer, but it was at moments like this when she saw the appeal of having a portable distraction in her hands. Then again, someone needed to keep an eye on the building.

Natalia pulled the binoculars to her eyes again and scanned the floors. As she did so, one of the lights went out. So. There *was* someone inside. Good to know.

Natalia tucked the binoculars next to her thighs. She glanced at Miriam's phone again, taking note of the colossal monsters and the oversized sword Miriam's character was swinging. "What game is that?"

"*Genshin Impact.*"

"You say it like I'm supposed to know what that is."

"I mean, you kind of should," said Miriam, casting her a quick glance. "It's only one of the most successful mobile games of all time."

"What kind of game is it?"

"I don't know," said Miriam. "It's like an open-world action RPG. The kind where you kill monsters and collect loot."

"Is it fun?"

Miriam sighed. "You don't have to do this."

Natalia frowned. "Do what?"

Miriam kept tapping at her phone's screen. "Talk to me. Try to make friends. I'm perfectly happy sitting in this car in silence."

"I wouldn't exactly call this silence..." said Natalia. "I can hear everything going on in that game of yours."

Miriam snorted. She tapped one of the side buttons on her phone until the sound all but disappeared. "Better?"

"Yeah, but..."

"But what?" said Miriam.

Natalia wasn't sure she should bother, but she still had another couple days of working alongside Miriam. Even though she thought teams of one worked best, it was probably beneficial to make sure she was on good terms with everyone. For now, anyway. "I don't really understand this animosity you're showing. I thought we were getting along pretty well this afternoon."

"I'm not being animous... animoss... animositous? Whatever. I've got nothing against you."

"You have a unique way of showing it," said Natalia.

Miriam sighed and put her phone to sleep with a flick of her index finger. "Okay. Let's clear the air. Earlier, when we were working on your loop closing doohickey and making plans and trying to hack into The Matthiessen Group, that was cool. I was excited because I like my work, and you're actually competent at what you do, which I respect. But ultimately, it's just work. I'm here to do a job. You're here to do a job. We make bank, we part ways, we never see each other again. That's just how it is. So why should I bother investing my time and energy trying to make friends with you when you're just passing through my life for a few days? Why not invest my time and effort into this game instead? At least there the progress saves."

"I get that," said Natalia. "I mean, I work alone for the most part. I don't go out of my way to form lasting relationships with the people I collaborate with, or... anyone really. But that doesn't explain Eddie and Diego."

Miriam frowned. "That's different. I've known Eddie and Diego a long time. We've been through some shit."

"Well, of course you have," said Natalia. "But unless you simultaneously grew up in London's East End and somewhere in Andalusia, there was a time when you hadn't. A time when Diego and Eddie were just two guys who you were going to do a job with, make bank, and never see again."

Miriam rolled her eyes. "Touché. Yeah, of course there was a time when I didn't know them but... what can I say? They earned my trust. It's a long story."

There was that T word again. First Diego had drilled it into her. Then Eddie had talked about it during the blind driving incident, and now Miriam was bringing it up. It was if the word had transformed into a bloodhound via a strange, anthropomorphic ritual and now the dog had gotten her scent and wouldn't leave her alone.

She glanced at the offices across the street. The lights stubbornly remained on. "As it turns out, I kind of like long stories."

Miriam shook her head. "Nah-uh. I don't know what kind of long-winded bullshit Diego has been plying you with, but I am *not* a storyteller. Suffice it to say they hired me for a job, and when things went sideways, they didn't bail on me. They were there for me. They showed up, and if they hadn't, I would've been in deep, *deep* shit. That's why I trust them."

Natalia was skilled at hearing what wasn't said, but she didn't have to be to pick up what Miriam was laying down. "And that's why you don't trust me."

"*Duh,*" said Miriam. "No offense, but you haven't proven yourself for crap so far. I mean, you clearly know what you're doing. If I didn't already think that, this afternoon proved it. You saw a path toward getting into the National Museum and you attacked it head on. I'm not doubting your skills. But as far as when the shit hits the fan? How do I know you're not going to cut and run?"

Miriam couldn't know that, because that was exactly what Natalia planned on doing. Natalia was not to be trusted. She shouldn't be. She *couldn't* be. She would cut and run, and she'd do so before the crap and the fan ever got close to one another. It was why she needed to keep Diego at arm's length, because she *would* betray him, even if she didn't want to. But it wasn't really Natalia's fault. She was a product of her environment, of all the people who'd ignored her and used her and abandoned her throughout the years. She'd been molded this way, and the shell that surrounded her was not going to be broken. Besides, Diego should've known better. He was a grifter, for God's sake. It was his job to trick and rob people. He would do it to Natalia sooner or later, as sure as the sun would rise. Natalia was simply going to do it to him first.

But if she really believed that, then why did her heart ache at the thought of what she was going to do? Why was there a pit in her stomach that had been gnawing at her all day? Why had she slept fitfully, accosted by nightmares after she'd broken into Diego's phone? Why was the voice inside her pleading with her to bail this instant, to sneak into the offices down the street and disappear out the back before she made everything a million times worse?

Natalia took a deep breath, hoping the shuddering nature of it didn't tip Miriam off to her thoughts. She kept her gaze on the building across from them, not trusting her eyes not to give anything away. She probably should've remained silent and let Miriam go back to her game, but some part of her was so desperate to confide in someone, to share even the slightest smidgen of her fears and hopes and desires. To make her feel as if she wasn't so damn *alone*.

"I..." Natalia swallowed and wet her lips. God, why was this so difficult? "I have a hard time trusting people."

"No shit," said Miriam. "We all do."

Natalia turned, her face scrunching up in confusion. "You do?"

Miriam looked at her as if she was dense. *"Hello?* Have you not been listening to anything I've been telling you? Of course I have a hard time trusting people. But you can't go through life never trusting *anyone.* I mean, what kind of life is that?"

A lonely one, thought Natalia. "Easier said than done."

"Tell me about it. But my point is that when someone shows you who they are, that's when you can trust them, even if they are a liar or a thief or a thug. And..." Miriam sighed. "Sometimes you have to take a leap of faith. Which is what I'm *trying* to do with you."

Natalia lifted an eyebrow. "That's what this is? You extending an olive branch?"

"No," said Miriam. "This conversation is about me secretly hoping you'll shut up so I can get back to my game. The olive branch is me trying to make myself believe you're going to go into those offices and get the blueprints we need without leaving any evidence, which I'm *mostly* confident in." Miriam paused. "Besides, if Diego trusts you, I suppose I can, too."

Natalia's second brow joined the first. "You think Diego trusts me?"

"Strangely enough, yeah. Which is odd because he normally doesn't trust anyone. But he seems to trust you." Miriam snorted. "I mean, he really, *really* trusts you."

Dawn broke over Natalia. "What did he tell you?"

Miriam unsuccessfully tried to hide a smirk. "Nothing. But I have eyes. It's not too difficult to spot that quintessential post-bone awkwardness."

Natalia groaned. "Great. Just great."

"Don't get me wrong," said Miriam. "I'm not judging. Get it wherever you can, I say. And Diego is pretty handsome..."

A suspicion Natalia hadn't wanted to consider reared its ugly head. "Wait... this isn't something he makes a habit of, is it? Like... with the new girl?"

"Not to my knowledge," said Miriam. "Maybe with some of his marks, but I kind of doubt it. He usually doesn't let it go that far. As far as our team is concerned, I don't have a lot of data to go on. You're the first woman we've brought in to work alongside us."

"So... you and him. You never...?"

Miriam's eyed widened. *"What?* No. No, no, no. Diego is handsome and all, but he is *not* my type." Her gaze drifted off, and her voice got small. "Not him, anyway."

Natalia blinked, trying to figure out what had caused her to say that. "Okay. Good. I just wanted to make sure."

Miriam cleared her throat. She seemed to have shrunken in on herself, but her voice was no longer soft and self-conscious when she spoke. "No worries. You're all good."

Natalia waited a moment, but Miriam didn't offer anything else. "So, were you pulling my leg about Diego trusting me, or do you think he actually does?"

Miriam shrugged. "I don't know. I think so. It's hard to tell. But what I can tell you is I've never seen him act around anyone else the way he does around you."

Natalia's heart fluttered. "What do you mean?"

"He seems flustered. Caught off guard. Less than perfect. He's never shown any chinks in his armor before you came along. And now..." Miriam shook her head. "I don't know. I'm not worried, but it's only recently I've been able to see it's all an act."

Natalia furrowed her brow. "Huh."

"What do you mean, huh?"

"It's just that... Sometimes I get the feeling part of it isn't."

Miriam was silent, and Natalia feared she might've shared too much. She wasn't used to being honest after all. Just when Natalia thought the silence had stretched beyond awkward into uncomfortable, Miriam pointed. "Hey. Look."

The last light in the building had gone out. Natalia lifted her binoculars and spotted a middle-aged gentleman locking up the front doors. As he finished, he turned down the street, heading in the direction opposite the sedan.

"Time to put up or shut up," said Miriam.

Natalia swallowed back the lump in her throat. "Yeah. Time to earn a little trust." With a flick of her hand, she opened the door and headed to the trunk for her tools.

Chapter Twenty-Six

DIEGO SAT IN FRONT OF THE BANK OF MONITORS IN THE loft, his legs stretched out before him. The windows which looked over the industrial park were dark, lit only by the glow of a single streetlight near the parking lot's entrance. Other than the gentle hum of the computers the loft was quiet. Even the occasional rumble of heavy trucks had long since gone away, having faded with the setting sun.

Part of Diego wished he could kick off his shoes and nurse a drink. It had been a long day. The security system Miriam had uncovered had thrown a wrench in Diego's plans, but thanks to Natalia's quick thinking and Miriam's resourcefulness, they were on track to pull the heist off in three days, before Kovalyov's ultimatum expired. Getting the race underway had taken a lot of effort, though. Beyond the planning of the various steps, they'd had to procure more equipment than Diego had expected. While some of it could be overnighted, other pieces had to be sourced from around town. He and Eddie had driven across the city and back. Palms had been greased, and items had been pocketed while people looked the other way. Even more effort would be required to reach the finish line.

But for all the physical efforts, the day had been even more emotionally draining. Whenever he'd been around Natalia, it had been a challenge to focus on the work in front of him, to think clearly and provide pertinent input. Every moment spent in her presence he'd wanted nothing more than to snuggle beside her, to relish in the scent of her hair and the press of her body against his. Even when he'd left with Eddie to complete their errands, his mind had wandered from the task at hand to the evening of passion they'd shared. What made it worse was that during the moments he and Natalia shared throughout the day, she'd done her best to ignore him. Why? Was she that motivated by her work? If she was that professional, why had she slept with him in the first place?

More importantly, perhaps, was why Diego had allowed himself to get this way. He wasn't the sort to moon over women, to pine for them and spend every waking thought on them. More often than not, the women in his life were targets. Marks to be tricked and fooled. Yes, he'd gotten physically involved with a couple of them over the years, but he'd never found himself distracted and befuddled in the aftermath.

But Natalia was different. He knew it in his core that she wasn't like any woman he'd ever met, even if he didn't know exactly why that was the case. It was that knowledge that made it so painful that she insisted on pushing him away.

The door creaked, and in walked Eddie. He dusted his hands as he walked toward Diego. "Well, 'at's the last of the unis. Figger we've got all our ducks plum placed s'long as Natalia gets 'em blueprints. You 'eard from 'er, yet?"

Diego picked his phone off the desk and waved it. "Still waiting on confirmation."

"And nofin' from Midge?"

Diego shrugged.

"Well, I'm sure 'ey would'a let us know if it'd all gone to pot."

Diego nodded.

Eddie pulled up a chair. "Y'alright, D? You look like a jam jar done run over your cherry."

Diego blinked. "Sorry, my what?"

"Cherry Hogg. Your dog." Eddie leaned in. "Seriously, y'alright?"

Diego waved his hand. "I'm fine, Eddie. It's been a long day."

Eddie snorted. "No offense, but 'ats bollocks. I can tell when me china's off, and you've straight gone to the dogs."

"Really, Eddie, it's nothing. I'm just... I don't know. Distracted, I guess."

Eddie nodded. "It's Natalia, innit?"

Diego sat up straighter in his chair. "Yeah. How did you know?"

"Ain't 'ard to see, D. 'Ere's somefin' in the air, 'ere is. So what's the matter? You tried to get your jollies off and she got all spuds on ya?"

"No," said Diego. "I mean, I don't know. I'm not entirely sure what that means. The point is I thought we were growing closer, and today all of a sudden she pulls away."

Eddie smiled knowingly. "'Cause you shagged?"

Diego shrugged. "Maybe. I don't know."

Eddie frowned. "You're not sure if you shagged or if 'at's why she's pullin' back?"

"For crying out loud, Eddie. Yes, we were intimate, and I remember the encounter. We were both lucid and clear headed going into it. But I have no idea if that's what's making her act the way she is."

Eddie looked a little uncomfortable. "Well, did you 'ave any, y'know... *problems?*" He pointed downwards for emphasis.

"No. The sex was phenomenal. For both of us."

Eddie smiled and clapped Diego across the shoulder with the strength of a horse's kick. "Yeah, it was, mate!"

Diego grimaced. "Eddie. Come on."

The big man's face fell and he removed his giant mitt. "Sorry. Just excited for ya. But if 'at was all good, 'en I don't know what the problem might be."

Diego rolled his shoulder. He might need an ice pack later. "Have you been in many relationships?"

"Depends what you mean by 'at," said Eddie. "You askin' 'bout more 'an just shaggin', I take it?"

Diego nodded. "Serious relationships."

Eddie leaned back in his chair. The poor thing squealed in protest. "Not many. Did spend a few monfs wif one bird, name of Jenny, after the Florence job but afore the one in Belgrade." Eddie shrugged. "It didn't work out."

"But you liked her?" asked Diego.

Eddie thought it over and nodded. "I did, but it wasn't meant to be."

"What happened?"

"'At's a complicated question, but the simple answer is I told 'er the truf."

Diego's heart spasmed, causing his body to twitch. "What do you mean you told her the truth? About what?"

"About bein' a criminal, mate. Jenny was a good li'l bird. Came from a good family. So when I broke the pews 'at I was up to me eyeballs in lemon and lime, she frew a wobbly. Never talked to me again."

Diego's heart constricted, causing discomfort and pain throughout. "So... you came clean about who you really are, and she couldn't handle it."

Eddie hacked a hand across his arm. "Cut me off, mate. Like an amputated limb, she did."

Diego sighed and leaned back in his chair. "I assume you regret opening up to her."

Eddie rolled his shoulders in a massive shrug. "Not really, mate. Me and 'er, we wasn't meant for each ofer. Besides, what was I supposed to do? Keep tellin' 'er porkies me 'ole life?"

Diego snorted. "It's an option."

Eddie shook his head. "For you, maybe, but not for me. Jenny would'a found me out sooner rafer 'en la'er. And even if she didn't, what kinda life is 'at? Sneakin' and lyin' all the lemon? Spendin' your donkey's ears with a bird who don't even know the real you?"

"It's better than the alternative," said Diego. "At least you'd have someone by your side, someone who cares about you, even if the you they care for isn't the real one. It's better than not having anyone."

Eddie pshawed. "Trust me, D, I been down almost 'at exact same road afore, but I gots to believe 'er's someone out 'er for everyone. It ain't worf tryin' a make it work wif someone who won't love ya for who you are."

Diego spun his phone on the desk with a finger. "Sure. Lots of fish in the sea, right?" *And maybe there are for most people,* thought Diego. *Maybe even for you, Eddie. Maybe you can find someone who can accept the real you, because the real you while rough around the edges is exciting and authentic. You know who you are, and you wear it proudly. But me? I'm a grifter through and through, and that's all there is. Without my persona, I'm nothing. An insignificant speck of dust that wouldn't attract notice if it floated in front of someone's face. And I know because no one ever did notice. No one ever cared until I became someone else. Someone better and more clever and more interesting than who I really am.*

"So?" Eddie leaned in. "You feelin' any be'er, mate?"

Diego forced himself to smile. "Of course, Eddie. You're quite the motivational speaker."

The big man laughed. "Me mum always said I 'ad a way with dicky birds."

Diego's phone buzzed. He stopped spinning it and picked it up, checking the text.

Eddie leaned over further. "Well? 'S'it Midge or Natalia?"

"The latter."

Diego showed Eddie the text, which read: *We got what we needed. We're on for tomorrow.*

Eddie nodded. "Right. Sounds like it's time for a li'l shut eye, 'en."

"That it is." Or at least, it would be for Eddie. Diego knew what he had to do to keep Natalia on the hook, and he couldn't wing it this time. He'd need to prepare.

Chapter Twenty-Seven

NATALIA WALKED ALONG THE WIDE OPEN *RÅDHUSPLASSEN*, her eyes locked on the tiled gray exterior of the National Gallery. A sling bag hung over her shoulder, the weight of the contents pressing across the length of the strap. Around her, individuals strolled through the plaza in the mid-morning sun, chatting with each other as they enjoyed their morning coffees.

Natalia spoke softly but clearly. "Alright, everyone. Final comms check."

Miriam's voice crackled through her earpiece. It was small enough no one would notice it, but even if they did, they'd probably think it a hearing aid. "I hear you loud and clear from the sedan."

Diego spoke. "And I can hear you from the control center. Eddie?"

"Control cen'er?" said Eddie. "You're in the bloody van, mate."

"Which is the control center," said Diego. "Last I checked, this is where we store the surveillance equipment and where I'll be taking the call you redirect, assuming you do your job."

"Ya don't 'ave to worry about me, mate. I'm on the bloody dog pole. Windy as the devil's own arsehole up 'ere, it is."

"Better you than me," said Miriam. "I don't like heights."

"Ya don't?" said Eddie. "Never knew 'at about you, Midge."

Natalia rolled her eyes. "I'll take that as a confirmation that every-one's comms are working. Miriam, do you have control of the cameras?"

"Yup," said Miriam. "Got them all pulled up on my laptop."

"You know, I'm the one in the control center," said Diego. "I don't know why you're asking Miriam."

"Maybe because Miriam has experience in this sort of thing," said Natalia.

Diego sniffed. "That's a bit rude. Do you think I've never run an operation like this before? I do more than smile and gain people's confidence, you know. I'm a multi-talented individual, good at a wide variety of things."

Natalia had been on the verge of making a snide remark, but a memory of their passionate night together flashed through her mind. As much as she might not want to admit it, he'd been very good at that, too, so she held her tongue. "I guess I misspoke. Miriam has *more* experience than you, is that accurate?"

"It's fair," said Diego.

Natalia approached the front of the museum. "I'm getting ready to go in. Miriam?"

"You're good. I'll splice a video loop into camera thirteen as soon as you're in position."

"Perfect." Natalia entered the museum. She'd already purchased a ticket on her phone, so instead of approaching the front desk, she veered into the ground floor exhibits. Natalia hadn't given much attention to the items on display, but there was plenty to look at: imperial porcelain from China, 18th-century Norwegian glass goblets, historical attire, armor, tapestries, and crafts. Some of it was certainly art, but none of it really appealed to Natalia. Still, she might've given a few of the displays more than a passing glance if she wasn't fully focused on the people around her, especially the guards. There weren't many of them, and she was quickly able to pick them out and estimate their patrol routes, but there were a decent number of visitors today. They wouldn't be paying close attention to her, but they could still pose a problem if she didn't account for them.

Natalia glanced at the security cameras as she approached the northeastern edge of the building. "I've passed the Baldishol Tapestry. Now approaching camera thirteen."

"You're looking good as far as I can tell," said Diego. "No security in the vicinity."

"Miriam?" asked Natalia.

"Give me a second," she replied. "I'm waiting for a couple to exit the frame so I can splice the loop in seamlessly. And... you're good to go."

Natalia took one more look around, locking the positions of everyone she could spot in her mind. Once she'd established their locations, she moved quickly and with purpose. She approached a door at the far side of the hall, one that looked no different to the one she'd broken into with Diego on their first trip inside the museum. With a deft hand, she slipped her lock picking tools from her backpack into her hand. After one last glance down the hallway, she tucked the pick and torsion wrench into the keyhole. With a couple flicks of her fingers, she heard a click and pushed her way inside.

She swiped the lights on and found herself in a maintenance closet, though the room was larger than most. In addition to racks full of cleaning supplies and carts with built-in mop buckets, there was an abundance of paper towels and toilet paper stacked in piles. A number of large metal tanks had been fastened to the wall with galvanized steel straps. A pump hummed steadily, though Natalia couldn't locate it on first glance.

"We don't have eyes on you anymore," said Diego. "Have you found the hatch?"

Natalia tucked her lock picks into her bag. Her eyes drifted toward a square panel in the ceiling, above a rack in the furthest corner. There were a number of access points into the crawl space between the first and second floors, but this one had the benefit of being hidden where no one would see her as she clambered into it.

"Yeah, I found it."

"Is it accessible?" asked Miriam.

Natalia tested the rack, but it didn't wobble. Someone had been smart and bolted it to the floor. "It is. Give me a moment."

Natalia hopped onto the third shelf, reaching for the ceiling. The panel above her slid to the side at her touch. She climbed one more shelf—carefully, as the shelf had finally started to wobble—before reaching up, grabbing the edge of the hatch, and pulling herself through.

The space she found herself in wasn't high, less than three feet for sure, but it was expansive. Natalia pulled an LED headlamp from her backpack and slipped it over her head. As she turned it on, it illuminated the gloom, lighting up thick steel beams, spray-foam insulation, the sub-flooring above her, and of course, all the guts of the building: conduits full of wires, plumbing, and galvanized steel ductwork. Contrary to popular opinion, the air ducts weren't remotely large enough for a thief to sneak inside and crawl along, no matter what any popular TV show or movie might otherwise suggest.

"Alright," said Natalia as she shoved the hatch back into place. "I'm in."

"You've got the blueprints on your phone?" asked Diego.

She pulled her phone from her pocket and brought them up. "I do. Might take me a moment before I get to the right conduit. I won't be able to move quickly."

"Take your time," said Diego. "We're in no rush."

"Speak for yerself, mate," said Eddie. "It's so Mindy up 'ere, I'm freezin' me bollocks off."

"You don't have to say at the top of the pole, Eddie," said Miriam. "If the tap is in place, you're welcome to come down."

"And what if somefin' needs adjustin', eh? Or what if 'is 'ere bloody wind blows the tap plum off? What 'en? 'S'not as if I can shimmy back up 'is dog pole right quick, not with 'ese soddin' crampons on, or wha'ever you call 'em."

"I think those are just called pole climbing shoes," said Miriam.

Natalia ignored their banter as she pawed her way, catlike, across the crawl space. It had been a while since she'd found herself trapped in a tight space, but there was something strangely comforting about the sensation. It wasn't so much the tightness or the darkness of the space she appreciated but the isolation. So long as she didn't make a racket, no one would interrupt her. No one would bother her. No one would intrude upon her. It was in moments like this that she truly felt free, even if she might be physically confined.

She'd need every ounce of that freedom for what was to come.

Diego spoke in her ear. "Are you getting close?"

"I think so." Natalia consulted her phone again. With nothing to orient herself with but the ductwork, it was a challenge to get her bearings, but she'd gained experience doing so in tighter spaces. "Okay... A little to the west. That duct leads to the Dahl exhibit. The security offices are to the north, so that means..."

Natalia padded along further. She checked her phone again. She thought she might've gone too far, but as she reoriented herself she saw it. A thin grey tube running along the underside of the sub-flooring above her.

Natalia smiled. "Got you."

"You found it?" asked Diego.

"Pretty sure. Now there's the question of access." Natalia followed the tube to the nearest connection point. She loosened the fitting, trying to see if she could get the two pieces apart, but there wasn't enough play. With a multitool from her backpack, she loosened the fasteners that kept the conduit in place. That created more play in the tubes, and she was able to spread them an inch apart. A series of wires resided inside. Using a small hook from her bag, Natalia snagged the wire coated in green plastic. Luckily, there was enough slack in the line that when she tugged, she was able to tease the wire out of the gap.

"Any success?" asked Diego.

Natalia wished he'd stay quiet. This was *her* time, where she was supposed to be alone with her work, but she told herself he was just doing his job as team leader. "I'm about to install the device in a minute or two."

"Great," he said. "Miriam. Is everything set with the call routing software?"

"Yes," Miriam said, "but it's going to take them a while before they reach out. They're going to try and resolve the problem themselves, first."

"Just making sure we're set," said Diego. "Whenever you're ready, Natalia."

Natalia reached into her bag and extracted the device Miriam had constructed. It was a simple thing, basically an alligator clip attached to a couple loops of conductive wire. What made it special was the rotary motor, wirelessly-controlled and battery-operated, which drove a tiny conductive paddle that vibrated between the two loops. When on one side, the signal from *The Scream's* contact sensor would travel to the alarm, and on the other, it would bypass it entirely, though the alarm would still think it was connected.

Natalia took a pair of wire strippers and a scalpel from her backpack. Without making contact with the conductive wire underneath, she cut two slits into the green plastic casing, then sliced it crosswise with the scalpel and peeled it off. She hadn't heard any alarms yet, but she wasn't entirely sure she'd be able to through the flooring. Diego and the others would've notified her if anything happened, though.

With the wire exposed, Natalia opened the app that Miriam had coded. As soon as she tapped it, the motor would start vibrating intermittently, and once attached to the wire, it would make it seem as if the connection was loose.

Natalia's finger hovered over the app as she held the device in her other hand. "Here goes nothing."

She attached the clip to the wire and simultaneously tapped the app. Almost immediately, she heard the clanging of an alarm. It was muffled by the flooring overhead, but she could hear it nonetheless. It clanged for a second or two, then stopped as the motor shut off. Then it started up again and stopped just as suddenly.

"Oh, man, this is working like a charm," said Miriam. "People look super confused in the security cameras. And... yup. A couple nearby guards are on their walkie-talkies. They're booking it to *The Scream*. Give me a second." Miriam laughed, the sound pealing in Natalia's earpiece. "Oh, this is great. They looked terrified a moment ago, and now they're super confused. Nobody near the painting has any idea what's going on. Neither do the guards. They're on their two-ways again."

Above her, Natalia could hear the intermittent peal of the alarm.

"Perfect," said Diego. "We'll have to see if they evacuate the entire museum or just the *Scream* exhibit. I imagine they'll have someone take a look at the sensors on the display as well. Either way, now we wait."

Natalia peered into her backpack, which was filled with a variety of other tools and devices the purpose of which she hadn't deigned to share with the crew. While it might be time for Diego to sit back and wait, she'd just gotten started.

Her voice felt thick in her throat as she spoke. "Yes. Now we wait."

Natalia cinched the bag shut, looped it over her shoulder, and after a glance at her phone to orient herself, she set back out, padding across the steel girders as if she were a monkey on a branch. Somewhere above her, muffled by sub-flooring and foam pads and the wooden floors above, the alarm continued to blare, only for a second to a second and a half at a time. Probably the hardest part of engineering Miriam's device was coding it to run for random intervals of time, something that was beyond Natalia's expertise but which Miriam didn't seem to think was any big deal.

Only about thirty seconds had passed before Diego spoke again. "You know, given that we don't know how long it'll take for security to call the problem in, this might be a good time to continue a certain story that's been on hold for a couple days."

Miriam groaned. "Oh, for Christ's sake, Diego. Nobody wants to hear your bullshit made up yarns about your old jobs or whatever."

"'S true, D. The wind's torture enough up on 'is bloody pole."

"For one thing," said Diego, "every part of the story I'm about to tell is one hundred percent true, something I've made clear to Natalia already. For another, I know for a fact Natalia is interested in hearing these stories, because she's made a point of asking me to continue them in the past."

That was true. Natalia *had* asked Diego to continue his stories. Almost begged him at one point, but that was before she'd slept with him. Before she'd stopped to consider the consequences of her actions. To let him continue to tell them, to lead him on in such a fashion as she actively worked to screw him over was vicious. Heinous. *Cruel.*

But Natalia had a lot of work to do, and it wasn't clear how much time she had available to her. If she turned Diego down now, she wouldn't hear the end of it. She knew him well enough to know he'd needle and cajole her until she finally relented and allowed him to tell the story, and she couldn't handle that distraction right now. Not when she had so many more wires to locate and so many more of her own devices to install.

She tried to swallow back the growing lump in her throat, but she couldn't. It stuck in her neck like a giant mouthful of food. When she spoke, her voice was pained. "Yeah. I'd love to hear the story."

Miriam groaned again, but Diego cut her off. "Don't worry. I have the perfect solution, Miriam. You see, since I'm the one in the command center—"

"Van," said Eddie.

"—I'm perfectly capable of temporarily removing you and Eddie from the comms." Natalia's earpiece crackled. "There we go. Just you and me now, Natalia."

She blinked. "You took Miriam and Eddie off? Is that wise?"

"I split them onto their own separate channel," said Diego. "I can splice them back in whenever I need to, or send them a text message. There won't be any need to communicate until the security office makes the call, anyway."

Somehow, the lump in Natalia's throat grew even thicker. "So it's just you and me, then."

Diego's voice had a light, cheery quality to it that made Natalia feel like an even greater monster. "Indeed. Now, let's see. Where was I..."

Interlude 5

OR THE TALE OF THE TEN DEADLY TRIALS

When last I left off, I'd just stolen Señor de la Paz's family signet ring from Principal Rosales's office, but I have to admit, I left myself in a precarious state. Because even though I'd obtained the ring, I was still shirtless, sweaty, and covered with cobwebs, engine grease, and soot from the tunnels underneath the school. The assembly was ongoing, but I had to assume it wouldn't be for long. More of an issue than the hundreds of students in the gymnasium pouring back into the school, however, was the fact that I needed to return the ring to Señor de la Paz before the parent teacher assembly that evening.

Now while I'd implied to de la Paz's son Hernando that I'd return the ring to him so he could return it to his father, I never explicitly promised that, just that I would make sure the ring was returned. In all honesty, I'd never intended to let Hernando take credit for the score. The ring was my ticket into Señor de la Paz's sordid, illicit, and thoroughly enticing world, and I wasn't about to throw it away.

With the ring gripped tight in hand, I took off, blasting through the school's front doors and turning down Camino Suárez in the direction of my parent's house. I must've looked quite the lunatic, a shirtless, dirty youth tearing down the street at full speed with a look of unbridled satisfaction on my face. I can't say it's the fastest I've ever run—there was an incident with a Bengal tiger that occurred a few years ago that probably takes the crown—but it's certainly the fastest I've ever moved for a sustained period. When I finally arrived at my house, my lungs were working like a bellows. Sweat poured down my body, plastering my hair to my brow and my pants to my legs. My parents weren't yet home and wouldn't be for another hour, so I didn't have to explain myself as I rushed upstairs and turned the shower on full blast, all cold water of course. I stripped my sodden clothing off and jumped in the frigid cascade, and after a couple minutes of that, the heat I'd generated during my run had wicked clean off. I scrubbed myself thoroughly, wiping every ounce of grime off me before hopping out, drying off, and combing my hair. I pulled my Sunday best from my closet—I'm not particularly religious, but my parents are devout Catholics—and dressed myself quickly. After checking myself in the mirror, I tucked the signet ring in the bottom of my pocket and headed downstairs to the garage.

I wish I could say I drove something eye-catching to Señor de la Paz's estate, something that was worthy of the treasure I brought him, perhaps a sleek 1954 Pegaso Z-102 coupe, but—

And here I thought you weren't a car guy...

Well, I'm not really, but a good story is entirely in the details. The point is, we didn't have a Pegaso Z-102. We didn't have a second car at all. We only had one, a bland, boxy Opel my father drove to work and used to drop my mother off at her job along the way. So the only option available to me other than taking public transportation, which would've taken far too long, was to ride my bike.

Now I know what you're thinking. Here I am in my best suit riding across town to Señor de la Paz's estate with the signet ring in my pocket. Any number of things could've gone wrong. The ring could've jumped out of my pocket as I hit a bump in the road. The fine cloth of my pants could've caught in my bicycle's gears and torn. I could've drenched myself in sweat, defeating the purpose of the shower I'd taken. But none of those things happened. That isn't where this particular story acquires its conflict. Suffice to say, I didn't push the pace, and I arrived at de la Paz's mansion safe and in a presentable condition at what I deemed was at least an hour shy of the moment he'd leave for the school. I ditched my bike in the bushes at the street and made my way to the front of the house on foot.

And what a house it was. Picture a fine Spanish villa with lush, manicured shrubs. A wide brick driveway that curves around a central fountain. Stucco walls, terra cotta tiles, Moorish arches, and decorative mosaics. Señor de la Paz's abode had all that and more. I'd seen it before in passing, but as I walked along the brick walkway, it struck me just how wealthy the Señor was. I should've been intimated, but for perhaps the first time in my life, I wasn't. I had the man's ring in my pocket, and I'd just pulled off the heist of the century, even if it had gone a little sideways. I felt excellent about my chances to ingratiate myself to the man, and from there, who knew where life would take me?

I arrived at the door. There was no doorbell to speak of, but there was an enormous cast iron knocker shaped like a lion, so I grabbed it and gave it three solid raps. It didn't take but fifteen seconds for the door to open. Though I'd expected a butler, the man who greeted me was rougher around the edges than that. He was broad in the shoulders and swarthy, with a three day old beard. He stared at me, a mite of curiosity working into his eyebrows. "Can I help you?"

Call it youthful ignorance, but my confidence didn't waver. "Yes. My name is Diego Cabrera. I'm here to see Señor de la Paz."

"Are you now?" said the man. "Do you have an appointment?"

"I do not," I admitted.

"And what makes you think Don de la Paz would be interested in meeting with you?"

"Because I am the future of his organization, and I'm going to make him so much money that he won't know what to do with it."

A smile spread across the big man's face, and he bust out in a jovial laugh. When his mirth faded he tipped his head to me and said, "Well, you're a cheeky little bastard, I'll give you that. Are you one of Hernando's friends?"

I shook my head. "If anything, I'm more of a rival."

The big man nodded. "That fits. Most of Hernando's friends are witless cronies who couldn't tell you how many fingers are on their own hands. They certainly don't have the moxie you do. Well, go on. Spread your arms and legs."

That was the first thing that caught me off guard. "Pardon?"

The man looked at me as if some of his esteem had bled away. "So I can check you for weapons?"

"Oh. Of course."

I did as the man asked. He patted me down, and when he was satisfied I wasn't hiding a pistol or a knife underneath my jacket, he waved me in. The home was even more beautiful on the inside than the out, but I won't bore you with the details. You can imagine them for yourself. What matters is the big man led me through a series of open hallways before eventually stopping at an enormous pair of wooden doors inlaid with hand-carved designs. He knocked, and when a voice responded, muffled by the doors, he poked his head in. "Don de la Paz. There's a young man here to see you."

I couldn't hear the Don's response, but I did hear the big man's reply. "Yes, I know, but he's making outlandish claims, and there's a certain moxie to him I admire. I thought I would bring him to you."

There was more discussion. The big man pulled his head back, opened the door further, and waved me in. "He's giving you five minutes. Don't waste his time."

I stepped into Señor de la Paz's office. The place was full of dark wood, black leather, and heavy curtains. A quiet tension hung in the air, thick as fog, as well as the unmistakable scent of cigar smoke. De la Paz sat behind a massive desk, a man with slicked back graying hair and sunken eyes. His cigar glowed orange as he inhaled, then died down as he pulled it from his lips and exhaled, spewing a purplish smoke into the air.

"So," he spoke is a soft, gravelly voice. "You're here to change my life, are you boy?"

Soft? Gravelly? Oh, for crying out loud, don't make him the Godfather.

The Godfather? Absolutely not. Señor de la Paz was nothing like Marlon Brando's character. For one thing, his voice was soft, not breathy or strained like Brando's. For another, de la Paz was hard as a rock. Lean in body, mind, and spirit. He was focused, intense, and sharp as a tack despite his years. He didn't speak the way he did as a way to intimidate. It was simply that he knew when he spoke people were listening, so he had no need to exert himself to make his voice carry.

I sat at one of the two chairs in front of his desk, my confidence starting to waver, but I held my head high regardless. "Yes, Señor. At least, that's my hope."

The Don took another drag from his cigar. "So you push your way into my presence, a proclaimed enemy of my son, making wild claims and bearing no gifts. What am I to make of you?"

A lightbulb appeared over me. "Actually, I do come bearing a gift, Señor. One I think you'll be happy to have returned."

I dug into my pocket and produced his signet ring. I reached over and placed it on the desk in front of him before sitting back down.

De la Paz's brow furrowed as he picked it up. He stared at it for a long moment before turning his cold eyes onto me. "I have a question, and think carefully before you answer, young man. How exactly has this ring come into your possession?"

And so I told him. I told him the whole tale just as I've told you, without embellishment, from when I saw Hernando flashing the ring to the point at which I stood in Principal Rosales's office. At first, de la Paz was dubious of my story, but as I went along, the sheer conviction with which I told it convinced him. When finally I finished my tale, he sat in his chair for a long moment, smoking his cigar and staring at the ring.

Eventually, he affixed me with that cold gaze of his again. "Assuming this is true, son, what is it you hope to gain by returning it to me? Money?"

I shook my head. "No, Señor. I don't wish for a reward of any kind, just an opportunity."

"What kind of opportunity?" asked de la Paz.

"The opportunity to learn at your side," I said. "The opportunity to show you that what I've done today is no fluke, and that I'm capable of much more. Of daring heists and lucrative robberies. That I can bend people to my will and wrap them around my finger. I promise you I can do all this and more, if only I'm given a chance."

If anything, de la Paz's eyes grew colder. His body even harder. He took one last drag of his cigar before leaning forward in his chair. He pointed at me with a bony finger, and I'll never forget the words he said to me. He said—

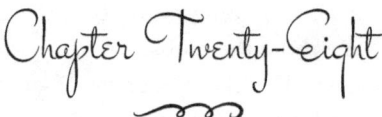

Chapter Twenty-Eight

A TRILL SOUNDED IN DIEGO EAR, AND HE SAT UP straighter in his chair. "Hold on a second. I think this is the security office calling."

A number of monitors were built into the side of the van in front of him. Most of them were occupied with museum security camera footage, but one of them was dedicated to monitoring information being fed to the van through Eddie's tap. Diego checked the number to make sure it was the one he expected before answering.

"FTS Security Services, customer service division. How may I help you?"

A youthful voice responded in a musical gait. "Yes, this is Einar Jacobsen at the National Museum of Oslo. We're having a problem with one of your alarms."

"I'm sorry to hear that," said Diego. "Before we proceed, is there an imminent security risk? Is the location secure and have police been alerted, if necessary?"

"It's not that sort of problem, thankfully," said Einar. "More of a glitch, really."

"I see," said Diego. "What's the model of the alarm you're having issues with?"

"Let me check." Diego heard Einar tapping at a keyboard on the other end of the line. "It's a T Four Thirty contact sensor, from the Sterling line."

"Give me one moment while I bring up the documentation," said Diego, even though he was doing nothing of the sort. "While I do that, could you tell me about the problem?"

"Sure," said Einar. "The alarm is going off intermittently, for a second or two at a time before turning back off. It seems as if perhaps there's a loose connection."

"Hmm," said Diego. "The T Four Thirty is installed at the point of display. Have you checked to make sure the display case is firmly in place?"

"Yes," said Einar. "Nothing is loose."

"What about the resistance through the display? Has that been affected?"

"I'm sorry, *resistance?*" said Einar. "Do you mean electrical resistance?"

"Yes," said Diego. "Has the display case been cracked or broken?"

"Nothing of that nature," said Einar. "Nobody has even touched the display. We've checked our video logs to confirm. The alarm just started going off on its own."

Diego hummed again. "That *is* odd. Has anyone inspected the actual alarm yet?"

"Yes, we've taken a look. We thought perhaps a wire was loose, but everything seems to be connected securely."

"What about the battery pack?" asked Diego. "Was there any corrosion to speak of?"

"No, none."

"Well, that's good, but I have to admit I'm running short on ideas. We may have to send a technician to help address the problem."

"How long will that take?"

"Let me check." Diego clacked his keyboard loudly, inputting a bunch of random gibberish on the keys. "We do have an authorized technician in Oslo. I can get them there in twenty to twenty-five minutes."

Einar sighed with relief. "That would be appreciated."

"I'll send them straight away," said Diego. "In the meantime, would you like me to walk you through how to disable the alarm? In case the sound is bothering you?"

"No, it's fine," said Einar. "We've cleared the second floor where we host the exhibit. Because the alarm is intermittent, it isn't overwhelming. If the technician will arrive within a half hour, I think we'll simply wait."

"I understand," said Diego. "The good thing is I've gotten confirmation the technician has received the maintenance request and they're on their way. Is there anything else I can help you with while I'm on the line?"

"Not at the moment," said Einar. "Thank you."

"Of course. Once again, I'm terribly sorry for the inconvenience, and we'll have that technician there as quickly as we can. Thank you for using FTS Security."

Diego hung up. He went back into the controls for the comms and reactivated Miriam and Eddie. "Good news, Miriam. You're officially en route to the museum."

"Yeah, I got it, jackass," said Miriam. "No thanks to you."

"You don't need to be so snippy," said Diego. "I figured you'd be listening to the call, and you were. Would you rather I'd left you on the comms while I regaled Natalia with tales of my youth?"

Miriam snorted. "It's the principle of the thing, Diego. That said, feel free to remove me from the comms again whenever you're ready to keep spouting your bullshit. I can handle things from here."

"Does 'at mean I can get down 'is bloody dog pole, now?" said Eddie.

"For Christ's sake, Eddie," said Miriam. "How many times did I tell you to come wait in the car with me? Yes, you can come down."

"But not to the jam jar," said Eddie. "You'll be 'eadin' to the gallery, soon."

"Correct. Not anymore. You missed your chance to spend some time with me, big guy. Better hope there's a next time."

"Alright," said Diego. "I'm going to put you two back on a separate channel unless there's something pressing that needs addressing. No? Perfect." Diego tapped a few keys on the board in front of him. "That should do it. Just you and me again, Natalia. Now, where was I? Oh, right. Señor de la Paz was about to tell me something that was going to change my life *forever.*"

Diego imagined Natalia waiting with bated breath for the rest of his story, but her anticipation must've been enormous for her to remain so thoroughly silent. Come to think of it, Natalia hadn't said anything in a while.

"Natalia? Did I lose you?" Diego checked his control panel. The system claimed he was still on the same band she was.

Diego had already pulled up a troubleshooting panel when finally Natalia spoke in his ear. Her voice was breathy and strained, almost as if she was in pain. "I'm here, Diego."

A wave of relief washed through him, not just at the prospect of not having lost Natalia from the line—Miriam would've given him hell if he'd screwed up something as simple as managing the comms— but at the sound of her voice. He'd gotten used to it. Having it suddenly gone felt as if a piece of him had been snatched away.

"Oh, good," said Diego. "Is everything all right? They only evacuated the second floor, so you're clear to sneak out if you'd like. Of course, if you'd rather kick back and relax in a quiet crawl space while I lavish you with my tale, I'd understand completely. I've been told I have a very soothing voice."

"Diego..." Natalia's voice cracked. "I can't. I just... I can't do this."

"Do what?" asked Diego. "Are you having a panic attack? God, you're not claustrophobic are you? You have to tell me these sorts of things."

Natalia's voice came back angry but still thick with pain. "I'm not claustrophobic, Diego. I just... *I can't do this.* I can't listen to these ridiculous stories of yours any longer. *Fuck!*"

Ridiculous? Diego felt as if a hot knife had been thrust into his belly. His stories were an integral part of who he was, an integral part of the persona he'd built for himself. Were they embellished and inflated? Sure, and if Natalia had asked him to dial back his flair for the dramatic, that would be one thing. But to call them *ridiculous?* That was an assault not only on the person he'd become but to his intellect, his wit, his fundamental sense of creativity. It was an insult of the highest degree.

But that wasn't what made Diego's pulse race. He'd seen it from the beginning. The shield Natalia carried in front of herself, trying to protect her vulnerable core from even being seen much less intruded upon. The nervousness with which she viewed the world, hidden though it was under a veneer of competence and professionalism. From the beginning she'd reminded Diego of a bird on a thin branch, ready to take flight at the slightest sign of trouble, and his stories had been what had kept her from flying. He was Scheherazade in *One Thousand and One Nights,* and the sultan had finally tired of his tale.

Diego swallowed back the lump in his throat. "Natalia, I haven't told you about the ten deadly trials yet. Not even *one* of them. What's going on? You can talk to me."

"I..." Natalia sighed, heavily enough that her microphone picked it up. "I can't. I'm sorry, Diego. I'm sorry..."

"Natalia, whatever this is, we can figure it out. Just talk to me."

Silence.

"Natalia? *Natalia?*"

Still nothing.

"Shit." Diego switched his attention to the monitors that showed security camera footage from inside the museum. He checked camera thirteen first, but Natalia wasn't on it. Nor was she on any of the cameras in the nearby galleries and hallways. Damnit, where was she?

As it turned out, Diego had been too quick on the draw. After a minute, she appeared on camera thirteen, sneaking out of the maintenance closet. She took a quick look around to make sure no one had noticed her, then headed for the exit. She started at a brisk walk, but with each step she took, her gait increased, turning into a jog as she approached the lobby.

She was running. She was *literally* running out of Diego's life— just as he'd feared she always would.

Chapter Twenty-Nine

NATALIA WALKED BRISKLY ALONG THE DOWNTOWN OSLO avenue, not entirely sure where she was going. She'd broken into a brisk jog at one point, on the verge of entering into a full-fledged run, but she'd forced herself to slow. Even though she was dressed in running attire, it wasn't the time of day when many other runners were out, nor did many have sling bags across their shoulders, and Natalia didn't want to attract attention. Even though her heart screamed at her to bolt in any direction until her lungs burned and her heart hammered like a drum inside her chest, to keep running and never look back, her mind refused to let her. She still had her wits about her, and they reminded her she was a thief first and foremost. She had to keep up appearances, even when it was nigh impossible to do so.

Natalia truly believed she'd be able to until she heard the squeal of brakes at her side, followed by the call of a familiar voice. "Natalia! *Natalia!*"

Natalia's heart sank as she turned toward the street. Driving slowly beside her was Diego, the windows on the van rolled down. He leaned across the console in her direction, his face wracked with worry.

Natalia groaned and shook her head. "Oh, for God's sake. Don't you know when to leave a woman alone?"

"What's going on?" asked Diego. "Did you throw away your earpiece?"

Natalia looked up and down the street. No one was staring at them—yet—but they would if this went on for long. "Would you stop following me in that unmarked van? It looks like you're going to kidnap me."

Natalia picked up her pace, hoping to lose him even though she knew it was impossible. Even with her focus elsewhere, she heard the rumble of the engine, the squeal of tires on asphalt again, followed by the slap of shoes against pavement. "Natalia! Wait!"

Natalia turned to see the van parked haphazardly on the side of the street. Diego rushed toward her, his suit jacket flapping in the breeze. Natalia groaned, rolled her eyes, and increased her pace yet again.

"Hey! Would you please slow down for a moment!"

Natalia felt Diego's strong hand close on her upper arm, forcing her to stop. Part of her wanted to shake him off and give him a hard shove for good measure, but another part of her wanted anything but. A part of her wanted to let herself be pulled back, to fold into his arms and bury her face in his chest and cry or scream or maybe do a little of both.

Instead, she stood there, staring at Diego as he held her. "What do you want?"

"I just want to talk," said Diego. "I don't understand what's going on."

"What's going on is I'm upset, and I want to be by myself, so please let go."

Diego didn't. "I can see you're upset, but that doesn't explain why. What did I do? What's eating you?"

What was eating her was the realization that she was a cold, heartless bitch who cared for no one but herself. The realization that she was absolutely, *definitely* going to screw Diego over now. She'd always known she would, from the moment she got his initial message about coming to Oslo to steal *The Scream,* but that had been a theoretical betrayal. A future screwing. Now, with the devices from her once overloaded sling bag fully in place, it was set in stone. She *was* going to betray him, and Miriam and Eddie, too. Maybe Diego deserved it. He tricked people for a living. Left them holding the bag, time after time. What did he honestly think would happen if he worked alongside people like himself for long enough? Of course someone would betray him. Why shouldn't it be her?

But Natalia knew the answer to that. Because they'd connected on a fundamental level. It was more than the sex. People betrayed each other after sex all the time. Maybe that's why they called it screwing. But she and Diego had shared something special. Something meaningful and genuine. It wasn't the aching desire between her legs that confirmed it, but the yawning, black pit where her stomach was supposed to be, the gaping maw that nearly swallowed her whole. Every time she was in Diego's presence the sensation accosted her, now more than ever. Even the sound of his voice in her ear wracked her with guilt, because she knew Diego didn't deserve what she was doing to him.

But she was going to do it anyway.

"I just..." Natalia needed to push him away, for good this time, but her brain wasn't working properly. Diego still hadn't let go of her arm. She could feel the heat of his body, feel the intensity of his gaze, smell that familiar, woodsy musk that had intensified since the last time she smelled it, maybe because he'd worked up a bit of a sweat chasing her. What could she tell him? What could she say that would really hurt him, make him turn away and never look back? "I can't keep listening to your stories. They're insipid and bland and boring."

Diego's hand snapped open, as did his eyes. *"What?"*

"You heard me," said Natalia as she wrapped herself in a hug. Her fingers trailed along her own arm, over the spot where Diego had touched her. "They're trash, and I don't want to hear them anymore."

Diego's brow furrowed, and his eyelashes shaded his eyes. "Don't do this."

"Do what?" said Natalia.

"Lie to me about this," said Diego. "You can lie about anything else. I've been lying to you about any number of things. It's who I am. You know it and I know it, and it's only fair you return the favor every now and then. And it's fine. I like it. This back and forth we've got. It's fun and flirty and... it feels real, even though it's false. But don't lie to me about hating my stories. Not when I've worked so hard on crafting them."

"So you admit they're all a pack of lies."

"Of course they are," said Diego. "But they're a pack of lies I spun for *you.* Because I could see the way your face lit up when I started spinning them. I could feel the weight of your interest hanging on my every word. I could see the desire in your eyes every time I left you hanging from the edge of a cliff and telling you I'd finish the story later. Don't deny it."

Natalia gritted her teeth. "Well, I do deny it. I never cared for any of them."

Diego cocked his head, sadness growing in his eyes. "Be honest with me. What happened? What changed?"

The look on Diego's face, like that of a wounded dog, made her stomach cramp all the harder, but she had to keep going. "What changed is I got tired of you being false. Being fake. Can't you be genuine for once?"

Diego took a step back, as if he'd been rocked with a heavyweight punch. Natalia had hit a weak spot. *Good.* She hated herself for going there, hated herself with the fire of ten thousand burning suns, but she had to. She had no choice.

Diego's body sagged, and his head hung toward the ground. "You don't understand what you're asking. There aren't many genuine parts of me worth sharing. That are worth... *liking.* The parts that I've shared? Those are the good parts. The exciting parts. The intriguing parts."

"Well, maybe I don't want to hear the good parts. Maybe I don't deserve the good parts." Natalia hadn't meant to say that. It just slipped out, but there it was. An admission of her own self-worth.

Diego's brow furrowed again. "Is that what this is about? You think you're somehow undeserving of... what? Care? Compassion? *Love?*"

You're god-damned right I'm undeserving of love, she wanted to scream, *especially after everything I've done and plan to do to you!* But she couldn't say it. She couldn't tell him, no matter how much it hurt.

"You wouldn't understand, Diego," she said with as much ire as she could muster. "I've been through things. Bad things. I didn't grow up with a loving family who had beautiful talents and who loved me dearly. Unlike you, I've been hurt."

Diego scoffed. "You think you're the only one who's ever been hurt? I just admitted to you the stories about my childhood are all lies. Why do you think I'd tell those instead of the truth? Because the reality was *too good?* Give me a break. You don't know the first thing about me!"

Natalia's heart felt as if it was tearing in two. Her lungs burned as if she'd just finished a ten kilometer run. Her fingertips tingled, and that voice inside her that normally advocated for caution screamed at her to stop. But she pushed on. "I know you haven't been hurt the way I was. That you didn't have to look out for yourself the way I've had to. That you had support along the way. From friends, from family. I know that whatever lies you spin to hide your failings are just that. A shroud of bullshit to keep from having to look at the real you. The you that you don't seem to like, and you only have yourself to blame for that."

Diego's jaw snapped shut with a clack. He shook his head and looked away. "Wow. *Wow.* You are something else, you know that?"

Natalia wanted to say something. She wanted to admit it was all a lie. That she didn't mean anything she'd said, that she'd only done it to hurt him and push him further away, but she couldn't. Her mouth was shut tight as if it had been glued. Her lips wouldn't have moved no matter how hard she tried, and she knew because she *did* try. She needed to spout more hatred and vitriol to seal the deal, but she couldn't do that, either. She'd spewed every last ounce of her spite and anger, leaving nothing left inside. She was an empty husk. One big aching stomach pit, nothing but pain and fear and loneliness on spindly legs.

Diego took a few steps toward the van before he stopped and turned. In that brief moment, Natalia's heart soared, but the look on Diego's face wasn't one of reconciliation or hope. It was one of realization. Of recognition. Of disappointment.

"You know, when you told me you work alone, live alone, do everything alone? I should've known. Because there's always a constant with people who are perpetually alone. It's them. *You're* the constant in the empty void around you, Natalia. You want to tell *me* that I only have myself to blame for who I am? Take a long hard look in the mirror."

With that, Diego turned away. He didn't look back as he crossed to the van. He didn't look back as he cranked the engine to life and pulled away, either. Throughout all of it, Natalia remained rooted in place, wallowing in her wretchedness and guilt, still hugging herself so tight that she thought she might break. Only once Diego had gone did she allow a tormented sob to escape her chest. Her hand rose to her breast, massaging the muscles in an effort to help her breathe. It was only then that she noticed the thin wet trails along her neck. She followed them to her jaw, then her cheeks. She tried to wipe them away, but they kept flowing, streaming down her face as the sobs grew fiercer.

Apparently, she'd been wrong. She wasn't empty after all. It was simply that all that was left was sorrow.

Chapter Thirty

NATALIA WASN'T SURE HOW LONG SHE WALKED BECAUSE the normal indicators that might've given her some clue didn't function properly. If her stomach growled from hunger, what was that next to the aching pit that already resided there? If her feet hurt from overuse, what was that next to the pain that ripped at her heart and the sorrow that lay over her like a mantle? All she knew was that she walked, and she cried. She walked in a single direction for all far as she could, until she reached the water's edge. Even then, she wasn't done walking, so she let the geography of the coast dictate her path. The wind whipped off the water, chilling her more thoroughly than any day since she'd arrived in Oslo, but even that didn't bother her. After all, what was nature's feeble attempt at a chill compared to the icy cold inside her?

As she walked, all she could think about was Diego. Those dark, mysterious eyes of his. The little dimples that appeared in his cheeks when he smiled, visible through his several day old beard. The smooth line of his nose, the curve of his jaw. Mostly, she thought about the look he'd given her as he'd walked away, that look of complete, profound, and utter disappointment. It would've been easier if he'd yelled at her. If he'd screamed and lifted his hand before thinking twice and pulling it away. At least that she could've understood, but that *look?* Natalia had never had a father figure in her life, but it was true what all those books and movies depicted. It was so much worse when someone you cared about told you they weren't angry, just disappointed.

The worst part was that it was entirely her fault. She'd intended to go for a swim and ended up diving to the depths of the ocean. If she'd never let Diego in in the first place, she wouldn't have had to push him away, certainly not as hard as she had. But she'd been weak. Helpless against his charms. It wasn't just the longing looks he'd given her, the ones that made her feel as if she was more than a scrawny thief without any semblance of family or friends. It wasn't just the elaborate stories he told her, which she *did* love, damnit all. It was the way he'd confided in her. When she'd stood in his arms on the ballroom floor of the Hotel Maximillian, when she'd asked him to tell her the truth for once.

And he had.

It had been so hard for him. She'd seen the pain it had put him in to reveal that true slice of himself, but he'd done it for her. *Just for her,* all because she'd asked. And knowing he was willing to go to those lengths for her, lengths he wouldn't attempt for anyone else? Well, she'd just about melted in his arms. She'd never stood a chance after that.

And yet she'd pushed him away. She'd done more than pushed. She'd ripped and torn and stomped because she needed the message to stick, none of which she would've had to do if she'd stayed at arm's length in the first place.

Another sob escaped Natalia's lungs as she thought about what she'd done, but she couldn't change it now. Besides, the split had needed to be made. She tilted her head toward the breeze coming off the water, dragging a thumb across her cheeks to wipe away her tears, but for once her thumb came back dry. It wasn't for lack of sorrow that she'd finally stopped crying, but perhaps her body's reserves had run dry.

As she tilted her head up, she found herself standing in front of an eye-catching contemporary building with lots of glass and concrete fitted together at strange angles. She would've recognized it as the Oslo Opera House even without the letters *OPERAEN* that hung over the entrance. And if she was near the opera house, that meant the Munch Museum was right around the corner.

Natalia picked up her pace, catching sight of the off-kilter thirteen story museum as she cleared the bulk of the opera house. It was odd that such a large building would be dedicated to a single artist, especially given that some of Munch's most famous works were on display at the National Gallery, but Munch had been incredibly prolific. By some estimates, he'd created over seventy-five hundred drawings and close to nineteen hundred paintings, rivaling even the great Pablo Picasso in terms of productivity.

With everything else she'd had going on, Natalia hadn't found the opportunity to visit the museum yet. Was it chance that brought her to its door, or something else?

Natalia crossed the remaining stretch of wharf between herself and the museum and pushed through the front doors. There were shops and a café in the lobby, but she stopped by the cloakroom first to put her sling bag in one of the lockers. As she did so, she purchased a ticket on her phone before heading up the elevators to the fourth floor to what the museum called the Munch Infinite exhibit. There, Munch's most famous works were on display, but there was only one she wanted to see. Natalia wandered the floor until she found it: the gallery that contained *The Scream*.

The Munch Museum actually had eight versions of the painting in their collection: the pastel preliminary study from 1893, the second painted version of *The Scream* from 1910, and six copies of the original lithograph. The museum rotated which version was on display, as the pastel and painted versions were prone to deterioration due to exposure to light, all because of Munch's choice to paint on inexpensive cardboard rather than canvas. Thankfully, it was the painted version on display today. The lithographs didn't speak to her the same way the originals did.

A number of people stood in the gallery, drawn to the painting the same way Natalia was, so she settled beside them and gazed upon the work.

This was why she was in Oslo. Not this specific iteration of the painting. Obviously, she was going to steal the more valuable original from the National Gallery, but it was this work, this expression of the human experience that had drawn her across borders to chilly Norway. *The Scream's* enigmatic protagonist, free of gender or race or class, expressed the sorrow and angst that lived inside everyone, especially in Natalia. So many times she'd felt like the individual in the painting, alone, desperate, wanting to scream, *to be heard,* but unable to find the voice with which to do so. There were times when she wanted little else than to scream.

Until she'd met Diego. With him, there were so many more emotions that roiled inside her. There were the funny ones, the silly ones, the ones that made her want to needle and prod him, to joke and jest and snicker and leer. Then there were the heartfelt ones, the tender emotions as he'd held his arm out for her to hold, as he'd pressed her body against his on the dance floor, and the more physical needs and desires they'd expressed in bed. And there were plenty of raw and painful emotions, too, including the desire to scream. She'd wanted to cry out as he'd roared off in the van, even though it was only a tortured sob that escaped her breast, but mostly she'd wanted to cry.

Was crying better than screaming? It had to be, didn't it? A scream was born of rage, of hopelessness, of invisibility, but a sob? A sob was a product of loss. It meant that even though your life was miserable and wretched now, it hadn't always been. Once upon a time there had been light and love and laughter, and wasn't that better than never having any of that at all? 'Tis better to have loved and lost than never to have loved at all, wrote Alfred Tennyson. It seemed logical to believe him, even if the truth of his statement escaped Natalia at the moment. Because for her, right now, the loss of Diego was still too fresh, too raw. As it stood right now, she would've rather never loved at all.

Never loved. No. That wasn't right. Lust, maybe. Attraction, sure, but she'd only met Diego a few days ago. She didn't love him. She wasn't even sure she knew what love was. It wasn't an emotion she had a lot of experience with, but even with her limited knowledge of the subject matter, she could state with confidence that she didn't love him. Love was for people who were caring and tender, people who shared and compromised, people who were truthful and trusting in one another. She wasn't *in love.*

Right?

Natalia's phone buzzed, which elicited a judgmental look from the middle-aged gentleman who stood beside her. Natalia cast a final look at the painting before retreating to a less occupied hallway. She pulled out her phone to find she had a text message, from Diego of all people. It read, very simply:

We need to talk.

Natalia punched in her response.

I don't know what else there is to say.

Circles appeared under her message, indicating Diego was typing. Soon:

Not about us. About the job. Everything is in place for tomorrow, but we need to know you're in the right frame of mind to continue. Can you meet me, Eddie, and Miriam at the loft in an hour?

Natalia took a shuddering breath and batted away a tear as she typed.

You don't need to worry about me. Tomorrow, I'll do the job I came here to do. See you in an hour.

Chapter Thirty-One

⟞⟝⟞

NATALIA HAD MOSTLY PUT HERSELF BACK TOGETHER WHEN she arrived at the industrial loft, but she still wasn't prepared for the looks she got as she stepped through the front door. Eddie's face was all scrunched up as if he'd eaten a particularly sour grapefruit, Miriam looked downright angry, and Diego? Well, Diego didn't look upset at all. He wore that calm, collected look Natalia had come to associate with his grifter persona, and seeing that on him was perhaps a bigger slap than seeing him dejected and forlorn. Couldn't he be pining for her, even a little?

"Well, 'ere she is," said Eddie. "Fought we'd lost you for a bit, Natalia. What 'appened? You get a bit narked or somefin'?"

"Yeah, seriously," said Miriam, who was still wearing her technician's uniform. "What the fuck?"

Diego lifted his hands. "Everybody calm down. Natalia needed a little space, that's all. It's no surprise given how I wouldn't stop badgering her with my stories that nobody else wanted to hear. Isn't that right?" Diego shot her a raised eyebrow.

Was he... *covering for her?* Why would Diego do that, after everything she'd said to him?

Natalia exhaled as she gathered herself. "Yeah. Diego was driving me up a wall. Still, I shouldn't have run off, especially not before Miriam was done with her work on the alarms. That was unprofessional. I'm sorry."

Miriam's disgruntled look didn't go anywhere, but Eddie's face broke out in a wide grin. "Aw, it's alright. 'Eaven knows Diego's brassed us all off with 'em stories o' 'is."

"Yes, I have quite a way with words," said Diego. "That said, I'd like to have a word with Natalia before we get down to the final brass tacks, as long as that's all right with the two of you. Natalia?" He nodded toward the door.

Natalia nodded back. "Ah... sure."

Natalia followed Diego as he opened the door onto the landing outside the loft, and she was instantly swallowed by a sense of dread. Standing with him on that small landing, being mere inches from his body, smelling his gentle musk, all while he affixed her with his midnight pools? She'd break down again. Lash out and rely on instinct to keep her safe, like a wolf threatened with a cage.

But Diego surprised her. He nodded and headed down the stairs as she closed the door behind her. "Let's go for a walk."

"Yeah. Sure."

The industrial park wasn't particularly scenic, but Diego led them behind the loft to a roadside path lined with trees. The sun was falling low, ushering in more of the chill Natalia had experienced on her walk to the Munch Museum, but at least the wind had abated.

Diego slowed his gait for Natalia to join him, but he didn't say anything, nor did he look her in the eyes. He kept his gaze either in front of him or pointed toward the ground at his feet.

Natalia didn't know what to say to him—she'd already emptied her heart—but she got the impression he was waiting for her to start. "Look, Diego—"

He lifted a hand, his index finger extended. "No. Let me start, if you don't mind."

Natalia pressed her lips together. Apparently he was having a hard time organizing his thoughts. That seemed fair enough given what she'd put him through today.

Diego waited another forty-five seconds before he spoke. "First of all, I'd like to apologize."

Natalia stopped in her tracks, completely caught off guard. "What?"

Diego stopped and turned, finally looking at her. "I said I'd like to apologize."

"I heard you," said Natalia, her confusion swamping her overloaded emotions. "But I don't think... I mean, I'm not sure you're the one who should be apologizing."

"What we entered into was mutual, I think you'll agree," said Diego. "But that doesn't mean I'm not the one responsible for the outcome. I put this crew together. I'm the leader. Everything that happens under my purview falls on my shoulders, whether it has to do with the outcome of our job or the relationships that form during it. And I should've known better. I should've known better than to..."

Than to fall for me? "Than to what?"

Diego sighed. "Than to let my emotions cloud my judgement. Than to make decisions based on the way I felt rather than what was the smartest course of action. Do you know what I mean?"

Yes, she did. Lord, but she did.

"Yes," she said, her voice whisper quiet.

Diego wiped a hand across his jaw. "Don't get me wrong. I care for you. Really, I do, and I think that you... well, I suppose it doesn't matter how you feel."

The tension on Natalia's heart grew, and she could almost feel it tearing. *But I do care for you, Diego,* she thought. *God, I care so much!*

"The point is," continued Diego, "that it's in both our best interests, not to mention Eddie and Miriam's, if we set aside everything between us and focus on the work. That's why we're here, after all. It's why you're here."

It was, thought Natalia, *but now I'm not so sure. If all I cared about was the painting, then why does my heart ache so much right now?*

Why do I still want to leap into your arms and feel you wrap me in a strong, tender embrace? Why do I want to feel your lips upon mine and sink into a kiss that leaves me breathless and faint, a kiss so deep that I never rise up from it? Why do I still want things I can't have? Why do I still care *about you, Diego?*

Natalia looked away, swallowing a thick lump in her throat and doing her best to ignore the searing agony in her chest. "Yes. That'll be for the best."

Diego sighed again, his breath sounding as labored as hers. "Right. That's good. Now, let's talk about the job. Eddie and Miriam are on edge after what happened today, Miriam more so than Eddie. They need to know your head is in the right place."

Natalia didn't know where she found the mettle. Maybe it was because she'd lusted after *The Scream* her entire adult life, because she'd seen the power in artwork from an even younger age, from the moment she stared at the tattered reproduction of Claude Monet's *Water-Lilies* in her foster home, but she spoke without a single hitch in her voice. "As I told you over the phone, I'm going to do the job I came here to do. It's as simple as that."

Diego looked at her, his eyes burrowing through her facade into her core. After a moment, he nodded. "Okay. I'll sell them on it."

Natalia's heart finally snapped. She gasped a little at the distinct, physical pain it put her under. Her voice was small in her own ears. "You... *you will?*"

"Yeah," said Diego as he started back toward the loft. "They trust me, and I trust you. I'll smooth things over. It'll be fine."

Sure, they trust you, thought Natalia. *But why do you trust* me?

Natalia had to force her feet into motion to avoid being left behind. She knew she should keep her mouth shut, but if she did, she'd never forgive herself. For once in her life she had to know the truth, and damn the consequences. "Why do you put so much faith in me, Diego?"

Diego snorted, giving her a sly smile as they walked. "I'm a grifter. It's my job to con people, but more importantly, it's my job to read people. You might think you're opaque, but I can see more of you than you might think."

Natalia had already stepped onto shaky footing. She'd already revealed more of herself than she'd intended, and she needed some way to deflect attention. To make this about trivialities rather than the real her. "So you read I was a good lay?"

Diego didn't seem to think that was funny. "I could tell you were complex. That there was something intriguing under your surface, and for lack of a better word, something genuine. That there was something within you of value that was worth exploring."

Natalia's voice squeaked. "Like with you?"

Diego sighed. "I don't know. Maybe a little bit like me. Regardless, I wasn't able to fully uncover that gem inside you, but I got some glimpses. And it was worth it. I don't regret anything with you, Natalia. Nothing I've said, nor anything I've done, even if I know the choices weren't the wisest."

Natalia hung back, tipping her head to the side so Diego wouldn't see the tears in her eyes. *You may not regret your choices now, but you will, Diego. You will.*

Chapter Thirty-Two

IT WAS THE LONGEST DAY OF DIEGO'S LIFE. EVEN THOUGH the heist wasn't set to be executed until after dark, they started early. They had to pantomime the steps they would take to get in and out of the National Gallery, making sure everyone knew exactly where they'd be and what they'd be doing at all times. They had to ensure comms were functional. That the control center was tied into all the museum's security, and that all the security functions they needed access to were enabled. They had to discuss contingency plans for any number of failures or unexpected events that might take place, each one with its own set of responses.

But the work alone wasn't what made the day interminable. Diego had put in eighteen, even twenty hour days before. The difference was *this* day was spent in the company of Natalia.

The day before, following their fight in the streets of downtown Oslo, Natalia had come across as vulnerable, unsure, pained even, all of which made sense given their sudden breakup, if it could be called that. But today she'd come into the loft wearing a calm mask, one which she refused to let drop. She didn't avoid him. Didn't snarl or yell or choke back any sobs. But she didn't engage with him, either.

She spoke when spoken to, responding only when necessary, doing so in a tranquil yet detached sort of way.

All of it made interacting with her, simply being in her presence, that much harder. Perhaps if he could sense her sorrow, feel the suppressed desire in her eyes, that might make him feel better. To know she was going through the same thing he was, but if she was, she kept it hidden, stashed away behind a pane of opaque glass that he couldn't see through no matter how hard he tried.

And Diego *was* hurting. He'd made the right call, he knew that. He owed it to Miriam and Eddie to deliver on their payday. To Natalia too, and that was even before thinking about his debts to Kovalyov, but God, he'd wanted to throw caution to the wind. With Natalia standing before him outside the loft, clearly torn over their brief, passionate fling, he'd wanted to say screw *The Scream*. Who cared about the painting anyway? What was one piece of art and millions of dollars compared to the possibility of true passion? Money couldn't buy that, nor could it soothe the heartache that had crippled him since he'd told Natalia they should call things off.

But even though he was a grifter, he was a man of honor in his own way. He'd made promises he intended to follow through on, so he kept his mouth shut, ignored the ache in his chest, and focused on the work. Somehow, minute by minute, the day ticked by, until it was time to make the final preparations before leaving. As the sun dipped below the horizon, Diego changed out of his suit into a pair of jeans, a long-sleeved shirt, and a close-fitting jacket, which would be far more practical than his usual attire for the evening's tasks. Natalia was already dressed in her running attire, and Miriam and Eddie planned on staying in the van the whole time, so he was the only one who required a new look. If Natalia liked his casual attire less than his usual fare, she didn't make any mention of it. They checked their gear one final time before passing out earpieces, loading into the van, and setting out for the *Nasjonalmuseet*.

Eddie drove. Diego sat next to him in the passenger's seat, while Miriam and Natalia hung out in back. Eddie worked his jaw while he manned the wheel, doing his best to spark conversation, but Diego wasn't in the mood. Only Miriam was willing to trade barbs with the big guy, but even she quieted as they worked their way deeper downtown.

Eddie parked as close as he could, in a lot that was underneath an overpass on the northwestern edge of the museum. There was a loading area next to it that accessed the museum's lower levels, but the lot was closed, and a security kiosk at the forefront of it still had a light on inside. They'd decided it wasn't worth the trouble to enter that way.

"Alright," said Diego as Eddie killed the engine. "Is everyone ready?"

"I'm be'ind the wheel, aren't I?" said Eddie.

Miriam brought the museum security cameras onto the monitors. "Looks like we're still in. We're a go as far as I'm concerned."

Diego turned in his seat. "Natalia?"

She gave him a curt nod. "Let's get this over with."

He nodded back. "Final comms check."

Diego put his finger to his ear as Miriam rattled off everyone's names. They all gave confirmation that their earpieces were working, and she gave back confirmation that she'd heard them.

"Watches?" said Diego.

Everyone checked their timepieces. It was nine oh-seven, and everyone's clocks were synced.

"Okay," said Diego. "Miriam. Keep us apprised. Natalia?"

Natalia nodded and cracked the van's side door. She climbed out, her sling bag cinched tight across her chest. Diego met her on the sidewalk, shrugging into the backpack that contained his own supplies. Together, they headed up the nearest stairwell to street level, then followed the sidewalk in the direction of the museum. Streetlamps burned bright overhead, bathing the road in a cool yellow glow. A nippy chill had set in with the darkness, so the sidewalks weren't as busy as they might've been during the day, but foot traffic hadn't evaporated either. Still, no one paid any attention to Diego and

Natalia as they hooked into a service corridor between the National Gallery and the nearby Nobel Peace Prize museum.

Diego was concerned his feelings for Natalia might become problematic once the two of them were alone, but a sense of focus had overtaken him as soon as he'd left the van, same as it did every time he was about to pull off a well-planned heist. It was as if his body knew this was not the time for hesitation or doubt, that the only thing that mattered was the theft and getting out cleanly.

Diego slowed as he reached an emergency exit in the side of the building. There were security cameras located on the museum exterior, but they were controlled by the same system as the interior ones. Thankfully, the door locks were also electronically controlled.

Diego checked the service corridor, but there was no one there. "How do we look inside, Miriam?"

"You're good," came Miriam's voice. "Nearest guard is in the Scandinavian design gallery."

Diego knew exactly where that was in relation to their entrance. He also knew where the guard's path would take him, as they'd memorized their routes thanks to the footage they'd skimmed from the security cameras.

"Natalia," he said. "Gloves."

They both pulled thin gloves from their pockets and drew then on. They were technically designed for touchscreen use, but the gloves provided good grip while preventing them from leaving any unwanted prints.

"Okay, Miriam," he said. "Open the door."

"You got it," said Miriam.

The door clicked, and when Diego pulled, it opened. No alarms sounded. He nodded to Natalia. "Come on."

They entered together, climbing the stairs to the second floor. They waited for Miriam to give them the go ahead before padding to the gallery that contained *The Scream*. It lay there in the middle of the exhibit, protected by a thick case of museum-grade glass. With a quick nod to each other, Diego and Natalia got to work. They pulled off their packs, removing from each a pair of tools that would help them pry up and lift the glass. They shared another look as they attached them into place, as if to say, *Let's hope Miriam's device works.*

When they lifted, no alarms sounded. The glass was heavy, but the tools gave them good purchase, and he and Natalia were able to set the cover next to the exhibit without difficulty. As they straightened, he and Natalia paused to stare at the painting before them, though it seemed to Diego that Natalia's eyes were stretched wider than his.

"Get the case prepped," said Diego, his voice barely more than a whisper. "Miriam, how are we doing on guards?"

"Everyone is where they're supposed to be," said Miriam. "You have at least another fifteen minutes before anyone stumbles across you."

Natalia pulled the travel case for the painting from her sling bag, essentially a garment bag with collapsible walls that would provide the painting with a little structure. She unfolded it while Diego spoke.

"And no alarms?" asked Diego.

"Nope. You're invisible on all the cameras thanks to the loops I spliced in. The security team is completely unaware you're here. Although..."

Diego's heart skipped a beat, and Natalia hesitated, too. Her hands hovered over the edges of the painting. "Although what?"

"I just checked the exterior cameras. There are a couple guys loitering near one of the museum's emergency doors. Not the one you guys entered through. One on the eastern edge."

"Cops?" said Diego.

"I don't think so," said Miriam, as Natalia slid *The Scream* into the collapsible bag. "Probably just a couple dudes hanging around. I'm going to keep an eye on them."

"Good," said Diego. "Let me know if anything changes. Now, Natalia. Let's get—"

That was the moment the lights went out.

Chapter Thirty-Three

NATALIA WAS USED TO WORKING WHILE CHAOS SWIRLED around her. She was used to working in the dark and under intense psychological pressure. She knew exactly what would happen when the lights went out. She'd predicted the far off cries of the guards, Miriam's confused gasp over the comms, even that Diego would curse as it happened, but she hadn't predicted how deflated he would sound, as if he stood at the top of a skyscraper and the floor had just fallen out from under him. "Oh, *shit.*"

Even as the words escaped his lips, Natalia had already broken into a run, the handles of the reinforced bag containing *The Scream* gripped tight in her fist. She knew exactly how many steps to take and in what direction. She knew when to turn. Knew exactly where the stairwell was as she raced toward it. As she neared the edge of the building, a trickle of light filtered into the museum through the exterior windows, creating a glimmer that rippled along the polished floors.

As she ran, the confusion intensified. The panicked cries of the night guards echoed through the museum, but it was the voices in Natalia's ear that were most prominent—and hardest to bear.

"Jesus, what the hell just happened?" said Miriam.

"Bloody 'ell, did a fuse pop or somefin?" said Eddie.

"I've still got camera control," said Miriam. "Can't see the guards well but they're coming! And those dudes I saw outside are up to something! They're circling the building!"

"Fuck me," said Eddie. "D, you know the backup plan. Meet me at the loadin' entrance. I'm comin' in."

Throughout it all, Diego spoke, but not to Eddie and Miriam. He ignored them completely, calling into the darkened void of the museum. "Natalia! *Natalia!*"

As Natalia approached the stairwell, she pulled the comms piece from her ear canal and stuffed it into her pocket. She wanted to throw it as far as she could or maybe smash it underfoot, but she knew better than to leave evidence of her presence behind. Even so, she could still hear Diego's calls echoing through the corridors as she pushed into the stairwell and raced for the ground floor.

Her hand snuck into her pocket to her smartphone, same as it had before the lights cut out. She'd set up her phone so she only needed a single press of a button to kill the lights, but now she needed a little more finesse. She woke her device, opened the app that controlled the other devices she'd installed in the crawl space, and pressed another button, cutting out the security camera that watched the museum's exterior western wall.

She slowed her pace as she pushed through the emergency exit onto the street. It was a different entrance than the one through which she and Diego had entered, spitting her onto a thoroughfare rather than an alley, but there weren't many people out and about. A quick glance up the street showed no one nearby, and the few in the distance didn't seem to be paying her any attention.

Natalia increased her pace again as she darted across the street, then slowed as she reached the sidewalk on the other side. There was a large glass building there that contained cafes and restaurants and several small businesses. Natalia skirted it before slipping into the alley behind it, making a beeline for a pair of dumpsters tucked against its side. With another glance behind her to make sure she wasn't being followed, she tucked the modified garment bag behind the nearest dumpster, checking to make sure no part of it was visible to passing pedestrians. She'd already verified the trash removal calendar. She knew the dumpsters would be emptied in five days, at which point someone might notice the bag. Until then, no one would have reason to look in the crevice between them and the wall, and Natalia wouldn't be leaving *The Scream* out of her sight for that long. Just long enough for the raging storm that was barreling toward them to pass.

In fact, even as Natalia stepped onto the wharf and began walking toward The Scoundrel, she heard the distant blare of police sirens. Natalia didn't increase her pace at the sound of them. The most fundamental rule of avoiding detection was to act indifferent to the world around you. To walk with purpose and confidence, yet to maintain a clueless attitude to the chaos that surrounded you.

And so Natalia ignored the sirens as she walked at a brisk but steady pace toward her hotel, and as she did so, it hit her.

She'd done it.

She'd stolen *The Scream*. Not only was it arguably one of the world's most valuable paintings, but it was the piece of art that spoke to her more than any other. The one that invoked in her a profound sense of longing and sorrow and dread. A beautiful, painful, soul-crushing masterpiece that had inspired and horrified audiences for well over a century.

And it was hers. She'd executed her plan perfectly, and she'd earned her prize.

By all accounts, she should've been ecstatic. The culmination of years of effort honing her skills as a thief, learning new technologies, working on her ability to lie and deceive had all come together tonight, resulting in her taking possession of the one thing she wanted most in life. So why was it that with every step she took, the pain in her chest intensified? Why was it that her heart felt like a violin string that had been wound too tight and every step wound it tighter, right on the verge of snapping? Why was it the black pit in her stomach that she thought she'd banished had opened back up underneath her, like a sinkhole that swallowed whole homes in the span of seconds? Why was it the saliva in her throat had turned as thick as molasses and her lungs seemed incapable of filling with anything more than gasping breaths? Why was it she felt like the physical embodiment of human garbage?

She didn't really have to wonder. She knew the reason why, even if she didn't want to admit it. It was because her gain had come at Diego's expense. She'd used him. She'd lied and cheated and stolen. Not in general, but *to him*. She'd abused his trust. God, he'd even used that very same T word, the word which she hated more than any other! But he'd uttered those very words. *I trust you.* She'd taken that trust and stomped on it. Befouled it. Ripped it to shreds and thrown it in his face. And for what? For a painting? For a depiction of the misery she felt on a daily basis? So she could hang it on her wall and stare at it day in and day out and wonder what life was like for people who didn't hate every aspect of their lives?

Natalia shook her head, her breath coming in ragged gasps. Well, Diego had been right. About many things, but especially about what he'd told her in anger before he drove off in the van. The only constant in her loneliness was her. She'd been responsible for every action she'd taken. She'd fallen for Diego willingly, even if she let herself fall further and harder than she'd intended, and she'd been clearheaded when she chose to screw him over. It wasn't something that just happened. She hadn't been caught in a tsunami she was powerless to stop. She'd chosen this. She'd chosen *The Scream* over Diego. Misery over a chance at something else. Not happiness necessarily, but something less painful than sorrow.

The sirens sounded faint behind her as Natalia pushed through the revolving glass doors into The Scoundrel. She stumbled toward the elevators, but a concerned voice stopped her. "Miss... are you okay?"

A young man stood behind the reception desk, his blonde hair parted on the side. He looked at her with pursed lips, his brow furrowed with concern.

Fear shot through Natalia, making her wonder if she'd missed something. Had she torn her clothes while racing from the National Gallery? Was she bleeding, and she hadn't noticed due to the all-consuming ache in her chest? After everything she'd gone through, all her planning and hard work, was something silly going to give her away?

"I... Ah..." Natalia lifted a gloved hand to her face, and that's when she felt them. The tears streaming down her face, wetting her cheeks and trailing down her jaw. For the second time in as many days, she'd found herself crying without noticing. It wasn't something she made a habit of. She couldn't remember the last time she'd cried before yesterday. Maybe when she'd stubbed her toe particularly badly and tears squeezed out of their own volition, but to cry because of her emotions? When was the last time? When she still a child, angry at the lot the world had given her? Yet here she was, sobbing like a schoolgirl who'd been dumped, even though she'd been the one to do the dumping.

Natalia pulled her gloves off and wiped the tears away with her fingers, though now that she was focused on them, she felt new tears spring to her eyes. Apparently, this was something she was going to have to deal with. "I'm fine. It's just... it's been an emotional few days. Thank you for asking."

The hotel clerk looked at her, the desire to help apparent on his young face, but there was nothing he could do. There was nothing anyone could do. Natalia had made her bed, and the only ones who would be lying in it were her and the enigmatic, faceless protagonist from *The Scream.*

Chapter Thirty-Four

WHEN NATALIA ARRIVED AT HER ROOM, THE FIRST THING she did was wash her face. She tried not to look at herself too closely in the mirror, for one because her eyes were puffy and swollen from crying and for another because she wasn't sure she'd like the person staring back at her, regardless of her physical condition.

The second thing she did was pack. The trunk that contained her bulkier equipment was still mostly packed, as few of the items had been necessarily to steal *The Scream,* but her nylon suitcase was in need of attention. She pulled the hand tools and electronic devices from her sling bag, securing them in the compartment at the bottom of her suitcase before turning her attention to her clothing. As she pulled her shirts and leggings and underwear from the dresser drawers, she went through the steps that lay before her.

Retrieving the painting would be simple, so long as she was patient. Police and news crews would swarm the *Nasjonalmuseet* for at least a day, maybe two, but she had five until the garbage crews came to empty the dumpsters. As long as she waited, she could come in and snag the converted garment bag without anyone wondering what she was carrying. In the meantime, she couldn't rest on her laurels. Diego and the crew knew where she was staying. They'd come for her as soon as they had their wits about them, which meant she needed to disappear. That meant changing hotels, signing in under a new alias, and generally going into hiding until she could secure the painting. Being in public was an unnecessary risk, so she'd be taking advantage of room service a lot for the next forty-eight hours. Natalia wasn't sure how good Miriam's hacking skills were, but she expected she and Diego would be keeping eyes on Oslo Gardermoen Airport. Diego might not try to capture her in such a public place, but they could track her to her final destination, which was just as dangerous. Better to rent a car, drive to Gothenburg, Sweden, and fly from there. Diego might also be keeping an eye on local shipping companies, so she couldn't risk packing *The Scream* and mailing it from Oslo. She'd be better off hiding it in her rental car and smuggling it across the Swedish border with the rest of her things. That might be a challenge given the physical dimensions and fragility of the painting, but she could figure something out. Maybe she'd rent an SUV and put in a fake floor.

As Natalia stuffed the last of the dresser contents into her suitcase, she crossed to the closet, which contained her jackets. As she opened the door, she paused, her eyes falling upon the violet dress she'd worn to the charity ball and the golden shoes on the floor underneath it. She reached out and took the fine satin fabric in her hands, feeling the silky cloth between her fingers. The sensation sent a shiver up her arm that was followed by goosebumps, not from the feel of the fabric but from the memory of Diego's touch. His hand on her thigh. His breath on her lips. Was it her imagination, or was there a touch of his scent on the dress?

Natalia swallowed hard as more tears threatened to spill onto her cheeks, but she batted them back through a few quick blinks. She wanted to burn the dress, or barring that leave it in the hotel and forget it completely, but she couldn't. She couldn't leave anything behind that might provide insight into her identity, so with her heart in her throat she folded the dress tightly and stuffed it into her suitcase alongside her clothes, adding the shoes on top before zipping it shut.

She scanned the room with one last shuddering breath, then grabbed her suitcase and headed for the elevators.

When she reached the lobby, the receptionist's focus was no longer on the door. Instead, he watched a breaking news report on a muted television in the corner. Natalia peered at it, noting the reporter standing outside the *Nasjonalmuseet* and the words "Brazen Theft" scrolling in the ticker underneath her, but as quickly as she glanced at the screen, she turned her attention away. None of it mattered to her any longer. She needed to focus on the path before her, not the past.

"Excuse me," she said.

The young man with the blonde hair turned toward her. His eyes stretched in recognition. "Oh. It's you, Miss. And... you brought your suitcase?"

"I'm checking out," said Natalia. "Room five-oh-five."

"At this time of night?" said the young man. "But you have already paid for the evening."

"My plans have changed," said Natalia. "I no longer have need to stay here."

The young man's face collapsed, as if the narrative he'd built based on her previous crying session was starting to come together. "I am terribly sorry to hear that. I will get to work on checking you out right away. I do hope your stay with us was pleasant, however."

There were so many ways she could've answered that question, but she knew what the young man meant. "Your hotel is lovely. If ever I'm in Oslo again, I'll be sure to stay here again." Though she wouldn't, because the hotel would remind her of... *everything*.

The clerk bobbed his head and began to type.

"One more thing," said Natalia as she summoned an Uber on her phone. "I have a heavy trunk in my room. I'll need someone to bring it down."

"Of course." The young man picked up a phone hidden by the front desk and spoke a few words into it in Norwegian. He kept typing as he hung up, but his gaze kept drifting to the television in the corner.

His brow furrowed, and he sighed. "Have you been watching the news, Miss?"

"A little," she lied.

The young man shook his head. "It is so hard to believe this sort of thing would happen in Oslo, right in this very neighborhood. I thought we as Norwegians were more civilized than this."

Natalia shrugged. "Items have been stolen from the National Gallery before, as they have been from the Munch Museum."

"Yes," said the young man. "But not like this. Not with armed thugs and car chases and violence in the streets. What is our city coming to?"

"Armed thugs? *Car chases?*"

Natalia turned toward the television. The scene had shifted from the National Gallery to what appeared to be a shaky cell phone video. Either she hadn't caught the start of it, or the video hadn't caught the start of the action. Regardless, despite the poor quality and the relative distance of it from the scene, Natalia could easily pick out the people involved. The white van Eddie had been driving had pulled over at the side of a street, but it hadn't crashed. It looked as if it had been forced off the road by two black SUVs with tinted windows. The side of the van had been thrown open, and Eddie and Diego were outside it, grappling with a quartet of large men wearing black ski masks. A fifth one climbed out of the side of the van, dragging Miriam along with him. That's when Eddie went nuts. He kneed one of his attackers and threw the other to the ground before lunging and slamming into the one that held Miriam. Even if the video had been taken close enough to have caught the nuance of the struggle, Natalia couldn't hear anything with the television muted, but she could imagine Eddie's angry bellow as he told Miriam to run. And run she did. She took off, disappearing out of the frame while three attackers dove onto Eddie to subdue him. The man fought like a bear, but just when Natalia thought he might drive them off, he shuddered violently and collapsed to the ground as if he'd been tased. One of the masked men pointed as if giving instructions. Still-struggling Diego and the now limp Eddie were stuffed into the black SUVs. One of the masked men jumped into the van and the others into the SUVs and all three vehicles took off.

As Natalia watched the video, her heart sank deeper and deeper into her stomach. No. *No, no, no.* This was not supposed to happen. She'd planned everything. She'd executed her portion of the heist to perfection, and she'd counted on Diego, Eddie, and Miriam to keep their wits about them when things went wrong. They should've escaped with ease, been gone long before the police arrived without leaving any trace of their presence. They should've faded into nothingness by now.

But these men weren't police. She didn't know who they were, even if she had a strong suspicion, but regardless of who they worked for, they were bad news. Very, *very* bad news, and their involvement was absolutely *not* what Natalia had signed up for. She'd planned on screwing Diego over, sure, and she'd dealt with the emotional fallout of that, but he was supposed to get away scot-free. To hate and despise her with all of his being for the rest of his days for the way she'd betrayed him, but she'd never intended for *this* to happen. For him to be captured? And then what? Tortured? *Killed?*

Natalia's breath caught in her throat. Her pulse quickened, and her vision went fuzzy. "Oh, no. Oh, God, no."

"I told you," said the young man behind the desk. "The violence. It is very disconcerting, isn't it?"

Natalia's legs grew weak. She grabbed at the desk to help support her weight even as she found it difficult to take a breath. Her vision blurred more, so she closed her eyes, focusing on her breathing. This was a panic attack. She could work her way out of it, but she had to steady her breathing. Fill her lungs with air, then let it out slowly. In, then out.

She heard the young man's voice at her back, blissfully unaware of the state she'd entered into. "You know, as a people I think we Norwegians try to be forward thinking. We try to solve society's ills by treating everyone with a measure of compassion and respect. For example, our prisons are not like the rest of the world's. We try to rehabilitate rather than punish criminals for their mistakes. But when you see an act like this? It makes me wonder if we are wrong to put so much faith in others. Perhaps as a people, we are simply too trusting."

At the mention of that dreaded word, the T word, Natalia's pulse slowed. Air entered her lungs more easily with each of her breaths, and when she opened her eyes, her vision was no longer blurred. Though her legs felt weak, she willed a little strength into them and stood up taller. "What did you say?"

The young man's focus shifted from the television to her, apparently having missed her entire episode. "I said perhaps we put too much trust in others."

Over the past two days, Natalia had learned what heartbreak felt like. After she'd slept with Diego and spied on him through his phone, she'd felt a hint of it. It hit her in force when she'd broken things off after setting up her devices in the bowels of the National Gallery, then again a little while ago as she'd walked away from the museum. She'd tried to hold her poor, broken heart together, but the fixes she'd put into place were temporary and futile, like trying to piece a shattered vase together with strips of clear plastic tape. But what she felt now was the opposite of heartbreak. A warm feeling suffused her chest, as if her heart was fusing back together, not into the state it was before she'd met Diego but a new, more powerful form. A form that was fuller, stronger, and more capable than ever.

And she knew exactly what she had to do.

"No," said Natalia to the receptionist. "We are not too trusting. If anything, we don't trust enough. We need to put more trust in others, especially those who've shown they care about us."

The young man blinked a few times. "Well, ah… Perhaps you are correct."

"I know I am," said Natalia, conviction suffusing her voice. "For maybe the first time in my life, I'm absolutely, *positively* sure I'm right about this. I'm sorry to be such a bother, but I'm going to keep my room after all. You can leave my trunk there. Take my suitcase up, too."

The young man lifted an eyebrow. "Are you sure, Miss?"

Natalia took a few steps toward the door, checking the location of her Uber as she walked. "Yes. I'm terribly sorry for the inconvenience, but please know you've helped me, much more than I think you'll ever realize."

The desk clerk's mouth fell open in surprise, but Natalia didn't wait to see what he did next. She didn't have the time. She needed to act *now* if she was going to have any hope of saving Diego. She burst through the front doors, racing into the chilly September evening. A smile crept onto her face as she ran toward the bus stop, but she pushed it away. Nothing had been fixed yet, and Diego's fate wasn't sealed.

Besides, she wasn't going to be able to save him on her own. She'd need help.

Chapter Thirty-Five

THE DOOR SQUEALED AS NATALIA PUSHED HER WAY INTO the loft. Before she'd even made it inside, she heard a shout of sheer terror. A nervous shiver shot up Natalia's spine, but it was just Miriam, who was cowering behind the bank of computers at the far side of the room, her face frozen into a grimace. The computers were in a state of disarray: their sides pried open, cables everywhere, and assorted parts scattered across the floor.

Miriam stood when she caught sight of Natalia, the pained look on her face melting into one of confusion. "Natalia? Fucking hell, you scared the shit out of me. What are you doing here? I thought the Russians nabbed you at the museum."

"So it *is* the Russians," said Natalia. "I figured as much."

"*You figured as much?*" said Miriam. "Jesus, did they not say anything to you? Whatever. It doesn't matter. We've got to get the fuck out of here. You can help me pull the last few hard drives from these computers. There's no time to format them, so we'll have to smash them. Then we need to slather this whole room in industrial clearer to get rid of our prints and DNA. Just soak the fuck out of every surface. I don't know what to do about the couch. Maybe burn it."

"Calm down, Miriam," said Natalia as she padded across the room. "I need to talk to you."

"Calm down? *Calm down?*" Miriam stared at Natalia with wild eyes. "Are you not paying attention to what's going on? The Russians have Diego and Eddie. Big nasty Russians with guns, okay? If they're not looking for us already, they will be soon. They could be on their way right now for all I know, and when they get here, they're not going to pussyfoot around. They're going to kidnap us and kill us, and that's if they don't do some unspeakable shit to us first. We need to get the fuck out, *now!* Like, yesterday. Seriously, how are you not *less* calm? And how are you even here? How did you get away from them?"

Natalia took another step forward. "I didn't get away from the Russians, Miriam."

"What do you mean you didn't get away from the Russians?" said Miriam. "If you didn't get away, then what... How did you...?"

Miriam's eyes widened, but a fraction of a second later they narrowed as her jaw clenched and her entire face tightened. "You *bitch.*"

Natalia held her hands out. "Please give me thirty seconds to explain. I promise I have nothing to do with the Russians, and I had no intention of anything bad happening to you or Diego or Eddie."

Miriam snarled. "Girl, I am not prone to violence, but I can pull some hood shit if I need to. *Start talking.*"

"You were right not to trust me," said Natalia. "I've been lying to you guys from the start. My goal since I arrived was to steal *The Scream* for myself, but I promise I'm working alone. I cut the lights in the National Gallery. I took the painting. I stashed it in a safe place, but I'm not working with anyone else. If Russians attacked, it's probably the mobsters Diego was fencing the painting to. I'm guessing they decided they weren't willing to pay the ninety million they promised and figured they could take it by force instead."

"No shit, Sherlock," said Miriam. "And if this is supposed to be an apology, it's anything fucking but."

"Look, I'm not going to lie to you," said Natalia. "Not anymore. My plan was to leave you guys in the lurch and take the painting for myself, that's the truth. And I'm sorry. I'm a bitch. A cruel, cold-hearted bitch who's never done anything but lie, cheat, and steal. I've never thought of anyone other than myself because... *because that's how I thought the world works.* Everyone I've ever known, ever cared about in my whole life has screwed me, taken advantage of me, and stabbed me in the back, so I figured, what the hell? What does it matter if I do the same? Everybody deserves it, right? But that was before I met Diego. The world's sleaziest conman who lied to me constantly and told me these stupid made up stories about his childhood, but in the moments that mattered, he showed me his true self. He confided in me, and *for fuck's sake, he trusted me!* He actually trusted me! And I... I..."

Miriam's face screwed up in a mixture of anger and disgust. "What the fuck, Natalia? *Are you crying?*"

Natalia felt her cheeks and found them to be wet. She *was* crying. Again. *Third time's the charm, I guess.* "God damnit, Miriam. I'm in love with him. *I'm in love with Diego!*"

Miriam's eyes widened again, except this time they stayed that way. *"What?"*

"I know," said Natalia, the tears now freely flowing down her face. "It's stupid. It's stupid to fall for someone you've just met, and it's even stupider to fall for a two-faced conman, but it's true. I never would've stolen the stupid painting from you guys if I'd realized it sooner, but I didn't know what the hell was going on! I've never been in love before. I've never wanted to be honest with someone. I've never wanted to share myself, the true self, not the pale imitation I show the world. But I do now. And I know I've screwed Diego over more than anyone has ever gotten screwed in the history of screwing, but I have to try and save him. I can't leave him to those Russian mobsters, I just can't! Even if he never forgives me. Even if he hates me for the rest of his life, I have to help him, because that's what love is, right? It's irrational and nonsensical and... selfless, I guess. And it's the right thing to do."

Miriam blew air forcefully from between her lips as she shook her head. "Christ. This is fucked up."

Natalia wiped the tears from her face and took another step toward Miriam. "I can't save him and Eddie by myself, though. I'm good at a lot of things, but not that good. I need your help."

Miriam's jaw clenched again, and her eyes flashed red. "Whoa. First you screw us over to the tune of ninety million dollars, then when bloodthirsty Russians swoop in and threaten to kill us, all of a sudden you want *my* help? Are you insane?"

"I'm a thief," said Natalia. "But if we're going to save Diego and Eddie, we're going to need your hacking skills, too."

Miriam's hands balled into fists at her sides. "What. THE. FUCK. Makes you think I'm going to help you?"

Natalia took another deep breath to soothe her nerves. "It's not about helping me. Hate me all you want. I deserve it, but do it for Diego and Eddie. You know they don't deserve this. Not after what they did for you. You told me yourself outside The Matthiessen Group offices. When the shit hit the fan, they didn't abandon you. They came back for you. They saved you."

"Yeah, from getting caught by the cops!" shouted Miriam. "Not from getting raped and murdered by a bunch of gun-toting Russian psychopaths!"

"Which is why it's so important you help me save them," said Natalia. "Come on. This is Eddie we're talking about. *Eddie.*"

Miriam frowned, crossing her arms and tucking them close to her body. "Yeah, I know who we're talking about. I don't know why you're so focused on Eddie when you apparently fell in love with Diego."

"Because as someone who only recently started being honest with herself about her feelings, I can tell you it's not worth running away from the people you care about. I see the way you look at him. The way you two banter with each other. For crying out loud, he's the only person you let call you Midge. You care about him, and he risked his life to free you from the Russians. There's a cell phone video. I saw it on the news."

Miriam hugged herself harder, chewing on her lip as she did so. She looked away, but when she turned back in Natalia's direction, there were unshed tears in her eyes. "God damnit. *Fuuuuuuuuuck.*" She thumped down in the chair in front of the desk, putting her head into her hands.

Natalia gave her a moment, but as Miriam herself had made clear, they didn't have a lot of time. "So is that a yes? Are you going to help me save Eddie and Diego?"

Miriam surreptitiously wiped her eyes as she lifted her lead. "Look, even if I *was* willing to help you, I wouldn't know where to start. We don't have any guns. That's not the kind of crew we are. I don't even know where the Russians took Diego and Eddie! I mean, I could track the van, assuming the Russians haven't torched it and left it in a ditch somewhere, but that doesn't mean I have any idea where the guys are."

"Oh, that part's easy," said Natalia. "I know exactly where Diego is."

Miriam's eyes narrowed. "I thought you said you weren't working with the Russians."

"I'm not. I installed a tracking app on his phone."

Miriam lifted an eyebrow. "Before or after you slept with him?"

"After. That same night, actually."

Miriam shook her head. "I'd remind you you're a cold bitch again, but honestly, I'm impressed. So we know where they are, assuming Diego still has his phone on him. Do you have a plan to free them? Preferably one that doesn't involve us getting shot?"

"I do," said Natalia. "But we'll need some equipment. Do you have any drones? Maybe some high intensity LED flashlights?"

Miriam frowned. *"Drones?* No. But I know a store that carries them if you don't mind breaking and entering."

"Great," said Natalia. "Is the sedan still here? Or Diego's Aston Martin?"

"The sedan is," said Miriam. "You plan on explaining what's going on in that noodle of yours?"

"I'll explain everything on the way," said Natalia. "Just grab your laptop, phone, and whatever else you think you might need. We need to move."

Chapter Thirty-Six

DIEGO HURT. HIS FACE HURT. HIS RIBS HURT. HIS stomach hurt. He just hurt all over. Strangely enough, he didn't think he was bleeding, because when he looked down at himself he didn't see any red spots on the collar of his jacket. He also didn't think any of his ribs or his facial bones were broken, as they didn't hurt from simply moving, but he was sure he'd sport an attractive bruise or twenty in the morning.

Assuming he made it to the morning.

Diego rolled his shoulders and flexed the muscles in his arms, trying to force blood flow into fingers that were slowly losing all sensation. His wrists were tied behind his back, stretched around the back of the hard, wooden chair upon which he sat. As he wriggled, he felt Eddie respond to his touch. The big guy was tied in a chair at his back, their wrists wrapped together in a confused knot of hemp and human flesh.

Diego heard Eddie's voice over his shoulder, little more than a whisper but gruff and weighty as always. "Are we goin' to come up wif a Jackie Chan to get outta 'ere, D, or what?"

Diego glanced across the expanse of the warehouse in which they sat toward the white van. After running them off the road, the

Russians who'd accosted them had stuffed him and Eddie into the backs of their SUVs and driven them to this abandoned warehouse. There wasn't much in the space around them: a number of pallets piled high with boxes wrapped in cellophane, at least fifty black garbage bags that were likely filled with non-biodegradable waste given the lack of a smell in the air, and a forklift that looked as if it had been manufactured in the 1970s. Though the Russians had parked their cars around the back, they'd driven the white van inside through one of the loading doors. All five of the men who'd assaulted them were currently in the process of tearing the van apart in search of *The Scream*. One or two of them would pop out every now and then to cast a glance in their direction, but they didn't seem terribly worried about them escaping. To be fair, it was a reasonable assumption that they wouldn't. Before strapping them to the chairs, the Russians had patted him and Eddie down for weapons, and even though Diego wasn't an expert on knots, the numbness creeping through his fingers into his arms told him the ones the Russians had tied were pretty solid.

"I don't know, Eddie," said Diego. "Unless you're strong enough to smash the chair you're sitting in with your ass cheeks, I think we might've reached the end off the road."

"Bollocks, mate," said Eddie. "'At ain't no way to talk. Just 'cause fings seem a mite bleak don't mean we're well and truly buggered."

A large clang sounded. Diego glanced at the van again as one of the Russians threw a piece of their electronic equipment out the back onto the concrete floor, resulting in another crash. "I don't want to burst your bubble, pal, but we're outnumbered five to two by guys who have guns, not to mention we're currently tied to a pair of chairs and we can't even see each other face to face."

"So let's deal wif each problem one by one, eh? Can you loosen yer ropes a' all, mate?"

Diego tried to shift his wrists again, but the sensation in his fingers was well and truly gone. What he did feel was a set of bindings that weren't budging. "That's a no on my end. I don't suppose you have a knife tucked at the end of your sleeve."

"If I 'ad 'at, I'd 'a used it already."

"What about a lighter?"

Eddie snorted. "Why? You fancy an oily rag?"

"Not to smoke, Eddie. To burn through these bindings."

"Burn 'em? 'At'd never work, mate. You'd just burn me 'ands."

"It worked in *Indiana Jones and the Last Crusade*."

"Bollocks," said Eddie. "Indy set fire to 'at 'ole Nazi castle and almost killed 'isself and 'is old man."

A smile crept onto Diego lips. "You know, Eddie, we may be about to die, but it gives me a great deal of pleasure to know you watched that movie. How long ago did I recommend that series to you? Four years ago?"

"Five," he said. "Fough you should've told me to skip the second one, and the fourf."

"Eh, that one doesn't even count."

There was another clang from the van, then one of the Russians jumped out the back. A moment later, another joined him, then the remaining three. All five of them approached Diego, with the one whom Diego had identified as their leader taking point. He was a man of middling height, but he was thickly muscled as Diego had learned when he'd wrestled him into the SUV. His face was weathered and a thin scar ran down the length of his cheek to his jaw.

He stopped in front of Diego and clasped his hands loosely before him. He spoke English with a heavy Russian accent. "So. Diego. We have looked through van, top to bottom now, and yet... no painting. How do you explain zis?"

"I've already explained it," said Diego. "I told you we didn't leave the National Gallery with *The Scream*. Someone else was working the same job. When my collaborator and I were getting ready to extract the painting, the lights went out. Guards rushed the scene. I fled, as did my collaborator. I made it to the van. Eddie drove us away, but we didn't escape you. You know the rest."

The Russian frowned. "News reports say painting is missing, but you do not have zis. So who has painting?"

"I don't know," said Diego. "As I said, someone was working a job on all of us independently. We all got screwed."

The Russian shook his head. "I do not believe you. I zink you are lying to me. Why do you insult Mr. Kovalyov zis way? Is very rude, given everyzing he has done for you. So I ask one more time, where is painting?"

The fact of the matter was, Diego *was* lying. He knew exactly what happened, and he wasn't being honest with the Russians, just as he hadn't been honest with Eddie and Miriam in the aftermath of the heist. He'd told both of them that when the lights went out, he'd heard shouting and footsteps and that Natalia had taken off to avoid capture, but that wasn't what happened. Natalia had betrayed them, plain and simple. She'd made off with *The Scream* during a moment of confusion she'd most certainly planned and implemented herself. At this very moment, she was probably on her way to the airport or maybe driving to some secluded port where she could take a chartered ship to a foreign country. She and the painting were long gone. He'd never see either again, *ever*. So why was he still covering for her?

The pragmatic answer was there was no point in giving her up. Diego knew where this interrogation was going. The thugs had pulled their masks off as soon as they'd arrived at the warehouse, not worried in the least about being identified. They'd even made it clear they were working for Kovalyov, and since Kovalyov had decided to take *The Scream* from them instead of paying them the ninety million dollars he'd agreed to made it clear he'd never intended to follow through on his promises. The thugs were going to kill him and Eddie, and if he gave up Natalia, or Miriam for that matter, the thugs would track the pair of them down and kill them, too. It was always possible they'd do so without his cooperation, but why would he willingly provide information that would result in the harm of people he cared about?

And that was what it boiled down to. He still cared about Natalia. Even after she lied to his face, over and over again. Even after she betrayed him and left him to fend off the wolves on his own, he still cared for her. Even as he sat bound in this uncomfortable chair, his body aching with nascent bruises, the thought of Natalia sailing around the world living off the proceeds of her sale of *The Scream* brought a smile to his lips. What difference did it make, after all? If she hadn't run off with the painting, the Russians still would've hunted them down. All four of them would already be dead, in fact, as the Russians would've gunned them down as soon as they took possession of the piece.

Of course, none of that explained *why* he still cared for Natalia, but Diego had a pretty good idea of that, too. It was because in her presence, he finally felt as if he could be himself. A liar and a thief, sure, but an authentic one. An honest one. One that wasn't scared to shed the facade he'd worn for so long and embrace the parts of him that weren't suave and sophisticated and clever, the side that loved movies and could admit nervousness and fear and could talk about the life he'd actually led as a youth rather than the fanciful tales he'd spun for her. As Diego stared death in the face, that was his only real regret. That he'd leaned into his persona until the end rather than telling Natalia the truth about how he felt when he'd had the chance.

Diego sighed. "I don't know where the painting is. That's the honest truth. And quite frankly, I hope you never find it, because a group of dishonest, backstabbing thugs such as you has no right to a painting as expressive as that. You can tell Kovalyov that to his face."

Behind him, Eddie rumbled his agreement. "You tell 'em, D."

The Russian ringleader shook his head. "Zis is very disappointing. I was hoping we could all deal with zis like men, but you refuse to see reason. Zankfully, we have ozer methods we can try."

He turned to one of the men and spoke a few words in Russian. Diego didn't catch all of it, but he understood the general gist, and it wasn't good. He gritted his teeth, wishing there was some way to get it all over with faster, but as the thug retreated, presumably to find implements of torture, the lights went out.

Diego looked up, squinting into the sudden darkness. There were murmurs from the Russians, and the leader spoke to one of the others. *"Chto za chert?"*

The lights hadn't been off for more than fifteen seconds before bright white lights flooded into the warehouse through windows set high in the walls. Diego squinted, trying to protect his eyes as a booming voice projected through a bull horn from outside. "This is the Oslo police! We have you surrounded. Come out with your hands up!"

Several of the Russians cursed. As they did so, a metallic rattle filled the air, and one of the loading doors flew up on its roller wheels. A siren blared, an engine roared, and flashing red and blue lights spilled into the warehouse as a police cruiser barreled into the warehouse. Tires squealed as the car turned sharply, the engine bellowing as the car raced across the empty floor toward them.

The Russian curses turned into full-on panic. They shouted and fled, racing toward the exits in the back of the warehouse. The cruiser's tires squealed as the car screeched to a stop in front of him, bare feet from his chair.

The engine idled. The passenger door flew open, and out popped... *Natalia?*

Chapter Thirty-Seven

NATALIA RUSHED TOWARD DIEGO, A SERRATED KNIFE IN hand. Diego's hair was mussed, there was a cut across one of his cheeks, and the tissue around one of his eyes was swelling. He wasn't unharmed, but he was alive. *Thank God, he was alive.*

Diego looked at her in confusion, his face lit by the alternating red and blue lights. "Natalia? What are you doing here? Where are the police?"

"No time to explain," said Natalia as she sawed at the bindings holding Diego and Eddie in place. "We've only got thirty seconds, maybe sixty before the Russians figure out this is a scam."

"A scam?" said Diego. "What scam?"

By this point, Miriam had jumped from the driver's seat with a plastic jug of gasoline in hand. There was a makeshift device attached to the top with wires sticking into a crude timer. She chucked it into the open back door of the van.

"Holy crap," Diego said. "Is that an explosive?"

The knife nearly slipped in Natalia's hand as it sliced through the last of the bindings. *"Move.* Diego, backseat with me. Eddie, front passenger seat."

Eddie rubbed his hands as he jogged to the car. "Shouldn't I be drivin'?"

"I've got this," said Miriam as she jumped into the open driver's side door. *"Let's go!"*

Natalia shoved Diego into the back seat as she plowed in behind him. She'd barely pulled her door closed before Miriam slammed the cruiser into reverse and gunned the engine. The car almost lifted onto two wheels as Miriam pulled off a reverse ninety degree turn, knocking over several pallets full of boxes in the process. She slammed the car into drive and hit the accelerator, throwing Natalia into the back of her seat. The car roared, catching air as it flew off the loading ramp. Tires squealed again as Miriam cranked on the wheel, pulling a hairpin turn in the lot outside. The siren wailed as she pulled onto the street, accelerating to a hundred and thirty kilometers per hour in a matter of seconds. An explosion tore through the air, and when Natalia glanced back, she could see an orange glow in the warehouse windows.

Diego stared out the back of the cruiser at the rapidly receding warehouse, too. "I don't get it. Who's manning the floodlights? And the bullhorn?"

"We mounted high intensity LEDs on drones," said Natalia. "And the bullhorn was a speaker with a recording playing through it."

Diego turned his focus back into the car. "So it's just the two of you."

"Damn right," said Miriam.

"And the police car?"

"Stole it," said Natalia.

"Borrowed it, really," said Miriam. "We'll leave it where the Oslo police can find it when we're done."

Miriam pulled the car into another sharp turn, rocketing onto a smaller, less inhabited thoroughfare. She flicked the siren off and eased off the gas.

Eddie sat in the front seat, staring at Miriam as if he'd never seen her until that very moment. *"Bloody 'ell, Midge.* Where'd ya learn to drive like 'at?"

Miriam smiled as she looked into Eddie's eyes. "Oh, I picked it up over time. Learned from the best, I guess."

"'At you did, Midge," said Eddie. "'At you did."

Eddie reached out and laid an arm across Miriam's shoulders, causing Miriam's smile to grow. She stared at him, her eyes looking a little misty, all while a smile grew across Eddie's weathered mug. Good thing Miriam had reduced her speed and turned onto a quiet street, otherwise Natalia would've feared for her life given her current level of focus.

Diego stared at the two of them through the screen separating the front of the car from the back, his brow furrowed. "I hate to interrupt whatever's going on up there, but I'm a little confused about what's happening in general."

Miriam snorted, breaking contact with Eddie for long enough to shoot a glance into the back of the vehicle. "What's happening is we saved your ass from those murderous Russians. You're welcome, by the way."

Diego nodded. "I figured that part out, thanks. The question is..." Diego turned his dark eyes onto Natalia. "What are *you* doing here?"

This was the moment Natalia had been dreading. Until now, she hadn't allowed herself to think about what would happen once she freed Diego. She hadn't even allowed herself to believe she and Miriam would succeed. There was too much riding on the outcome, and there hadn't been any time to spend thinking about failure, anyway. Normally, Natalia spent weeks preparing for a heist, so to break into an electronics store, steal a police car, and set up a raid on a warehouse in a span of an hour and a half was completely ludicrous. Adrenaline had taken over. Her desperate need to see Diego safe had driven all other thoughts from her mind, letting her focus only on the work, but now that they'd escaped and the tingling rush of her body's fight or flight response had faded, the emotions she'd tried to hide resurfaced. She felt all of them, naked and raw as never before, but she wasn't scared of them anymore. In fact, she embraced them.

Natalia took a deep breath, trying to still her nerves. "Look, Diego, I'm just going to come out and say it, but please give me a chance to explain. I betrayed you. I stole *The Scream*, but I never set you up to get caught. I had nothing to do with the Russians. I promise."

Eddie turned around in his seat, his face scrunched up in confusion. "*You* stole the paintin'? *Cor blimey*, Diego said the Ruskies nabbed ya."

"Eddie, shut up," said Miriam. "This is between Natalia and Diego, got it?"

Eddie snorted, but he shut his trap.

Diego peered at Natalia, his body carefully positioned on his side of the cruiser. He wasn't wearing the mask of confidence and charm he usually did. He seemed pensive. Reserved. Cautious. "I knew what was happening as soon as the lights went out in the National Gallery. Maybe I'd suspected what you were up to for a while and didn't want to admit it to myself, but I believe you weren't working with Kovalyov's men. None of that needs explanation. What I don't understand is why you came back."

"I came back because I had to," said Natalia. "Jesus, Diego, I couldn't leave you and Eddie to that fate. When I'd planned to run off with *The Scream*, I'd assumed you'd fade into the background. Disappear completely. A crew as competent as yours would never get caught by the police, but I didn't count on the Russians, although maybe I should've. I did have some idea of how far in debt you were to them..."

"You did?" said Diego.

"I looked through your phone," said Natalia. "I'm not proud of it. The point is, I'm cold and self-centered. I've only ever cared for and looked out for myself, but I couldn't leave you there. I just couldn't."

Diego let out a sigh, and his body slumped. "So... you springing us loose was an issue of morals. Honor among thieves, so to speak."

"Yes. I mean, no. Maybe a little, but mostly no."

Diego straightened, one of his eyebrows inching upward. "No?"

Natalia tried to take a deep breath, but once again her lungs seemed to have lost some of their capacity. She felt as if she was going to break out in a cold sweat. God, why was this so difficult? Did most people have such a hard time telling the truth, or was there more to it? Was it being honest that was difficult, or was it baring herself to *this man* who sat before her, maybe the first man in her entire life whose opinion actually mattered to her?

Natalia wouldn't let herself back down. Not now.

"Diego, my entire life I've suffered from trust issues. I was given up at birth. My mother didn't want me. I don't know why. Maybe she was poor. Maybe I was a reminder of something that wasn't supposed to have happened. Regardless, I was left in an orphanage. A few years later, when I was three or four, I was adopted and sent to Australia. You'd think if someone went to all that trouble to adopt from overseas, they'd be desperate to start a loving family, but that never happened for me. Maybe I was a problem child, I don't know. But I never found a family. I bounced from foster home to foster home, from a social welfare scam to an abusive foster parent and back. I didn't have anybody to rely on. No family, no friends. Or rather, there were a few people I considered friends, but when the chips were down, they showed me who they really were. They abandoned me and looked the other way when I needed them most. My entire life has been one long lesson in why trusting anyone to have your back is utter and complete foolishness. So don't. I never have, and I protect myself, at whatever cost is necessary.

"So when you messaged me about coming together to steal *The Scream,* a painting I've long admired, that has spoken to me on a fundamental level for as long as I've known of its existence, I thought it would be easy. I thought it would be easy to fly here and lie through my teeth and steal it out from under you. But that was before I met *you.*"

Natalia felt her eyes welling up with tears, but at least she was aware of it this time. Her chest ached as she took another shuddering breath, willing her conviction to last another few minutes. "Diego, you're unlike anyone I've ever met. You lie constantly. You lie *for a living*. But there's also a part of you that's so unbelievably honest and real and genuine. I haven't seen as much of it as I'd like to, but the glimpses I've gotten make me want to melt. You run a team of thieves and hackers and criminals who by their nature are dishonest and untrustworthy, but they trust and believe *in you*. They put their life in your hands, and they'd do it again. It's nonsensical and baffling and utterly endearing. But there's more than that. You're charming and funny and cute, not when you don that persona you wear like a cloak but when the real you shines through. You make my heart feel weird and unsteady when I'm around you. My pulse gets quicker for some reason, as if I have an undisclosed medical condition. My fingertips get all tingly and I have a hard time breathing. But even that's not the crazy part! The crazy part is that when I'm around you, you make me want to be... *not me*. Someone who gives a damn and is willing to stick her neck out to save you and who against all logic actually trusts you sometimes. Someone who *wants* to trust you, maybe all of the time."

Diego sat there throughout Natalia's speech, his body holding onto that guarded posture, his brow getting steadily more creased, his gaze fixed in the direction of his feet. The car swayed as Miriam took another turn, and Diego lifted his dark, unreadable eyes. "Let me see if I understand this correctly. Everything you've told me since we met is a lie. You actively worked to undermine everything Eddie, Miriam, and I worked for. Even at the last moment, when you could've chosen a different path, you stayed the course. And now, finally, you want to talk to me about trust?"

Natalia's eyelashes could no longer hold back the tears. A fat droplet escaped and rolled down her cheek, falling free and splattering onto her leggings. Her entire torso ached with the knowledge that she'd let this man down. Was this what it was like to open herself to her emotions? To constantly be in pain, all the time?

Natalia's voice felt small when she spoke. "It wasn't all a lie,

Diego. The way I felt about you wasn't a lie. The smiles we shared. The jokes. Our night together. That was all genuine. That was the real me. I don't expect you to forgive me. I don't expect you to... *care* for me after any of this. But I couldn't live the rest of my life without coming clean. Without telling you the truth for once. Even if it makes you hate me that much more, it was worth it. It was worth giving honesty a chance."

Diego turned his gaze out the window. The car purred underneath them. The city hummed with a quiet energy. Natalia's breath sounded raspy in her throat, and she thought she felt the silent weight of Miriam and Eddie's eyes on her through the rear view mirror. More tears rolled down her cheeks, and her heart, which once she thought she'd put back together, now felt on the verge of breaking again.

"Diego, please say something."

Diego turned his gaze upon her, a sad, wistful expression on his face. "I'd like to tell you a story, Natalia."

Natalia shook her head, sending more droplets falling. "Not now, Diego. I like your stories—I lied when I said I didn't—but I don't want that now. I want something real, even if it hurts."

"You're going to want to hear this story." Diego's face softened. "Trust me."

Strangely enough, against all odds, Natalia did. She really and truly did trust him, so she nodded. "Okay. Tell me, Diego."

Chapter Thirty-Eight

DIEGO TOOK A DEEP BREATH. HE'D NEVER TOLD ANYONE this story. He'd never even told it to himself, not since adopting the suave, sophisticated persona he now wore like a second skin, but if Natalia could bare her soul to him, he should be able to do the same, shouldn't he?

"This story starts with me as a small child," said Diego, "same as the first one did. But unlike in that story, I don't remember the details of this one. Like any other child I don't have memories of things that happened before I was about five, but my parents and siblings have told it to me. You see, I did fall down the stairs when I was a year old. My parents were home, not at the movies, but they lost track of me for a moment and I wandered off. When I fell, somehow I managed not to break any bones, but I did hit my head quite hard, causing a massive *chichon* to grow upon my head. In addition to crying quite loudly, I also seemed to be confused and disoriented. My parents were terrified. They rushed me to the hospital, at which point their worries grew. Not only did they have to worry about my wellbeing, but they also had to deal with the police who justifiably wanted to see if my injuries were the result of malice or neglect. Unfortunately, the impressive lump didn't grant me a superior intellect. On the contrary, the doctors were concerned it might've given me brain damage, though they wouldn't know for many years. So what the *chichon* really implanted in me was doubt.

"Not just in me, but in my parents. I was coddled as I grew up. If I acted antisocial or angry or didn't achieve academic expectations, it was attributed to the fall, not to me. But I was always doubted. Always made to think that I wouldn't achieve much in life, all because of a traumatic event that happened which I couldn't even remember. I was put into different classes in those early years, the same classes as the special needs children. The same classes as Rojo, Chiquitín, and Maria, all of whom really exist. They were some of my only friends at the time. They all had their own difficulties, problems controlling emotions, putting together coherent speech, understanding difficult concepts, but they were kind and they accepted me. They didn't judge me the way the adults did. If I was quiet or had an outburst, they understood, and they didn't turn away from me the next time I approached them.

"All through that time, I kept having sessions with doctors and therapists. After many years and many tests, they determined that the hit I took as a child hadn't impacted my development, so whatever flaws and personality issues I exhibited were my own fault, not a lingering medical problem. But the damage had been done. My family didn't believe in me, and more importantly, I didn't believe in myself. As any youth who doesn't fit in can tell you, I didn't react in the most healthy ways. I acted out. I got into fights. I stole things, and I got into trouble for it. Quite frankly, nobody thought I would amount to anything, and I agreed with them.

"That's when I realized that instead of fixing my problems, it would be easier to just... *be someone else.* Change who I was. Adopt a new persona. Someone who was confident and charming and wasn't a total screwup at life. So I did. It wasn't an easy process. There were hiccups and bumps in the road. I fell on my face, a lot. But I learned. I got better at lying and at hiding my true self. That's about the time I got caught up in Señor de la Paz's enterprise. I did recover his family signet ring, believe it or not, but not in the fashion I told you. He showed me the ropes, and when I felt I'd learned all I could from him, I set sail on my own. After a few years, I met Eddie, then Miriam a year or so after that. We did a few jobs, and that's that. That's the story. The *real* story of how I became a grifter."

There was a moment of silence before Natalia spoke. "That's it? No magical spells or gravelly-voiced strangers or duels to the death?"

Diego's gaze had drifted to his feet again as he told his tale. When he looked up, he found Natalia's eyes brimming with tears and looking all the more blue because of them, but a smile graced her lips, a wounded one but radiant nonetheless.

"That's it," said Diego. "That's the honest truth. I'm sorry the reality isn't as strange as fiction."

Natalia shook her head. "I don't care. I liked all of your stories, Diego, I truly did. But I *loved* the truth. It's all I've ever wanted, even though I didn't even know it."

Diego looked into Natalia's eyes, feeling very exposed and very confused. "You said you didn't expect me to forgive you. Well, I do. I forgive you for everything. How couldn't I after all you've done tonight and everything you've told me? But you have to understand, I'm not the guy you think I am. This guy that makes you feel weird and unsteady and makes your heart race? That's not me. That's the man I became so I wouldn't have to be me anymore. The brave face I show to the world. *This* is the real me. A kid who nobody thought was smart enough or strong enough or compassionate enough to make it. I'm a fraud, Natalia. A liar. That's all I am."

Natalia wiped the tears from her eyes and scooted toward him on the bench seat. "No, Diego, that's not all you are. You think you're not smart enough? You engineered a heist to steal one of the most beloved paintings in the world, a heist that *worked,* by the way. One of countless cons you've executed to perfection. You're not strong enough? You held it together so many times when my heart was breaking, when I couldn't stop the tears from flowing, but you held firm. You were a rock standing strong against my storm. Not compassionate enough? You believed in me when no one else would, when I didn't even believe in myself. And you know what? Even if all you were was a liar, that would still be something to be proud of, because you're the best damn liar I've ever met."

Natalia's smile grew. She held out her hand expectantly, and Diego took it.

Natalia scooted closer on the bench seat. "Diego, I know this is crazy because we only just met and because I stole a priceless piece of art from you, but I'll regret it for the rest of my life if I don't say anything. I... I think I love you. Maybe it's just the emotions of the moment. Maybe I'm out of my right mind, and maybe I don't even know what love is. Certainly I've never felt the way I have before, but—"

Diego squeezed Natalia's hand. "I love you, too, Natalia."

It came out of him so easily, so freely. Without any hesitation or regret. That's how Diego knew it was the truth. He didn't have to think about it. Didn't have to remind himself it was a con. It just was. It was the truth. He loved her. He loved everything about her. He loved her eyes, her smile, the way she looked at him that dimpled her cheeks and crinkled the corners of her lips. He loved the way she pushed him and challenged him and made him question his preconceptions. He loved that she was the only woman he'd ever met who was better than he was at the skills on which he prided himself most, but more than anything, he loved that she brought him out of his shell. She made him want to be himself, not the persona he'd spent years perfecting that he'd been sure was all the world wanted of him. She made him believe that he didn't need to be Diego Cabrera, grifter and conman extraordinaire, to be deserving of love. That just Diego was enough. That he'd always been enough.

Natalia leaned toward him, her eyes as big and soulful as he'd ever seen them. She paused, inches from his face, her mouth slightly open, her eyes full of desire, and Diego closed the gap. He wrapped his arms around her, pressing her against him. He closed his eyes as his lips met hers.

Diego had kissed Natalia before, the night of their passionate love-making. He'd kissed her over and over again, on more than her lips, but it hadn't been like this. Those kisses were fueled by hunger and need and lust, but this one? It made the other kisses feel like pale facsimiles of the real thing. This kiss was tender and passionate and *real.* Natalia's lips felt soft and pliant against his own, not greedy but content to live in the moment, to share in the taste of his skin and his very presence. Natalia sighed in his arms, the tension fleeing her body, but Diego gave her support. Her breath escaped her nostrils in a puff, and Diego breathed it in, relishing in her scent, her warmth, her tender embrace.

Diego wasn't sure how long they kissed. Part of him was sure it had only been a few seconds, but when Natalia pulled back, Diego realized it could've been minutes. Hours. He could've spent his entire lifetime in that embrace and been happy, never having need of food or water or sleep. As long as he had Natalia, his soul would be fulfilled, and that would be enough.

Natalia didn't pull back far, just enough so she could look Diego in the eyes. Her fingers played with the short hairs at the nape of his neck. She flashed him the sweetest, most heartfelt smile he'd ever seen. "I'm sorry. For the lying. The stealing. For everything."

"Don't be," said Diego. "You made me realize who I am. And besides. You came back."

Natalia's smile grew. She leaned forward for another kiss, only for Eddie's forceful clearing of his throat to stop her in her tracks. "Breaks me strawberry tart to intrude upon a tender moment such as 'is, but seems to me as if we should pause on the lockin' o' lips and fink about the angry Ruskies chasin' us for a lemon."

It was as difficult as pulling a boulder apart with his bare hands, but somehow Diego tore his gaze off Natalia and took in his surroundings. Miriam had stopped the car, parking on the side of the street in a commercial portion of the city.

"Right," said Diego. "We've bought ourselves some time, but

Kovalyov's men aren't going to be happy. They're going to come after us. We have to hide our tracks."

"I got started on that before Natalia showed up," said Miriam, turning around in her seat. "But there's still work to do at the loft. Did you or Eddie give them anything?"

"Ya mean did we squeal?" said Eddie. "Come on, Midge. We's made of stronger stuff 'an 'at."

"We didn't tell them about our headquarters," said Diego, "and I don't think they have any way to track us, so we've got a window to operate. But..." Diego turned his gaze back onto Natalia. "We should probably talk about the painting."

"It's safe," said Natalia. "I stashed it behind a dumpster across the street from the National Gallery. I figured I'd pick it up in a few days once the heat died down."

"I assume you lined up another buyer?" said Diego.

Natalia shook her head. "I was going to keep it for myself."

Diego blinked. "You were? Why?"

Natalia shrugged. "The painting has always spoken to me. My whole life I've felt so alone and desperate, and *The Scream* symbolized that feeling succinctly. But I don't feel that way anymore. There's no voice inside me yearning to scream. I feel..." She smiled, that same demure, heartfelt smile she'd so recently shared. "Happy."

"Well, 'at's some bloody good news," said Eddie. "If Natalia don't need the paintin' no more, we can sell it to the Ruskies. Problem solved."

"I think that ship has sailed, Eddie," said Diego. "Honestly, I don't think they ever had any intention of paying us. Sorry about that, by the way. Apparently, I need to vet my buyers better."

"Maybe just make sure your buyer and your bookie are different people," said Miriam.

"If we don't have a need for the painting," said Natalia, "then I have an idea about what we could do with it to get the Russians off our back permanently."

"I like the sound of that," said Diego, "but Kovalyov isn't the only person I owe a debt to. I was banking on the proceeds of *The Scream* to take care of that. And before any of you say anything, I acknowledge I have a gambling problem. I'm going to get help for it, but unfortunately, me addressing my personal flaws doesn't make the debts disappear."

Natalia smiled, not the heartfelt smile he'd so recently come to love, but the devious, malicious smile that had drawn him to her in the first place. "It sounds to me as if we'll have to steal another painting then. But if it's alright with you, let's pick something more joyful this time. Maybe something that celebrates love instead of sorrow."

Diego snorted. "I don't know. Do you promise not to steal it from me if we do?"

Natalia leaned in, her grin widening. "I promise the only thing I'll steal from you from now on is your heart. Deal?"

Diego figured the best way to answer that was with another kiss, and he was right. It was even better than the last.

Chapter Thirty-Nine

NATALIA STRODE ARM IN ARM WITH DIEGO THROUGH Paris's Musée d'Orsay. Early afternoon light flooded the gallery, trickling through the translucent arched roof overhead and the tall windows as the sides. People packed the gallery floor: young couples holding hands, parents pushing strollers, tourists snapping pictures with their phones, elderly locals reading on benches. Diego led Natalia by the arm, weaving through traffic at a relaxed pace, pausing any time he felt Natalia's gaze wander. Natalia loved that she didn't have to tell him when she wanted to stop and enjoy a piece. He seemed to know, either because he'd deduced her preference in art or because he was so in tune to her wandering eye. Either would've been fine, but she suspected it was a bit of both.

Natalia paused in front of a popular painting, one with distinctive yellow swirls in a field of midnight blue. Her eyes widened in surprise. "Wait a second... That's not Vincent Van Gogh's *Starry Night.*"

Diego followed her gaze. "Nope. *The Starry Night* is in the Museum of Modern Art in New York City. That's *Starry Night Over the Rhône,* which Van Gogh painted a year before."

Natalia snorted. "Wow. It's beautiful. I think I might like it better than *Starry Night.*"

Diego's brow furrowed. "Hold on. Are you telling me you've never laid eyes on *Starry Night Over the Rhône?* A classic piece of impressionist art, which happens to be one of your favorite movements?"

Natalia shook her head. "I never knew it existed."

Diego's eyes widened, and a grin spread across his face. "But that means..." He gasped. "You *don't* know everything about art."

Natalia slapped him playfully across the arm. "I've never claimed to, but maybe you can teach me more about it later. Perhaps while we share drinks under a Parisian night sky of our own?"

"It's a date," said Diego. "But for now, we should keep going. What we came here for is just up ahead."

Natalia nodded, enjoying the strength of Diego's arm as he led her across the gallery. They passed a few more couples, then skirted a beautiful bronze by Auguste Rodin before stopping at a pair of paintings that had a section of wall to themselves. They each depicted a couple arm in arm while dancing, painted at slightly less than life size. The women wore light colored dresses, neither anywhere near as revealing as the gown Natalia had worn to the gala with Diego, but the men in the paintings did have a bit of that dark-haired mystique Diego possessed, even if they weren't as attractive as he was.

"*Dance in the Country* and *Dance in the City* by Pierre-Auguste Renoir," said Natalia. "Aren't they lovely?"

"Very much so," said Diego. "Which do you like best?"

Natalia filled her lungs with a breath. "It's hard to say. *Dance in the City* is more elegant, but I think I prefer *Dance in the Country.* The embrace the couple shares is more intimate. See the way he kisses her cheek? And the look on the woman's face? She's so happy. You can tell she's in love."

"But she's staring at the painter, not her dance partner," said Diego.

Natalia smiled. "That's because the woman in the painting is Aline Charigot who later married Renoir. So she *was* in love."

Diego snorted. "And here I thought I might trip you up."

"I may not know *everything* about art," said Natalia, "but I learn what I can about the pieces I enjoy. I find that knowledge helps you better understand the piece, and thus makes it easier to fall in love with. Men are a little bit like art in that way."

Natalia lifted herself onto her tiptoes, and Diego leaned down to give her a kiss. As soon as their lips locked, a voice spoke in Natalia's ear. "Hey guys. I've sent you a news clip. I think you're going to want to check it out."

Diego sighed as Natalia returned her heels to the ground. "Impeccable timing, as always Miriam." He dug his phone out of his pocket as it dinged. Once Diego awakened it, he clicked on Miriam's message and followed the link.

It took him to a video, one of a Norwegian news broadcast. A woman was speaking, narrating the scene, but it was a familiar one to Natalia. The video showed security camera footage of the dumpster across the street from the National Gallery (a security camera that hadn't been in place when Natalia left *The Scream* there, to be clear). A black SUV pulled up, and a heavyset man hopped out the back. He searched behind the dumpster and came back with the painting. As he returned to the SUV, two police cars came careening in behind it. Their doors popped open, and officers starting yelling, their pistols drawn and pointed at the SUV. More armed officers poured in from off camera, pulling the SUV doors open and dragging the men out onto the ground.

Natalia clicked her tongue. "That's a real shame. Those poor Russians. I have to think this'll get them off our backs, though."

"Hey, I gave Kovalyov the location of the painting," said Diego. "It's not my fault someone tipped the police off about it."

Natalia felt a smile grow on her lips. "Nope. That's *my* fault."

"Don't get too confident," said Miriam. "Those guys always have impeccable lawyers, though I don't know how they'll weasel their way out of this one... Hey. Eddie. *Stop...*"

Natalia heard what sounded like slapping sounds coming through the earpiece. She shot a questioning glance toward Diego. "Uh... Miriam? Is everything okay over there?"

"Yes." She grunted. "But this job would be a lot easier if Eddie would *keep his hands to himself* while I'm trying to perform surveillance."

Eddie's meaty chuckle joined Miriam through the earpiece. *"Shh, Midge.* You know the rule. What 'appens in the van, stays in the van."

Miriam giggled, then cut loose with a yelp. "Eddie. Seriously. Guys? I'm going to, ah... leave you to yourselves for a bit. Don't steal anything while I'm not paying attention."

Diego rolled his eyes. "Don't get arrested for public indecency, you two."

The earpiece clicked, and Diego looked at Natalia. "You know, this job was a lot easier when everyone on the crew kept to themselves."

"Easier," said Natalia with a smile. "But a lot less fun, I imagine."

"You imagine right."

Diego leaned down again, and this time, Natalia took her time with the kiss. She didn't care if anyone saw. Didn't care about anything except sharing that moment with Diego and holding onto it for the rest of her life.

When she finally pulled back, she found herself a little dizzy, and she had to take a deep breath to steady herself. "Wow. Those keep getting better, don't they?"

Diego gave her a sly smile. "Imagine how good they'll be ten years from now."

"Ten years?" Natalia scoffed. "I don't know about you, but I'm young. I plan on living a lot longer than that."

Diego laughed, a heartfelt, joyous sound. When he was done, he nodded toward the art. "So. Are you ready to steal another couple paintings?"

"Well... three," said Natalia.

"Three?"

"We can't ignore *Dance at Bougival,*" said Natalia. "It's part of the collection, even if it happens to be on display at the Museum of Fine Arts in Boston. We'll have to make a separate trip."

Diego laughed again. "I suppose we will. But you didn't answer my question. Are you ready to pull off another heist?"

"With you at my side?" Natalia leaned in for another kiss. *"Always."*

About the Author

Hi, folks. I'm Alex Berg, author of *The Confidence Game*. My romances feature clever, capable female protagonists and flawed male protagonists with hearts of gold. I try to keep them fun and flirty, and of course, every single one comes with a happily-ever-after ending.

So you might be wondering... what about Miriam and Eddie? Don't worry. I'll get to their story soon, but first, let me introduce you to Brooke Neal, the FBI agent who hopes to crack the mystery behind the stolen *Scream*. Don't miss the second White-Collar Crimes romance, Dream Big, the first chapter of which is included at the end of this novel!

Word of mouth is **critical** to my success. If you enjoyed this novel, please consider leaving a positive review on Amazon. Even if it's only a line or two, it would be a *huge* help. Thanks!

Want to learn more about me? Visit me at www.alexpberg.com or follow me on social media.

For a complete list of my romance novels, please visit: www.alexpberg.com/romance/.

Excerpt from Dream Pig

BOOK 2 OF WHITE-COLLAR CRIMES

Brooke stood in Gabby's office, checking her reflection in the sixth story window overlooking 10th Street. She moved to the side as she smoothed her hair, angling toward Pennsylvania Avenue, but the morning shadows that draped the J. Edgar Hoover building weren't conducive to producing a quality reflection.

"You should really get a mirror in here," said Brooke. "Frankly, this window isn't cutting it."

Gabby's exasperated sigh rolled off her back. "Maybe if you want to check yourself in a mirror, you should try the bathroom."

Brooke moved another foot to her right. "But the bathroom mirror can't provide me with insight into how I look."

"Yes it can," said Gabby. "That's what it does. It *mirrors* reality."

Brooke snorted. "You know what I mean. I need verbal feedback." Brooke turned and splayed her hands. "So... How do I look?"

Gabby Calderón sat on the edge of her desk, a look of resignation on her soft-featured face. "You look great, Brooke."

Brooke's brow furrowed. "Okay, but like... *how great?* Extraordinary great or regular great? Because I need way better than run-of-the-mill great today. I need *spectacular*. I need to walk into that meeting like a god-damned typhoon, blowing people into their seats so hard their butts hurt. I need them dazed and confused and utterly gobsmacked by how powerful and professional I look. I need them to know just from setting eyes on me that I'm the one who's going to crack the Oslo job. Not that I'm the best one for the job. That I'm the *only* one for it. I need them to *feel it*, Gabby."

Gabby rolled her eyes. "Well, that's going to be challenging given that—"

"Don't say it."

Gabby blinked. "Say what?"

"Do not imply I can't impress Monica and Rusty and everyone else in that room because of my size. I am *not* tiny."

Gabby crossed her arms over her ample chest. "That was *not* what I was going to say. That's your insecurity, not mine. Don't try to pin it on me. You should know by now that it doesn't matter if you're seven feet tall or four foot eleven—"

"Five foot," corrected Brooke.

"Whatever," said Gabby. "My point is, your size doesn't affect how good of an agent you are. It doesn't affect how smart you are. It doesn't affect your case closure rate. What matters is how much you've prepared, and trust me, Brooke, *you are ready for this.* You are going to blow everyone away, okay? You've got this."

Brooke sighed. Sometimes she wished she possessed Gabby's unbridled optimism, but in her opinion, a more pessimistic worldview protected you better in the inevitable event of failure. Besides, no amount of encouragement would convince her looks didn't matter. Maybe Gabby had never experienced much discrimination in that regard. She had a normal female figure, full and curvy in the places a woman was supposed to be, with glossy black hair and mysterious dark eyes and naturally tan skin that Brooke couldn't replicate even if she was a full-time shell collector on a beach in the Caribbean. More importantly, Gabby was a totally normal five foot six, and Brooke... wasn't.

She was, in fact, four foot eleven, even if she'd claimed she was an inch taller (all of which Gabby knew—what best friend wouldn't?).

But perhaps more importantly, Brooke *was* tiny. She was a hundred and five pounds soaking wet, and that was *after* a hearty meal. Maybe that wouldn't have been a bad thing if she'd pursued a career as a cheerleader or a gymnast, but she hadn't. She'd gone into law enforcement, specifically the FBI, and while her day-to-day duties didn't involve tackling perps or wrestling meth-addled gangsters, she was nonetheless expected to handle herself in a tussle. While Brooke was perfectly capable of pulling a trigger, there was an assumption that she wouldn't be able to handle herself the way someone bigger might be able to, even though she'd proven herself in the past. And so the other agents in the bureau looked down at her, literally as well as figuratively, and doubted her, just as people had done pretty much her entire life.

Brooke shook her head. "What I wouldn't give for your positive outlook. Be grateful you haven't experienced the same size discrimination I have."

Gabby lifted an eyebrow. *"Size discrimination?* Maybe not, but girl, I am a *Latina*. Emphasis on the '*a*', which means I am a woman. In the FBI. So yeah, I've been passed over for assignments, promotions, you name it. You're not alone in that regard."

Brooke sighed. "I didn't mean to imply I was a charity case. But you have to admit that in this job as much as any other, looks matter."

"Of course they do." Gabby hopped off the edge of her desk and grasped Brooke by the upper arms. "But they don't matter nearly as much as competence. Other people might disagree, but I'll die on that hill. Brooke you may be small, but you're talented and tenacious and fierce. You're my best friend. I believe in you, and you're going to get the Oslo job. Six hours from now, you'll be sipping a crappy rum and Coke on a jet to Europe, and twelve hours after that, you'll be beating off a horde of sexy European intelligence officers, all of whom are going to be very eager to get to know you better."

Brooke snorted. "Excuse me, what? I'll be *beating off* how many guys?"

Gabby flushed. "I meant it in the sense of you shooing them away, not the other thing."

"Seriously. A *horde?*"

Gabby gave a sheepish smile. "You know I didn't mean it that way, but if you insist on being dirty, sure, a horde. I have faith in you. You've got great stamina."

Brooke laughed out loud. She knew Gabby had been trying to pump her up with a pep talk, but her unintentional gaffe had calmed her better than any inspirational speech could've. She leaned in and wrapped Gabby in a tight hug. "Thanks for believing in me, Gabby."

"Always." After returning the hug, Gabby pushed back, tucking a strand of Brooke's shoulder-length chestnut hair behind her ear. "Now get moving. Because the only thing that might keep you from getting the job and doing... whatever you please with those hot European intelligence officers is being late for your meeting."

"Right." Brooke checked her pocket for her thumb drive, then grabbed her laptop from Gabby's desk and headed for the door. With one final nod and a smile of encouragement from Gabby, she headed into the hall and set off for the conference room.

As she walked, Brooke felt a lightness in her step that hadn't been there all day. As she'd gone on her morning run, she'd felt nervous. As she'd eaten breakfast, she'd felt more nervous. Her stomach had sprung backflips as she'd arrived at her desk, but now, finally, after speaking with Gabby, she felt confident. She'd prepped her presentation. She'd memorized the facts. She was ready. Might was well call her Hurricane Brooke because she was going to blow everyone away, goddamnit.

Brooke felt tall and powerful and breezy as she reached the meeting room overlooking Pennsylvania Avenue. Through the glass windows separating the room from the hall, she could see Rusty had beaten her, but Monica was nowhere to be seen yet. Neither was—

"Good morning, Brooke. Almost didn't see you down there."

Brooke turned. Lurking behind her was the final agent scheduled to be present: *Mitchell White.* He stood there, all six feet, one inch of him, his blonde hair perfectly coifed as he flashed his sleazy, shit-eating grin. God, even his stupid teeth were as pearly white as his surname. His smug grin grew as he caught Brooke's look of disdain, clearly delighted by the offhand way his comment about her height landed. Brooke wished she could brush it off—he made fun of her height almost every time they interacted—but Mitchell's tongue remained as razor sharp as when they'd first met. With one hurtful swipe, he'd cut her down to her true stature. Gone was the glorious sense of power she'd found in Gabby's office, cast overboard as if by a sudden squall, and now she had to hold onto her confidence for dear life.

Disgust seeped into her voice as she gave him a nod. "Mitchell."

Mitchell adjusted his jacket cuffs as he peered down his nose at her. "I'm surprised to see you. Figured you would've given up. It'd be a lot less painful to learn I got the Oslo job through an email instead of having it rubbed in your face in person, after all."

Brooke swallowed a snarl. Mitchell White was no athlete, but he *was* the Tom Brady of having the world's most punchable face. "Laugh it up. A few hours from now, I'll be soaring across the Atlantic while you'll be stuck filing paperwork wishing you weren't suffering through another muggy end-of-summer heatwave. Once Monica hears my presentation, she's going to forget you even work for the art crimes team."

Mitchell's eyes sparkled, as if he knew something Brooke didn't. "I don't think anyone could forget a face like mine. You, on the other hand, are completely forgettable. You know what they say. Out of sight, out of mind. And you? You're *always* out of sight down there."

Brooke clenched her teeth, her jaw muscles bulging. She wanted to roast Mitchell with a devastating burn, but there were only so many times she could come up with a clever retort before all that was left was a burning desire to tell him to go fuck himself.

Not that Mitchell gave her a chance to come up with anything. He swept past her, calling over his shoulder. "Remember, stand tall when you present. And project. I wouldn't want to miss what you're about to share."

White paused at the door and made eye contact again, his crystal blue eyes twinkling with malice. Now Brooke *knew* something was up. What the hell did that weasel have up his sleeve?

Brooke closed her eyes and took a deep breath to cool the anger inside her. It took a few more to cobble together the wind-scattered shards of her confidence. When she felt her internal temperature returning to normal, she followed Mitchell into the conference room. He'd taken a seat near the front by the projector—the perfect spot for a brown-noser like him—which in turn dictated the seat Brooke would take: the one furthest away. Brooke picked a free chair at the opposite end of the table, next to Rusty.

The old guy tipped his head at her. "Morning, Brooke."

"Morning, Rusty."

Gregory Arbuckle, better known to everyone on the art crimes team as Rusty, was about as senior of an agent as you could get. The mandatory retirement age for an FBI special agent was fifty-seven, which placed Rusty four months shy of leaving the team for good, but frankly, Rusty looked as if he were a decade older than the limit already. His skin was wrinkled and weathered, his beard grizzled, and his hair as white as snow, which made his nickname all the more amusing. Still, Brooke had it on good authority his follicles had been a ruddy ginger once upon a time, back when giant sloths and saber-toothed tigers roamed the earth.

Rusty leaned back, his arms casually crossed over his chest. "So. You decided to put your hat into the ring for the Oslo job."

"Honestly, I'm surprised *you* did," said Brooke. "You might be sipping Mai Tais on a beach on Oahu before this gets resolved."

Rusty laughed. He had a reputation as a grump, but Brooke had never seen it. He'd always exuded a grandfatherly vibe to her. "You have lofty ideas about how much you earn off an FBI pension. More likely I'll be sipping Miller Lites on my back porch."

"Well, you could close your eyes and imagine you're on a beach," said Brooke. "It's been so warm that envisioning Hawaii shouldn't require too many mental gymnastics."

"Are you kidding?" said Rusty. "Next time you see ninety-eight percent humidity in Honolulu, you give me a call."

Brooke snickered. "So you're *not* angling for the Oslo case?"

Rusty shook his head. "It's just you and pretty boy over there, far as I know."

Brooke shot a glance at Mitchell White, who appeared to be paying them no attention. "So why are you here?"

Rusty lifted an eyebrow. "This is the most exciting art theft in years. You think I'm not following the case?"

Brooke's lips curled in a smirk. "So you're going to peer over my shoulder and enjoy the fruits of my labors without doing a damn thing?"

Rusty winked at her. "Call it a seniority perk. Pay attention and you might learn how to reach retirement doing as little as I have."

Brooke knew it was a joke, but she couldn't help but think if anyone had learned how to get by doing the bare minimum, it was Mitchell. He was completely useless, yet he rode his charm to all the cushiest assignments. But not this time. This time Brooke was ready. Even with her confidence pieced together and patched with duct tape, she was going to blow Monica out of the water with her presentation, just as Gabby had told her to.

As if on cue, Monica appeared from around the corner, sweeping into the conference room with a briefcase in hand. Monica Harcourt was the division lead for the art crimes team. Early-forties, African-American, and with a practiced glare that could freeze a lake, she was more politician than agent. She played the internal game as well as anyone, which was probably why she'd risen to her position at a relatively young age. While she came across as cold and severe, Brooke rarely butted heads with her, mostly because her decisions were based on cold hard facts, something Brooke planned to exploit. She'd peppered her presentation with loads of enticing data points that would prove without a shadow of a doubt that she was ready to take charge in Oslo.

Of course as Brooke looked at Monica, she suffered a hint of creeping doubt. Monica was normally unflappable, but not today. She'd rushed into the conference room at close to a jog. Several strands of her normally perfectly arranged hair were out of place, and she hadn't greeted anyone upon entering, instead setting her briefcase on the conference table with a thud while furiously texting on her phone.

Brooke shared a glance with Rusty, who responded with a raised eyebrow. Meanwhile, Mitchell leaned back in his chair looking cool as a cucumber, a canned smile plastered across his face.

After a minute, Monica slipped her phone into her pocket and looked up. "Sorry, everyone. It's been *a morning,* and I have a million things on my plate already. The good news is I won't keep you trapped here for the next hour. A few minutes should suffice."

The doubt inside Brooke multiplied like a virus. *"A few minutes?* I can't condense my presentation to an elevator pitch."

"You won't have to," said Monica. "The presentations have been cancelled. A decision has been reached. Agent White? You're heading to Oslo in two hours. I hope you've packed a bag."

Brooke's heart spasmed. She rocketed to her feet, her chair squeaking as it rolled back. *"WHAT?"*

"It's not my call, Agent Neal," said Monica. "The decision came from above. Apparently someone thought we'd waited too long to act, and they didn't want to waste any more time on inaction. Congratulations, Agent White."

Rusty spoke under his breath. *"Son of a bitch..."*

"Thank you. I won't let the bureau down." Mitchell flashed Monica that smarmy grin of his, but he adopted a look of mock pity as he spun toward Brooke. "But I'm disappointed for Brooke. I was *really* looking forward to hearing her presentation."

Mitchell's eyes twinkled again, and Brooke knew without a shadow of a doubt he was behind this. Like every other time in his life, Mitchell had bootlicked his way to the top. Anger boiled inside her at the sight of his sleazy grin, threatening to explode like ash and brimstone from a volcano. She wanted to scream, to pound her fists against the table, but mostly she wanted to pummel Mitchell White's obsequious face into a paste.

But she couldn't. She couldn't fight him, she couldn't beat him, and she sure as hell wasn't getting the Oslo job, so before she erupted she snatched her laptop and stormed out of the room, all while Monica's voice called after her.

Buy Dream Big — Available February 16, 2023!